D0732432

Tillamook Passage

Far Side of The Pacific

Brian D. Ratty

AuthorHouse™
1663 Liberty Drive
Bloomington, IN 47403
www.authorhouse.com
Phone: 1-800-839-8640

First published by AuthorHouse 6/21/2011

ISBN: 978-1-4634-0615-8 (sc)
ISBN: 978-1-4634-0616-5 (hc)

Library of Congress Control Number: 2011908544

Printed in the United States of America

This book is printed on acid-free paper.

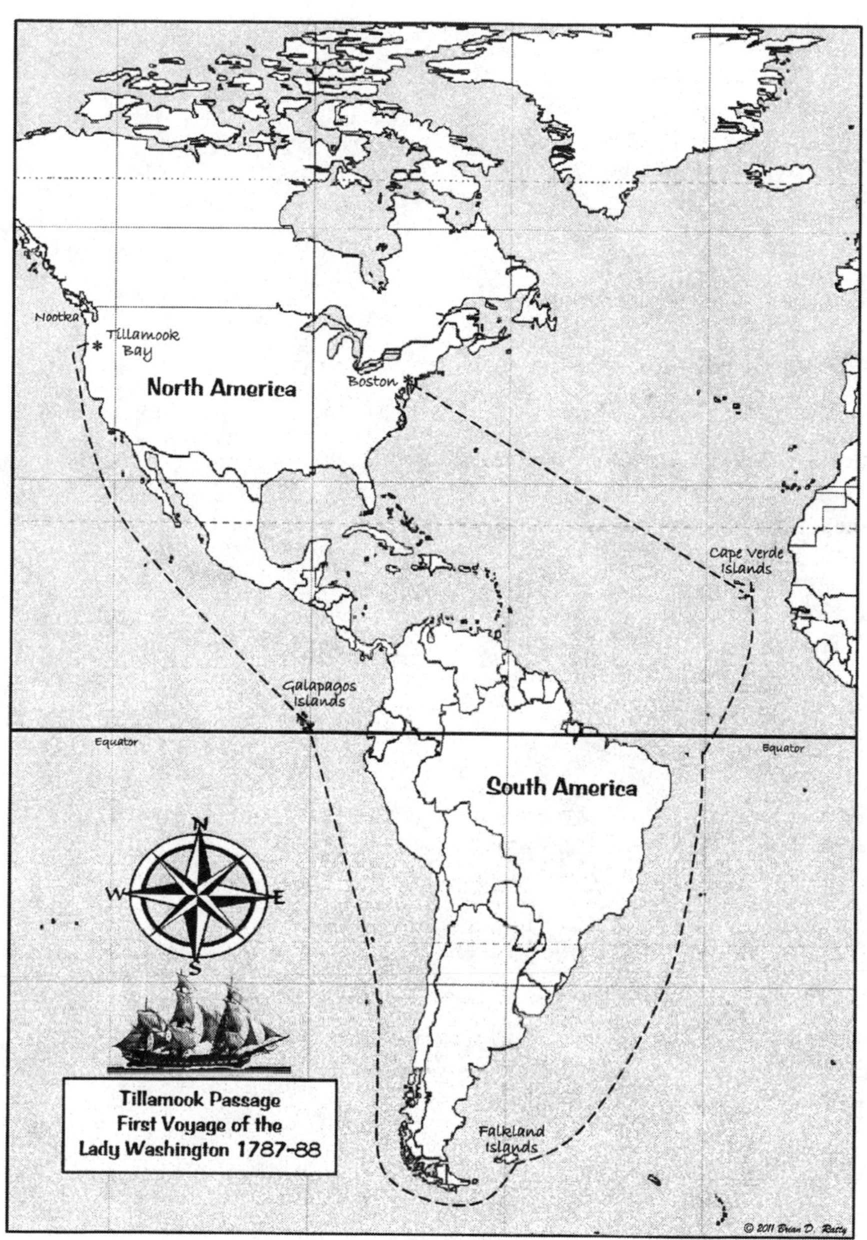
Nootka
Tillamook Bay
North America
Boston
Cape Verde Islands
Galapagos Islands
Equator
Equator
South America
N
W
E
S
Falkland Islands
Tillamook Passage
First Voyage of the
Lady Washington 1787-88
© 2011 Brian D. Ratty

For my loving wife Tess of two score years.
Love brought us together
as husband and wife
and gave us each
a best friend for life

And for baby Roan Elizabeth, our newest grandchild

Introduction

Tillamook Passage is my third book and a departure from my first two novels. The seeds of this story started many years ago, when I read about Captain Robert Gray and his discovery of a pristine Pacific coastal bay that he named, after the local Indians, as Tillamook. Then, some years later, the story took root after my wife, Tess, and I found an out-of-print book about the culture and rituals of the Tillamook Indians. These two events forged the general premise of a story that is steeped in history while rich in adventure.

Writing historical fiction, in this age of political correctness, can be a tricky enterprise. Some readers wish to overlook the past, pretending that our forefathers were without fault and that the world was always a peaceful, gentle place. Unfortunately, that isn't how history works. Remember, for example, that the very first 'cash crop' shipped back to Europe from the fledging colony of Jamestown, in the seventeenth century, was tobacco. America's early financial foundation was primarily built upon the growth and sale of tobacco. Then, immediately after the Revolutionary War, ships were sent to the Pacific Northwest for the taking and trading of pelts. Essentially, the Pacific coast frontier was opened because of the skins of small animals like the otter and beaver. At that time, the local Indians, thousands of them, lived peacefully up and down the Pacific coastal plain. Most of them had never seen a ship or a white man, and they had no concept of guns or money. They were a simple people, living off the land and raising their families just as their ancestors had done for over five hundred generations. These Indians became tragic victims of the fur trade and the opening of the frontier. Within a single generation, the culture and lives of these people would be changed forever. No, history isn't always pretty, but it's always fascinating, and it is a window to what has already been. For if we don't truly come to understand our checkered past, we will be doomed to repeat it.

Tillamook Passage presented other challenges, such as working with eighteenth century language usage and the many seafaring terms of the day. And finding resources that could shed light on the culture and jargon of the local Indians was an even more daunting task. But as Tess and I undertook extensive research trips, we found clues to the Indians' lives that helped me to depict a civilization rich with courage and strong in faith.

Tillamook Passage is written in three voices. At the beginning of each chapter, a brief narrative highlights the history of the time, while the story itself is told through the voice of my main subject and, later, his son. As to my characters, many are historical, some arise from folklore, and still others come from my imagination. Their development and my plot will hopefully take the reader back to a savage wilderness of endless forests, rugged mountains and bountiful waters. In this land of long ago, they will discover Indians with proud spirits, steeped in savaged traditions. These natives must now face their fate, dealing with white men and their ships that spit fire. *Tillamook Passage* is a thrilling testament to the iron wills, brave hearts and sharp wits of the gritty explorers who came before us. Two worlds… one destiny.

Acknowledgments

WRITING HISTORICAL FICTION IS A REWARDING ENTERPRISE for anyone who loves history. Once the general story line is set and a rough outline has been written, the leg-work begins. For the first of many research trips, my wife Tess and I visited the Tillamook County Library in search of information on the coastal Indians of Pacific Northwest. We were pleasantly surprised by this modern library and the many valuable research documents it had to offer. It was here that one of the librarians told us of an out-of-print book which contained rare information on the rituals, ceremonies and culture of the Tillamook Indian nation. Soon, an old, dog-eared copy of this book was found in a local bookstore, and it proved to be invaluable.

The first part of my story is about tall ships and sailors. Being only a fair-weather power boater myself, I needed much guidance regarding sailing terms and the lifestyles of the jack-tars of the seventeenth century. For help, I turned to my old friend, David White, who is a world-renowned sailor in his own right. David was one of the first to sail solo around the world, and became one of the founders of a world-famous sailing competition. I thank him deeply for the time and effort he gave to each of my chapters.

Many thanks to Scott McBride who, over the past two years as the manuscript took form, read my story and provided enthusiastic support. His questions were always thought-provoking, and his positive input encouraging.

During our extensive research trips, we often were joined by family and friends. On one such trip to the Garibaldi Maritime Museum, I am grateful to my cousin Lori Olson, for pointing out the work of a fine maritime artist. Visiting this artist's website, I found the perfect image for the cover of my book. This artist is Gordon Miller. For more information on his outstanding work, go to www.gordonmiller.ca. He is a fine artist of the tall ships of yesterday.

My story editor, Judith Myers, has helped me with all three of my novels. She has a magic touch with our language and is a joy to work with. One way or another, her changes and suggestions always made the read much better. Judy is one of my biggest fans and has given me new insights into the power of the written word.

My appreciation also goes to Gary Adams, an award winning writer and author of the new book, *Felicity*. As a friend and fellow writer, his input and insight was invaluable.

To Commander Rick Jacobson, who keeps me 'real,' and his brave wife, Gayle, and to all my other family and friends for their kindness, support and good wishes… I thank you all.

Tess has always been the first to read my story before it goes to edit. Over the months-turned-to years of my writing, we've had long and spirited conversations about my storyline, the characters and the pace of the plot. Her constructive feedback kept me focused, and her heartfelt enthusiasm kept me hopeful. As always, I am grateful for her non-stop encouragement and unwavering support.

Having expressed my gratitude to all those who helped me with this project, it is still my name on the title page, and I am responsible and accountable for every word.

Many Thanks to the Staff, Volunteers and Historians at:
Alsea Bay Interpretive Center
Burrows House Museum
Cape Mears State Park, Octopus Tree
Columbia River Maritime Museum
Clatsop County Historical Society
Fort Stevens State Park and Museum
Garibaldi Maritime Museum
Lewis & Clark National Historical Park at Fort Clatsop
Oregon Coast History Center
Seaside Library
Seaside Historical Society Museum
Siuslaw Pioneer Museum
Tillamook County Library
Tillamook County Pioneer Museum
Umpqua Discovery Center

Contents

Chapter One: The Winds of Change

THE EAGLE'S LOUD CRY WAS DEFIANT AS it swooped down with outstretched talons to begin the struggle of the American Revolution. But the first clamors of the Great War were not cannon or musket balls: they were words. Stirring words, like those from Patrick Henry in 1775, who denounced the British rule by saying, "Is life so dear, or peace so sweet, as to be purchased at the price of chains and slavery? Forbid it, Almighty God. I know not what course others may take, but as for me, give me liberty or give me death."

With these words, and thousands more like them, the dark shroud of war draped over the colonies. When the dove of peace next reappeared, some six years later, colonial America was no more. With the English royal yoke removed, the colonies rose from the ashes as the thirteen independent States of America. These States were as different and uncommon as the nearly three million people who inhabited the land. Each State, each region, each person looked to the future with optimistic determination. It was now time for prosperity, exploration and expansion. There would be no seas too vast, no mountains too high, or rivers too deep to stop this march forward. The sleeping giant of the United States was awakening to its future and all that it might hold.

This promise of a better life was made by ordinary people who had bold visions, courageous convictions and faith of purpose. These God-fearing individuals had survived the crown and the costly years of the war of independence, and now they were determined to thrive and rise. This belief in a divine destiny was found in every hamlet, every town, every state, but nowhere more so than in Massachusetts and her bustling seaport of Boston in 1787.

Wharf Rats

My boots made a muffled clopping noise on the damp cobblestones as I walked towards my father's home. The February day had been dark, cold, and foggy, and I was chilled to my bone. My mood was as miserable as the weather, for I had spent eleven hours hunched over my clerk's desk, and now I relished the hope of a hot meal and a warm fire. But it was more than just the day and weather, as I had not been joyful since my mother's death, almost four years before. A Puritan woman in both heart and soul, she had been the center of my universe; she had taught me the joy of reading and writing, how to use my numbers, the rhythm of good music and the fine lines of great art. She had been my spiritual beacon in an otherwise dreary childhood. Now, at eighteen, I still couldn't envision a future without her.

Turning the corner at Fulton, I looked down the long, deserted street. Only the oil lamps from a few public houses lit the dark way. The light fog that hung low over the stones made for a ghostly and shadowy journey. At nearly eight o'clock, most folks were cozy at home, enjoying fire and food.

My father had been a drunk during my mother's life and had worsened after her passing. Now his wrath was pointed only at me and my younger brother, Frederic. At least Momma was spared those indignities…the only good thing about her passing. After her funeral, I thought about running away and going to sea, but I feared for Frederic's well-being. No, I would stay and become the foil between father and brother. It was a job that I hated, but it had to be done until Frederic could find the courage to stand up to our father.

After Momma's death, I was obliged to work for my father in his blacksmith shop. As his apprentice, I was taught what he called "real skills, not fancies from books." With his massive, filthy hands, he showed me how to work the forge, and to cut, bend and shape the iron and bronze. As always, I was a quick study, and I soon learned the blacksmith's dance in the molten sparks of the spitting forge and hammer. It was heavy, hot, and dirty work. The days were long and the rewards few. But my tall, lean body soon grew strong, with muscular limbs and powerful hands—hands that I washed three times a day so as not to have them look like the grimy paws of my father.

Over the sounds from my boots, I heard eight bells ring out from one of the ships moored at the piers, only blocks away. The high-pitched sounds bounced off the brick buildings that lined my way, producing an echoing effect.

Two years had passed since I'd left my father's blacksmith shop to clerk for the merchant Joseph Barrel… and what did I have to show for it? Nothing! My father confiscated my wages for rum, and my back ached from the long hours I spent hunched over my desk. Soon I would look like Mr. Crumwell, the old, rawboned chief clerk, who could no longer stand erect. He was a wretched man with a deplorable job.

My thoughts were interrupted by sounds of gaiety coming from the opening door of a public house, a half-block down. By the light spilling into the street, I could just make out the tavern's carved sign: *Sea Witch*. The figure of a man, dressed in a heavy coat and tricorne hat, stumbled into the night. From my position across the street, he was difficult to make out. Slowly, he turned his back to me and staggered down Fulton, holding onto the buildings for stability. He soon disappeared into the gloom.

Such a sight reminded me of my father on most Saturday nights. The only thing more pathetic than a drunk in public was a lone drunk on a cold, dark night. Rum was for the weak, and I would have none of it!

As I passed directly across from the public house, its door opened again, releasing more sounds of merriment. Stopping in the shadows, I watched two young men emerge from the tavern. Both looked like jack-tars, in their striped blouses, tattered jackets, and baggy breeches. As the door closed behind them, one turned and peered up Fulton, while the other turned and looked down the avenue. One whispered loudly, "He went this way, mate. Come on, let's get him." Turning, both men moved briskly into the darkness, following the drunk.

I crossed the street, knowing full well what was happening. It had become a nightly custom for some to beat and rob the many drunks found on the docks. It had happened to my father more than once, and I hadn't liked it. A hapless drunk made an easy but unfair target, one that I found shameful. These scourges of the wharfs had to be stopped.

Picking up my pace, I rapidly reached the next cross-street, but I could neither see nor hear which direction the sailors had gone. It was so dark that I could hardly make out the lines of the buildings, let alone moving shapes. Looking up at the sky, I prayed for moonlight and moved farther down Fulton.

Halfway along the next block, I heard a dog bark, and then the faint sounds of a person crying out. Moving towards the sounds, tracing the passing shop fronts with my fingertips, I found an alley just down the street. As I rounded its corner, the clouds briefly parted, and a sliver of blue moonlight helped me see the way.

Twenty feet into the lane, a shadowy figure lay prone on the cobbles. One jack-tar, to the left of him, was kicking the drunk with his boot. With each kick, I heard a muffled cry. The other sailor, closer to me, knelt by the figure, apparently rummaging through his clothes.

"What the hell goes on here?" I shouted.

The ruffian on his knees turned quickly at my approaching steps and shouted back, "No concern of yours, mate. Move on, before I spoil your guts."

"Stop kicking that man!" I demanded.

In the blink of an eye, the kneeling sailor jumped to his feet and turned to face me. In the pale moonlight, I saw a quick flash from a knife in his right hand.

He lunged at me, trying to stick me with the blade, but I jumped to the side. As he stumbled by me, I kicked him hard in his groin with my boot. He let out a loud cry and hit the stones with a thud, face down. When he landed, I heard the knife clink out of his hand. Looking down in the faint light, I spotted the blade not three feet from me and moved to it, kicking it out of the alley and onto Fulton. Then, twisting back, I found the second thug moving towards me over the stranger's body. But as he did so, the drunk raised one of his legs, tripping him. The sailor landed hard on the stones and scrambled in an effort to get to his knees. Rushing to him, I punched the side of his head before he could rise. The force from my blow threw the man across the alley, where he crumpled against the opposite wall.

Rounding on the first thug, I saw that he was still moaning, holding his crotch as he tried to stand. Reaching down with trembling hands, I pulled the second jack-tar up the bricks until we were face to face. He was dazed and only half conscious, the fight gone from his eyes. Grabbing him by his jacket, I pushed him in the direction of the other wavering sailor.

The entire brawl had lasted only a few breaths, and I was shaking but ready for more. Herding the two groaning men towards the street, I angrily shouted, "You guttersnipes get the hell out of here… and if you touch that dagger in the street, I'll stick you both."

Helping one another, they slowly retreated out to the street and vanished into the darkness.

Turning, I rushed back to the stranger, who had pulled himself up to a sitting position, his back braced against the alley wall. When I knelt, I found him groggy and groaning.

"Let me help you, sir," I said quietly.

He just sat there a moment, shaking his head in the dark. Slowly, he moved his hands down to the cobbles and finally looked up at me. "You've got a hell of a punch, lad. Thanks. Let's see if I can get up."

Putting my hands under his arms, I gently helped him stand, with his back to the bricks. Then, after a brief rest, we stumbled out of the alley to the street. Here I propped him against a building, and we took another respite. By the faint moonlight, I finally got a look at his face, and what I found startled me. He had blood trickling down one side of his dirty forehead, and he wore a pearl stud in his left ear. On the right side, his badly scarred eye was mauled shut. His face, hair, and thick beard were covered with filth, as was his black wool coat.

Concerned, I said, "Your forehead is bleeding, sir, and your eye looks mangled."

With a slight grin, he replied, "Aye, the blinker has been like that for years. Go back and retrieve my hat, lad… and my eye-patch, so I can cover it up."

Steadying the stranger against the wall, I watched as he reached into his pocket and retrieved a handkerchief, which he then held to his bleeding head.

"Are you sure you're alright, sir?"

"Aye. The rum got the best of me, and those varmints thought me an easy mark. My head will heal. It's my innards that hurt. They got a couple good whacks at my ribs before you came along. Now, go get my belongings, boy. I'll be fine."

Returning with his gear, I watched as he slipped the black patch over his dead eye and placed his hat on his head. When he finished, he looked every bit like the pirates I had read about. Laughing to myself, I thought, *what have I done here—saved one buccaneer from other pirates?*

After straightening his filthy coat, he finally said, "Okay, lad, let's sail for home."

"Where would that be, sir?"

"The Morrison House, just a few blocks down."

With the stranger's right arm draped around my shoulders, I steadied him as we slowly stumbled farther down Fulton. The man was short and stout, but I could feel his powerful muscles under his coat. With every step of his left leg, he let out a grunt or a cry. I was sure that those vicious wharf rats had cracked a few of his ribs, and I hoped he wouldn't pass out from the pain.

Finally we reached the boarding house, where I knocked loudly on the small front door.

Within seconds, an older man opened the way. The expression on his wrinkled face when he saw us was one of shock. He stood there a moment, staring at the scruffy drunk, and finally said, "Captain, is that you? Come in, come in." Helping me get the stranger through the doorway, he pointed down a small hall. "Put him in the parlor by the fire and get his coat off. I'll get a basin to clean him up."

We bumped down the narrow hall and into a large, warm, well-lit room. Here I steadied the standing captain in front of a chair while I helped him remove his heavy coat.

Once done, he collapsed into the overstuffed armchair and mumbled, "I need some rum, boy. It's over there on the sideboard. Pour me mug, there's a good lad."

Studying the stranger slumped in the chair, I found that he was a man in his early thirties, and I was surprised to see that, under his dirty coat, he was dressed in clean gentleman's togs. That's when I remembered a passage from one of my books: *Never trust a gentleman with a black eye-patch.* Shaking off the notion, I moved to the sideboard for his rum.

As I poured, I asked, "What are you a captain of… sir?"

Shaking his head, he slurred, "Right now… nothing. But I still have my purse, thanks to you."

Returning to his chair, I handed him the mug. After taking a large swig, he slowly reached into his trouser pocket and pulled out a coin, which he flipped into the air in my direction.

Reaching out instinctively, I snatched it just as he added, "That's for you, lad, for your help. But I'm still in your debt. You're a hell of an alley fighter. You can run along now. Mr. Morrison will care for my needs."

Looking down at the coin, I saw a new, silver Continental Dollar, a week's wages for just a few moments of help. I was overwhelmed by his generosity.

Just then, the proprietor returned with a tray of soap, water, and towels. Nodding to the captain with a surprised smile, I thanked him and rushed out of the boarding house, clutching my good fortune.

Shortly, I was climbing the stairs to our small flat above my father's blacksmith shop. Still excited about the events and the reward, I wanted to share the news with my family. However, when I opened the door, I found the drab main room lit only with firelight, and my father, Samuel, seated in the shadows at the eating table. In the dim light, I could see a clay jug next to him.

When I entered, he looked up at me and snarled, "Where the hell you been, boy? There's still some stew in the pot, but it's cold by now. You're just too damn late."

Taking off my coat, I hung it on a wall peg. "Why is it so dark in here? Why aren't the lamps lit?"

Samuel snapped back, "Oil costs money, boy—money we don't have, with the lousy wages you bring home."

Taking a punk from the fire, I lit the candle on the mantel, and then used the candle to light the oil lamp next to a chair and the other lamp on the eating table. As I did so, I noticed a flagon in front of my father, half full of rum, with his dirty paws wrapped possessively around it.

With the light on his face, I realized just how old and pathetic he looked. He smelled of sweat, and his clothes were dirty and worn. His eyes were deep-set, with dark rings beneath them, and his black hair was matted, showing strands of gray. Not many years before, he had been regarded as a handsome and vigorous man, but now he was full of self pity. His quick downfall frightened me.

"What are you staring at?" he asked angrily.

"Father, you need to get washed up. You're filthy."

He took a swig from the mug. "Watch your tongue, boy. You don't know anything. You're not my equal."

Just then, the bedroom door opened and my brother Frederic came into the room.

Moving towards the fire, he said, "Joseph! I'm pleased you're home. I was getting worried. What kept you?"

In answer to his question, I told him the tale of the alley fight and the reward that I had received. Finishing, I handed the coin to him, and he examined it in the firelight.

"Blimey!" he exclaimed. "I've never seen a Continental Dollar before."

At those words, Father surged out of his chair and snatched the dollar out of Frederic's hand. He looked at the bright coin in the light, and then closed his large, filthy fingers around it.

When he turned to move back to the table, I blocked his path. "It's my coin, Father, and I'll have it back now."

Without hesitation, Frederic joined me. "Yes, Father, it's Joe's money. Give it back to him."

Father turned his head and looked at us in the flickering firelight. What he saw was my brother and me standing shoulder to shoulder, staring back at him, blink for blink. After a moment, a strange expression crossed his face; it wasn't his usual look of anger, but one of nervous uncertainty. For the first time, I think he realized that standing before him, making this demand, were two men, not two boys.

Opening his hand, he gazed at the coin again and then flipped it to me. "Foolish pay for a foolish deed. Helping strangers is not your business. Just remember, boy – if you get hurt, I ain't caring for ya."

Grabbing the coin, I grinned at Frederic, thanking him silently for his support. He nodded back and returned to the bedroom.

I kept my face straight as I ate warmed-up stew, while my father sat at the table in complete silence, consuming his spirits. Eventually, without another word, he got up and staggered to his bedroom.

Moving to the fire, I stoked the remaining wood, then sat and watched the flames. It had been an eventful evening. It wasn't just the scuffle in the alley, although my quick reactions and powerful fist had surprised even me. And it wasn't just that the mysterious captain had rewarded me so well. No, the most important thing had been how Frederic had stood up to father. This was the first time that I had seen such courage from him. Maybe – just maybe – there might yet be a future for us both.

Prospects

Of all the seasons, my mother loved spring the best. She called it a time of new life and of hope for new prospects. As winter faded and the flowers of spring started to bloom, I had to agree with her. It was an exciting time of both colors and smells. Now I prayed for those new prospects, as well.

Unfortunately, no new opportunities were apt to come from where I worked, as I hated my position. The job was monotonous and offered little chance for promotion. The merchant Joseph Barrel was a major importer and exporter in Boston, and I was one of five clerks that worked for him. Our task was to keep detailed accountings of each shipment in and out of port. Working with the ship manifests, we wrote out long columns of items, and then placed a value on each entry. From that total, detailed expenses were deducted so that a shipment value could be determined. I had wanted to resign many times, but Father would not hear of it, as the little money I brought home was gravely needed. So I was marooned at Barrel's under the watchful eye of the head clerk, Mr. Crumwell.

All of the clerks worked in a cramped nook of the main offices on Commercial Street, just across from the piers. Here we had three high windows that provided light during the day; at night, we used oil lamps. Even my young eyes found the light insufficient for the detailed entries we were required to make. Many a night, I would walk home with a roaring headache from eyestrain. Further, the drab offices were part of an old brick warehouse that was cold in the winter and stifling in the summer.

Despite all of my silent complaints, there were two aspects of my position that I enjoyed. The first was reading all the ports of calls from the ships' manifests. The places they traveled sounded exotic, and I daydreamed for hours about those ports. Someday, I hoped to travel the same sea lanes and experience the unknown.

The second aspect was more personal; her name was Becky. She was the daughter of Mr. Barrel, and came to visit him quite often. I could only catch a few glimpses when she came, as she always went directly into her father's office. Miss Becky had long blonde hair that touched her creamy shoulders, and a delicate face. I guessed her age to be close to mine but, from my across-the-room view, I couldn't be sure. Her visits always brightened my day, for she was as beautiful as a swan.

She had no idea of my watchful gaze, or even that I existed. But why should she? Other than my bright red hair, I was just a common John without prospects.

In the forenoon, one April day, I looked up from my columns to find Miss Becky talking to a gentleman in front of her father's office door. The man's back was to me, but that really didn't matter, as my attention was focused solely on her pretty face. Just then, Mr. Barrel joined them, and the gentleman turned my way.

The unexpected sight of my mysterious captain nearly made me fall off my stool. There he stood, black patch and all, dressed in a blue naval coat with sleeves adorned with gold braid. He looked bigger and more dashing than I remembered. Who was this man and why was he here?

Getting up from my desk, I quietly approached Mr. Crumwell and cleared my throat. He was a sour faced hunchback who didn't like being disturbed, as I well knew, but there was a question that I simply had to ask.

Finally, he raised his bony face from his work. "Yes, Joseph?"

"Sorry, sir, but I was wondering if you know the man speaking with Mr. Barrel."

He twisted his head in their direction, reached for his monocle and placed it over his right eye. Then, turning back to me, he answered, "That would be Captain Robert Gray."

"Do you know why he's here, sir?"

Crumwell looked startled by my question, but replied, "I believe Captain Gray is commanding a new undertaking that Mr. Barrel has organized."

"Do you know the nature of the venture, sir?"

His pale eyes turned angry. "Alas, they don't pay me to speculate, nor you to talk. All I know is that it has something to do with sea-otter pelts. Now get back to work."

By the time I returned to my desk, the three had departed. Shuffling through a stack of ship's manifests, I thought, *I've never seen a single sea-otter pelt come in or go out of this office... so what goes on here?*

All that afternoon, I daydreamed about the new venture and how I could make myself a part of it. Certainly the undertaking had to do with ships or they wouldn't need the services of Captain Gray… and that was a problem, for I had never been to sea. There must be something they needed that I could provide… but how would they know, if I didn't ask?

I had walked past the Morrison House many times since that February night, thinking about the mysterious captain. Now I wondered if I could muster the courage to stop and talk to him again. I found myself riddled with doubts. Was he still residing there? Would he even remember me? As I approached the house, something deep inside told me to just keep walking. But, a block down, I turned back, remembering what mother had once told me of life: *Hesitation is failure; action is success.*

With my heart in my throat, I knocked on the small front door. Soon, the old proprietor opened it and peered out at me.

"Good evening, sir. Do you remember me? I helped Captain Gray here, a few months back, after he was waylaid and set upon. I was wondering whether he still lives here and, if so, whether I might see him."

Grinning while nodding his head, he answered, "Yes, I remember you, boy. And yes, the Captain is still here. Come in. I'll ask if he'll see you."

Directed to the parlor, I waited for the Captain by a bright fire. The interval was nerve-racking, as my mind was still full of doubts.

When he finally entered the room, wearing the same uniform I had seen earlier that day, I bowed. "Thank you, Captain Gray, for seeing me."

When I straightened, he stared sternly at me and answered, "You have the advantage, sir."

Puzzled, I replied, "I beg your pardon?"

"You know my name, while I do not yet know yours."

"Oh, I see, sir," I said, smiling. "My name is Joseph Blackwell."

He stood there a moment, looking me up and down, and then asked, "Well, Joseph Blackwell, what can I do for you?"

"Do you remember me, sir, from that February night? How are your ribs?"

"Aye, how could I forget that red hair? My innards are still sore but much better, thanks to you. You saved my purse and perhaps my life. I did pay you something for your trouble, did I not?"

Mustering my courage, I answered, "Yes, sir…but I saw you today at Mr. Barrel's offices and heard that you are leading a new venture for him. I was wondering if you might need my services."

Walking farther into the room, he stopped in front a chair next to the fire and gestured to another across from it.

"Have a seat, young Joe. How do you know Mr. Barrel?"

Taking the opposite seat, I answered, "I clerk for him, sir."

He stared at me for a good long moment and then said, "So, you want to sign on. Well, lad, before you leap into those waters, you should know what's swimming. It's an undertaking not for the faint of heart or for those seeking comforts. While our voyage will be historic and hopefully profitable, it will also be long, hard and dangerous. Shall I explain? "

And that's what he did for the next half-hour. I sat, enthralled, watching his weathered face and listening to his powerful voice as he gave an exciting and detailed account of what was expected of the expedition. Two ships were to leave Boston Harbor, laden with trading supplies. They would sail around Cape Horn, passing from the Atlantic Ocean to the Pacific, and then travel up the west coast of South America to the Pacific Northwest of North America. There, they would trade with the local Indians for sea-otter pelts. Once the hulls were filled, the ships would carry their cargo to China via the Sandwich Islands. In Canton, they would sell the valuable animal skins and buy tea for the return trip to Boston via the Cape of

Good Hope. If they accomplished this three-year voyage, they would be the first American ships to circumnavigate the globe, and the company would surely make large profits from selling the China tea.

The Captain ended his explanation with a stern warning. "Along the sea lanes, we will have many potential enemies – Spanish authorities, local natives, diseases, mishaps … and, worst of all, loneliness. This expedition is only for those who are stout in heart and mind. So, what say you now, Joe Blackwell?"

Unhesitatingly, with visions of high adventure swirling in my head, I stammered, "I…I want to jump in, sir."

The Captain's expression turned serious, and his one good eye seemed to search my soul. "Well then, what skills would you bring to such an undertaking? Are you a seaman?"

Shaking my head, I answered honestly, "No, sir. I've never been to sea. But I'm an excellent clerk and a good artist. I could help with map making. Also, I can play a lively flute for the entertainment of the crew, sir."

"The mate usually clerks my ships, and I have no berths for artists or musicians. No, Joe, other than being a courageous alley fighter, it seems you have no skills that we need. This endeavor demands that our ships be crewed by experienced seaman."

His words saddened my heart, but I knew that what he said was true. Nevertheless, I heard myself say, "Please, sir… this prospect is for me."

Shaking his head slowly, he looked into the fire. Then, turning back to me, he asked, "What does your father do, lad?"

"He's a blacksmith, sir."

"Have you worked with him?"

"Yes, sir. I was his apprentice for two years."

"Were you good at the trade?"

"Yes, sir, but my family needed the wages that I could earn from Mr. Barrel."

Getting up from his chair, the Captain moved to the sideboard, where he poured himself a tankard of rum. Returning to the fireplace, he looked down at me. "Joe, I'm still in your debt from the alley fight. You saved me a great deal of money, that night. So here's what I'm going to offer – but it must be approved by Mr. Barrel. I'll sign you on as my cabin boy and pay your wages out of my pocket. Then, if you prove yourself during the voyage, I'll promote you to seaman and you can share in the ship's profits. Your duties will include taking care of my personal needs and serving as the ship's blacksmith and clerk. What say you to that, Joe Blackwell?"

Jumping to my feet, I extended my hand eagerly. "I say yes, sir! And I won't let you down."

Shaking my hand, the Captain grinned. "Very well, lad. We'll see what Mr. Barrel has to say about the matter."

As I was leaving, I stopped at the door and turned back to Captain Gray. "What would my wages be, sir?"

Looking up from his mug, he shrugged and answered, "A bit late in asking, don't you think?" He grinned, then asked, "What are you paid now?"

"Four dollars a month, sir."

Thinking a moment, he cocked his head and replied, "I'll pay you five. It's the most I've ever paid for a cabin boy, but you will have other duties, as well. Good night, Mr. Blackwell."

Blimey. "Yes, sir."

That evening, I explained the expedition to Frederic and Father, and told them of Captain Gray's offer and my acceptance. Father's only concerns were about the wages, so I assured him that I would make arrangements to have four of my five dollars paid directly to him. This seemed to appease him, as he made no further comment other than, "Where you are going, there are no maps. You should have demanded more pay."

My brother, on the other hand, was quite excited, for he realized that it was my prospect for freedom. Over a book I owned that described Captain Cook's chronicles, we spent hours speculating about Captain Gray's mission. That evening, before falling asleep, I had only two concerns: Mr. Barrel's reaction and what my duties as a cabin boy might be.

But I did not see or hear from the captain for weeks, and Mr. Barrel never glanced my way. My excitement over the voyage soon turned to apprehension, then sank into disappointment. Had I only dreamt of the offer from Captain Gray? But no, it was real. It had to be!

Finally, in the second week of May, Mr. Crumwell approached my desk and announced that Mr. Barrel wanted to see me in his office. Putting on my coat and straightening my blouse, I slowly crossed the large room. Along the way, I could feel the eyes of my startled coworkers. The only other time I had been in Mr. Barrel's office was when I was first hired, and the others seemed to assume that being summoned now could only be a bad omen.

I knocked softly on the door and heard from the other side, "Enter."

As I swung the door open, my heart was pounding like a rainstorm. The inner room looked smaller than I remembered but was still filled with books and nautical whatnots. Mr. Barrel's hand carved teak desk was enormous. Just behind it, a large window looked out over the wharves.

Mr. Barrel himself was seated behind his desk, chewing on a cigar while he read a piece of paper. And across from him sat Captain Gray.

I stared at him in surprise, realizing that he must have slipped in while I was out running an errand for Mr. Crumwell. Coming to a stop in front of the desk, I stood there for a long moment while Mr. Barrel continued to read. My employer was a big man, dressed in a black coat with a frilled silk blouse. His face was round, and he had a full head of dark brown hair. But it was his long, dark mustache that everyone's gaze was drawn to. He always reminded me of a drawing of a walrus that I had once seen.

Putting the paper down, Mr. Barrel looked up at me. "Captain Gray tells me that you want to sign on for our expedition."

"Yes, sir," was my quick reply.

"Well, there have been a few changes to our venture. Captain Gray will be commanding the sloop *Lady Washington* and will be second in command on the expedition. Captain John Kendrick will be the Commodore, commanding the ship *Columbia*. Because of these changes, and other circumstances, I am going to look favorably on his request. Beginning on the first of September, you will be placed in his employ on the sloop. Until that time, you will remain in your current position as my clerk. Is that satisfactory, Mr. Blackwell?"

With gusto, I answered, "Yes, sir!"

Mr. Barrel seemed surprised by my loud answer, and a tight smile crossed his lips.

Captain Gray inserted, "I told you he was earnest."

Shaking his head, Mr. Barrel continued, "You will not be required to sign the ship's articles, because you will be working directly for Captain Gray. If he promotes you to a seaman during the voyage, you can sign the articles then."

Later, I learned that Mr. Barrel had formed a company by selling fourteen shares at $3,500 each. Mr. Barrel had subscribed to four shares, while five other Boston businessmen had purchased two shares apiece. That capital, a total of $49,000, was being used to purchase, refit, and supply the two ships for the expedition. It had been those other partners who convinced Mr. Barrel to hire Captain Kendrick as Commodore, because they felt he was more experienced. At the time, they had no notion of the folly of that decision.

Standing, Mr. Barrel extended his hand to me across the desk. "I wish you fair winds and a following sea. May this venture be profitable for all."

Shaking his firm grip, I answered, "Aye, aye, sir." Then, turning to Captain Gray, who had also stood, I offered him the same handclasp.

Just then, I heard the office door open. When I turned that way, I saw Miss Becky gliding through the doorway. She was wearing a pale green dress with a white lace collar and a dark-green feathered bonnet. Her beauty took my breath away and turned my tongue to stone.

In a sweet, soft tone, she said, "Hello, Father. Hello, Captain Gray. So nice seeing you again."

Then she glanced my way, and I heard Mr. Barrel say, "This is Mr. Joseph Blackwell. After clerking for us for a number of years, he has just signed on with Captain Gray for our expedition. Mr. Blackwell, this is my daughter, Becky."

She extended her small hand to me. "How nice to finally meet you, Mr. Blackwell. I've noticed your red hair many times…and now you're going to sail away."

Shaking her soft, gloved hand, I was afraid she would notice the cold sweat on my brow as I meekly answered, "Thank you, Miss Becky. Nice to meet you."

"That will be all, Mr. Blackwell," I heard Mr. Barrel say.

Backing out of the room, I bowed and thanked everyone. By the time I closed the door behind myself, I was about ready to explode. Miss. Becky had noticed my hair and had talked to me. I could not believe the pounding of my heart!

Lady Washington

It was hard, returning to my clerking duties with the knowledge that in a few months I would be at sea. And those months seemed to drag on and on, with the only news of the venture coming from Mr. Crumwell. In late June, he told me that both the *Columbia* and the *Lady Washington* were receiving extensive repairs and reconditioning in a shipyard up the coast. He added that the work was proceeding on schedule and should be completed by the end of August. That bit of news lifted my spirits and filled my head with visions of what was to come.

On the third of July, I turned nineteen. I mention this for only one reason: it wasn't our family's tradition to celebrate birthdays. On this occasion, however, both my brother and father gave me a gift, and we had a gleeful time. My brother had stitched a leather pouch for me, complete with shoulder strap. The inside was for my drawing paper and charcoals, so that I could bring back sketches of where I went and what I saw. He had even added two small compartments that were for my flute halves, so that I might always have my music by my side. It was a heartfelt gift, one I deeply appreciated.

But my father's gift was the most surprising. He had forged a steel and bronze sea-knife for me. The steel blade was nine inches long and razor-sharp on one edge, while the other edge was deeply serrated, good for what he called "gutting fish or fowl." The hilt of the steel was riveted between two pieces of bronze and flattened on the butt end for cracking or pounding. The grip was tightly wrapped with leather cord to insure a good grasp. He had even stitched a leather sheath, made from some scraps from the pouch, so that I could hang the knife on my hip. It was a beautiful piece of workmanship, and it caused me to ponder my opinion of father. While he didn't count for much, maybe he cared for me, after all.

In the middle of August, the local newspapers ran stories about the upcoming venture and how the owners had petitioned the Continental Congress for a sea-letter that explained the peaceful nature of the voyage. Such a letter was granted, and days later a similar document was secured from the Commonwealth of Massachusetts. Then the owners had commemorative coins and medallions struck that would be carried by the *Columbia* for distribution at places we touched along our route. While only the owners were named in the stories, the undertaking had gained great public support, and I was proud to be a part of it. Even my father and brother seemed impressed.

With my pouch on my shoulder and the sea-knife on my hip, I reported, as instructed, to the deck watch of the sloop two hours after sunrise on September 1, 1787. Actually, in my excitement, I showed up an hour early. With the morning fog lifting, I saw both ships moored across Commercial Street from the offices of Mr. Barrel. The docks beside the ships were stacked with containers, bales, and barrels, which I navigated in my search for a good view. Through the moving mist, the *Lady Washington* was dwarfed by the *Columbia* in size and sails, but I found the sloop as sleek as a sea bird, with gentle lines and bright colors. Her single mast towered over her deck, and her timbers looked clean and freshly painted. She was big, as big as any sloop I had ever seen, and she pulled on her moorings and moaned loudly, seeming eager to sail. I stood on the dock a good long time, gazing at her lines and dreaming of adventure. Finally, I walked up the dock to her bow, and then paced slowly to her stern, noting every detail of her construction and rigging.

With my dock inspection complete, I walked to the gangway and shouted across to the deserted deck. "Is anybody here?"

Moments later, a skinny sailor with a bald head appeared from the aft stair hatch and stepped lively to the ship-end of the gangway.

"Would you be the deck watch?" I called.

He glared at me before answering in a high pitched voice, "Aye… and you would be Mr. Blackwell. Ya look too old to be a cabin boy… and you're early, lad. I was having my morning tea. But come aboard."

Stepping along the plank, I asked, "How do you know my name?"

"Captain asked me to keep an eye out. I'm to give ya a tour and show ya yer duties."

Extending my hand, I said, "I'm Joe Blackwell."

Shaking it, he answered, "I'm Hayes, but everybody calls me Sandy." Pointing to his bald head he continued, "Use to have a full head of sandy hair. Now all I got is a head full of skin." Smiling, he let out a chuckle. "Oh well. Indians won't get anything from me. Welcome aboard the Orphan."

"Why do you call her an orphan?"

"Let's go to the bow and I'll show you."

As we walked forward, I noticed his red knickers, which were cut off at the knees, showing his bowed bird-like legs. He was thin and short, and I doubted that he weighed a hundred pounds dripping wet.

At the bowsprit, we turned to look astern. In his squeaky voice, he said, "Take a good look at her, lad. This deck will be yer home for the next three years. She's sixty-four feet long and twenty feet wide and can carry ninety tons. That makes the *Lady Washington* the biggest sloop every built. She's one of a kind, an orphan of the sea. Hell, boy, she's so big that she should have been built a brigantine."

With the morning light on his face, Sandy's eyes twinkled as he spoke proudly of his ship. And speak he did, for the next few hours, non-stop. The pitch of his voice nearly drove me overboard, but the information it spilled was fascinating. The Orphan was big, so big that she required lots of canvas. She had a large mainsail with a square topsail and three headsails. Sandy guessed, in good conditions, that she would do twelve knots.

After walking the deck, he took me below and showed me the layout. Astern was the captain's cabin, with one window looking aft. The compartment was compact and well designed, with a small berth, eating table, and desk. Next to it was the mate's cabin, half the size of the captain's, also with a single window looking aft. Forward of the companionway, on the port side, was the galley, with its large iron cook stove and mess table. On the starboard side were lockers for foul-weather gear, firearms, and ship supplies.

In this area, Sandy opened a door to a cubbyhole. "And this be the cabin boy's berth."

It was a small, dark, dingy nook with a narrow, wooden berth, but I said nothing.

Amidships were two holds – a smaller one for foodstuffs, firewood, water, and other sailing needs, and the main hold, where we would carry our trading supplies and all else. Forward of the holds were the crew's quarters and sail lockers. On her deck, she was armed with one six-pound canon and four swivel guns. The Orphan would have a crew of thirteen: the Captain, the Mate, ten seamen, and me. Sandy didn't like me being the thirteenth member of the crew, as he felt the number was unlucky. By then, however, he had already told me about half a dozen other superstitions he held. He was a queer little man, but I took to him easily, and he was a fountain of information. By the time we completed the tour, my only thought was that his nickname should have been Gabby, as he talked so much.

Later that morning, the Mate, Davis Coolidge, came aboard, and Sandy introduced me. Mr. Coolidge was tall and looked to be in his late twenties. He had a dark, ruddy face and broad, square shoulders. But his personality was as cold as the rain. He told us that two other crew members would soon come aboard, and that the four of us would begin to load the supplies. Preparing the Orphan to go to sea would be our task over the next few weeks. He stressed that we would load the ship backwards, putting the things we wouldn't need for a good while into the holds first, and the things we would need frequently on top. He also added that the heaviest cargo items should be loaded first and deepest.

Turning to me, he concluded, "Mr. Blackwell, the Captain wants you to maintain a complete accounting of the supplies we've received and where you place them. I have other business in town, so you're in charge."

Then, while my mouth was still open in disbelief, he turned and walked off the ship.

As he disappeared into the sunshine, I said to Sandy, "What the thunder do I know about loading a ship? Why would he leave me in charge?"

Shaking his head, he answered, "It's all about the numbers, boy. Most of the crew knows nothing about ciphering and such things. We know how to load the ship, but we need you to keep the accounts. And, Joe..." He hesitated. "Give Mr. Coolidge a wide berth. I've heard he's mean-spirited."

That afternoon, seamen Owens and Taylor came aboard, and we began the task of loading the ship. Working on the dock, I used shipping receipts to inspect and count all of the supplies already received. On the sloop, the three sailors set up a block-and-tackle rigging to lift the containers into the holds. As each item was hoisted, I marked it with chalk, giving it a number. Then I wrote the number and where it was placed on each receipt. It was a dirty, sweaty job, as both the dock and the ship baked in the hot September sun. But, ever so slowly, we made progress.

The items we hoisted were all different in size, shape and weight. Our trading goods included cloth, beads, blankets, axes, knives, saws and hundreds of iron chisels. We even loaded raw iron and brass for making more implements. Then there was firewood for the cook stove, and barrels of rum, wine, and brandy. Next came barrels of cheese, oil, flower, sugar, molasses, and animal feed. The endless list of dry goods and sailing provisions had been carefully crafted by Captain Gray, and I marveled at his foresight and attention to detail.

Each morning, the Captain or Mr. Coolidge would come aboard and check the work from the day before. Then they would give us instructions for the day ahead. I found Captain Gray to be friendly and direct, while Mr. Coolidge was cool and aloof. The crew was always pleased when the Mate left the ship for what he called "other business in town."

Most redheaded people have fair skin that doesn't take to the sun, but for some reason my skin took to it and I would easily color. I had thought about this before, because my father had olive skin and black hair while my mother had creamy skin with light auburn hair. Why did I have red hair and medium skin? With my mother dead, it was a question with no answer, so I shoved it from my mind.

That first week, I worked on the docks without my shirt, and my body soon browned. Late Friday morning, I looked up from counting blankets to find Miss Becky approaching the sloop. She held a parasol above her head, shading her face, and wore a light blue summer dress. At first, she didn't notice me watching from my perch atop the bale. Then she did and turned my way. As she approached, I froze in place, my mouth dry and my heart racing.

"Good morning, Mr. Blackwell," she said, peering up at my bare-skinned torso.

Her strange look sank to my toes. Jumping off the bale, I quickly reached for my shirt and put it on. I didn't know whether to feel embarrassed or proud. Mumbling, I answered, "Good morning, Miss Becky. Can I help you?"

"Is Captain Gray aboard? Father wants me to deliver some papers to him."

"No, Miss. He's ashore. But you could leave the papers in his stateroom, and I'll tell him you came by."

Standing face to face with me, she smiled and her green eyes twinkled. "Could you show me the way?"

"It'll be my pleasure."

After leaving the papers in the Captain's compartment, Becky asked if I would give her a tour of the ship, which I was delighted to do. We walked from stern to stem, and I told her all I knew of the Orphan. With the crew watching our every step, she made comments and asked questions as we went along. I even introduced her to Sandy and the other boys, and she was warm and friendly to all. As we were finishing up, strolling towards the gangway, Mr. Coolidge came aboard.

Before I could present Miss Becky to him, he angrily asked, "What the hell goes on here, Mr. Blackwell? You're not paid to lollygag."

As I fumbled for a response, Becky quickly turned to Mr. Coolidge and said, "My father, Mr. Barrel, asked me to drop off some papers for Captain Gray, and I asked Mr. Blackwell for a tour. Is that a problem, sir?"

Mr. Coolidge had not previously met the owner's daughter, and she had now put him in his place in front of the crew. He glared at me for a good long moment, then grunted, "No, ma'am," and walked away, clasping his hands behind his back.

As we descended the gangway, Becky stopped and whispered, "Oh, Joseph, did I get you in trouble?"

"Not at all. It was my pleasure."

"May I visit you again before you sail?"

She was smart and spirited, and I liked that. "Please do," was my humbled response.

"But my visits will have to be our secret," she continued, "as Father would not approve."

"I understand. I'm currently a man with no fortune. But this voyage will change all of that."

Twirling her parasol, she smiled and turned down the dock. With my heart in my mouth, I watched her leave. That's when I realized that something special had just happened: our two lives were now intertwined.

A few days later, Miss Becky reappeared just before the noon meal. This time, she had used her influence to get the mate of the *Columbia* to give her a tour, and she wanted me to join them. I jumped at the chance to meet other crew members and see the Commodore's flagship. We found Mr. Woodruff, the mate, aboard, and he walked us around. He seemed very friendly and full of information. At two hundred and twelve tons, the square-rigged *Columbia* was much bigger than the Orphan. She had a deck eighty-three feet long, with a width of twenty-four feet and a depth of twelve feet. When I commented on her size, the Mate informed us that the *Columbia* was small for her class, as most similarly rigged ships ranged anywhere from three hundred to four hundred tons.

The ship was armed with four six-pound cannons and four swivel guns, which made her firepower much greater than the Orphan's. The total complement of her crew was forty, consisting of Captain Kendrick, five officers, an astronomer, a surgeon, a furrier, a clerk, and thirty seamen. The Captain had two of his sons sailing with him; one was the fifth mate, while the other was a seaman.

Finishing the tour, we thanked Mr. Woodruff and moved down the gangway. At the bottom, Miss Becky turned to me and asked, "Do you wish you were sailing on the *Columbia*?"

Looking up at the ship's brownish color and square shape, I answered, "No… she's too bleak and boxy. While the Orphan is as graceful and colorful as a mallard duck."

A smile curled her soft lips as she replied, "Why, Joseph... you're a romantic."

I saw Miss Becky twice more. The following week, she came by with a basket of food, and we shared our first meal together in the shadows of the ships. For our final outing, I arranged shore time, and we walked the shops of the waterfront. With full knowledge that I would depart within the week, we enjoyed our time together, filling it with laughter and conversation. In one of the shops, Becky found a necklace with a small gold cross that she admired. Taking out the Continental Dollar I had received from Captain Gray, I bought it for her. She seemed overwhelmed by my gift, and allowed me to help her put it on. Then she turned and gave me a hug, whispering, "I shall cherish your gift, and will be wearing it when you return."

It was an afternoon that I would relish forever.

The next day, Captain Kendrick called the ships' crews to a meeting aboard the *Columbia* — the first and only time that all fifty-three sailors would assemble. The Commodore had been in the Continental Navy as a privateer and had distinguished himself many times. After the war, he had returned to whaling and coastal shipping. At forty-eight years old, he had experience commanding sailors and the sea. On paper, he had all of the right qualifications, and the assembled crew showed him great respect.

On the quarterdeck, the men gathered round him as, with Captain Gray at his side, he addressed the crew: "We shall sail with the tide on Saturday morning for Nantasket Roads. There, we will load fresh meat, produce, water, and livestock." As he talked, he twitched his nose. "Nantasket will be the last place to say farewell to family and friends. We sail the following morning to begin our expedition, taking leave of American soil." Removing his hat, he wiped his brow with a handkerchief and continued. "At four bells on Friday, the owners will host a farewell party on these decks. Your families and sweethearts are invited. But hear this – there will be ladies and gentleman aboard this ship, so I expect to see my crew dressed in clean denims and shirts. There will be no over-imbibing or profanities. Do you understand?"

"Yes, sir," was our loud response.

Tucking his head, he turned and mumbled, "Very well. Dismissed."

My first impression of the Commodore was one of caution. He seemed like a strange little man with a strange manner. I could only hope his sea skills would prove to be better than his oratory.

On Friday, the whole crew set to work, polishing both the ships and themselves. Although the days had been warm, autumn was in the air. The crew was ready to depart, but only after the gleeful celebration.

That afternoon, our ship's cook, a seaman named Gayle, was sent to the *Columbia* to help with the preparations, while most of the other crew went ashore. Earlier, I had brought aboard all of my personal belongings, and I was trying to stow them in my small, dingy cubbyhole when Sandy shouted down the hatch, "Joe, you have visitors."

Rushing up the ladder, I found my father and Fredric waiting on the quarterdeck.

Pleasantly surprised – and pleased to see that my father appeared sober – I said, "You're early. But I'm glad you came."

My father smiled – something he rarely did – and answered, "Closed up the shop at three so we could see your ship. Will you give us a tour?"

My brother added, "Please, Joseph?"

Grinning at their enthusiasm, I agreed. We slowly walked the Orphan, with me spouting information as if I were an old salt. Below deck, I even introduced them to Captain Gray, who was in his compartment. He was cordial and shook their hands.

Once we were back on deck, Father and I strolled to the stern while Fredric wandered off towards the bow.

"I like your captain, Joe. I hope you'll heed his orders and do a good job."

Just then, the sound of fiddle music rolled over the transom from the *Columbia*.

"Well, I guess I had better get properly dressed," I said to him. "It sounds like the soirée is getting underway."

With a serious expression, my father answered, "Before you do, I have something for you." Reaching into his pocket, he pulled out a folded, wax-sealed envelope and handed it to me. On it, I saw the delicate handwriting of my mother. She had written: *For my son, Joseph Blackwell: To be opened upon the death of my husband, Samuel Blackwell.*

"Your mother gave this to me on her deathbed, and I promised to take care of it."

The look on his face was so serious that it scared me.

"But, Father, you're still alive."

"Aye… but three years is a long time. Maybe I won't be here when you come home. Or maybe you won't come back. Keep it in your pouch. You can give it back to me if – or when – I see you next." With music swirling in our ears, he extended his hand and concluded, "Do we have an agreement, Son?"

Taking his hand, I shook it, and he embraced me, with tears in his eyes.

As we parted, he whispered, "We live by accident or we live by purpose. Dig deep, to find your way."

We had an agreement; I would cherish his words and Mother's mysterious letter.

After I had changed into my finest togs, my family and I walked over to the *Columbia* to join the party. We climbed the gangway and found a crowd of well over one hundred guests on deck.

Slipping through the people, I led my father and brother to the food tables, where the owners had provided meats, fruits, cheese, and breads, along with wine and ale. As my brother loaded up a food plate, my father took a tankard of wine.

Noticing that I was watching, he grinned and softly said, "There will be no problems tonight, Son."

I nodded my approval as Fredric join us.

Between bites of fruit and cheese, he asked, "Joseph, why don't you play your flute with the fiddler?"

Turning, I watched the musician as he strolled from group to group, with lively music spilling from his instrument. It was tempting, but I was too shy to play for this many strangers.

"No, I don't think I'm good enough."

Just then, Captain Gray approached us and pulled me aside. With a grin on his face, he whispered in my ear, "Miss Becky is aboard the sloop and would like to speak with you." Then, drawing back, he winked with his good eye.

Clearly, he knew our secret. She must have told him. Turning to my family, I made an excuse and rushed back to the Orphan.

When I reached the deserted deck, I found her waiting at the bowsprit.

As I approached, I asked, "Is everything alright?"

"Yes. I wanted to talk to you one last time… but not in front of all those people."

"The Captain knows our secret."

"I suppose he does. But who would he tell?"

Undoing her bonnet, she shook her head and let her long, blonde hair fall to her shoulders. She wore a russet dress that accented her figure, and my necklace encircled her soft throat. In the golden afternoon light, she looked as if she had a halo.

"I have something for you, Joseph."

Reaching into her handbag, she retrieved a gold locket and placed it in my hand.

"My grandmother gave this to my grandfather when he went off to the Indian Wars. Later, he told me that it brought him luck during his time away. When he died, Grandmother gave it to me. Inside, I have replaced her likeness with mine, and on the back there is an engraving."

The locket was oblong, with a hinged front cover of gold that featured a black porcelain emblem of a woman in silhouette. Clicking it open, I found an inked picture of Becky. It was a beautiful likeness.

Flipping the locket over, I held it to the sunlight to read the small, scrolling letters. It simply asked, *Why Is the Eagle Feared?*

Looking up at her, I said, "A riddle. Did your grandfather find the answer?"

"Yes."

"And what was it?"

"That's for you to find out."

Snapping the locket closed, I curled my palm around it. "I will keep your likeness close to me for all my days... and I will protect this locket with my life."

She stood there a moment, staring at me with her deep-green eyes. "I will be here when you return, Joe Blackwell. And when you do... you will have many prospects." Delicate color stained her cheeks. "I'd give you a kiss now... but there are too many prying eyes. We had best join the party before we are missed."

Becky returned to the flagship first, while I followed a few minutes later. For the rest of the evening, we kept a respectful distance from each other, although our eyes met several times. At one point, she placed her hand over her necklace and flashed me a look that spoke volumes.

A few hours later, with the sun setting and a chill in the air, the Barrel family departed. I watched from the ship's rail as they boarded their luxurious carriage and rode off into the night. While Becky's departure saddened me, I relished the thought of our future together.

Soon, many other guests were leaving. At eight, my father and Fredric started their walk home, but not before one last embrace and an exchange of encouraging words. What remained after nine o'clock were only the hard drinkers, so I walked back to the sloop to spend my first night aboard.

Lying in my cramped berth, listening to the distant merriment and the groans of the Orphan, I held Becky's locket in one hand and my mother's letter in the other. It had been an emotional evening and I was ready to sail, if only so that I could begin counting down the days until my return. My last thought of the night was: *Why is the eagle feared?*

At sunrise the next morning, I served my first morning meal to the Captain. He was quiet and withdrawn as he ate his food, not saying a word about the party or Becky. His attention was fixed on the charts of Boston Harbor, which he had spread out on his desk. After he finished his breakfast, he climbed the steps to the helm and prepared to get the Orphan underway.

A few hours later, I staggered up the listing stairs and poked my head above the deck. The waters of the harbor were calm, and I spotted Deer Island on the port and Boston astern. Looking up into the crisp sunlight, I saw that the sails were filled with a fresh breeze, and that crew members were aloft in the rigging, answering the orders from the helm. It was exciting to be underway, and I could have watched for hours, but Sandy called me below to finish my duties.

Just before noon, we tied up at the piers of Nantasket Roads. This peninsula was the last easterly land connecting the countryside to the sea. Here, farmers and ranchers sold their produce and livestock to ships leaving Boston Harbor. When we arrived, the docks were stacked with provisions, and they kept coming, all afternoon. First the holds were filled, then the lockers, and finally the decks. Straw was place on the planks, then packed with livestock. There were crates of chickens, pigs, sheep, and goats, all producing their own robust noises and smells. By early evening, everything was aboard and secured for sea. Now all we had to do was wait for the tide.

Late in the afternoon, carriages arrived from town with many of the partners. Even Mr. Barrel came out for one last meeting with the captains, but without his family. Soon we could hear more cheerfulness coming from the deck of the flagship, as the partners enjoyed more spirits and food. With the work complete on both ships, many of the crew passed the time by wandering the docks and the few public houses. Waiting can be difficult for sailors on land when they know that the next tide will bear them out to sea.

After finishing up a few last accounts, I strolled to the bowsprit and gazed out to a rising new moon. While the sea lamps were being lit, I took out my flute and began playing softly. My mind and music were soon filled with thoughts of my unknown future.

From behind me, Captain Gray interrupted. "Your notes sound sad. Are you worried about the voyage, lad?"

In the fading light, I turned to him and answered, "No, sir. Just thinking about three years from now and the long sail home."

He smiled. "I'm pleased you have someone to come home to. She's a beautiful young lady. I'll get you home, lad. But it's getting late, and we sail at dawn."

Chapter Two: The Fur Trade

CHINA HAD BEEN TRADING FOR FUR PELTS for centuries, first with Russia and then with Spain. While the Celestial Kingdom loathed trading with western nations, there were certain commodities that the mandarins demanded, chief among them medicinal herbs, ginseng, and the soft, durable pelts of sea otters.

The Russians sent the pelts overland in trading caverns by way of Manchuria, while the Spanish church shipped the New World furs by way of Macao. Russia and Spain managed to keep this fur trading with China secret until Captain James Cook's expedition returned to England after its third voyage in 1780. Among the crew of Captain Cook's flagship, *Resolution* was an American, John Ledyard, who was a corporal in the Royal Marines. During the expedition, the ship traded with northwest natives for sea otter pelts. Then, on the homeward journey (after the death of Captain Cook in the Sandwich Islands), the ship called at Macao. There Mr. Ledyard watched as Chinese fur traders purchased the sea-otter skins for over a hundred dollars per pelt. That high purchase price astounded all who witnessed it.

In 1782, after being promoted to the rank of sergeant, Mr. Ledyard was attached to a British frigate that sailed for America. Once the frigate had anchored in a bay off Long Island, Ledyard deserted and returned to his home in Connecticut. There he wrote a journal of Captain Cook's last voyage, which was published in 1783. It was this account that fired the imaginations of the merchant Joseph Barrel and of Captain Gray.

With sails filling, the Boston ships weighed anchor at daybreak on

October 1, 1787, beginning the first American expedition to the Pacific and northwest coast of the continent.

Outward Bound

Bang!

The sloop's bow slapped the curling waves with such force that the deck timbers shook all the way to the stern. The boat raised itself high into the sky and then dropped down like a rock, twisting and rolling with each swell. The spray from the foaming sea rushed across the deck, drenching the crew with a coldness that they felt to their toes. The endless blue sky seemed to blend with the vast teal-green ocean, taking away all sense of distance. From horizon to horizon, the Orphan was lost in the vastness of sea and sky. Like a snake in the water, she swam away from home and towards her first destination, a cluster of tiny islands just west of North Africa.

With the outward passage from Boston, we found fair winds and moderate seas. But the constant pitching and rolling of the ship was unexpected, and it took me almost a week to find my sea legs.

The first few days were the worst; my head never stopped spinning, and my stomach never stopped twisting. All of the crew noticed the "green gills" of seasickness on my face and mocked me endlessly. They felt no pity and showed no mercy, and no matter how awful I might feel, my duties needed to be performed. On the second day, I had gone into the Captain's cabin to clean up from the morning meal, but soon found myself sitting with my head on his table instead.

When Sandy opened the door and saw my slumped body, he angrily ordered me topside. Standing me by the rail, he shouted over the roaring wake from the bow, "There will be no slackers on this ship. Puke it up, lad. It's the only way it will stop."

Hanging on the halyards, with the cold ocean spray on my face, that's exactly what I did for the next hour. When I finished, my gut felt as if a horse had kicked it, but I did feel better. After that time at the rail, I found my stomach of steel.

My duties aboard ship were simple enough, as Sandy had trained me well for being a cabin boy. I served the Captain three meals a day, made sure he had ample spirits and candles, cleaned his cabin, made up his bunk, and tended to his clothes.

Sandy told me that the added bonus was providing scuttlebutt to the forecastle. Most evenings, the Captain dined with the Mate, where their conversations, liberally oiled with wine and brandy, touched on all aspects of the voyage. Sandy wanted me to share all this news with my shipmates. At first I hesitated but then agreed, as I wanted desperately to be viewed as a member of the crew.

Shortly after our departure, the Captain added to my duties by asking, "Were you raised on a farm, Joe?"

"No, sir."

"Have you ever tended animals or slaughtered livestock?"

"No, sir."

"Well, beginning today, you will learn. After the morning meals, you will tend the animals on deck by feeding them fodder and changing their soiled straw. Then you will learn to dress them for the table. The cook will show you how."

I looked at the skipper with puzzlement; this wasn't a chore I had expected.

He noticed my quizzical expression and added, "Where we are going, we will need hunters for killing and dressing wild game. I want you ready for such a task."

Sensing his wisdom, I replied, "Aye sir."

Working with Mr. Gayle, our cook, proved to be more important than I realized at the time. He had been a ship's cook for over twenty years, and he knew how to provide hardy meals for stout crews. What he put in his pot was never fancy, but it was always tasty. The men wanted simple meals of meat, breads, cheeses, and heavy vegetables such as potatoes, onions, cabbage, and turnips. To satisfy those needs, nothing was wasted or overlooked. Between his baking and cooking, Mr. Gayle worked with me at a cutting board, where we butchered the livestock as needed. With my sea knife in hand, the cook showed me in great detail the finer points of cutting, removing, and using all that each animal had to offer. At first, I found the bloody, slimy work offensive, but I was soon intrigued by the skills needed to slaughter livestock correctly.

Mr. Gayle was a burly man with powerful hands that could kill the animals with one quick twist of their heads. His arms and neck were thick, covered with strands of black hair, and the apron he wore was always bloody and soiled. Unlike Sandy, Mr. Gayle was usually quiet, but when he spoke, I listened. He told captivating tales of voyages past and of all the exotic foods he had prepared.

"I've cooked fifty-pound turtles, harpooned hundred-pound squid, and eaten fruit bigger than your head and sweeter than pie," he told me proudly.

Mr. Gayle always had fishing lines dragging off the stern, and it was my job to check them every few hours. Whatever we caught was put into his pots and served fresh. The cook had a flavor all his own; he was a different kind of sailor, one that I took to right away.

Because of my duties, I ate my meals with the cook, before or after mess call. With this distraction, it took me weeks to meet the whole crew. They seemed to be good enough mates and expert sailors, with varying skills: one was a carpenter, one a sail-maker and mender, while others were helmsmen and riggers. Their nationalities were as different as the night stars. We had Dutchmen, Brits, Irish, French, and even a half-breed Wampanoag Indian who had tattoos all over his body. Some were joyful and loud, while others were quiet and reserved.

There were only two crewmembers I steered clear of: the Mate, who I found sour and demanding, and a seaman named William Wayne. He was a scoundrel who used lewd language, told bawdy stories and was always complaining. If he got hold of your ear, his nasty breath would follow you around, sounding off about every person aboard, the food, the weather and even the venture itself. He was one unhappy jack-tar, with a storm cloud over his head that we all tried to avoid. From the crew, I learned that every ship had a bilge rat, and that Mr. Wayne was ours.

If I had one close friend aboard ship, it was Sandy. Since that first day, he had watched out for me, giving both instruction and advice. While his high-pitched voice was still annoying, what it said was always fascinating – like when I asked him why the ships weren't sailing due south to round the Cape to the Pacific.

"Been like this forever, lad. If ya wanta go to the Pacific, ya gotta go to Africa to catch the currents to the Cape. It's God's highway."

He was a funny little man, full of knowledge and fables. And when I watched him in the shrouds, I learned why his legs were bowed. He was the fastest sailor in the rigging and could climb like a spider. While he was twenty years older than most, he was nimble and knew the ships needs before the Captain could shout them out.

What little free time I had was spent with Sandy. He slowly taught me the ways of a seaman. Soon, I knew all the parts of the sloop and all the knots used. He even had me in the shrouds, climbing like a monkey.

I took to his instruction and enjoyed our time together. The crew had great respect for Sandy, and he had great loyalty for Captain Gray. I was fortunate to call him my mate.

At the end of the second week, the Mate announced that all the fresh vegetables and fruit had been consumed. Therefore, beginning that afternoon, each crew member would receive a rum ration. The crew seemed delighted with the news as their faces shined like a church window. All except me; I wanted no part of the devil's brew.

Gathering around a crock, the men were given putter mugs and, under the watchful eye of the Mate, told to fill them. Not wanting to draw attention to myself, I complied. With mugs in hand, the happy crew milled around the main hatch, talking in small groups in the sunshine. Joining them, I sat next to Sandy on the hatch cover, gazing at the liquid I despised.

"Play us a tune, Joe," Sandy requested joyfully.

"Yes! Yes!" a few others shouted.

Putting down my cup, I smiled my agreement and reached inside my pouch for my flute. Within moments, the lively melody of "Yankee Doodle" filled the air. Soon, even the skipper was on deck, enjoying the comradeship.

I gazed around the deck as I played; some jack-tars were dancing while others were slapping their hands. It was a sweet distraction. By the end of the third chorus, Sandy was done with his rum and set his empty cup on the cover. As I ended the song, I reached down and slid my mug to him.

With a surprised look, he grabbed it and asked, "Are you sure, lad?"

Nodding my happy approval, I began playing another jig for the crew.

For a few short minutes, with the Orphan slicing through calm seas and with a tepid breeze on our faces, we forgot the ship's business and enjoyed our fellowship. It was an occasion that we would repeat many times on the voyage.

That evening, as I was preparing the Captain's cabin, he entered, and I was amazed to see he was clean shaven. He looked much different – younger and more dashing. I was unable to take my eyes off his bare face. He removed his eye patch, poured some wine, and finally said, "Where we are going, it's too hot for chin whiskers."

"Yes, sir."

Slumping in a chair, he turned his head to look at me. "I liked your flute playing. It's good for the men's spirits. But I saw what you did with your ration, and that has to stop. When we give rum out, you will drink it. Do you understand?"

The Captain had turned serious, with his good eye staring at me.

"Sorry, sir. I've never taken to hard spirits. I think of them as the devil's brew."

"Devil or not, you will drink your rum. I ration it out not as a favor, but as medicine. It helps prevent scurvy, a disease you do not want."

"I didn't know that, sir."

Finally, a small grin chased his face. "Sandy should have told you, but I'm afraid your ration was too tempting. I will eat now."

The next afternoon, I drank my first cup of rum. The liquor was like a flame in my mouth, and a lump of hot coal in my windpipe. At first, I could not understand its hold on some men. But soon my innards warmed like a summer's day, and I felt a deep a sense of well-being. It *was* an evil brew, but a drink I could come to love, medicine or not.

As the two ships moved further southeast, the winds moderated and the weather turned cloudy. Sandy called the area the "horse" latitudes. This well-known position boasted a broad belt of light, variable winds with frequent rain squalls. The *Columbia* was about a mile ahead of the sloop and never out of sight. With the storms, however, she sometimes got lost in the mist, only to reappear after the quick-moving squalls.

The flagship was given close watch for both her direction and her signal flags. These pennants of different shapes and colors were flown from her stern. They told us of course corrections, approaching weather, danger, and if the commodore wanted a council. These councils happened weekly, with the two ships reefing sails and coming alongside one another. Then we would lower the longboat and, with four seamen rowing, transfer the Captain to the *Columbia*. I sometimes went over with the longboat, as well, as our cook was always trading supplies with the flagship's cook. And it was a good way for me to get to know the much larger crew of the *Columbia*.

A few hours later, after much drinking, the meeting would be over, and Captain Gray would stagger into the longboat and return to the Orphan. It always surprised me to see how many corks were pulled by the officers of both ships. Spirits flowed like water.

After each of these councils, the Captain would brief the Mate over the evening meal. With my ears open, I'd listened intently to the details. But as the weeks passed, the news grew more disturbing. The astronomer aboard the flagship, Mr. Nutting, was failing to work his navigation charts correctly, and at times the ships were well off-course. It was Captain Gray, an expert navigator, who brought this problem to the Commodore, but little or no corrective action was taken. As a result, the constant course corrections were costing time and frustrating the skipper.

Then there was the pace of the flagship. For some reason, she always ran with shortened sails, which was slowing down the voyage. The Captain asked many times that she sail with full sheets but the Commodore was concerned that the sloop wouldn't be able to keep up. The truth, however, was that the *Lady Washington*, in good conditions, could out-sail the *Columbia*.

And, finally, there was the matter of the surgeon, Dr. Roberts, who had suffered many verbal indignities from the Commodore and wanted to quit the expedition. Captain Gray described these and other tensions aboard the *Columbia* and hoped that their outcomes would not affect the enterprise.

The cook's fishing lines, dragging off the stern, usually caught a few fish each day. They were never very big, but they were tasty morsels for the crew.

I had just pulled in a three-pound flounder and placed it in a wooden bucket to take below and clean. On the quarterdeck that afternoon was the Mate, with Seaman Taylor at the helm. After rebaiting the hook and playing out the line, I stood in the sun, sharpening my sea knife. Soon, the Mate swaggered over and looked down at the bucket, then up at me.

"You're not much of a fisherman. They're always so small."

Dragging my blade across the stone, I nodded at his comment without saying a word.

"That's a nice looking knife. Can I see it?"

Flipping the handle his way, I answered, "Yes, sir. It's very sharp."

Taking the handle, he twisted the knife in his palm. Then, making a few jabbing motions, he added, "It's got a nice feel and good balance... I've noticed it on your hip before. I want to buy it."

"It's not for sale, sir."

Mr. Coolidge towered over me by a good six inches, with his brown eyes glaring. Then he looked down at the knife in his hand. "I'll give you five dollars for it."

"It's not for sale, sir."

Anger crossed his weathered face, with blood vessels protruding from his sweating brow. "I could just toss it overboard," he said. "Then neither of us would own it."

I tried to keep my words calm. "Yes, sir. But then I would have to toss you overboard…sir."

The look on his surly face reminded me of my father. He just stood there, staring like an angry rooster, as if he didn't know what to do next. Finally, he threw the blade to the deck planks.

It made a loud twang and stuck straight up.

"I don't know how you weaseled your way onto this ship, but hear this – it's going to be a long voyage, and I will have that knife before it's over."

Turning, he walked back to the helm, while I stooped and removed the blade from the timbers. Then, still enraged, I returned the knife to my hip, picked up the bucket and went below.

That evening, as I was pouring fresh coffee for the Captain, the Mate looked up from his plate with his mouth full, and said, "You've got a stupid cabin boy, Captain."

"Indeed? Why's that?" The skipper responded, without looking up from his food.

"See that knife on his hip? I offered him five dollars for it, and he wouldn't sell."

The Captain looked my way, and I suspected that he could see the anger on my face. I was tempted to pour the hot brew over the Mate's head. But I didn't. Instead, I slowly freshened his coffee, as well, and stepped away.

"Well, it's his knife."

"A month's wages for a dagger," the Mate answered back, shaking his head. "No, he's just stupid. Guess it really doesn't matter, though, as he'll lose it in some dingy alley before the trip's over."

The square of the skipper's shoulders told me that he sensed the threat. With a serious expression, he gazed directly across to the Mate. "I wouldn't worry about that. I've seen Mr. Blackwell in an alley fight. If anyone tries to waylay him, they'll get their guts spoiled."

The Mate quickly twisted his head towards me. "You've seen *him* in a fight?"

"Yes, and when it was over, two sailors could hardly walk. I'd have him at my back anytime. Therefore, if I were you, I'd drop this business of the knife. It would be healthier for all concerned."

And that's what happened. The Mate never again said a word about my sea knife, and he seemed to respect me more after the Captain's warning. While we weren't friends, whatever fear I had of him disappeared that night.

After cleaning up from each evening's meals, I liked to walk the deck on clear days and watch the spectacular sunsets. Looking astern, I watched the thousand twinkles of colorful sunlight dancing off the water. Then I'd marvel at the color and size of the sun as it descended into the western sky. Sometimes I played my flute and dreamed that the breeze would blow my music home. If it was cloudy, with a fresh wind, I'd walk to the bowsprit and ride it like a bull. With the wind and spray on my face, I watched the porpoise play in our wake. As their sleek bodies twisted in the coral-blue seas, I dreamed of home and what the future might bring. These were special times for thinking of special people. Sometimes loneliness adds beauty to life. It adds an extraordinary meaning to sunsets and seas, while making the night air smell better.

A few mornings later, while checking the fishing lines, I heard the lookout, aloft in the crosstree, report land two points off the weather bow. It was the Island of Saõ Vicente of Portuguese-controlled Cape Verdes. The next day, we entered the fourteen-mile channel between the islands of Saõ Thiago and Maio. The length of the passage from the Boston Light had been forty-two days.

Cape Verdes

With the flagship in the lead, we steered close to Maio Island. An hour later, we found four ships anchored in a protected cove close to the shore. As the *Columbia* reefed sails and came close to the ships, Captain Kendrick used a voice horn to make inquiries.

He learned that three of the ships were American whalers, awaiting livestock that they had purchased from a local dealer. In the shouted-out conversation, the Commodore was told that the price being paid to the dealer was quite reasonable, so he came about and dropped anchor in the inlet. The sloop did the same and came to rest just a hundred yards from the flagship.

When the Mate removed the long glass from his eye, I overheard him ask Captain Gray, "Why the hell are we stopping?"

"I have no idea," the skipper answered. "I'm sure the Commodore will let us know."

Sure enough, the flags of council were soon flying.

After returning from the meeting, the skipper briefed Mr. Coolidge.

"The Commodore has the notion to purchase the livestock here and then continue on to Porto Praya for the other supplies."

The Mate looked confused. "Sir, didn't you tell me that the owners gave specific instructions to buy all ships supplies at Porto Praya?"

"Yes... but I'm not disagreeing with Captain Kendrick, as he's in a foul mood. There's something afoot on his ship...so let's load the livestock and get on with it."

The next day, the Commodore purchased one hundred and forty goats, two bulls, a cow, three hogs, and three sheep. But it took six days before the animals were delivered. By that time we were alone in the cove. As each of the other ships departed, they held farewell parties for all the officers. Much merriment and drinking could be heard over the still, coral waters of the inlet.

Standing at the rail, waiting for the animals on that last day, Captain Gray approached and asked how I had found the first leg of our voyage.

"I enjoyed it, sir. Forty-two days at sea passed quickly. How many miles did we travel?"

"From the Boston Light, forty-one-hundred miles."

Without really thinking, I answered back, "So we averaged just over four miles an hour, or about three knots."

The Captain was surprised by my quick calculations. "You've got a good mind for numbers, Joe. But it was a slow passage. With full sheets, I could have made it in thirty-six days."

His face showed frustration as he turned and walked away.

Early that afternoon, with the decks filled with livestock, we weighed anchor. With a fresh, warm breeze, we reached the mouth of the harbor of Porto Praya late the next morning and dropped anchor. Then both ships shot their signal cannons and raised the Q-flags. These yellow pennants requested permission to enter the port. An hour later, the authorities rowed out and inspected the ships' papers, crew, and cargo. Finding no reason for quarantine, the ships were granted a *pratique*, or license, to enter the harbor.

As we approached the bright, colorful port, I was taken with her beauty. The green hills that surrounded the little harbor were dotted with small, white stucco cottages and a few tall churches with red tile roofs. All the streets seemed to snake down the hillside to the main square of the town, just up from the piers. The air was filled with sweetness, and the white sandy beaches glistened in the sun. It looked very much the way I had envisioned a Mediterranean seaport might be, and I hoped for shore leave to do some exploring.

After making arrangements with the harbormaster, both ships were moored at the public docks in front of the town square. Here, many of the local Africans came to look with curiosity at the two American ships. They were strange-looking people, with skin as black as midnight and clothes as colorful as a rainbow. But they were friendly bunch, waving and smiling at the crew.

After helping to secure the Orphan, I went back to work, tending the animals in the tropical sun. As I went from crate to crate, giving them water, Captain Gray approached.

"I have a job for you, Mr. Blackwell."

"Yes, sir."

"Do you remember the three bales of tobacco you stowed in the forward hold?"

"Yes, sir."

"Get the hatch-cover off and bring two bales to dock. When that's done, call me so we can deliver them to a local merchant."

Knowing that one bale weighed around fifty pounds, I asked, "Can I have Sandy help, sir?"

"Yes… but let's turn to."

Thirty minutes later, both bales rested on a wooden cart with wheels. As we waited for the Captain, I paced the dock with dizzy steps. After weeks of the pitching and rolling of the ship, it would take some time for me to find my land legs.

When the skipper joined us, we began pushing the dolly over the rough cobbles towards the town square. As we walked, the Captain explained the task. Many years before, Mr. Barrel had sailed into this port and made friends with a local merchant who was a renowned cigar maker. Over the years, they had kept in contact, with a few letters delivered by merchant ships traveling to each side of the Atlantic. The cigar maker wanted to add some Virginian leaf to his African tobacco to make a more flavorful roll. Therefore, arrangements had been made for the Virginia tobacco to be delivered to him at thirty dollars a bale. The Captain was to be paid in African cigars that could then be traded with the Pacific natives. The whole scheme was well-thought-out endeavor and fascinating to hear.

As we moved through an open market, I begin noticing our surroundings in more detail. The market was filled with fruits, meats, and vegetables of every kind, color, and shape. The Africans were all dressed in their bright-colored clothing, and many of the women had large flowers in their hair, making the air smell of jasmine. As we pushed through the busy crowd, I saw some locals pointing our way and then frowning, speaking in a language I didn't understand. At first I thought it was just normal curiosity at seeing Americans, but it happened so many times that I began to feel uncomfortable.

Finally, we reached a tobacco shop and stopped. All three of us were sweating from the afternoon sun, so we took a moment to wipe our brows.

As we did, the Captain asked, "Joe, do you know what those people were pointing at?"

"No, sir."

"Your red hair. They thought you were the Devil himself!"

Chuckling, Sandy added, "You should cut it all off, lad. You're frightening the Afer-cans."

After the Captain talked to the proprietor, we were told to push the bales down a side alley to the rear of his shop. When we got to the back, we found a large, open-air tent with five men sitting at tables in the shade, rolling cigars. With Captain Gray and the proprietor waiting for us, we quickly unloaded the dolly. Then they began cutting open the bales to inspect the tobacco. The proprietor was a lean, older African with short, gray, curly hair. His black skin was shiny, and he had huge hands with white palms.

Obviously, he was the master cigar maker and Mr. Barrel's old friend. He held a few leaves up to the sky and then smelt them and rolled them in his hand. He seemed quite pleased, as he had a broad smile on his face. As he worked, I turned and watched the other makers. It was delightful to gaze at the way their nimble fingers rolled, tucked, and packed the dark tobacco. When they finished each cigar, trimmed to just the right length, it was given a paper band and placed in a small wooden box. When that box was filled, it would be packed in one of the larger wooden boxes that were stacked all around the tent. From my calculations, each large box held two hundred and forty cigars.

The Captain spoke to the proprietor in both English and Portuguese, a language that sounded similar to Spanish. When their business was completed, the old man invited all of us into the shop for a cup of coffee.

Inside the sweet-smelling store, we found shelves lined with all things tobacco. As we waited for the coffee to brew, Sandy and I walked around, looking at the many items. In one area, I found forty or more pipes for sale. They all looked like the work of fine craftsmen, with highly polished stems and bowls made from different woods. But, to my surprise, one looked to have its bowl made out of corn husk. Holding the pipe up, I showed it to Sandy and commented on its design. Just then, the old man moved in my direction and said something to me in Portuguese.

The Captain translated. "If you like that pipe, Joe, he wants to give it to you as a gift. He will also select a good tobacco to go with it. Sandy, you do the same. It's their way."

Turning to the old man, I smiled, bowed and thanked him. It was an unexpected gift that I would cherish.

Finally, after we drank the strongest coffee I'd ever tasted, the Captain told us to take two of the larger boxes of cigars back to the ship. As we loaded the dolly, he added that he had more business with the old man and would return later.

The way back was much easier with the lighter load. But as we wove in and out of the crowded marketplace, many of the townspeople still stared and pointed our way. It gave me a sinister feeling to know I was being compared to the Devil.

Just a block from the docks, Sandy spotted a public house and wanted to stop for a tankard. At first I hesitated, as we couldn't take the load inside, but then agreed to stay with the dolly while he slipped in for a quick flagon. Standing in the shade of the building, I reached into my pouch and took out my new gift. I was amazed at the workmanship and wondered if I would enjoy smoking the African tobacco.

Then I heard a loud cry. "*Braaak*! Hello, sailor."

Looking up, I saw a tall, shapely woman approaching me, with a red-and-yellow parrot on her shoulder. She had a soft brown complexion and midnight hair piled high on her head, with an orchid woven in. Twisting her yellow parasol, she stopped right front of me. With my heart racing I stared at her green floral dress, which accentuated her breasts and bright-red lipstick. She was as stunning as any woman I had ever seen.

"I like your red hair, sailor. And your skin is almost as brown as mine," she said with a smile, in near perfect English.

Her parrot repeated, "*Braaak*! Hello, sailor."

Searching for my tongue, I finally stammered, "Thank you, ma'am."

"Why don't you buy me a drink?"

"Sorry, ma'am. I can't leave my crates."

"What's in the boxes?"

"Cigars for my ship, ma'am."

"I love a good cigar," she said with a strange look on her face. Then, fast as a fox, she reached out and touched my cheek. "Right after I have a good sailor."

With her hovering over me like a bee at a jam pot, I felt my face flush and wondered what to say next.

Just then, a Portuguese soldier approached and, in the King's English, demanded, "Move on, Louie."

The lady twisted to look at him and angrily replied, "It's none of your affair. I mean this lad no harm."

Her bird added, "*Braaak*! Hello, soldier."

The Portuguese officer had a stern look on his face as he repeated, "Move on, Louie. Now, before I run you in."

She glared at the officer for a moment and then turned and huffed down the street towards the docks.

As she was leaving, I said to the officer, "You called her 'Louie.' Why?"

He grinned back at me. "Because 'she' is a he."

"A 'he'? I don't understand."

"Louie is a Frenchman. The chap likes to dress up like a woman to waylay and shanghai sailors like you."

With my mouth open in disbelief, I sputtered, "That can't be. She's so beautiful!"

"In the tropics, lad, beauty can kill. You better run along to your ship."

Thanking the officer, I shouted into the tavern for Sandy. Moments later, as we rushed towards the ship, I told him my story. As we reached dockside, my mind was still reeling from the experience. It was the first time in my life that I'd gazed upon a rose that turned out to be a weed. One thing was for sure – I had much to learn about life.

The skipper missed the evening meal and came aboard around eight bells. As he walked by me in the lamplight, I told him that I had stowed the cigars in one of the aft lockers. He was pleased, and showed me the two small boxes of cigars he carried under his arm. They were made with the new Virginian blend and were a gift from the old man.

After saying good night, I walked to the bow and smoked my first pipe with the African tobacco. Just like the rum, I found the flavor bold, bitter, and harsh.

The next evening, Captain Gray told the Mate disturbing news. Someone had over-stowed four water casks on the flagship, and the main hold would now have to be uploaded to retrieve the barrels. But because the deck was crowded with livestock, there was no room to stack the supplies. Captain Gray had suggested stowing the animals on the dock, but Captain Kendrick thought the livestock would be a temptation for harbor thieves. And, worst of all, the Commodore blamed the problem on his chief mate, Mr. Woodruff. Those two officers had had a strained passage, and now they were going at each other, verbally, in front of the crew. The skipper worried about the rancor and the delay it would bring.

Later the next morning, we learned that Mr. Woodruff had resigned and was demanding his pay. Captain Kendrick had agreed but was disputing the amount owed. Over the transoms, we could all hear the yelling of the two angry men.

Finally, out of frustration, Captain Gray went aboard the flagship and mediated an agreement. When he returned, I overheard him telling the Mate that the loss of Mr. Woodruff was a blow to the expedition. He had been third in command, was an expert navigator, and been with Captain Cook on his last voyage, when they had traded for sea otters pelts. Now he was gone.

That afternoon, the *Columbia* slipped her moorings and sailed to a small, grassy island in harbor. Captain Kendrick had made arrangements with the harbormaster to rent this strip of land for the livestock. After the animals were unloaded, the hatch cover could be opened and the cargo uploaded to the deck. This would take many days.

Late in the afternoon, the skipper took the longboat over to the flagship to see if they needed any help. When he arrived, he found the Commodore, bare-skinned, working with the crew in the hot hold. Mr. Haswell, the new second mate, stood topside watching the work party and talked to Captain Gray. Mr. Haswell assured him that they had more than enough hands for the uploading, although, because of the Commodore's interference with the work gang, the process was slow going. He added that there was much discontent aboard the ship. It seemed that when the officers moved up from the vacancy of Mr. Woodruff, the Commodore's son had gone from fifth officer to third, and that nepotism was not well received by the officers and crew.

Captain Gray gave assurances that he would talk to Captain Kendrick after the cargo problem was resolved. The skipper hoped that his words might inspire confidence and calm the dissention.

I learned all this news during the evening meal, and by eight bells the whole crew knew the scuttlebutt.

But that clamor for calm didn't last. A few days later, the Surgeon, Dr. Roberts, asked for his discharge, claiming ill health. Captain Kendrick seemed accommodating, but only if the doctor paid for his passage. The surgeon refused, and the two men had a heated argument. Later in the day, the doctor left the flagship and reported his problems to the Portuguese governor. When the doctor failed to return from shore by the next morning, the fuming Captain listed him as a deserter. Moments after that, the governor's brig pulled alongside the flagship with a summons for the Commodore.

When Captain Kendrick reached the government offices, he found the doctor having tea with the governor. As the Viceroy tried to mediate the difficulty, another loud argument broke out. With no hope of a resolution, the Commodore stormed out of the office, screaming obscenities at Dr. Roberts.

A short time later, while the surgeon was leaving the government house, he was approached again by Captain Kendrick. The Commodore calmly asked that he return to the ship. The good doctor declined. Irritated by his response, the Captain drew his sword and started shouting more obscenities. Luckily, some Portuguese soldiers, who had witnessed the confrontation, stepped in and broke them up.

Now the doctor was gone for good.

During all these delays, the Orphan remained quietly moored to the pier. With only light duty needed, Captain Gray began granting the crew some limited shore leave. All of those with liberty were to return to the ship by eight bells.

On my first leave, I wrapped a bandana over my hair and walked the streets, making sketches of the quaint little town. There were markets to mingle, churches to wander, and shops to explore. Now that I wasn't the center of unwanted attention, I had a grand time.

After returning to the ship, I learned that Captain Gray had made arrangements for sending mail home. There was an American whaling ship out of Nantucket in the harbor, and she would be returning home within the year. Her Captain had agreed to take our mail at ten cents a letter. This was delightful news.

The next day, I sat at the mess table writing my letters. The first was to Father and Fredrick. It was short and chatty, telling them about the passage and the beauty of Porto Praya. I kept it all upbeat and didn't mention any of the problems. In closing, I told them that I was learning seaman's ways and that, when I gazed at the sunsets, I always thought of them.

Miss Becky's letter was written more carefully, as I didn't want to invite her father's disapproval. In it, I wrote with praise of Captain Gray's seamanship, and told her of the fair seas and gentle breezes of the tropics. I talked of the quaint town and its colorful people. In my final line, I wrote, "This prospect looks promising, and I'll keep a keen eye out for that Eagle." There was so much more I wanted to say, so many more words I wanted to write…but I couldn't.

Having completed my letters, I took them to Captain Gray in his compartment.

When he looked up from his log, I said, "I beg your pardon sir. Here are my letters. But I have a problem."

"And what would that be?"

Reaching into my pocket, I pulled out all the coins I had. "I only have seventeen cents, sir."

A grin crossed his face. "I guess that's because I haven't paid you yet."

Reaching into a drawer, he removed a handful of coins and counted them out. "Here's for two months, less the twenty cents for your mail. You should have reminded me earlier."

As he handed me the money, I smiled back. "Yes, sir."

A week later, I went on liberty with Sandy. We walked around town for a while, but it was so beastly hot that Sandy convinced me to seek the shade of a public house. Just up from the piers, we found a tavern named The Salty Dog, and went in. As we sat down at a table, the bartender moved from behind the bar.

"You chaps look hot. Want to try a Coconut Harpoon?"

He was a Brit, with gray hair and a ruby scar across his forehead. He had a belly so large that it rolled over his belt and jiggled when he walked.

"What the hell's a Coconut Harpoon?" Sandy asked.

"It's a tropical brew, made from coconut rum and pineapple juice."

"Why do they call it a Harpoon?" I asked.

The bartender chuckled, "Well, lad, when ya drink a few, you'll feel like you've been harpooned."

"Okay, we'll dive in," Sandy ordered.

Against my better judgment, I agreed. When the drinks came, I found the taste to be delicious and refreshing. The usual bitterness of alcohol was gone, and the flavors were much like a fruit punch.

Over our drinks, Sandy started talking of home, and I was surprised to learn that he had a wife and two grown children. He told me he had been married for twenty-three years, and that his wife was always the happiest when he was at sea.

I asked if he had written her a letter.

"Na," he said, "don't know my words."

I told him I would be glad to write it for him.

But he shook his head. "Na… there's nothing to say."

I grinned at his comment and smartly answered back, "Oh, Sandy, you're such a quiet man." With that, we both roared with laughter.

Over the second round of drinks, I learned that this was Sandy's third cruise with Captain Gray. They had first shipped out, during the Revolution, when the skipper was a privateer. After the war, Sandy had shipped with him on a whaler for three years in the Atlantic. "He's a fair man, and almost as good a sailor as me. And that one good eye can see more than most."

Over my strong protest, Sandy ordered a third round. With dusk approaching, I thought of my berth and hoped for an end to my spinning head. But no, Sandy kept jabbering while the rum kept flowing. Finally, Mr. Gayle, the cook, staggered into the tavern and plopped down in a chair at our table. He was thrilled about his new tattoo from the shop next door. Lifting his sleeve, he proudly showed us a poorly drawn blue anchor running down his left forearm.

"Did that hurt?" I asked.

"Na, it's my fourth tat. It tickled."

"I've got two," Sandy slurred, "Joe, let's go next door and get one."

Vaguely, I remember saying no, but by the time my flagon was empty, I couldn't recall. It was as if I had lost all reason… along with my ability to walk.

I was in a deep sleep, having disjointed dreams of colorful parrots and tall, chocolate ladies. Then I became aware of something licking me. Opening my eyes, I saw a big rat resting on my chest, licking my shoulder.

Startled, I sat straight up in my bunk and flung the rat into the passageway. Unharmed, it turned and scurried towards the bilges.

There was fire in my arm, and my head was spinning like a tornado. Slowly, I gazed down at my left shoulder and was confronted by a crude tattoo of a perched eagle. The blue ink from the needle blended with the dried blood that the rat had been sampling. The tattoo hurt like hell.

By God, what the hell have I done? What will Becky say? I thought.

Carefully, I reached for the pitcher of water and took a long, cool drink. *I must have been thinking about that eagle riddle*, I reflected. Shaking my head gingerly, I blamed my condition not on myself, but on the rum and the riddle.

The Orphan was not spared the problems of the harbor. A few days later, the Mate reported that Seaman Wayne had failed to return from shore leave. Quickly, the skipper organized a shore party to search him out. But after hours of looking in flop houses, public houses, and sporting houses, the detail returned empty-handed. That evening, Mr. Wayne was officially listed as a deserter.

The next day, with her reloading tasks completed, the flagship returned to the pier, where both ships began taking on water and fresh supplies. Soon we learned that two of the *Columbia's* crew had also deserted. This was disturbing news, and I silently wondered if Louie had had a hand in those desertions.

Finally, I took my concerns to the Captain. He listened intently to my story of the scoundrel parrot "lady" and what the Portuguese soldier had told me. In the end, he told me that he would notify the authorities so that they could search out Louie and, with luck retrieve the deserters.

As I was preparing to leave the cabin, he stopped me and asked, "With

Mr. Wayne's departure, there's an empty hammock in the forecastle. Sandy has a high option of you and tells me you're ready. Do you want the berth?"

A broad smile spread across my face. "Yes, sir. What would be the pay?"

Smiling, the skipper replied, "Good, you're learning. A seaman apprentice is paid seven dollars a month plus one percent of the ship's share of the profits."

"And how much might that be, sir?"

"It could be a sizable amount, maybe four or five hundred dollars."

Extending my hand, I answered, "You can sign me on, sir."

"Good," the Captain replied with a handclasp. "You can move your sea bag forward and sign the ship's articles."

"But what of your needs, sir?"

"I'll hire a new cabin boy, and you will need to train him."

With my head spinning from this upturn in my fortunes, all I could say was, "Aye, sir."

Because of the desertions, the Commodore canceled all shore leave. And the next day, as a further precaution, after the two ships were fully loaded, they slipped their moorings and anchored out in the harbor. Late that afternoon, three newly hired seamen reported to the flagship, and one new cabin boy, Marcus Lopez, reported to the Orphan. He was an African, with skin as black as coal, hair as curly as waves and teeth as white as cotton. At thirteen years old, he was a puny little scrap, and I wondered if he would be able to carry his load. Later, I found out that he was the grandson of the cigar maker. His arrival would prove to be a twist of my fate.

After forty-one days of prolonged delays, the ships prepared to get underway from Cape Verdes on December 21st. But Porto Praya had one last indignity for Captain Kendrick. When heaving away, *Columbia's* anchor dragged, causing an imminent danger of collision with another ship. The Commodore shouted orders to cut the cable. The command was obeyed instantly and, thanks to some smart seamanship, the flagship maneuvered clear.

Captain Kendrick was in no mood to anchor again and grapple in the mud for his lost bower and cable. He had another anchor aboard and was determined to depart the harbor with all due haste.

The Falklands

As the two ships reached open water, they heaved smartly before the northwest trade winds. The expedition was now in a race for time, as the best weather for rounding the stormy Cape Horn came at the end of the southern summer season. And the Falkland Islands were still forty-seven hundred miles away.

I spent the next few days training the new cabin boy. Marcus was a smart enough lad but, because of the language barrier, some of my instruction was not understood. He only spoke his native Portuguese and what I called "pigeon English." But with the help of Captain Gray as translator and lots of sign language, we soon had a savvy with each other. He was a fine-looking boy, with big brown eyes and a face that always smiled, showing off his near-perfect, bone-white teeth. Marcus was a skinny fella, and seemed to have no fear of the sea or the strange environment of ship and crew. He worked hard and didn't complain. Even Mr. Gayle took to the lad and cooked a few special meals to remind him of home.

Living conditions in the forecastle proved to be much better than in my dingy aft berth. Each sailor had his own hammock with a wooden foot-locker for storage, just under the swinging canvas. There was even a table for eating, playing cards, and writing. While it wasn't posh, it was a great improvement over my narrow cubbyhole.

The only problem with my promotion was that my ears were no longer privy to the evening meals'. I tried to teach Marcus to listen carefully, but he always told me that they talked too fast and he couldn't understand. After much thought, I decided that the cunning Captain had planned all along to stop the scuttlebutt by hiring a Portuguese-speaking cabin boy at the first opportunity.

After I moved forward, Sandy took Mr. Wayne's sea bag and dumped the contents on the table. Then the crew divided up the items. With Wayne listed as a deserter, he had no further use for the gear. I was hesitant to rummage through his belongings, but in the end, I took a foul-weather coat and a pair of wool gloves.

The crew worked by rotating four-hour watches. There was always an officer on deck, with one seaman at the helm and another usually in the crosstrees as a lookout, leaving one or two other sailors for the rigging.

Each watch checked for sea depth and speed of the ship. These results were then written in the daily log book. If there was an emergency, the deck officer would blow his whistle and ring the ship's bell; then all sailors would report to quarters.

I enjoyed having my feet in the shrouds and my face to the wind, and wondered if I could fill my future days with the sea. *As long as you're good at something*, I thought, *my prospects would always be bright.*

Christmas came and went with hardly a nod. While the cook made a special meal of beef and potatoes, and even passed out some sugarplums, for the most part the crew didn't celebrate. When I was on watch that day, I gazed at the vast horizon, reminded myself of the meaning of the day, and thought of home. But Christmas in the tropics just didn't seem to fit.

To celebrate the New Year, the skipper passed out a double rum ration for all of the men getting off the watch. But the day was so hot and the winds so calm that most of the crew retreated to shade of the forecastle to drink their brew. Out of sight of the watchful eye of Captain Gray, I shared half my ration with Sandy. Sitting at the table, he told me that the ships had entered the doldrums, an area close to the equator that had light and variable winds.

"If we get becalmed, we'll have to use the longboat to tow the Orphan."

"In this heat? The skipper wouldn't let that happen," I answered.

"He can only harness the wind, not create it. I've done it before."

And like providence, that's what we did for the next three days. With our bodies sweltering, we pushed and pulled the oars of the longboat, dragging the Orphan ever so slowly. Each watch seemed longer than the last, and each pull seemed harder than the one before. The sea was as flat as a lake and the wind as calm as death. There was no beginning or end, only rowing.

On the third long day, Sandy looked up from his oars with sweat running down his face and mumbled, "Sunshine or thunder, a sailor always wonders when the fair winds will blow." And then, like a miracle, just when I thought my arms could take no more, we caught a breeze that filled the headsails. The longboat was recalled and the spent but gleeful crew returned to the deck.

A few days later, having just come off the morning watch, I went forward to shave. Just as I finished, the ship's bell started ringing, and the deck officer's whistle blew. Dropping everything, I quickly ran up the ladder to turn to. By the time I got to the quarterdeck, the whole crew was gathered around – all except Mr. Gayle.

Just then, he popped up from the stern hatch, wearing a white sheet. Just below his rosy red cheeks, a mop head was tied to his chin. The crew snickered as he moved to address the ship's company.

"I be King Neptune," he shouted in a deep voice. "Who among you wishes to cross my line?"

"We do!" the sailors shouted back.

"Who has crossed my line before?"

All hands went up, except for Marcus and me.

The silly-looking cook made his way through the crew and stopped in front of me.

Motioning for Marcus to stand by me, he said, "Well, lads, you will have to pay me tribute to cross my equator for the first time."

"And what tribute would that be?" I asked with a grin.

"A week of your rum rations?" He paused and slowly glanced towards the sour-faced Captain. "Well, no… I guess not."

The crew laughed.

"A week of your food prepared by that great ship's cook?" He paused, shaking his head. "No."

The crew laughed again.

"Let me see… What tribute can you give me?" Turning, he walked to the stern, where I noticed that two ropes had been tied to the rail. "I have it! You will swim with my fish until you find your scepters."

The crew yelled their approval, grinning, and began herding Marcus and me to the stern. Once there, King Neptune tied a belaying pin – a long wooden dowel – to the end of each rope. "These pins will be the scepters that will give you leave to cross my line." Turning, he threw the pins overboard and let the rope rush out. "Once you return with your scepters, you will be allowed over."

I looked at Marcus and noticed fear on his face. He had no idea of what was happening. Glancing over to the skipper, I nodded my head in Marcus's direction.

He got the idea, and was soon telling the boy in Portuguese not to worry, that this was all in good fun.

Or was it? That's when I noticed the Mate by the rail with a musket.

"Why the musket, King Neptune?" I asked.

"So none of me fish thinks ye to be their dinner. Now, over the side, lads."

As we grabbed onto the ropes, I could still see fear on Marcus' face. I yelled to him, "Do as I do."

He nodded back.

The morning was hot, the water looked cool, and, with a soft breeze, the sloop was only making a few knots. Like monkeys, we scrambled down the ropes and into the ship's wake. The green coral sea was refreshing, and I discovered that if I let go of the line, the speed of the ship pulled the hundred-foot end of the rope to my hands. When it did, I untied the pin and placed it in my month.

Marcus watched and did the same.

Now the hard part started – going hand-over-hand, against the oncoming sea. As we surfed and struggled forward, I felt a fish pock against my body. Startled, I looked over to find a porpoise swimming playfully next to me. The animal dove and twisted in the crystal-clear water, then bumped me again. It was glorious.

Looking up, I spotted the Mate with his musket pointed our way. Taking the pin from my mouth I shouted, "Only a dolphin." He withdrew his aim.

A few moments later, we reached the stern. With the crew at the rail, laughing and yelling, we were dragged aboard, dripping wet. When we handed the pins to a smiling King Neptune, he gave us each a crown of seaweed and a cup of rum. Then he welcomed us to his equator. I had read about this whimsical ceremony before, and now I had experienced it.

We slowly moved in a southwesterly direction, but, with the light and variable winds, we traveled only fifty or sixty miles a day. A week later, the Orphan was helped by the southeast trade winds, and our daily runs increased.

Finally, the island of Fernando de Noronha was spotted on the leeward side, which told the Captain that we had reached the broad shoulder of Brazil. Here, a course correction was made to follow the South American currents. By sailing south with the contour of continent, our daily runs increased to over one hundred and twenty miles. But these long runs proved tiring for the crew, and the ship still had sixteen hundred miles to travel. Soon, many of the crew started griping disrespectfully about the Captain, the food, the weather, and everything else. All this rancor made me uncomfortable, even though Sandy took me aside and told me that this was normal for a crew on a long voyage. But I still didn't like hearing all the insults and laments.

A few days after changing course, the flagship came to an abrupt halt and raised its emergency signal flags. Quickly, the sloop came alongside and reefed sails. Then the two captains talked, using the voice horns.

From their conversation, we learned that Mr. Nutting, the astronomer, was missing. The Commodore had dispatched a party to search the ship and was waiting for their report.

Shortly, he called across that the party couldn't find the astronomer and that they guessed that he had fallen overboard. "He was last seen by the midwatch," the Commodore shouted.

"If he went in during the night, he's gone," replied Captain Gray.

"Aye…he must have drowned. Let's get underway."

Later, we learned that most of the crew on the *Columbia* believed that Mr. Nutting had gone mad and jumped overboard. He had been unstable during the voyage and an unusual addition to the expedition from the very start. He was probably the first American astronomer to view the southern skies, but there were no records to show that he had ever done so. Hopefully, with both Captains now navigating, the expedition would make more progress.

Being in the crosstree as the lookout when the seas were rough and the winds brisk was a miserable job. But when the seas were calm and the winds warm, I enjoyed the duty. Sitting in the crosstree always provided spectacular views. Some days I watched clouds stack up like firewood and see lighting behind them, like a tattered shade. Then came the thunder, rolling across the sky like cannon fire. During the night watches, there were the brilliant southern stars to admire and sometimes a bright moon. On one such night, just after a big, full moon had risen in the eastern sky, and with my mind reeling with thoughts of home, I lost all sense of time. When a bald Indian head popped up from the shrouds below, I was so startled that I about fell off my perch.

"Hopi, you gave me a start," I yelled.

"My watch," he said as he pulled himself to sitting position next to me.

Pointing out to the horizon, I said, "Look at that moon! Have you ever seen it so big and blue before?"

"Nay."

Hopi was a quiet, half-breed with Wampanoag Indian blood in his veins. He shaved his head each morning, leaving only a stump of black hair at the back of his skull. That stump was tied together with leather and small sticks, allowing the long hair to fall onto his back. Other than bushy black eyebrows, his bronze head was devoid of facial hair. On one cheek, he had a tattoo of a circular blue swirl, and he wore large, round earrings on both ears. If you didn't know him, you might think him a savage.

In the blue moonlight, I watched his face as he gazed at the moon. Then I asked, "What does your name mean in your native language?"

Turning to me, he answered, "Restless one."

"Are you restless? Is that why you're a sailor?"

"Aye, I search for answers."

"Answers to what?"

Turning his gazed back to the moon, he said, "Life."

"Have you found any?"

"Aye, many."

After thinking for a moment, I asked the question that had been on my mind all voyage. "Would you know why the eagle is feared?"

Looking back at me, the blue twinkling ocean reflecting on his face, he thought for a moment and then answered, "Aye… because he can soar."

This was the longest conversation I had ever had with Hopi, and his answer made me think. After all, Indians would know best about eagles.

A few days later, I helped row the skipper to the flagship for a council. After having coffee in the galley, I went to the forward rail, waiting for the meeting to end. As I heard the ship's bell signal a watch change, I observed Mr. Haswell, the second Mate, having a problem getting a sailor to turn to. At first, he calmly approached the forecastle hatch and ordered the crewman to the deck. When he received no response, he went down the ladder.

From where I stood, I could only hear what happened next. In a firm, loud voice, Mr. Haswell ordered the sailor topside. The seaman responded with loud and scurrilous language. For a few seconds, the two men just yelled at each other, and then I heard a scuffle and the cracking of a fist. Moments later, the Mate returned to the deck with the seaman, who was holding a handkerchief to his bleeding nose.

As this commotion was unfolding, Captain Gray and the Commodore came to the quarterdeck. When Captain Kendrick saw the bleeding sailor, he exploded with anger and rushed forward. He confronted the two men, but instead of supporting Mr. Haswell, he yelled at him. The Mate yelled back. With the two men now loudly cursing one another, and with all the crew watching, Captain Gray came forward to intercede. Finally, calm was restored, and the three officers moved back to the stern...but without anyone saying a word to the bleeding sailor who had started the fracas.

Still angry, Captain Kendrick would not let it go and soon ordered Mr. Haswell off the deck and told him to move from his cabin to the forecastle. The Mate agreed, if he was given leave of the ship's company. But Kendrick would not agree to that and, after much yelling, Mr. Haswell stormed off the deck.

As we rowed back to the Orphan, the skipper sat quietly, gazing at the flagship. We had just watched the Commodore go a little berserk, and we all knew it could be a bad omen of things to come.

A few days later, our two ships arrived at the easternmost coast of Argentina and changed course for West Falkland Island. As we traveled these waters, the overcast sky teemed with sea birds of all kinds and colors. Sandy pointed out one large albatross with a yellow head and told me that a legend claimed that these birds were the souls of drowned sailors.

Looking more closely at this big beaked bird as it soared, glided, and fished so close to the ship, I thought Sandy just might be right. There is something about stories of the sea and the men who give their lives so freely that always seemed to ring true, like the ship's bell.

In due course, the two vessels spotted West Falkland Island. The destination of the ships was to be Port Egmont on Saunders Island, just northwest of West Falkland Island. But upon entering a narrow channel that led to the port, the Commodore was confronted with strong headwinds and an adverse tide. He therefore bore away and set sail for Brett's Harbor, a protected anchorage on the same tongue of land as the port but on the opposite side of the island.

Here, with no other ships in sight, the vessels dropped anchor. Our passage from Port Praya had taken fifty-seven days.

After dropping the bowers, Captain Gray went ashore with the Commodore in search of fresh water. Upon their return, they reported finding many springs and of observing large flocks of duck and geese.

The next day, work parties were dispatched to fill the water casks and to hunt for game. The air was chilly when I went ashore with musket in hand as part of a hunting detail.

A heavy, gray layer of clouds hung over the rocky landscape that looked sparse and barren. There were a few small groves of trees and long, golden sea grass on the hillsides. How humans could survive on this wasteland, I did not know. One thing was certain: whatever game was on this bleak island would have to be searched out. We hunted all that afternoon and returned to the ship weary but with large bags of gutted and plucked game-birds, ready for the cook's pot. That same afternoon, other parties returned with firewood and with grass for the livestock.

The following day, Captain Gray set about preparing for the Orphan to round Cape Horn. He instructed me to set up a small forge on the deck to repair some of the ship's iron strapping that had been damaged during the passage.

As I worked the hammer and anvil, other crewmembers caulked the hull planking above the water line. Some timbers were replaced or repaired by the ship's carpenter while other sailors worked in the rigging, setting in heavy new canvas sails. For three long days, all the ship's activities were focused on making the sloop ready for its dangerous crossing to the Pacific. Finally, with deck planks fully sealed and the Captain's final inspection passed, the sloop was ready to sail.

Just as we completed our work, however, we learned that the Commodore was having misgivings about making the southern passage so late in the season. His idea was to winter in the Falklands and begin the passage in eight months.

Staying in this desolate harbor for eight months was not well-liked by the officers or by crew. Captain Gray warned the Commodore that it was a bad idea and that some of the men might take "French leave" – jump ship. He even asked permission for us to proceed alone in the Orphan, but his request was rejected. Captain Kendrick vacillated for days, and all the while the weather worsened in the southern seas.

One day, I asked Sandy why we couldn't sail to Argentina and winter there.

"It's the Spaniards, lad. They rule with an iron fist from Madrid. If we sailed into one of their ports, they might confiscate our ships, and we could be marooned for years."

As the days dragged on and we were running out of time, I knew that something had to happen. And then it did. On our ninth day at anchor, we learned that Mr. Haswell, the former second Mate of the flagship, had gone ashore with a hunting party and failed to return. A search detail was sent out, but at dark they returned alone. By now, most of the crew guessed that the Second Mate had walked the five miles across the island to Port Egmont, where he could simply sign on with another ship.

The next morning, when he still had not returned, the Commodore ordered his brig lowered, intending to sail to Port Egmont and retrieve the deserter. But just as the boat was ready to get underway, Mr. Haswell was spotted on the beach, waving his hands. Later, we learned that he had indeed walked the five miles, only to find a crumbling town with no souls and no ships. The British settlement of Port Egmont had been abandon a few years before.

With Mr. Haswell aboard the flagship again, Captain Gray rowed over to confront the Commodore. Reminding him that others would likely desert if there were further delays, he convinced Captain Kendrick to get underway. Then he asked that Mr. Haswell be assigned to the Orphan as the sloop's much-needed Second Mate.

The Commodore hesitated, then relented reluctantly.

When the skipper was rowed back to the Orphan, he brought with him both the longed-awaited sailing orders and a new Second Mate.

With the crew happy and singing jovially, we pulled together in preparing the ship to get underway. The two vessels sailed for the Pacific Ocean via the Drake Passage at daybreak on February 28, 1788.

Chapter Three: Cape Horn

Cape Horn is actually a small island well off the tip of Tierra del Fuego, which is the last large island at the very bottom of the South American continent. To round the Horn, at this very southern tip, is one of the most dangerous nautical passages in the world.

This route, circling beneath South America, was first discovered in 1615, by a Dutchman named Isaac Le Maire. At the time, most sailors believed that Tierra del Fuego was another continent. But Le Maire was convinced that it was just a large island and, therefore, could be rounded to the south. Since Sir Francis Drake, years earlier, had reported sailing in an open ocean far south of the island, therefore, this new route came to be the known as Drake Passage.

Before that discovery, the only way to the Pacific was by sailing through the Strait of Magellan. But this narrow inland passage, just north of Tierra del Fuego, was hampered by contrary winds, shallow depths and little room for the ships to maneuver.

When ships traveled to the Pacific, using the much wider Drake Passage, they rounded Horn Island to catch the prevailing winds and tides. If ships were heading east, into the Atlantic Ocean, they would travel well south of Horn Island for the prevailing winds and tides. However, due to violent and treacherous weather in the Cape passage, sailors navigated the route with great apprehension. The waves could reach heights of over 65 feet, and the Strait experienced clouds, ice and windy storms more than two hundred days out of the year. As a result, the area was littered with shipwrecks and the forgotten souls of hundreds of sailors. Rounding Cape Horn was not for the faint of heart.

Passage to the Pacific

With the addition of Mr. Haswell as the new second mate, cabin boy Marcus Lopez was moved to the forecastle. Marcus and I had developed a kinship after our King Neptune experience, so I was pleased with his arrival. Both Sandy and I hoped to help the lad with his English so that we might again be privy to the scuttlebutt. We knew the boy was smart enough to learn; we just didn't know if he was willing to share the news.

When Marcus first came aboard, in Porto Praya, he had carried a leather valise containing his personal belongings. During his move forward, I was lying in my bunk with Becky's locket in hand, daydreaming of home and family. Out of the corner of my eye, I sensed Marcus's presence as he stowed his belongings in the footlocker under his hammock. At first, he worked quietly and I paid him little heed. But then, suddenly, he started chanting in a low mumble, using words I could not understand. Twisting my head in his direction, I watched as he removed various small muslin pouches from the bottom of his valise. With each bag, he uttered a different chant before placing them into his locker. I counted seven pouches in all, and the placement of each was accompanied by a different hymn.

After the last one, I rolled out of my hammock and joined him where he knelt on the deck in front of his locker.

Pointing to the bags, I asked, "What's in the pouches?"

He looked at me for a moment, then smiled and answered, in his broken English, "Big spirit."

"Can I see?" I asked, and pantomimed opening the bags.

"Aye," he answered.

Each muslin sack had crude symbols embroidered on the fabric: on one side was the moon, and on the other side was the sun. Using sign language and a little English, Marcus explained to me that the symbols were the signs of his gods. As he opened each bag, he proudly showed me its contents. Two contained long strands of dried roots. Two others held different types of curled-up tree barks. The final three were filled with different kinds of dried leaves. They each had an odor that was bitter and unpleasant.

"Are these your gods?" I asked.

He looked at me strangely for a moment, and then seemed to understand. "No… Vodou."

His words startled me. Sandy had told me about the practice of Voodoo in many parts of the Dark Continent, and how the natives believed in its mystical powers. He had called it "witchcraft," and I wanted no part of it.

Pointing to the sewn symbols on the bags, I asked, as simply as I could, "What name…your gods?"

He pointed to the moon symbol and said, "*Mawu.*" Then he turned the bag over, pointed to the sun symbol, and said, "*Lisa.*"

The kid looked so proud to be sharing his gods with me that I didn't know what to say next. Finally, I asked bluntly, "Is this witchcraft?"

His brown eyes stared at me for a moment. Then, shaking his head, he slowly answered, "No…no. Big medicine."

Staring back at this curious little guy, I replied, "Yes, I understand."

But I really didn't. What kind of medicine? What was the name of this religion? Why wasn't he a Christian, like all the other Portuguese?

As I watched this strange black boy carefully stow away the bags, he started to chant again. Those pouches were big spirits to him, and I wanted to learn more. This dark side of Marcus frightened me a bit, but other questions about his beliefs would have to wait until he spoke better English or I learned more of his tongue.

With sea birds swarming after the ships like locusts, we moved south smartly. The winds were fresh and the currents favorable, so we ran with full sheets. During each watch, the officer of the deck and a crewmember would use a *chip log* to determine the ship's speed in knots. Then the depth of the sea, in fathoms, would be determined by using a *sounding line.* After these measurements were written into the daily log, if the weather was clear, the deck officer would then use a *quadrant* to fix the ship's latitude and correct any compass errors.

With all of this logged information, Captain Gray fixed the ship's longitude by dead reckoning. But his positions never seemed to match those of the flagship's logs. Because of that, he grumbled that the *Columbia* was always off course.

Early on the chilly morning of our sixth day of sailing, I was told to report to Captain Gray's compartment. When I arrived, I found the skipper and Hopi having coffee. The Captain motioned for me to sit next to the Indian, and then called out to Marcus for another mug.

Looking up from his brew the skipper, said, "Hear me now, lads, and hold on to my words. Our sails will soon carry us into an ocean like no other in the world. Here the seas will boil up like mountains, and the winds will scream with rain and snow. The storms will turn day into night and night into hell. And so, for these next few treacherous weeks, I will need my best eyes in the tree. I know this task will be unpleasant, but until we reach the Pacific you're going to be my lookouts. You'll work six-hour watches, relieving each other. I want keen eyes watching out for rocks, shoals, birds and ice."

As Marcus slid a mug of coffee in front of me, I repeated, "Birds and ice?"

"Aye. If you spot a flock of birds hovering over the sea, it could mean danger. Look for rocks and shoals where they fly. And in these southern waters, the tip of an iceberg can be as big as an island, under the surface. If the ship hits one, we could all be lost." The Captains expression was as somber as I had ever seen. He continued, "When the seas start to boil, you're going to have a crazy ride in your perch, so use your life line and stay alert! Your eyes are our fate, so no dozing off. Do you understand?"

"Aye," both Hopi and I answered.

"Tomorrow, we should raise Staten Island on the larboard quarter. Sing out with the voice horn when she comes into view."

With the Captain's sobering words ringing in our ears, Hopi and I departed his cabin. As we reached the aft hatch ladder, Marcus stopped us. Reaching into his pocket, he pulled out a chunk of tree bark and broke it in half.

"Ya sleepy, chew this. It keep ya awake. Big medicine."

Hopi and I looked at each other in amazement, but we nodded and took the chunks of bark. Thanking the little lad, I had no idea how tree bark could be big medicine, but if the time came when I needed it, I would give it a try.

With the winds brisk and the seas rolling, I was the first to climb to the tree and begin this new vigil. Wearing my foul-weather coat, tuque and wool gloves, I lashed myself to the main mast and gazed out to sea with the long glass. My innards twisted with each swell, and I feared the future and yearned for home. This current assignment was a notion I did not like, but

I understood that it was a task of great importance. We were now the eyes of the ship, eyes that could help guide her safely to the Pacific.

Despite twenty-four hours of searching, however, Staten Island was never raised. Captain Gray remarked that the convoy had missed the island because the flagship was off course and sailing too far east. This confusion with the ship's position caused many of the crew to grumble that we were lost, but Sandy kept assuring them that the skipper knew right where we were. Soon, the council flags were flying, and Captain Gray, along with both mates, were rowed to the flagship. After a contentious meeting that included much finger-pointing, both ships turned due west – hopefully, towards the Cape.

Two days later, the island of Tierra del Fuego was spotted off the starboard quarter, and both ships turned southwest. But this new course placed the ships in the direct path of ever-recurring storms of heavy seas and squalls of rain and snow. With the decks awash almost constantly, and with water seeping into the hull and bilges, it became necessary to man the pumps on each watch. As the weather got worse and the seas taller, this pumping never stopped. We feared that the bilges would overflow, causing damage to the contents of the hold and imperiling the safety of the vessels.

Working the pumps was a miserable two-man job on the dark, cold, pitching deck of the main hold. It was horrible duty, but I would have traded my lookout perch for a pump handle any time. Riding the tree in heavy seas was like riding a bucking horse. It was during these storms that I chewed my first chunk of Marcus's *Big Medicine*. I found the bark sweet, with a tough, stringy texture. Within moments, I was surprised by the results; gone was my weariness and even my fear. For some reason, I *was* more alert, and the icy shrouds and pitching ship no longer frightened me. This magical potion was a tonic like no other, and I was pleased to have it.

At times, these unrelenting gales and high-breaking seas all but overcame the efforts of our crew to keep the Orphan afloat. Soon, the seaworthiness of both ships became our utmost concern. Our progress was being impeded by the weather and currents, and also by the heavy growth of barnacles and grass on both ships hulls. On some days, we moved forward only a few miles; on others, we actually lost mileage. During these massive seas, there was no cook's fire, so the crew went without warm meals and hot coffee. And trying to sleep in the forecastle, with its leaking and twisting deck above, was out of the question. For four long, wet, deplorable days, we battled the raging seas and roaring winds, until we thought that neither the ship nor we could take any more.

Then it stopped, as quickly as it had started. The sky brightened, the seas turned calm and the winds blew gentle. It was as if God had finally heard our cries for mercy and blessed us with favorable conditions.

With the cook's fire lit again, we made repairs to the ship and finished pumping out the bilges. Then, when our bellies were full of warm food, Captain Gray whistled the crew to the quarterdeck and passed out a double ration of rum.

As we stood drinking the brew, he pointed aft and said, "The worst is over, lads. We will continue on this heading and, within the week, raise Horn Island, then turn west for the Pacific. There is no turning back, boys. Our destiny is upon us. We will be the first American ships to complete such a journey." Taking his cup he raised it over his head and concluded, "Here's to the crew of the *Lady Washington*."

The crew answered his salute with a loud yell, cups held high. Only a day earlier, we had all feared for our lives, but now we stood drinking rum and enjoying fellowship. Being a sailor was indeed a strange way of life.

But the worst was not over. Two days later, Mother Nature turned against us again. With howling, icy winds, gale succeeded gale out of the south. In this souring weather, I soon spotted chunks of ice in the sea. The farther south we moved, the bigger these chunks became, until some were indeed as big as islands.

Because of the strong, blustery winds, both ships moved with shortened storm sails. On the sloop, that meant using only one or two of the headsails. If conditions improved, other sails would be rigged.

At dusk, the two ships would heave-to and dragged a drogue. This slowing of the boats' forward progress helped the crew and lookouts keep a watchful eye for any dangers in the blackened sea. Then, when daylight returned, our sails would be hoisted again, and the sea anchor brought aboard.

This constant changing of sheets and rigging caused great hardship for the crew. Adding to their misery was the dropping temperature. The deck soon became a sheet of ice, with the rails garbed in white frost. Standing on the slippery, pitching deck, the crew had to break away the ice buildup before its weight could capsize the sloop. And as soon as the task was complete, they would have to start all over again. No one slept, no one even rested, as ship and crew struggled for their very survival.

With timbers moaning and the winds swirling, I climbed the slippery shrouds to relieve Hopi on the morning of the fifth day of the storms. Cautiously, we traded places on the icy, swaying platform.

As I strapped the life rope on, I noticed the Indian's frozen eyebrows. His face looked tired and empty.

Finally, Hopi shouted over the winds, "Do ya have any more tonic?"

Shaking my head yes, I reached into my pocket and took out my small remaining piece. Taking a bite from the bark, I handed the last part to Hopi.

Smiling, he put the chunk into his mouth and yelled, "I'll get more from the boy. See ya at two bells."

As the Indian gingerly descended the shrouds, I slowly turned and took my first view of the horrifying seas. Because of the heavy, black storm clouds, the ocean looked like ink. Other than a few dirty white caps, the sea itself blended into the horizon with a gloom that I had never before witnessed. Even while I was chewing the bark, this shroud of darkness frightened me to my bone. Day had been turned into night, and I feared we were sailing directly into the eye of a hurricane.

With the top sail furled, I was able to take the long glass and slowly pan the abyss for dangers. Hours passed as I swept from port quarter to starboard and then back again. With the flagship a half mile in front of us, I kept a close eye on her signal flags, for any signs of alert, but saw none. Soon, squalls begin to roll in, accompanied by heavy snows. At times, I would lose sight of the *Columbia* for long, terrifying moments. Then, out of the gloom, she would reappear, always plodding southwest.

As I heard four bells in the wind, I turned my glass again to the port quarter. At first I didn't notice anything amiss, but then I saw it: there in the murk, a large flock of birds was hovering over the sea. Straining my eyes, I watched as the birds flew straight up into the wind and then glided sideways down again. As the ships moved closer, my view improved. Finally, I was able to make out a long line of white water, just under their flight…and then the dark silhouettes of rocks.

Grabbing the horn with dark doubts, I shouted down to the quarterdeck. "Shoals tens points off the port bow." I repeated this frantic warning twice more before Mr. Coolidge answered my call.

Moments later, I was surprised to see the faint outline of a large island just behind the rocks. Its sight caused my heart to skip. The land looked to be no more than a few miles away, with both ships, sailing directly for it.

In the loudest voice that I could muster, I shouted down again, "Land ahoy, off the bow!" This I repeated three times before Captain Gray's voice answered back.

Looking down to the deck, I watched as all three officers rushed to the bowsprit to view this obscured island with their glasses. As I looked up again, I sighted the silhouette of a second menacing island just behind the first. Turning my view to the flagship, I saw no signal that they had seen the danger. Finally, I felt the Orphan change its course to west. But the *Columbia* continued on its course, making directly for the rocks.

With my adrenalin pumping, I shouted down, "Flagship off course."

This I repeated over and over again, until the sounds of our signal cannon answered back with a loud… *boom*. Moments later, the *Columbia* got the message and tacked sharply to a westerly course.

From the deck below, Captain Gray shouted up the mast with his horn, "Mr. Blackwell, those islands are Diego Ramirez. We are south of the Horn and have rounded her. Well done!"

With his words ringing in my ears, I looked again to the sea. The way now seemed brighter, and our future more promising. There was a feeling of pride in my heart, for I had helped save the ships from danger and guided them to the Pacific. On this nineteenth day of March, 1788, I was one of the first Americans to double Cape Horn. We were now on the far side of the world, and I had found the strength to do my duty. Thank God!

The next day, with temperatures moderating and the seas still boiling, both ships changed course again to the northwest. Two wet, miserable days later, we raised a group of craggy islands off our starboard quarter and began noticing large flocks of black-winged, white-bodied birds. From their size and the shape of their beaks, I guessed that they were a different kind of albatross.

Whatever they were, they were aggressive. As I stood on my platform, they would drive at me, making loud, high-pitched shrieks, while others perched above me on the top sail spar, dropping dung on me. At one point, a fat albatross landed at the very end of the boom above. He shook his body and cocked his head, with his beady eyes staring directly down at me.

Looking up at him, I shouted, "Why is your Pacific so violent?"

Spreading his gigantic wings, he cooed back at me. As I watched him,

I thought about him in the cook's pot, but then remembered that these birds were the lost souls of sailors. This thought gave me the creeps.

"I won't be joining you any time soon, so fly away."

With his golden beak, he groomed his black wings and then cooed back again.

"Why aren't you an eagle? Fly away. You are of no use to me."

He looked at me for another moment, as if he understood, and then flew away.

Shaking my head, I thought, *"How bad is this? Now I'm now talking to birds!"* With my own oddities in mind, I tolerated their annoyance until we passed their rocky nests.

With the bird islands in our wake, both the sea and the winds seemed to moderate. Soon, the flagship signaled for more speed, and Captain Gray answered with full sheets. He also ordered Hopi and me to return to our normal duties. He was pleased with our efforts, and believed the ship was now out of danger.

Relieved with the change, I looked forward to my time on deck. Standing for hours on that exposed and swaying lookout platform had been a duty I did not relish.

At dusk three days later, a sudden gale blew up from the south with such fury that it snapped off the top of our main mast. With the winds still roaring and the halyards damaged at the top, one storm sail broke loose and tangled in the riggings.

Quickly, Mr. Coolidge hove-to and sounded the emergency. By the time the crew got to the riggings, the light was fading and ship was pitching in near hurricane seas. Fearing that we might capsize, Captain Gray took the helm and managed to get the Orphan turned into the wind. For the next few hours, working in two-man teams with lanterns, we furled all canvas, cut away the top of the main mast, removed the damaged sails, and repaired the rigging.

Finally, with only one storm sail set, the skipper turned the ship again, tracking it with the wind. As we came about, lightning began to flash across the sky, with thunder close behind. Moments later came snow and hail. With visibility gone, the skipper ordered lookouts to the bow, armed with lamps, then reefed the storm sail to slow our progress even more. For many wet hours, we peered through murky flakes, watching for danger.

When dawn brightened the skies, the gale abated and we added a second storm sail. With conditions improving, the lookouts searched the horizon for the flagship, but reported she was gone.

This astonishing news didn't seem to upset the skipper, as he was more worried about his men. The entire crew had been on deck over twelve hours, and everyone was exhausted from work and weather. He was wise enough to realize that the proper tonic for us was dry clothes, hot food and rum. And so, with the first rays of daylight, he addressed crew. "Good job men. In the bedlam we lost contact with the *Columbia,* so we will proceed to the uninhabited island of Masafuera. There we will find provisions. For now, your watch is over. Dry yourselves and get some hot grub."

While my wet and weary crewmates shuffled towards the forecastle, Captain Gray ordered Mr. Haswell and Mr. Coolidge aloft to make further repairs. It was an extraordinary order, seldom given to ship's officers.

Later, we learned that the Commodore had given the skipper written orders, back at Brett's Harbor, instructing him to proceed to the Juan Fernandez Islands if the two ships became separated. If the ships didn't rendezvous there, the *Lady Washington* was to sail for the northwest coast and meet up with the *Columbia* in the autumn at Nootka Sound. The orders were clear and, to tell the truth, the crew was pleased to be out of the shadow of the flagship.

North by Northwest

The sloop had been badly mauled. We had lost twenty feet off the top of the main mast and, because of that, the rigging for two sails. Upon further inspection, we also found cracks on the main jib. Repairs had to be made, but we had no timbers aboard that could be crafted as replacements. Because of these problems, we could only proceed on our northerly course at four knots.

The other problem we had was food. We had lost all the livestock overboard in the many gales, and we had no fresh fruit or vegetables. The skipper worried about scurvy, and ordered double rations of rum daily.

A few dismal days after the damaging storm, I stood on the cold deck, alternately sipping rum and playing my flute. It had become my custom to play lively tunes on these dark days. The music seemed to help my shipmates forget their misery. It always surprised me how many smiles my simple songs could bring.

Sandy stood next to me at the rail, enjoying his rum and slapping to the beat. As I finished, the crew clapped and tipped their cups to me.

Reaching for my rum, I said to Sandy, "I don't understand how."

"How what?" he replied.

After taking a swig, I answered, "How can a deserted island have provisions? And where is this land? How many leagues away? I liked it better when we knew the scuttlebutt."

Sandy dripped the last of the rum from his putter. "Aye, I overheard the mates talking. They said the island chain is called Juan Fernandez. They're Spanish-controlled and about seven-hundred miles north of us. Mr. Haswell said the land is rich and warm, and that, over the years, it's been planted with fruit and vegetable seeds, and stocked with hogs and goats. He talked about those islands as being a paradise. But I'll believe it when I see it."

Making sure that no one was watching, I handed Sandy my remaining rum. "Well, it does sound like heaven…although, for that matter, I'd settle just for being warm and dry again."

In due course, Captain Gray announced that we had reached the fiftieth parallel. It had taken us forty seven days to round the Horn from the West Falklands. It had been a journey of terrifying green seas and storms of a magnitude I could not have imagined. At the time, I had sworn that I would never make such a passage again. Along the way, I had proved my worth and found my sea legs, but I still knew, deep inside, that rounding the Horn was a foolish task only suited for desperate sailors.

As we sailed north, the bite in the air was soon replaced by a warm and gentle Pacific breeze. The slow-moving Orphan was blessed with fair winds and long westerly swells on her larboard beam. The ship would roll heavily downward into the bowls of the waves and then, on the next surge, be lifted high enough to view the surrounding horizon. This slow, pitching progress seemed God-sent after the violent seas of the Horn. But during our journey, not another sail was sighted.

By the middle of April, we arrived at the Juan Fernandez Islands, and the skipper turned the Orphan east. Two days later we sighted Masafuera Island and hove-to, half mile off her shoreline. The island was a beautiful, lush green dot in a vast teal ocean. It had a craggy coastline, with one pale mountain in the background. But there was a problem; the island had a reef of crashing surf that surrounded its shore.

After surveying the sea conditions, the skipper ordered the longboat away, with the Chief Mate in charge, to search for a channel. From the deck, we watched as the small boat rowed away, parallel to the long line of white breakers.

Two hours later, the skiff returned and Mr. Coolidge reported his findings. During his search, he had found only one narrow channel. But there, the surf rolling through that opening was so violent that it rushed unobstructed onto a rock-strewn beach. Any attempt to land, even with just the longboat, would be pure madness. Reluctantly, he recommended that the sloop sail on.

Without further discussion, the skipper agreed and set sail for the main island, Masatierra. There we would find a Spanish port of entry. But Captain Gray became increasingly concerned about the prospect that the governor might detain – or even outright seize – his ship, and so, with our destination in sight, he hove-to again.

Walking the deck, the skipper pondered that, because of his decision not to call on the island, the crew would surely suffer short rations and probably scurvy. On the other hand, being under the Spanish thumb was an option that could destroy the very venture.

There was indecision written all over his face, and the crew could see it.

Finally, with evening fast approaching, he ordered the second mate and Mr. Gayle to make a complete inventory of all provisions. Then he announced that we would lay-off the island until next morning. His final order was rum-call. With the happy crew lining up with mugs in hand, Captain Gray departed the quarterdeck for the solitude of his cabin.

Early the next morning, while having coffee in the galley, Marcus came up to Sandy and me and whispered, "Much argument last night. Mates don't want to go to island, Captain does."

Smiling at the boy, we thanked him for the information, and he quickly departed.

Looking across the table to Sandy, I tipped my cup to him and remarked, "The boy's English is getting better... and we have a pigeon now. Here's to the lad."

"Aye," Sandy answered with a grin.

A few moments later, the skipper whistled the crew to the quarterdeck. In the early morning sun, he stood next to the wheel, waiting for us to gather. Under his tricorne, I saw a tired and unshaven face. He looked as if he hadn't slept properly for days.

After all of us had assembled, he spoke to us in a firm voice. "I have decided not to chance Masatierra. Instead, we sail for New Albion. With fair winds, we should make the journey in about two months. We have enough food for the passage, and along the way we will search other islands for fresh fruit, vegetables, water and timbers to make repairs. Until that time, you are rationed to two quarts of water per day. There will be no exceptions, do you understand?"

At first, the crew seemed stunned by his decision, as we desperately needed provisions. The disappointment showed on many faces but, slowly, each man nodded his head and said, "Aye."

"What about scurvy, sir?" one of the crew asked.

Before replying, the weary Captain scanned our faces. "We will have fresh provisions soon enough. Until then, drink your rum." Turning, he told the chief mate, "Mr. Coolidge get her into the wind and set your course north-by-northwest."

That evening, while standing watch with Mr. Haswell, I learned that New Albion was an area discovered by Sir Francis Drake in the 16th century. The land was north of the Spanish stronghold of San Francisco, and over 5500 miles away.

Doing some quick figuring in my head, I said to the mate, "Not sure we can make that in just two months."

"Aye," was his only response.

Walking away, I gazed at the golden sun just starting its slow journey over the horizon. The color and brilliance of the sky reminded me of the hot days and dangerous waters ahead. Stopping by the weather rail, with a warm breeze on my face, I pined for home. But this endeavor had been my choice, and no matter what the tides, I would stay the course.

A few days later, we raised the small charted island of San Ambrosio. This low-lying land looked barren and unproductive as we dropped anchor offshore. Plainly visible were rust-colored dunes and sandstone hillocks, sure signs of sterility. Still, the skipper thought that landing might be worthwhile, so Mr. Coolidge went ashore in the longboat, seeking water, fruit or any other provisions.

Waiting in the blistering sun, Marcus approached and asked if he could see my sketches of Porto Praya. Sandy had told him about my drawings of his hometown, a placed he missed very much.

Seeking the shade of the forecastle, we sat at the small table, where I opened my portfolio and let him leaf through my drawings.

The first few were sketches done aboard ship, and he pondered at my work. Next in the stack were those of his hometown, the waterfront, the old church and the public market. As he gazed at these images his face lit up like a lantern, and he made many comments. The final sheet was a sketch that I had drawn from memory of the bird lady. When he saw it, he started to chuckle.

"You know Louie?" he asked, with his teeth flashing and his eyes dancing.

"Aye," I responded.

"He a very strange man. My tribe threw sour fruit at him many times."

Delighted with our banter, I asked, "What's the name of your tribe?"

"We are Fon, many people."

"And your religion?"

He looked at me for a moment and then answered, "We Animism."

"That is your god's name?"

"No, no… I will draw for you."

Turning over the sketch of the bird lady, I handed him a charcoal stick.

He twisted the paper to a better slant and went to work. A few moments later, he turned the sheet my way again. On it, he had drawn a triangle. At the places where the lines came together, he had marked three different symbols that I couldn't grasp. In the center of the triangle, he had drawn a crude sun, moon, tree, and water.

Pointing to the symbol on top, he said, "Father." Then, pointing to the bottom left symbol, he said, "Me." Pointing to the right symbol he said, "Spirit." Then he indicated the center drawings and said, "Gods."

Staring at his design, I finally understood, "So nature is your god."

Slowly, with a grin and a nod, he answered, "Aye." Then, turning his drawing over to reveal the bird lady on the other side, he continued, "Not nature."

Just then, I heard Mr. Haswell sing out that the longboat was returning. Gathering my drawings, I put them back in my pouch, and we went topside. Marcus's words had been revealing, and I found his beliefs simple yet thought-provoking. In the future, we would have to talk more about his gods, and about those muslin sacks of magic remedies.

The chief mate's quest had again been futile. He returned with only a few fish and one dead seal. The fat of the seal would be boiled down for oil used in the lamps and cooking, and the small fish would be consumed that very day. The island had proven to be nearly worthless, and the skipper got underway immediately, calling out a compass course.

As days passed and the rations dwindled, the crew's mood became bitter. We all knew that the Orphan was racing the wind against hunger and thirst. Although the cook continually dragged four fishing lines off the bow, they provided very little. So, with salt-pork our only grub and near empty water casks, angers flared. More than a few times, the officers had to stop crew scuffles and profane arguments. No one had been flogged yet, but Mr. Coolidge was threatening it.

Weeks went by without spotting another sail or dot of green. Along the way, the Captain made corrections to the course almost every day. During one mid-watch, I asked Sandy if he knew where we were heading. His reply was simple, "No, but the skipper does." Later, when I repeated this answer to the crew, they laughed. We all knew that soon the water casts would be drained, and our bellies would be empty.

I prayed for rain or land. Something had to happen or we would surely be lost.

Then, on May 10th, our prayers were answered. The lookout reported land off the starboard quarter, and the whole crew rushed to the rail to view the news. But all we saw was a cloud-dotted horizon. Using our glasses, we finally made out a short green band just below one white cover. Then, as we moved closer, the outline of land came into view. Moments later, a second island was reported on the larboard quarter.

Soon, Captain Gray was standing with us, carrying his long glass. Placing it to his eye, he panned the two islands for a few moments. When he put the glass down, there was something on his face that I had not seen for weeks: a smile.

Pointing towards the first island he said, "Welcome to the Galapagos Islands, lads. Here we will find our needs."

As we slowly passed the first rocky island, more came into view. We counted seven, in all, each with volcanic mountains and fluffy white clouds on their peaks. The farther we sailed, the bigger and greener they seemed to grow.

Making a slight course correction, the skipper ordered the main sail reefed, and directed that soundings be made every five minutes. Then, as we moved towards the largest land, he called out all the island names, and went on to tell us that these islands had been used by whalers and pirates for hundreds of years.

"On these islands we will find wild hogs and goats, as well as strange animals the likes of which you have never seen before. Most sailors call these islands the Enchanted Isle." Then, turning to me, beaming, he asked, "Mr. Blackwell, how about a lively song?"

An hour later, we came about and dropped anchor in a large, crystal clear inlet near the center of Isabel Island. Just as the sheets were being furled, the sun darted behind a dark cloud and it started to rain. It was gentle whisper at first, but then with dispatch.

Instantly, the silent crew tipped their faces to sky and, mouths open, drank in the sweet, cool water.

Moments later, it stopped as suddenly as it had started. Drenched, we watched the shadow of the shower chase across the island, and we shouted with glee. Our deliverance was at hand.

We stayed at those amazing islands for seven days of recovery and replenishment. What we saw there was mysterious; what we reaped there was magnificent. The shoreline teemed with seals, penguins, birds, sea turtles and large, bizarre-looking lizards. In the highlands, we found iguanas, snakes, wild hogs and goats. The clear waters held an abundance of fish of many types and sizes, and shellfish from clams to crabs. It was the food basket we desperately needed.

During our stay, we didn't see another sail, although there were signs that sailors had visited the islands before. On the windward side of the big island, Mr. Haswell and his shore party discovered the remains of a whaling brig. She appeared to have crashed years before on some rocky shoals, and what still stood was only a skeleton. From these bones, our ship's carpenter was able to scrounge a new top mast and a replacement jib. While the crew cut other timbers for fuel and charcoal, I worked my forge to hammer out iron joint sleeves for both mast and jib. We had been fortunate to find the derelict, as she proved us with much-needed resources.

We found no fresh fruits or vegetables on the islands, although different types of cacti were plentiful. These green prickly plants were boiled by the cook in hopes that they would be nourishment and help prevent scurvy, but they tasted bitter, and soon the crew refused to eat them…that is, until Mr. Gayle crushed up the plants and fermented the juice into a brew that had more of a kick than did rum. He referred to his new ale as *Green Thunder,* and it quickly became a nightly favorite for both officers and crew.

On May 16th, we departed our inlet with barrels filled with water, brew, salted pork and fish. Caged on deck were five goats, two pigs and one very large sea turtle. During our week's stay, the crew had been cheerful, but as we sailed away they were clearly pleased to have the sea under their legs again.

As we approached the northern tip of Isabella, the skipper told us that we were crossing the Equator. Crossing the gray line again, I stood at the rail, watching this wondrous enchanted isle slip away. She had been good to us, and I wondered if the northwest coast would be so generous and bountiful. To find that out, I would have to wait another 3500 miles.

Returning to the northern latitudes was like a homecoming for the crew. The event reminded us that we were one step closer to our venture and then home. The winds and currents were with us for the first few weeks. But then we came upon the doldrums again. This broad belt of calm winds frustrated the crew, but not the Captain. As the ship bobbed up and down in the long, rolling ocean swells, he ordered the Orphan *hogged.* Lowering the longboat we worked at scraping and scrubbing off the heavy growths of barnacle and grass from the ship's hull. It was a difficult task, for it had to be timed with the rolling and pitching of the sea. The work consumed a few days, and fog rolled in as we completed the task.

The ship had to keep moving, and so, with visibility limited to a few hundred yards, the longboat began towing the sloop. For ten long days, fog and calm winds stayed with us. Then, one morning, we awoke to find the gray ocean gone and the water sparkling. Soon, the limp sails thrashed, then bellied and finally filled. With timbers groaning, the Orphan was on the move again. We had lost two full weeks in the doldrums.

It had been over five months since the *Lady Washington* and *Columbia* arrived in the Southern Ocean. By now, most of the food staples had been consumed or were no longer fit for consumption. During this period, we had not eaten any fruits or vegetables. Because of this, three crewmembers began showing early signs of scurvy. They all had bleeding gums, which the skipper said was a positive sign of the disease. The ship desperately needed to find fresh food if these men were to recover. Yet the passage seemed endless. The days became increasingly monotonous, as did the crew's tedious mood.

My twentieth birthday came and went without fanfare. Celebrating personal events aboard ship was not the wont, as it was a distraction to the business at hand. When standing dog watch that night, however, I fixed my eyes on the vast haven of twinkling stars, and reflected on my purpose and promise. Life's journey can be conflicting, and I prayed for wisdom.

In due course, the sloop arrived at the forty-second parallel, far north of the Spaniards' stronghold of San Francisco. The skipper judged that any danger of being intercepted by a Spanish man-of-war was remote, so he changed course for the still-unseen land of New Albion. Once the continent was sighted, he would, without haste, put ashore a party to search out wild fruits, vegetables and water. Also, there was a chance that the much-needed fresh staples could be procured from the local Indians.

After the easterly course change, we hit headwinds that delayed our approach to the still unseen land. What we did see were sea gulls in the sky and kelp in the now-gray sea, sure signs that terra firma lay ahead.

A few sunny days later, while standing the forenoon watch, the lookout aloft loudly reported land off our bow. Soon, the crew stood at the rail with ebullient shouts. Even the sick shuffled onto the deck so that they might see it and rejoice. What we viewed of the distant land was the thin white line of breakers that protected its shore. Just up from the beach were rolling hills of endless evergreen forests which spread yet further inland to merge with a far-off, pale gray, mountain range. This memorable date was August 2nd, 1788; we had been at sea for ten months and two days, and we were finally at our destination! It was a moment in my life never to be forgotten.

The Land of Tillamook's

Captain Gray approached the surf line cautiously, taking depth readings every five minutes. Once we were a few hundred yards from the breakers, he changed course to the north and began following the long line of white waves. We all knew that, before sustenance could be obtained, a coastal opening would have to be found and a sandbar crossed.

A few miles up the line, the lookout reported smoke drifting up from a beach. Moments later, he shouted down that he saw natives around a bonfire.

Weather conditions seemed favorable, so the skipper came about and dropped anchor in fifteen fathoms. Soon, the lookout reported that ten men in a dugout canoe were crossing the surf and traveling in our direction. As they approached in their canoe with upright ends, they tossed feathers overhead and sang out in a strange tongue. Watching from the rail, I noticed that the Indians were clad in deerskins and adorned with beads of European manufacture. My first impression of these natives was disappointing. They looked small in stature, with long matted black hair and dirty bull-dog faces. I had seen many Indians back home, and these new specimens were, without a doubt, the most primitive looking I had ever encountered.

As their bobbing skiff came alongside, the skipper shouted down in English and with hand signs. They responded only with the hand language. Soon, the man that seemed to be the chief invited the Captain to visit his village, but the onshore breeze was increasing and the tides were changing, so the skipper had to refuse.

Before the Indians shoved-off, they handed up fish they had brought with them, and Gray reciprocated with trinkets. We were all disappointed that the Captain couldn't go ashore but, with the conditions changing, the welfare of the Orphan came first. Quickly, the anchor was lifted, and the sloop moved to deeper waters, continuing our course up the coast.

The next morning the skipper ventured to take the sloop closer inshore. Before long, the watch reported a narrow inlet, leading to a long verdant beach. Once again, our hopes rose, and the longboat was dispatched to sound the depths of the inlet.

But Mr. Coolidge returned sooner than expected. He told the skipper that, when the boat approached the shore, they were threatened by a band of shouting, defiant Indians who brandished spears, bows and arrows. They made such menacing gestures that any attempt to land would have been foolhardy. Astounded by the threatening behavior of the Indians, the Captain resumed our course up the coast.

A few hours later, the Orphan was hailed from a sea canoe whose occupants held sea otter skins aloft on paddles. The sloop rounded to, and the canoe came alongside. Then Captain Gray engaged in our first trading transaction. In exchange for three pelts, he offered simple iron hand tools, which were accepted. But the Indians had no food or water, so the skipper got the Orphan promptly underway.

That afternoon, at rum call, I sat on the hatch examining the first otter pelt that I had ever touched. Its shape was much like a weasel, and while the coat was thick, with a dark, soft fur, it also had an odor that was offensive.

Taking a swallow of rum, I asked Sandy, "We came all this way for this? It doesn't seem worth it."

"That's black gold you're holding, lad," he answered back in his falsetto voice. "We fill the Orphan with pelts like those and we'll all be rich."

"But they smell so bad."

Putting the pelt to his nose and making a sour face, he answered, "Them savages didn't tan it right. Let it dry a bit, then do some scraping on the hide, and it will smell sweet as a wench on Saturday night."

I hoped Sandy was right, as sea otter pelts were now our enterprise. If they were black gold, I wanted all we could find, odor or not.

Two days later, another small, barely visible inlet was observed. Soon, Mr. Coolidge went in to sound, but the bar was too shallow for the sloop to enter. Wind and sea conditions permitted anchoring outside, however, so the longboat went in again. The party searched for food and water, but without success. Only firewood could be found. The mate filled two boatloads of the much-needed wood before we sailed on. This was the first landing by Americans on the Pacific coast of the New World.

At twilight the next day, we approached another inlet, but when we came abreast of it, we found only large, wind-swept waves breaking at the bar. In the dim light, the conditions looked too dangerous even for the longboat, so we sailed on.

The next morning, the wind shifted from the north, with choppy cross-seas that brought the sloop nearly to a standstill. The skipper had to choose whether to remain stalled, perhaps for days, or to take advantage of the north wind and double back to the inlet we had seen on the previous evening.

After conferring with the officers, Captain Gray promptly turned the Orphan before the wind and sailed south. When we arrived again at the inlet, we found moderate swells breaking at the bar. Beyond it, however, we could see a channel of quiet water and, inside the opening, the green waters of a bay. The north side of the slit was protected by a tall, rocky mountain, while the south side boasted a long, brush-covered sandbar that protruded into the inlet. The bay beyond seemed to offered safe refuge, and the land looked abundant. From the rail, the crew prayed that our hopes would not be dashed again.

Quickly the skipper heaved to and the longboat was hoisted out. As usual the chief mate went in to sound. Soon back alongside, Mr. Coolidge reported ample depth of water, both on the bar and at the bay's estuary. The longboat was swiftly recovered while the American flag was unfurled.

With favorable winds, the skipper slowly guided the Orphan in the direction of the bar. The channel of placid water was only 70 yards wide, so the sloop had to be carefully turned into the slit with soundings shouted out constantly. Sailing in the grove was like threading a needle, as we had pounding surf and swirling waters on each side of the ship.

Once over the bar, we approached the bay's entrance, which narrowed to about 50 yards. Here, the skipper skillfully avoided the tall rocks on both sides. On the north, the approach was dominated by granite cliffs, while a sandy peninsula protected by shoals on the south. When we were finally inside the bay, we sailed to within a half-mile of the eastern shore and dropped anchor in ten fathoms of water. It had been one hell of a ride!

Still musing the crossing, I couldn't believe what lay before us. The calm green inlet was wide and long. The bay's crystal-clear waters stretched south for miles, and its shoreline was rich with foliage. The hills alongside the eastern shore was forested as far as the eye could see; across the bay, the green-covered sand spit reached for miles, with bone-white beaches. We had arrived at this new frontier on August 14, 1788. The passage from Brett's Harbor had taken 168 days, over a distance of 10,900 miles. Exhausted, hungry and sick, we had finally found relief.

As the bower was being dropped, the lookout shouted down that he had spotted a village on the northeastern shore. Moments later, he added that a canoe was being launched.

The Captain hurriedly whistled the crew to the quarterdeck.

With the warm early sun on his determined face, he addressed the men. "We want no trouble with the locals. But when they come aboard, keep a watchful eye. I understand from Captain Cook that they can be thieves. I will ask them first for provisions and then the pelts." Turning to the officers, he continued, "Mr. Coolidge and Mr. Haswell, draw out side arms, and I want two swivel guns loaded and manned. If things turn sour, be prepared for a fight." Then, turning to me, he concluded, "Mr.

Blackwell, fetch me a lit lantern and a box of those cigars. We'll see how these Indians like Afra-can tobacco."

When I returned to the deck with cigars and a brass lantern, I saw that a huge cedar dugout containing a dozen men had pulled alongside. The Captain stood at the rail and signed with them for a few moments, and then invited three of the chiefs aboard.

The Indians glared up at Gray, with his black eye patch, with great trepidation. Then, slowly, three bronzed savages, with surly faces and feathered heads, climbed anxiously over the rail, carrying two baskets of crabs and another of wild blackberries. They placed this gift of food on the deck in front of the Captain. The Indians were dressed in buckskin with filthy sour faces, and they wore crude belts and necklaces of seashells.

While all the crew stared at the food, the Indians lifted a hand upward, a jester of peace, and said something in their native tongue. As they spoke, the skipper turned to Hopi, his gaze asking silently whether he understood their tongue; in response, Hopi shook his head 'no' in a reply.

The dismayed Indians scanned the ship with wide-eyed amazement. Their mouths hung open as they grunted to each other. The expressions on their gawking faces were as if they had just stepped onto the moon.

The surprised Captain answered with a palm skyward in response, thanking them for the food. "Mr. Blackwell, the cigars, please."

I handed the box to the skipper. He opened the wooden lid, removed a cigar and placed it in his month. Then, turning the box, he invited the savages to do the same.

The first Indian was the tallest, and on his scruffy face, he had a shell piercing his noise. With a stern look, he hesitated, then reached out, took a cigar, and placed it into his mouth. The two other chiefs, with earrings of shells, followed his lead.

Handing the box back to me, the skipper ordered, "Mr. Blackwell, light my cigar."

When I opened the tiny door of the lantern and brought it level with his face, the skipper stuck his cigar inside and lit it.

Puffing blue smoke, he continued, "Now do the same for our guests."

Turning to the tallest Indian, I noticed a faint ruby scar across his sloped forehead. His clothes were tattered and he had a dreadful odor. All in all, he made my skin crawl. Opening the little brass door, I pointed to the candle burning inside. Cocking his head, he seemed curious about the lantern and finally stuck his cigar into the flame. Taking his first drag, he wheezed, and his manic gaze went from the candle to my face. He glared at me for a few more puffs. The other two did the same, never taking their eyes off of me.

With a loud chuckle, the skipper said, "Joe, it be your red hair again... they think ye the fire God."

At that, the crew got boisterous and started laughing. At first, the Indians didn't know what to make of this, but soon they started smiling and laughing, as well. While the gaiety was at my expense, even I joined in. With the three amused chiefs puffing blue smoke, Captain Gray had broken the tension with simple cigars. Now, that was diplomacy.

As the men continued to powwow, we learned that the Indians were from the Killamook tribe, but Captain Gray pronounced it as Tillamook. They went on to tell us, using sign language, that five other villages were spotted around the bay. And just north of this inlet was another that had two villages. When the skipper asked how many people were in all the villages, they didn't seem to understand. My impression was that they were too primitive to know ciphers.

In due course, trading started for more food. From the hold, Sandy brought up a stack of wool blankets and a large iron cook pot. It was soon agreed that for each blanket we would receive a basket of food, including more berries and other greens. And, in exchange for the iron pot, we would be given as much water as we needed.

The final thing they wanted was all of the remaining cigars in the wooden box. For those, they bartered a freshly killed animal that was hanging in their village. From their signs, we guessed that the kill was a deer.

With trading completed, the skipper told them that we would come to their village with the trade goods and pick up our food. This they understood, and departed to make preparations.

As they rowed away, I noticed that the brass lantern had gone missing from the hatch cover. I quickly pointed this out to Captain Gray.

He shook his head, but his only comment was, "Blimey, these Tillamooks *are* thieves."

With the Indians gone, the skipper called for rum, and told us that we could eat. The crew rushed the baskets and started devouring the food. Sitting on the deck, we found the berries firm and sweet, but it was the fat crabs that surprised us the most. Their hard shells were bright red on the top with a creamy bottom, and the meat inside was as sweet and tasty as lobster. It was simply delicious. Even the officers took their share, all the while pouring rum for the crew. Half an hour later, all that remained was a pile of shells. It had been a picnic like no other I had ever known.

In the afternoon, I went with Mr. Coolidge's shore party. The cook and I were to butcher the deer, while other crewmembers filled the water casks and traded for food. Before leaving, the Captain told me to draw out a pistol, because Mr. Gayle and I would likely be separated from the party. My thoughts about carrying a gun were mixed, but it was the Captain's direction, so I complied.

As we rowed towards the village we passed a long, sandy beach with tall, blonde sea grass. Up from the grass was a large grove of trees that grew up the rolling hills to the rocky cliffs that protected the bay's entrance.

The native village was up from a shallow cove that was fed by a small fresh-water river. As we first approached, I found it picturesque. But as we drew closer, my opinion changed. The many wickiups were scattered across the high ground in no particular order, and their shabby construction was apparent as we pulled the longboat ashore. At the water's edge, we were greeted by a large crowd of curious Indians of all ages and both genders. They seemed friendly enough, offering the shore party handfuls of sea shells as a token of welcome. The women were the strangest looking, as they were dressed in petticoats made of straw with tops of tree bark, while the men and boys were dressed in hides. Almost all of them had sloping foreheads and were adorned with necklaces made of shells. Their faces were annular, with high cheekbones and brown eyes. Some sported feathers in their hair, while others wore hats made from baskets and had bones or shells pierced into their bodies. Many of the men carried animal bladders filled with water and they started filling our two casks. While that was happening, a group of the woman stepped forward, offering to trade baskets and nets full of food for blankets.

I carried the cigar box and was soon approached by one of the chiefs from the ship. He motioned for us to follow him into the village. Both Mr. Gayle and I were nervous about being separated from the other men, and for the first time the pistol in my belt gave me comfort.

As we walked pass the Indian huts, I noticed their construction. They were large enough; some round to the ground while others were square or oblong. The walls were framed with long, bentwood poles over which layers of tree bark and wood planks were fastened to hold out the weather. Where all the poles came together, at the top, there was an opening for smoke. I guessed that the village had about fifty such wickiups; many large, while a few quite small. They were crude-looking shanties, but most likely practical for this environment. As we walked further, I saw no gardens or livestock. In the distance, I did hear a few dogs bark, but I never actually saw one.

As we rounded one hut, we came to a large tree. There, hanging from a limb, was an animal, but it wasn't a deer. Rather, it was the largest elk I had ever seen. A good-sized deer can dress out at a couple hundred pounds, but this animal, with its seven-foot rack of antlers, would be closer to five.

Looking up at the elk, I marveled that these primitive Indians could down such a large and magnificent creature. *These Tillamooks must be great hunters,* I thought with respect. Turning to the chief, I handed him the box of cigars and thanked him.

He looked at me oddly for a moment, then reached out and touched my hair. When his fingers didn't burn, he smiled and walked away.

Mr. Gayle chuckled, "He wants your hair on his pole. I'll bet they call you 'fire head.'"

We spent the better part of the afternoon dressing out the animal. Soon, we even had a small gallery of Indian children, sitting on their haunches, watching us cut. When we returned to the boat, we took only the four quarters, liver and pelt of the elk. What we left behind, the offal, was quickly gathered up by the children, as the Indians used all of the animal's parts.

That afternoon, the longboat made three runs from the beach, loaded with food and water. During this time, Mr. Coolidge found an old Indian woman in the village who owned a goat. At first, she didn't want to trade, but after the mate showed her three blankets, another large iron cook pot and a bag of colorful beads, she relented. This animal would join the one emaciated goat remaining on deck from the Galapagos. It was a great find for our future needs.

In the early evening, the Captain invited the three chiefs to return. When they came aboard, the skipper directed Marcus to serve them mugs of Mr. Gayle's ale.

As he handed out the brew, the chiefs' looked stunned, unable to take their eyes off the boy. With great excitement, they talked amongst themselves, until the scar-faced Indian finally reached out and touched the boy's midnight skin. When he looked at his fingers and found no grime, his eyes bulged, and he showed his hand to the others. Their reaction was one of amazement and disbelief.

Once over this, however, they tasted the brew with hesitation and then with enjoyment. As the chiefs drank, the Captain revealed our otter-pelts and told them we would trade for more. Soon, Sandy brought out the iron tools we had for bartering and placed them on the hatch. There were cooking pots, tin cups, chisels, adzes, saws, hammers and other hand tools such as iron bars and bores. The chiefs held each items and talked to each other, but didn't seem impressed. With hand signs, they indicated to the Captain that they wanted knifes and swords, like other tribes had received from other ships.

The skipper was surprised by this request, as it was too dangerous to trade weapons with the Indians. But soon, over a second mug of ale, their demands softened. They would trade their pelts for the iron goods but they also wanted more brew.

After checking with Mr. Gayle as to how much remained, it was agreed that a half-bladder of ale would be traded for every three pelts, until the brew was gone, but only if the Indians traded otter pelts, in good faith, for the iron tools. The trading was to take place the next day, on the ship, and to be completed by noon. This the three chiefs agreed to.

In the waning evening light, the Indians rowed to shore. We all knew that trading sprits with the savages was a bad idea, but for a few gallons of ale we would receive many pelts, worth a great deal of money. And this enterprise, after all, was all about money.

Early the next morning, the canoes started coming. We didn't want the Indians onboard, fearing their thieving ways, so Captain Gray put the longboat next to the sloop. There he would stand, under the watchful eyes of the crew and swivels, making the trades. Next to him was Mr. Gayle, pouring out the brew. Sandy brought the trading goods up from the hold as needed, while I kept the written account. From the rail and rigging, the rest of the crew, armed with muskets, stood watch over the bartering.

In the warm morning sun, the trading went smoothly and without incident. During this time, Mr. Coolidge counted twenty-two canoes, large and small, coming to trade. Many came up from southern villages, as well as two large dugouts from the ocean, crossing the bar in heavy surf.

By late morning, the trading was finished. On deck, we had a pile of thirty-two otter pelts and eleven beaver pelts that had cost us forty-six iron implements and the last fifteen gallons of Green Thunder. The skipper was pleased and the crew relieved that there had been no trouble.

After the noon meal, Captain Gray dispatched Mr. Haswell, to make soundings of the bay. I was ordered to join the party and draw a map of his findings.

The day was bright and the breeze warm as we rowed south along the eastern shore. We stayed fifty yards out in the bay and took depth readings every quarter mile. When the mate shouted the depth, I added the number to my map. I also drew rock formations, coves and creeks that we saw. It was the type of work that I relished, and at every glance I found new points to add. At the southern end, we discovered five rivers that flowed into the bay, and we passed four villages. They were all quite small, and of the same construction as the northern hamlet. Some curious Indians came out from their huts and watched us pass, but we had no trouble. Turning north, we rowed up the western bank. Here, the landscape changed from rocky shoals to sandy beaches. The land around the shoreline was green and fertile, and the placid blue bay was teeming with fish. Indeed, we witnessed many of them rolling in the water. *Here a man had elbow room*, I thought, *someday this bay will be much like Boston Harbor.*

As we finished our survey and rowed towards the ship, I looked down on my map with great pride. It was detailed and accurate, and it had been a pleasure to draw. Might map-making be my calling? Looking back along the bay, I wondered if we were the first white men ever to see this lush land. In any event, I thanked God for the opportunity, and told myself that I was now a wilderness explorer.

Captain Gray seemed please with my parchment as he rolled it up with his other maps. Then he told me that we were sailing with the evening tide. Before parting, however, he was sending Marcus ashore to cut sea grass for the goats, and he wanted me to go with the boy for protection. While we worked, the mates would visit the village one last time. He emphasized that the shore party should be back aboard by the first dog watch, which meant that we would have only a few hours before leaving this wondrous bay.

With the afternoon came a cool breeze off the ocean. Before departing, I grabbed my coat and pistol, as Marcus secured a cutlass from the arms locker. Moments later, we were helping to row the longboat towards a grassy beach just up from the village. With us were both mates, and another seaman.

After securing the boat at the water's edge, the shore party started walking towards the hamlet, a few hundred yards farther down the beach.

As Marcus got busy cutting the grass with his cutlass, I spotted a rocky perch up the beach that could give me one last view of the bay. Pointing to the outcropping, I told the boy that I would be up there, drawing a sketch of the cove.

Tying up his first bale of grass, he nodded his approval.

The escarpment was about fifty feet above the bay, and it took me a few minutes to scale it. Once I reached that perch, I had a spectacular view, all the way down to the southern shore, and to my left I could look down to where the boy worked, and just beyond to the Indian village. On my right was the crystal-blue cove where the Orphan rested. With the sun dropping in the western sky, it was a pristine scene that needed tracing, but as I reached for paper and charcoal, I heard drums and chanting in the breeze. Looking towards the village, I guessed that the Indians were putting on a dance for the shore party. Glancing down to the boy, I saw him drag another bale to the longboat, then return for more. With the taste of salt on my lips and glory in my eyes, I felt deeply content, and confident that all was well.

Chapter Four: The Coastal Indians

The terrain of the Northwest Coastline is rugged and untamed, as forbidding in many ways as the natives that flourished on its shore. This land stretched north from San Francisco to Nootka (Vancouver Island), and was inhabited by dozens of different Indian nations. Just south of Tillamook Bay lived the Siletz tribe, while to the north were the Clatsop and Chinook tribes. Unlike most Indians, these costal people didn't nomadically follow the game they hunted, or move with the seasons. Instead, they stayed close to the bays and the sea, establishing permanent homes and villages. The common thread between these nations was that they all spoke some dialect of the Salishan tongue. Unfortunately, none of these tribes had a written language, so their idiom would eventually be lost to time.

Thousands of years before the white man discovered Tillamook Bay, the Indians had migrated from a mighty northern river controlled by the Chinooks. These native explorers occupied the sand spits and placid bays, reaping the harvest of both sea and shore.

From these rocky coastlines and coves, the land rose gently to a heavily forested mountain range that served as a divide between the sea and a vast, fertile valley to the east. Residing along that ridge, and in the valley, were many more inland tribes.

The Pacific Coastal Strip inhabited by the Indians was a narrow, rolling plain, engraved with twisting rivers and streams that flowed westward from the mountains into numerous lakes, bays and bogs, and eventually into the broad expanse of the shallow tidewaters. It was along a six-mile bay that the Tillamooks chose to make their home. The men worked the rivers for salmon and other fish while the women busily gathered clams and other crustaceans from the shallow, sheltered bays, and roots from the brackish, swampy bogs.

The tribes inhabited a land abundant with resources that provided a hard but good life. The meadows teemed with black-tailed deer, elk, bear and a variety of other animals that could be used for food and clothing. And while the climate was harsh, with more than a hundred inches of rain in a single year, the temperatures were mild, giving birth to thick rainforests of cedar, fir, hemlock and spruce. All of these materials could be used in making tools, canoes and homes.

But the shallow, narrow estuary to Tillamook Bay also isolated the Indians from the outside world. For hundreds of years, the Europeans had sailed ships just off the coast without noticing this pristine bay. A month before Captain Gray slipped across the bar, Captain John Meares, an English explorer, spotted the opening from his ship and made notes in his journal about the scant passage, but then moved on. It was only a twist of fate that forced the winds and tides to allow the *Lady Washington* across the spit, and that twist would not repeat itself again for many decades.

Turning Point

With the sun on my face, and my gaze darting from view to paper and back again, I sat on the perch, sketching the breathtaking vista. My mind was deep in contemplation of line and texture when yelling from below startled me.

Looking down to the grassy beach, I noticed Marcus's sword sticking up in the sand, then saw a young Indian boy approaching it. Marcus, a hundred yards away, stood by the boat with an arm full of grass, screaming at the boy to stay away. The lad paid him no heed; instead, he ran up, snatched the cutlass and headed for the grove of trees.

Still yelling, Marcus dropped his load and ran after the boy.

As I stuffed the paper and charcoal hurriedly into my pouch, I heard more uproar coming from the village. Peering that way, I saw my shipmates running away from the hamlet, towards the boat, with a large band of Indians giving chase.

Filled with dread, I rushed to descend the cliff. Before I could reach the ground, a pistol shot rang out, and I craned around to see a savage fall from the pursuing horde. Reaching solid ground, I raced toward the trees, heading in Marcus's direction. Once I was within the grove, I circled around, and spotted three Indians binding Marcus to a tree with thong. As I crept closer, they finished, and two of the Indians ran out of the trees, whooping, towards the beach. The lone Indian guard was the boy who had stolen the sword, which he now held in his hand.

With my half-cocked pistol in hand, I snuck up quietly to just behind the tree.

Boom! The Orphan's six-pound cannon roared to life. Its loud report shook the ground, and the young boy turned his frightened face towards the beach. As he did so, I rushed him from behind and brought the barrel of my pistol down hard on the top of his head. Like a reefed sail, he folded to the deck.

Hearing more yelling from the beach, I faced Marcus and said, "Are you okay, boy?"

With his eyes wide, he stammered, "Yeah...but what's happening, Joe?"

Sliding the pistol back into my belt, I removed my knife. Then, moving behind the tree, I cut the rawhide freeing his hands. "The shore party is under attack. We have to get out of here. Pick up your sword."

He reached down and grabbed the cutlass, clearly frightened. "Which way?"

"The beach is swarming with savages, so we can't make it to the boat. The village is down that way," I said, with a jerk of my head, "so we'll go up the beach to the rocks and see what's happening. Keep low."

Just then, from the soil, the Indian boy let out a groan and started to move.

Of one accord, Marcus and I ran off as quickly as we could.

Together, we climbed the escarpment to my perch. From there, we could look down and watch the whole battle. The longboat filled with our shipmates had left the shore and was desperately rowing towards the ship. At the water's edge, a large group of Indians stood, yelling after them and shooting arrows at the slow-moving boat.

Boom! The six-pounder came to life again. The cannon ball landed just in front of the savages, drenching them with bay water, and they skipped back in some confusion.

Looking out to the ship, I saw men in the halyards with rifles, but they were not firing, because of the range. Glancing to my left, I saw warrior-filled canoes rowing out swiftly from the village. With just three men rowing the longboat, I wasn't sure they would make the ship before the canoes reached them. Watching that life-and-death race, my heart beat like a drum.

Just as the war canoes were about to over take the longboat, Captain Gray opened up with two swivel shots and rifle fire from the deck. The lead canoe, hit, capsized with a dozen men aboard.

That well-timed volley slowed and then stopped the pursuing Indians. Soon, we heard shouts of joy from the Orphan as the longboat came alongside. The skiff was swiftly recovered.

But the battle wasn't over. Indian canoes soon surrounded the ship, staying just outside of rifle range. While this was happening, the ship made preparations for getting underway. They hoisted the anchor and the skipper turned the sloop but, with the wind against them, they had to drop the bower again.

"They going to leave us, Joe?" Marcus whispered in panic.

"Maybe," I answered back, as calmly as I could.

The Indians still on shore began to mill around, shouting angrily, and we ducked behind the rocks so as not to be seen. Marcus was frightened, and I was finding his fear contagious.

"Why Indians mad?" he asked.

"Don't know…maybe too much ale."

"How we get back?"

"When the wind shifts, the Orphan will head for the bar. We should move that way and swim out to her before she crosses the spit. But we'll have to wait until nightfall as not to be seen."

He looked down at the Indians below, who were milling about like a swarm of ants on a mound, then raised his troubled gaze again to me. "Aye."

Keeping a keen eye on the wind, we stayed on our perch until dusk. Then, under cover of the growing darkness, we started moving towards the mouth of the bay. As we were leaving, I noticed that more canoes had come from the south to join the picket line around the ship. On the beach, the Indians had built a series of bonfires that stretched from the sandy spit to the village. Each fire cast long shadows of the dancing warriors, their war cries and throbbing drums carrying on the breeze. It was an ominous sight that roused a depth of fear in me that I had never felt before.

With twilight upon us, we moved slowly up the hills towards the narrow entrance. The night was moonless, but soon we could see stars as we stumbled west. An hour later, we felt our way to a rocky cliff, high above the mouth of the bay. Looking down, we could just make out the glistening water of the inlet, and hear the crashing surf.

In the coal-black darkness, the way down looked too dangerous. Shortly, we found a large crevice in the rocks that would protect us from the cold wind off the sea. As we tried to relax on the rocks between the boulders, both of us pulled our coats tight to keep off the damp.

Huddling close, Marcus spoke, his white teeth flashing in the starlight. "I'm hungry, Joe."

"So am I."

After a long minute of silence, he spoke again. "Joe… I can't swim," he confessed, with terror in his voice.

"Well, lad," I answered, with a forced grin, "tomorrow you will learn."

The morning quiet was shattered by the sounds of swivel guns echoing off the cliffs.

I awoke with a start, covered with dew. It was just dawn, with the dim light brightening.

Bang! Bang!

The Orphan fired another salvo. Jumping to my feet, I looked to my left, over a boulder, trying to spot the ship, but the rocks to the entrance blocked my view. Twisting my head toward the sea, I felt the wind coming from the south, and knew that the ship would be on the move.

Marcus came to stand next to me in the faint morning light. "Is she move?" he asked.

"Aye… and we have to get down the cliff to the water's edge."

The way down looked to be more than a twenty foot drop-off. As we moved out from our protective boulders, I searched the crags, trying to find a path. At first I saw none, but then noticed a rock point, a hundred yards up from us, that looked scalable.

Boom!

The six-pounder roared again, and we moved quickly up the cliff to the point. Once there, I turned towards the bay and saw the sloop's tall mast slowly moving behind the rocks, coming towards us.

"Here she comes. Let's go!" I shouted.

With my first step down, the boy put his hand on my shoulder, pointing seaward with the other.

Looking out, I saw what Marcus had seen. In the surf of the sandbar, three war canoes filled with savages were heading right for our ship. I stepped back and turned towards the bay to watch the Orphan come through the narrow rocky entrance, with many canoes close behind.

Bang! Bang! The two aft swivels fired.

I wasn't sure that anyone on deck could see the canoes now crossing the spit. The Orphan looked trapped, and there wasn't a bloody thing I could do about it.

"Do we climb down?" Marcus asked, breathing heavily.

"With all those canoes? It be suicide." I sternly warned.

We watched grimly as the crew raised the main sail and the skipper trimmed the ship. Then – *Bang! Bang!* – the two forward swivels fired on the approaching Indian canoes. With the smell of gunpowder in our nostrils, we witnessed grapeshot hit one canoe, wounding many warriors. At that, the war canoes broke formation and paddled for the shoreline to get out of range.

Moments later, the Orphan sailed right past us, not a hundred yards away, firing her guns while all around her the howling savages shot arrows back.

From the rim of the cliff, we stood in mortified silence, staring as the sloop turned into the slit and then sailed through the surf and out to sea. Horrifying moments later, with the war canoes still in pursuit, she vanished in a curtain of ghostly fog.

The skirmish was over, and we were lost!

An hour later, Marcus and I were running north, up a wide, straight beach littered with log snags. With the ocean on our left and grassy, rolling sand dunes on our right, we sweated in the hot August morning. Not wanting to be seen, we ran between the driftwood and dunes, but moving across the soft sand made for slow going.

We had retreated from Tillamook Bay after I convinced myself, and then Marcus, that the ship would put in at the next cove and send out a search party for us. I reasoned that Captain Gray would never leave us marooned, and that doubling back was his only option.

I prayed that my logic was right.

When we came to a small creek that drained into the sea, we stopped to gain our breath and refresh. Removing our coats, we quickly sprawled on the sandy ground to drink the cool water from the stream. After we had swallowed our fill, we splashed our shirts and faces, which were dripping with sweat. Since leaving the bay, we had been focused inward and hadn't said a word to each other.

Finally Marcus spoke. "Why they leave us?"

With water dripping off my face, I answered as best I could. "The safety of the ship comes first. Everything depends on that. But they will come back for us. I feel it in my bones."

Marcus sighed. "I'm hungry."

Standing, I brushed the sand off my trousers and coat. "Right now, we have to keep moving. We'll look for food later."

We stumbled and ran for another few hours, crossing three more creeks, before we came to another inlet. Seeing the small sea opening from atop a dune made my heart skip. The bar across the opening looked about the same size as at Tillamook. If the depth was right, I knew the Orphan could cross it. Once over the sandbar, the estuary connected to a narrow bay that stretched due north. On our side of the bay, the grassy beach gave way to a rocky shore, while across the water was a long, sandy spit spotted with green scrub.

From my tall sand dune, it all looked promising…until I noticed, in the distance, some canoes on the bay. Quickly, the boy and I ducked behind the dunes and started to move slowly along the bay for a better view.

A half-mile up the shore, we came to a tall, rocky outcropping that blocked our way. Turning in among some trees, we climbed up a stony slope until we reached the top. From that higher ground, we had a good view of the entire bay, but what we saw was dispiriting. On the west shore, in a small cove, was an Indian village with dozens of huts. Across the bay was another, smaller village. Around the shoreline, many Indians were working, while three canoes plied the water, fishing. But it wasn't just the sight of the Indians that discouraged me. Reflected in the placid green waters to the north were tall granite mountains that would impede our way. Those peaks dominated the landscape, making any thought of travel in that direction foolhardy.

"What now?" the boy asked.

After thinking a moment, I answered, "This wilderness will not flog us. We'll go back down the beach, and at nightfall we'll build a signal fire for our shipmates."

"A fire? Indians will see."

"No, I have a notion. A way to keep it invisible."

We backtracked quickly to a creek that was about halfway between the two bays. In the late afternoon sun, I searched out a tall, grassy sand dune with a deep depression. Inside this hole, the boy and I built a V-shaped rampart out of driftwood. The log walls were about four feet high, with the opening of the bunker facing seaward. Inside the walls, we leveled out the sandy floor and laid out the twigs and sticks we would need for starting a signal fire. With our fire deep inside the bulwarks, no one on land would be able to see the flames but, with it being open to the sea, our shipmates could, and hopefully would send in the longboat. I prayed that my scheme would work, as we were running out of options.

While we waited for darkness, we searched for food. Looking around, I thought about shooting one of the many screaming seagulls, but dropped the idea because of the noise. Then, walking a few hundred yards up the creek, we found a few blackberry bushes. Carefully, we picked and ate the sweet berries until there were no more.

After we finished, we sat by the creek, washing our hands and drinking. That's when the boy noticed the little crayfish living under the rocks of the stream. They looked like baby lobsters and could swim like lighting. Finding a long stick, I used my knife to sharpen one end. Then the boy and I waded into the water and began to turn over rocks. As the crawdads swam away, we tried to spear them.

They were fast, but we were hungry. Just before dark, we returned to our bunker with a dozen crayfish to cook. Using a pistol flint, I soon had a small fire going. Then, using the spear, we roasted the crawdads. They were small but tasty, and in the end we could have eaten dozens more.

Under a red and orange sky with whisky clouds, we gathered more wood for our fire. It had been a long day but we had, at least, found some nourishment. Now we needed to start the vigil for our ship.

With the fire roaring and the surf pounding, I spent hours searching the dark horizon for a ship's lantern, but saw only stars. The inside of our bunker was cozy from the fire, and soon Marcus was slumped against the log walls, fast asleep. Watching the lad, I knew that I would be joining him soon. First, however, I added more wood to the fire, and took one last long walk down to the surf, dreaming of rescue.

Unfortunately, all that I found was an empty sea. As I squatted on my haunches in the wet sand, my head filled with foreboding thoughts, and I cursed the darkness.

With the early morning came a damp, cold fog. When I awoke, my mood was as gloomy as the weather. As the boy stirred, I walked into the sea grass and relieved myself, but as I came back, I heard muffled Indian voices in the foggy, still air. I jumped back into the bunker hastily and, with hand motions, told Marcus to be quiet. He soon heard the same voices, and we retreated from the hollow into some tall grass next to the creek. From there we quietly started walking east. Half an hour later, we came out of the mist to the sight of green forested hills and mountains as far as our eyes could see.

Stopping for a breakfast of blackberries, Marcus asked, "Now what, Joe? The ship not coming, we lost."

For the first time, I realized that the boy might be right and that our future could well be in doubt. After a moment of sober reflection, I replied, "I say we walk east. That's where my home is."

After a moment, he asked, "How far?"

I finished a mouthful of berries and answered with confidence, "Three thousand miles over those hills, we will find my people."

He stared at me, amazed, and finally pointed back to the sea. "We can stay with Indian people until another ship."

"No," I answered back quickly. "Those Tillamooks will enslave us or kill us."

He shook his head dolefully. "We lost, Joe… but I will follow."

Trekking east, we soon came to a forest as deep and tall as any I had ever seen. As we moved up a game trail, the canopy from the trees was so dense that we lost sight of the sun, and seemed to be moving in an endless emerald-green twilight.

Most of the forest floor was littered with massive trees and toppled snags, downed in many storms. Each dead or growing tree was covered with a thick layer of green moss. The smell of damp and rotting vegetation permeated the forest floor. Growing through and around the downed trees was a crowd of green underbrush, so moving through these obstacles was more challenging than I'd expected. Along the way, we'd lose one game trail, but then find another. As we climbed up the mountain, my mind filled with doubts. How could we walk three thousand miles in such conditions? What would we live on? How would we survive?

By early afternoon, we had crossed one mountain, emerging from the dark forest into a small valley. With the warm sun once again on our faces, we stumbled down the banks of a rocky stream which seemed to meander east. A few hours later, the stream emptied into a deep, narrow river moving south. Exhausted and hungry we searched out a sand bar on the river to camp for the night.

As I gathered wood for a fire, Marcus went looking for berries. My mind twirled with thoughts of survival, but I soon had a small blaze going. Taking off my pouch, I opened it carefully and laid out its contents. The entire inventory of my belongings consisted of my flute, my mother's letter, Becky's locket, drawing papers, my pipe and tobacco, a full powder horn, a few flints and fifteen lead balls. Other than my pistol and knife, that was all there was. No food, no compass and no warm clothes. How could we walk three thousand miles with just these provisions? It would be pure madness!

With death on the prowl, I thought about reading my mothers letter, but I resisted the notion, not wanting to give in. Finally, sitting alone in the sun, staring at my meager belongings, I started to weep. Where had my promise gone? I wasn't worth spit.

Just then, Marcus stumbled back into camp with his coat full of small blue berries.

As he put the coat next to me, he squatted and said, "They look like baby grapes. Taste real good, Joe."

With my head turned, I hastily wiped my tears, then turned back to face the boy. "Aye."

As we ate the bitter-sweet grapes, he added, "I see fish in water. We will eat well, tonight."

Turning to the boy, I soberly requested, "Show me what you have in your pouch."

He glanced at my own belongings on the sand and then, without hesitation, dumped out his pouch. All he had was a wool hat, a pair of gloves, a straight razor and two muslin sacks of his potions.

"Why the razor and gloves?" I asked.

"Find more medicine."

I sighed. "We don't have much, do we?"

Forcing a smile, he replied, "We stay with Tillamook people until next ship?"

Placing all my goods back into my poke, I answered, "Maybe. For now, let's fish."

We speared three fish, that evening. They were a kind of trout that I had never seen before, as they had blood-red markings on their gills. After cleaning them at the water's edge, I slid their fat bodies lengthways down the spear and cooked them over the fire. While I was doing this, Marcus used his sword to cut ferns for beds.

When the boy joined me by the fire, I handed him a cooked fish.

Taking the trout, he raised it to his lips and then mumbled something.

"Was that a prayer?" I asked.

"Yes. I speak to the fish's spirit."

"Last night, you didn't pray to the crayfish."

For a long moment, he looked at me thinking. Then he replied, "Shellfish have no souls."

In this crazy world, that almost makes sense, I thought.

In the last rays of daylight, we ate the fish and were delighted with the taste. One thing was certain – this land was plentiful, if you knew her ways. But what did a blacksmith's son and a cigar makers' grandson know about this wilderness? Nothing! Where had my legacy gone?

Later with Marcus asleep, I found myself beset with fresh tears, gazing up at a sky full of twinkling stars. In the distance, I heard an owl hoot. Then I became aware of the sound of the river rolling over its rocks. With my mind in a miserable place, I knew a decision had to be made. We were strangers in a strange land, and needed to find our way. If we tried to walk out, could we survive? If we surrendered, would we live? What of my shipmates? Why did they leave us?

Just then, a wolf cried out, his lonely song echoing through the gorge.

Throwing more wood on the fire, I thought, *if we must surrender, we'll do it with dignity and diplomacy, just like Captain Gray.*

Aboard the Orphan

On that fateful morning, Captain Gray had sailed out of the bay, heading due west. Within the hour, he lost sight of the pursuing war canoes, and then turned his ship north. After traveling an hour in that direction, he reefed the sails and turned the Orphan into the wind.

From the quarterdeck, he whistled the crew around. Mr. Coolidge, with his arm in a sling from an arrow wound, was the last to gather.

With great distress on his face, he addressed the men. "We are without Mr. Blackwell and the boy Marcus. Who was the last to see them?"

The first mate answered, "We took them ashore to cut some grass, but when we were attacked and ran back to the skiff, they weren't around."

"I saw them from the halyards after the first shot," Mr. Owens said. "The boy had been captured, and the savages were pulling him into the woods. Then I saw the flash of his cutlass, with an Indian standing over him. He be dead, Captain."

"And what of Mr. Blackwell?" the skipper asked.

"Saw him run into the woods and never come out. He's dead, too, sir," Mr. Owens stated.

In a loud, angry voice, Sandy yelled, "We don't know that! We have to go back for them."

"Go back and do what?" Mr. Gale asked.

"Send in a party and search them out. I'll volunteer." Sandy said with conviction.

Mr. Haswell raised his hand and angrily shouted, "Hold it… there is only eleven of us now. We can't go looking for trouble."

"What we can't do is leave them marooned with savages, sir!" Sandy answered back.

"They're dead," Mr. Owens shouted.

Captain Gray raised both of his hands, requesting order, and calmly said, "This be my decision. We will go back and look for a cove north of the bay. If we find one that we can anchor in, Sandy and I will go ashore and walk back to those woods, under cover of darkness."

Shaking his head, Mr. Coolidge answered, "Be a foolish move, sir. But you're the Captain, so let's come about and fill our sails."

The ship did find a scant opening of a bay, some dozen miles north of Tillamook. Mr. Haswell went in with the longboat and sounded the depth. Returning, he reported that the bar was too shallow and the tides adverse. He also said that he had seen Indian canoes on the waters inside the cove.

As the skiff was being recovered, Captain Gray paced the quarterdeck in deep thought, with a sour face. Finally, he walked over to Sandy. "It's too dangerous to cross the bar, and the safety of the ship must come first. I am sorry, Sandy. Even if we went ashore over the surf, we might not get back. And if they're dead, it would all be for naught. It's a damn rotten shame, but we have to move on."

Sandy stared back at the skipper with a blank face. He knew that the

Captain was right, but what of his mates? Being a sailor was a miserable job, suited only for dreamers and fools.

From the crosstree, the lookout shouted that two war canoes were moving north from Tillamook Bay. Within moments, the Orphan had turned into the wind and was setting a course northwest.

As Sandy stood at the rail, watching the land slip away, he told himself that Tillamook Bay would always be remembered by him as Murderous Harbor, God bless his mates.

Courage

DURING THE COLD NIGHT, I ADDED WOOD to the fire three times. With my final slumber came my father in a vision. His voice touched my heart as he whispered, 'Trust the Tillamooks. They will show you the way home. I wait for you.' At daybreak, I awoke with a clear head and with confidence in my decision. And suddenly, for some reason, I felt at peace with the ship for leaving us.

We would return to the bay and face the savages...but our surrender would have a twist.

Over a morning meal of berries, I told Marcus of my dream and my scheme. He eagerly agreed, and we started walking south, down the river. I reckoned that the river flowed into Tillamook Bay and that, once we had a village in sight, we could employ my plot.

At first, our way was a rocky, broken trail, but as we got closer to the bay, the path improved. At noon, we stopped and fished in a deep hole with clear eddies that showed many trout. Soon, we were sitting on boulders in the bright sun, eating more of the tasty fish. As we were about finished, I looked up to see an eagle perched high atop a fir tree. He, too, was fishing. With great patience, he waited and watched, and when his prey came close to the surface, he swooped down, with wings six feet across, and snatched the fish out of the water. As the bird flew by, with his talons full and his white tail fanned out, he turned his bald head and let out a cry that seemed to ask, 'Who is the best fisherman now?' It was a marvelous sight, and a hint for my riddle.

A few hours later, we reached tidal water. Not wanting to be seen, we moved off the trail. I guessed that we had walked eight or ten miles from our last camp, and the bay was close. Moving into the forest, we stayed parallel with the river for another half mile until we came to a wide, muddy bog. From the trees, we could see that this was where the river emptied into the bay. Just up the shore from the marsh was the main Indian village that I had visited.

Quietly, we moved deeper into the forest and came around behind the village. For over an hour, we searched for just the right hiding spot. Finally, under some brushes, we found a small burrow between two large rocks. Here we could safely place all of our worldly possessions. I had reasoned that, if we walked into the village with our weapons and belongings, we might be killed for what we carried. But if we walked in empty-handed, the Indians would see us as no threat.

Earlier, I had told Marcus, "We will walk into the village with dignity and no fear." Now that the march was at hand, however, I was nervous. Therefore, I pulled out my pipe and had one last taste of my African Tobacco. As we talked and smoked, I removed my flute from my poke before placing it into the hole. Marcus removed nothing before placing his pouch next to mine. Finally, we added our weapons, the coins from our pockets, and the still warm pipe. Then we covered the opening.

Our destiny was at hand.

It was early evening when we came to a well-traveled path behind the village. Stepping out of the bushes, we straightened our clothes and gave a last fond look at each other. Then we began walking towards the hamlet as I started playing "Yankee Doodle" on my flute. My idea was simple: just as Captain Gray had used cigars to break the tension, I would use my music.

As we emerged from the forest, we passed the first hut, and I could see the people inside staring out at us. We marched past a few more huts, and then turned for the shoreline. What a sight we were, both marching in step while I played the grand old tune. With the late afternoon sun on our faces, we choked down our fear and just kept moving. Soon, we had a crowd behind us and a larger group gathering beside us. The Indians seemed stunned, with open mouths and expressions of amazement. Some of the men grabbed spears, while others brandished bow and arrows.

As the bay came into view, we marched towards a group of Indians near the shore. Here we halted, and I stopped playing. With my final notes floating in the breeze, there was an eerie quiet. The savages just stood and glared at us for the longest while. We heard a loud voice from the rear, and the crowd parted, then the scar-faced Indian from the ship stepped forward. With that small bone pierced through his nose, his angry face was ugly. Soon, he started shouting out words that only they could understand.

Coming face to face with us, he suddenly reached out and grabbed my flute, hitting me with it alongside my forehead. *Crack.*

The crowd let out a loud gasp. I felt blood trickling down the side of my face. Although dizzied by the blow, I remained shoulder to shoulder with him, staring into his manic eyes. Soon, the two other chiefs from the ship pushed their way through the crowd and stood before us, as well. They called out to some braves behind us, who rushed forward and grabbed our arms. Then these Indians tied our hands behind our backs with a thong. As this was happening, the three chiefs started arguing with each other. I had a bitter copper taste in my mouth, and my legs began to tremble as I prayed that death would not soon find us.

With their dispute seemly resolved, the chiefs turned their glances to Marcus and said a few more loud words. Then the scar-faced chief reached out and ripped open the shirt the boy wore, exposing Marcus's chest.

All three Indians poked their fingers at his black skin. Twisting my sweating head, I saw a fear on the boy's face that scared me to my soul.

Then one of the braves behind us handed the scar-faced savage a small black stone with a sharp tip. With a sadistic smile, he cut the boy's skin with the edge.

Marcus screamed out words in Portuguese, while the chief smeared his hand with the boy's blood and then showed his crimson palm to the crowd. They let out a loud gasp and started to chant. One of the other chiefs put his finger into his blood and then tasted it. Grunting, he turned to the crowd and started whooping. They responded with more loud cries and war drums. With the savages now in a frenzy, I knew the worst was about to happen.

Instead, a sudden hush came over the camp. Then, from the rear of the crowd, I heard loud words in a tongue I could not understand. With little fanfare, the Indians parted behind the chiefs. Through this narrow opening walked an old Indian squaw. She was short, with long gray hair and a stoic face full of wrinkles. Around her neck was a long necklace of seashells that hung down in front of her blouse of bark and her skirt of grass. She didn't look at the chiefs, or say a word. Moving around us, she came between Marcus and me. Then, grabbing one of our arms in each hand, she began to gently lead us through the silent, shocked crowd.

The fuming chiefs just stood there with clutched fists. Moving past them, my heart raced with fear.

The old woman walked us between a few huts and down a lane to a large lodge with an open door made of cedar. Once inside, she untied our hands and directed us to sit on a split log in front of a small fire. Next to the fire, resting on the sand, I noticed an iron cooking pot from our ship. This squaw had to be the woman who traded her goat to Mr. Coolidge. This realization lifted my spirits.

We watched in silence as this odd woman placed two small pieces of cloth inside the pot. Then, wringing out the excess water, she handed the warm fabric to us. Making signs, she instructed us to clean our wounds. As we did, she put a flat stone on the log and took a small hanging pouch from the wall. Kneeling in front of us, she opened the pouch and searched its contents for a few dried leaves, then placed the leaves on the flat stone and crushed them with a second rock. Marcus watched with particular attention, as her actions were similar to his ways. After the leaves were ground, she added what appeared to be tree pitch to the mixture.

As she worked, I looked around the darkened room. It was about twenty-five feet long and fifteen feet wide, and devoid of any windows. In the center was a large fire pit ringed with stones, above which was an opening in the roof for the smoke to escape. On each side of the pit, split logs rested on a floor of sand. At the narrow end of the room was the door we had entered, and at the opposite end was another opening, covered with an elk hide. On one side there were long shelves, holding an assortment of baskets, wooden planks, bowls, cups and buckets. On the other side were more shelves, and these held mats, fur pelts, tools, and weapons. Under every shelf were stacks of fire wood. The walls of the room were made with crude cedar boards, running vertically and fastened to the tall poles that were the interior ribs of the lodge. With all the cedar, there was a sweetness in the air, and while the roof hip held some smoke, the living area was clear.

When the squaw finished preparing the mixture, she took a bone and rolled the gooey mix in and around the long slit on the boy's chest. Then she cut his piece of cloth into a small strip and pressed it hard over his wound. Because of the pitch, the cloth stuck tightly to the skin.

She then did the same with the gash on my forehead. Almost instantly, I felt relief, and I marveled at her doctoring.

Standing, the old woman placed the flat stone in the fire, apparently to burn off the sticky residue.

As she straightened and moved across the room, the scar-faced chief walked though the door. He said a few angry-sounding words and grunted a few times before the old woman finally spoke. What she said, I have no idea, but the pitch of her voice reminded me instantly of Sandy, and the way she talked was like rapid-fire gunshots. Whatever she said made him fume even more. Turning from her, he threw my flute onto the sand in front of me, then stormed out of the lodge with hatred on his face. This old woman had a lot of brass.

Examining the patch on his chest, Marcus asked, "What's happening, Joe?"

"Don't know... but I think we're safe."

From across the room, the old squaw yelled something and shook her head, indicating that talking was taboo.

While we rested quietly, the woman made us a meal. It wasn't much, but we were hungry. She served the food on short cedar planks. On each board, she placed a few strips of dry fish, a root that looked and tasted like a fat onion, and a small cake of dried berries. Along with this, we each got a wooden mug of spiced hot water.

When we finished our meal, she took us outside and walked us into some trees, a good distance behind the village. There, she pointed out the place that all the People used to relieve themselves. It was nothing but two deep slit trenches, with a long pole for a seat, and separated by some bushes. The left was for men, and the right for the women. The place stunk, but the boy and I quickly used it.

As we walked back to the village, the old woman stopped at a hut near her lodge. Scratching the door, she motioned us to wait, while she went inside.

"How's your cut?" I whispered to the Marcus.

"It no hurt or bleed."

"Aye, same with me. She has powerful medicine, just like you."

Quietly, we talked in the late sun until I noticed a young Indian girl walking our way, carrying two bladders of water. She looked different from the other squaws, wearing a dress of animal skins, and without bowlegs. As she approached, I noticed that her face was more oblong and without the sloping forehead, and while her hair was black, it was a shiny black. But it was her flesh that was most unusual; she had a light honey skin, not the reddish-brown of the Tillamooks. As she passed us, she shyly spoke, but her words weren't Indian. They sounded Portuguese. When Marcus answered back, the girl stopped and slowly turned to us.

She and Marcus talked for a few moments with much animation.

Finally, I interrupted, "Does she speak Portuguese?"

Marcus shook his head. "No, Spanish, but we understand."

They kept talking until the old woman came out of the hut. Then the young girl turned to the woman and spoke to her in her native tongue. As they talked, the old squaw smiled. Soon thereafter, the girl turned and continued down the lane with her water. Her departure disappointed me deeply, because there was so much we needed to know.

As we continued on, I wanted to ask Marcus about the girl and what she had said, but I knew that the old woman wanted no talking. When we arrived at the lodge, the sun was just setting, with a golden sky shimmering off the bay. Looking at the colors in the water reminded me of Boston Harbor, and I yearned for home.

Once inside the shanty, the old woman busied herself by adding wood to the fire, rolling out mats in front of the split logs, and dumping out the water from the iron pot. When it was empty, she moved it closer to the flames and poured in a bucket full of live clams in seawater. They were small-looking creatures, about the size of a Continental dollar. She then placed a cedar plank on top of the pot.

While she was working, the boy and I wandered around the room, looking at her belongings. There were piles of baskets in many sizes. Some were tall and ridged, while others were soft and flexible. All of them were crafted from straw, grass or strands of bark, and many had detailed patterns woven into their sides. I was astonished at the craftsmanship.

As we were looking at some wooden bowls, an Indian brave walked through the door, with the young maiden just behind. He wore buckskin and carried a stone tomahawk in a belt made of seashells. His weathered face looked young, but his bowlegs and flat bare feet looked painful. The brave and the squaw talked for a few moments, and then the old woman motioned for Marcus and me to sit next to the fire. As we did, the brave and girl sat on mats across the fire from us, and the old woman placed herself on a mat next to the cooking pot. There was silence for the longest of moments, and then the squaw said something to the young girl, who translated her words into Spanish. Marcus listened intently, and then told me what the words meant in English.

She wanted to know if we had fire sticks.

Before answering, I said to Marcus, "What are their names?"

The boy nodded and translated my question back to girl.

As she spoke to them, they seemed surprised by my question, but each answered with their Indian name while pointing at themselves.

Their spoken language was hard for me to grasp, so I told Marcus to ask what their names meant. When they understood this question, they smiled proudly and answered. The old woman was Woodpecker, a name that suited her well. The brave was known as Timber Wolf, and the young girl was Raven.

Pointing to myself, I said, "Joe." Then, pointing to the boy, I said, "Marcus." They smiled and asked what our names meant. Marcus and I grinned at each other with mischief in our eyes. I pointed to my hair and said, over the dancing flames, "Sunset." Then the boy pointed to his skin and said, "Midnight."

They seemed pleased, and smiled.

I asked Raven if she was a Tillamook, but Woodpecker interrupted, wanting an answer to her first question. So I explained that the ship had left us behind and that we had lost our weapons in the forest. My answer seemed to satisfy them, as I think they worried, very much, about the white man's fire sticks. I asked if we could stay in the village until another ship came. "What ship?" they asked. "When will it come?'

I told them that many ships would surely come. They seemed surprised by my comment, and said that ours was the first *white-bird* ever to cross the spit. To Marcus and me, hoping for an early rescue, this information was devastating.

This tedious conversation went on for hours, having to be translated into the different languages with the many subtle hand signs. As we talked, more Indians came into the room and squatted quietly, listening to our words. These curious locals were greatly interested in us, as they worried we might be a threat. At one point, Woodpecker served small wooden bowls filled with steamed clams to everyone in the room. The chewy little morsels were savory, and I could have eaten more.

By the time the fire finally turned to embers, we had learned many things. Woodpecker was a shaman or medicine woman and also a seer or prophet. She was a widow; her husband had been the chief and had died two summers before in a canoe mishap. Her three children had all died, many years before. Timber Wolf was a distant relative to Woodpecker, as were most of the other Indians in the lodge.

I asked about the scar-faced chief, and why he had cut Marcus. They told me that the chief's name was Hawk, and that no one in the tribe had ever seen a *midnight* person before. Being curious, they wanted to see if the boy would bleed red blood. Next, I asked why they had turned on our shipmates. Timber Wolf answered by saying that the sailors were stealing bear grass. These ugly answers reminded me how primitive a people they were. The Tillamooks had only vague concepts of right and wrong.

Timber Wolf's final assertion was astounding. He said that we belonged to the old woman now and that, if there was any trouble, he and the rest of the tribe would skin us alive. He said it with such a matter-of-fact look that I knew he meant every word. But, unlike Hawk, there was no hatred in his eyes.

After everyone was gone, Woodpecker closed the front door, lit a cedar torch and showed us through the doorway draped with the elk hide. Inside the darkened room, she used the flames from the stick to start a small fire in the center of the room.

As I blinked, my eyes adjusted, and I looked around. The room was about fifteen by fifteen feet. On each side of the room, there were two large shelves with firewood underneath. The shelves were about three feet off the sand, and each held a folded animal hide and one of the wool blankets from our ship. While unfolding a hide, the old woman pointed out two shelves across the room and told us with signs that these were our beds. Then Woodpecker turned, undressed and slipped on a baggy robe made of buckskins. Soon she was in her bed, with her back to us. Marcus and I, using our coats as pillows, crawled onto the hard planks. In the flickering firelight, my tired gaze moved around the little room. It had been a long day, full of discovery and fear, cruelness and kindness – and now we were slaves.

The old woman had us out bed before dawn, the next morning. With great urgency, she fed us dried fish, berry cakes and mugs of hot water. We were out the door just as the first signs of light reflected in the eastern sky. Marcus and I carried two baskets each, while Woodpecker had one. She led us down to the shore, where I noticed that it was low tide. Soon, we were joined by other squaws, all of them carrying baskets. As we stumbled west along the rocky waterline, the women talked and giggled while staring and pointing at Marcus and me. We had no idea what they were saying, but we reasoned that having men come along on such an outing was unusual.

In the morning twilight, we reached the narrow entrance to the bay. With the tide low, the monolith that protected the north shore was exposed almost to its base. And there were other boulders around the column that were now visible, as well. When the squaws waded into the water, Woodpecker motioned for us to take off our shoes. After we did, she gave us sharp stones and led us into the cold estuary. Carrying our baskets, we waded into waist-high water at the base of the pillar, where she showed us how to cut from the rocks a mussel in a blue-black shell. The mussels were small, about half the size of my fist, and their sharp shells were difficult to remove from the rock.

An hour later, we struggled back to shore with our baskets full. My legs were numb from the cold water, and my feet were bleeding from the jagged rocks, but it was my hands that stung the worst. The sharp shells had sliced a dozen small cuts on my fingers, and the salt water had made my hands swell. Once on shore, our feet were so swollen that we couldn't wear our shoes, so we walked back bare-footed. *Gathering mussels is a miserable job, only suited for squaws,* I thought. But the message of the morning was clear: everyone worked, and we were no exception.

As we walked through the village, Woodpecker traded three of our baskets of mussels for other food: a net full of crabs, a basket of greens and a bucket full of the dollar-sized clams. It amazed me to see how their commerce worked. They took what they wanted and bartered for what they needed. It was, in some ways, a savage but refreshing concept.

Once at the lodge, the old woman placed the food on a shelf, then searched out a small bowl that contained animal lard. With hand motions, she directed Marcus and me to wipe this fat onto the bottoms of our feet and the cuts on our hands. As we did so, I noticed that she didn't have a cut on her body, even though she had gathered more shells than we had. This woman was full of surprises, and was rapidly gaining my respect.

After a short rest and more hot water, she led us back through the village and up the path alongside the river. She carried a large basket with clothes inside. We followed her, but moving up this trail bare-footed was like waking across hot embers. Lesson learned. In the future I would keep my boots on, in or out of the water.

Soon, we came to a large flowering lilac tree, where we stopped while the old woman cut some leaves from it. The smell of the flowers made the air sweet, and the purple buds were beautiful.

We continued until we came to a place on the river that had a small cove and a rocky beach. Here the water gently flowed, with eddies that showed a deep hole. Woodpecker put her basket on the rocks and, with hand motions, told us to take off our clothes. Looking wide-eyed at each other, Marcus and I hesitated, but she approached us and started pulling at our coats. Soon, they were off, followed by our shirts and trousers. As we stood in front of the old woman in only our smallclothes, she demanded even those. She glared at us, yelling words we didn't understand, until we finally gave in. With a strange look on her face, she slowly surveyed our two naked bodies. Then she noticed the eagle tattoo on my left shoulder. Stepping forward, she gently touched the image with an expression of wonderment.

All the while, I stood there embarrassed. Finally, she smiled, reached down into her basket and handed us some of the leaves from the tree, then pointed to the water and made motions of using the leaves as soap.

We got the idea and went quickly into the water.

As we bathed, she washed clothes, including ours, then spread them on rocks in the sun to dry. The tree leaves worked like magic, and even lathered up as we rubbed them against our dirty bodies. Soon Marcus and I, laughing about the day's events, started playfully to splash water on each other. This joy was good for our souls as we had been so fearful since the ship departed. This bath lifted our spirits and gave us confidence that, by learning the Indians ways, we just might survive.

Our Fate

When we returned to the village, we found Timber Wolf working a bonfire next to the lodge. The day before, I had noticed a large pit in the sand, filled with rocks. Now I saw that he had removed half of those rocks and had built the fire on top of the remaining stones. The flames were tall and the embers hot. Soon, Woodpecker brought out baskets of food, while Timber Wolf went to the bay and brought back planks of cedar soaked in water. They placed crabs, clams, mussels and root greens on the soaked wood. After that, they covered the hot embers with a thick layer of wet seaweed. On top of the algae went the cedar planks. On top of those wood planks, they placed another layer of seaweed. Then they rolled the hot stones from the ring of the fire into the pit. Finally, they poured three buckets of bay water over the smoking pit and covered the top stones with a mound of sand. The process had taken about an hour, and they indicated with their hands that we would eat soon.

Resting in the shade of the lodge while rubbing more lard on our raw feet, Marcus and I witnessed this activity. It seemed a strange way to cook until we noticed other huts with the same pits. I wondered if they steamed all their food, as they had no iron grills.

Sometime later, Timber Wolf's family and Raven came to the lodge. As they approached, I noticed that the girl had her shiny, braided hair pulled tight at the back of her head. She wore buckskins, with a top sewn with beads of blue and white. She introduced Timber Wolf's wife, Sandpiper, to us, along with their two young children, a boy and a girl, named Buck and Doe. They were nice enough youngsters but very timid. Raven explained that they were frightened to meet the black boy and the man with fire in his hair. Soon, the children ran off to play, while Sandpiper went into the lodge to be with her husband.

Finally, we got a chance to talk to Raven alone. My first question, through Marcus, was how old she was. Her answer was sixteen seasons. Then I asked whether Timber Wolf was her father: She answered no, then sadly told us that she was a slave.

I had thought that might be the case, so I asked, "Are we also slaves?"

A grin crossed her lips and she shook her head, explaining that we weren't slaves, we were bucks.

"Bucks to what?" I demanded.

She said that Woodpecker had claimed us as her bucks from the chief, the night before. As an elder and shaman, she had such a right. Had she made us her slaves, we would have been killed if she died. Now we would live after her death. It was a great honor.

"Bucks…like lovers?" I stammered.

"If you want," Raven shyly answered.

Both Marcus and I looked at each other, shaking our heads with disbelief. Then, smiling, I told her, "No… we would not be her lovers. But how did you come to be a slave?"

Her face turned sour as she told us her tale. Two years before, Timber Wolf had won her while gambling with some Siletz Indians, far down the coast. These Indians had raided her village and stolen her when she was twelve. With great sadness, she explained that her tribe lived in a beautiful cove many leagues away. The small village was built next to a white man's trading post and had a small garrison of Spanish soldiers. Her father had been one of those soldiers, but he had retuned to Spain when she was nine. That was how she had learned Spanish. Her mother, a full-blooded Tolowa Indian, was left behind with two small children. Her brother was a year younger than Raven. After the garrison closed, the Siletz raided the village in the middle of the night, taking only horses and young girls. She and two other captives were forced to walk many leagues north to a bay where other Siletz people lived.

Finishing her story, she looked around carefully to see if any Indians were watching. When she saw none, she reached into her blouse and pulled out a crude wooden cross that dangled from a strand of rawhide. With tears in her eyes, she looked at me, and said through Marcus, "Me good Christian girl, baptized by priest."

This was astonishing news, for a priest meant civilization. I wanted to learn more. But the sight of her cross reminded me of Becky and a life now almost forgotten.

Just then, with a loud commotion, the children ran past us and into the lodge.

Suddenly, we were interrupted as Woodpecker called out for Raven, who quickly concealed her cross and wiped her eyes.

We talked for many hours over our food, but it was a conversation full of questions about the white man: his ships, his fire sticks and why he had come to the Indian lands. Woodpecker said she'd had a vision, right after her husband died. His spirit had told her to befriend the strangers that would come, as they would teach new ways. To her, our arrival had been foretold.

After our meal, the old woman asked me to play my flute, which I did gladly. Everyone enjoyed my music, and the children even warmed to me. With broad smiles and loud giggles, they blew into the flute, making funny notes. They even found the courage to ask if they could touch my hair and Marcus's skin.

After that, Woodpecker told them of the eagle that perched on my arm, and they all wanted to see it. When I exposed my shoulder, the Indians crowded around, looking with wide-eyed amazement at my skin. Then they started laughing and wanted to know how he had come to land on my skin. Whimsically, I made up a funny story about the eagle on my shoulder that everyone enjoyed. We had a grand time, that evening.

When we retired that night, I saw that Woodpecker had laid a robe made of animal hides on each bed. She didn't say a thing about the gifts, and was soon fast asleep with her back to us. She was one strange woman. Her vision had saved our lives, and her kindness would help us find our way home. We weren't slaves. No, we were bucks!

Chapter Five: The Spirit of the Indians

For the Tillamooks, each village was the social unit around which life revolved. Their communities varied in size from a few hundred people to much smaller hamlets. A typical village was usually an extended clan that had a loosely structured class system in which material wealth was the ruling force.

These villages had four social classes: the leaders, the middle class, the poor and the slaves. The power of the leaders, or chiefs, was limited by the elders, seers and shamans. "Chief" was a term used by the white man for any individual who exerted some degree of authority over his people. With the Tillamooks, this title seemed dependent on the task at hand: an expert warrior to lead an attack, an expert fisherman to oversee fishing, or a shrewd trader to deal with other tribes. One village could have many chiefs.

Most people in the villages were middle class. These Indians lived well, thanks to their personal property and their skills at hunting and gathering food. As a group, they wielded great political power, and had to be consulted before any changes were made that pertained to village life. Below this class were a few poor people who, because of fate or ill health, had been reduced to a lesser social status. These Indians lived in mat houses or abandoned lodges, doing odd jobs such as running errands or digging slit trenches. The final class was that of slave. The typical slave among the Tillamooks was not much worse off than a poor person, except that they could be sold or bartered. All slaves lived in the lodges of their owners and, in the case of female captives, often became wives of their captors. The children of slaves were also slaves, and the custom of killing slaves when the master died was common.

The Tillamooks believed that all people experienced three essential periods in their lives: birth, finding their guardian spirit and death. The guardian spirit was the core of their lives; once it was achieved, it would stay with them throughout life and into death. Therefore, the search for this protector was steeped in tradition and tribal rituals.

Because only half of all Indian children lived to be twenty-one, childhood was kept as short as possible. When a boy reached his early teens, he was sent into the forest alone, to fast for ten days. He brought only a knife and a blanket, and his quest was to have a vision during this time in the wilderness. If his spirit vision was a salmon or crane, he would be a great fisherman. If he saw a wolf, seal, bear or eagle, he would become a mighty hunter. Should the vision be a woodpecker or beaver, he would be an expert canoe-maker. Finally, if his spirit vision was a snake or serpent, he would become a shaman. While on this journey, the boy performed certain other tasks to prove to the spirits that he was strong enough to accept his guardian spirit.

An Indian girl's ascent to womanhood was governed by nature, marked by the beginning of her menstrual cycle. When the young woman wished to obtain her guardian spirit, she was placed on a large cedar board. Here she would squat for two days of fasting. During this time, her head was covered with a basket hat, and she was given a blanket adorned with abalone shells. She had her own fire and was required to stay by herself. During the night, she would dance around her fire and chant. At midnight of the second day, she would go up into the mountains and bathe in a pond. When she returned, the next morning, she was allowed into her family lodge but could not sit next to the fire for two more days. Finally, after swimming in a river at sunrise, she was deemed to have completed the rituals, and the village shaman would announce that she had obtained her guardian spirit.

These beliefs were so strong that, when the salmon returned to bays and rivers each year, the Indians believed that the fish were the spirits of their dead ancestors. Therefore, they were killed quickly so their souls could be released again and return to the other side. The Tillamooks were true to their spirits and had little tolerance for non-believers. If they captured people of a different faith, those individuals were likely to be killed.

Making My Way

It had been fortuitous to find the old squaw who foretold our coming. But the other Indians in the village didn't have such a vision, so they called us '*tlehonnipts*' or strangers who drifted ashore. They looked at Marcus and me with great suspicion. I could see it on their faces and hear it in their words, even though they were words that I couldn't understand. This mistrust, I feared, could become dangerous if we didn't prove our worthiness.

Early on and without explanation, two things happened to me. The tribe started calling me 'Fire-Head' and Woodpecker decided that until the first salmon returned, I would learn canoe-making. Also during this time, the old woman and Marcus stayed close together, as she explored the boy's culture and future.

Boat building was a task that I did not mind, as Raven told me that Timber Wolf and his brother, Coyote, were great craftsman. Toiling with them at the bays edge, I found their method of building a canoe fascinating: after carefully selecting a cedar log, they used fire and stone axes to cut it to length. The timber would be short and narrow for small dugouts, and long and thick for war canoes that could hold twenty or more men. After securing the log firmly to the shore, the men went to work, shaping the outside shell. To craft the hull, they used only stone chisels, beaver teeth and hammer stones. There were no plans or drawings; they just shaped the pirogue from pure instinct. Then, once the body was completed, they turned the canoe over and started digging out the inside. For this work, they used small, controlled fires, their stone tools and large bones that were sharpened at one end. This removal of the inside wood was a delicate task, for if they broke through the thin hull the canoe would be worthless. Once finished, the prow and the stern had upright ends that would be carved with their mark of animal symbols. Finally, they painted the canoe by mixing berry juice and other natural elements, producing a reddish type of lacquer.

This laborious process could take weeks, if not months. In the end, however, their efforts were rewarded with a lightweight canoe that rode high in the water and was, therefore, sleek and fast. They could then barter the finished boat for goods and services. These were prized items, and there were many of the brothers' canoes on the bay.

As I worked with them, I noticed that they didn't use the iron chisels or the axe they had traded with the ship to obtain. When I asked them why, they showed me their iron tools. In the damp climate, the metal had already started to rust, and all the edges were gone. They also indicated that the chisels were too flat for cutting the curves they needed in a dugout. They had tried the white man's tools, but preferred the old ways.

Their lack of understanding of the iron tools gave me an opening. At the bay, I found three pumice-type rocks; one stone was quite coarse, another had a rough texture, and the final one was smooth. Using these stones and some animal lard, I cleaned and sharpened their tools until they were like new. Then I showed them how to use and care for each implement. They seemed swayed by my instructions, and they soon realized that the iron tools could help speed up some of their work. My efforts gained me a little respect, although not the trust I so eagerly sought.

Soon, other Indians started coming by the lodge, asking me to sharpen and clean their iron tools. This I gladly did, always with a smile. Those contacts with the villagers gave me an insight into their personalities and their abilities to use each tool. They all seemed eager to learn, and thankful for my help.

Within the first week of my stay, I began grasping a little of the Tillamooks' difficult language. Their words were full of vowels with a sprinkling of consonants, like the name of our village: Kilharhurst. With patience, sign language and a lot of guessing, I began to understand a bit of what was being said.

A few days after we arrived, Raven explained that being Woodpecker's bucks brought us a great deal of protection from the other villagers. The old woman had told her people that if any harm came to us, she would conjure up an evil force to drive away the offender's guardian spirit. While we appreciated the old woman's protection, we still noticed hatred in the eyes of Hawk and a few other braves. With this in mind, Marcus and I decided to secretly retrieve our belongings from their hiding place. Then, when the old woman was out of the lodge, we hid the pistol, sword and gunpowder behind the firewood under our beds. When she returned that evening, we told her that we had found some of our belongings in the forest and showed her the contents of our pokes. She pondered my drawings but, as a shaman, her interest was more with Marcus's bag of potions. The old woman examined every leaf, piece of bark and stand of root, while Marcus tried his best to explain each substance's purpose.

At one point, Woodpecker asked the boy about his gods. Marcus answered, with details, that he was an Animist. Then she asked me the same question. Knowing that I was a Christian, Marcus brown eyes flashed warnings to me. At that, I remembered Raven and how quickly she had hidden her wooden cross. Turning to the squaw, while fearing my damnation, I said that my religion was the same as the boy's. The old woman's withered face looked pleased by my answer.

After this conversation, I filled my pipe and shared it with all. The old woman loved the African mix and explained that tobacco was a prized native item. As she smoked, I used some warm water and my sea knife to shave away my week-old red stubble. In the dim firelight, Woodpecker watched with wide-eyed awe, as Indians did not have chin whiskers. When I had finished, she touched my smooth face and then carefully examined my sharp knife. Handing the blade back to me, she shook her head and told me to keep the blade secreted in my pouch. Her sad instruction told me she knew of the dangerous undertow lurking in the village.

A few days later, while I was working on a canoe, a runner appeared. With a twisted tongue and sign language, the young boy told me that I was needed back at the lodge. As we ran back towards the village, I felt a cool breeze and could see dark clouds building over the bay. A summer storm was brewing.

Once at the lodge, I found Marcus and Woodpecker waiting. As we hurried to the bay, the old woman told me that a warrior in the northern village was dying. She had been summoned by a runner and asked to come and help save his life. Marcus and I were coming along because the man had been wounded by one of the ship's fire-sticks, and she wanted our wisdom.

At the water's edge, a large war canoe with Hawk and five other braves waited. He grunted and glared at my approach. As we got into the center of the boat, the chief handed us paddles and signed for us to do what the warrior in front of us did.

As we rowed across the bay, Hawk barked out orders from the stern, and the paddlers quickly answered his commands. With the old woman and the runner from the north sitting behind us, we did the same.

By the time we got to the bar, the winds were roaring across the slit. The towering waves of blowing green water reminded me of our passage around the horn, and my heart filled with fear. The closer we got, the louder Hawk shouted over the pounding surf. The first wave, that we hit straight on, lifted us skyward and then crashed us down on the other side of the curl. As we slammed against the sea's surface, we got drenched with cold saltwater. But there was no time to recover, as we pulled and paddled quickly into the next wave. Up we would go, and down we would crash. Soon there was ankle deep water in the bottom of the canoe. As it boiled around, we kept rowing from one breaker to the next. Twice, we almost floundered when the boat got pushed sideways at the crest of a wave, but with great teamwork we righted the canoe for the next surge. We rode out the last and largest breaker just before it curled and finally crashed down into calmer waters.

It had taken us almost ten terrifying minutes to cross the bar into the sea. With my soaked hair matted against my face, we stopped for a few moments to bail out the almost knee-deep water. My body was shaking and I was wet from head to toe. But as I looked around the boat, I saw no fear on the Indians' faces. They looked as though this was a normal happening when crossing the spit. I prayed that my face hadn't shown my inner terror.

Moving again in unison, we rowed due north in choppy seas for about a half hour. Then we turned into the slit for the northern bay. Hawk guided the boat atop a large wave and we shot through the tongue with surging currents in less than two minutes. The ride was swift, and I was amazed by the boat's seaworthiness and the seamanship of the Indians.

Once inside the estuary, Woodpecker told us that we were in a bay named *Nehalem*. We paddled up this placid green inlet until we came to a small village on the east side. Here we put ashore in front of five small lodges. The voyage from Tillamook to this location had taken just under an hour – the same distance that Marcus and I had run in six hours.

Waiting on the shore were the dying man's young wife and the local shaman, an older brave named Bright Cloud. Getting out of the canoe, Marcus and I took off our wet coats and spread them on some rocks to dry in the cloudy morning air. While we were doing this, Woodpecker and Bright Cloud went inside one of the huts, and we quickly followed.

The shanty was tiny and dark, about twelve feet square. There was a small fire burning in the center of the room, with a man sprawled on a reed mat next to the pit. The top of his buckskin was open, exposing his right shoulder. He was quietly moaning and seemed semiconscious. A stench of rotting flesh hung heavy in the smoky room.

Woodpecker motioned for us to take a look at the man, so Marcus and I knelt by his head. In the dim light, we could make out a large swollen wound on his right shoulder but not much more. Then I noticed his face in the firelight, and was shocked to find that the 'man' was a young boy. He looked to be no older than his early teens.

Turning to Marcus, I said, "Hand me a stick from the fire."

When he did, I lowered the flame close to the boy's skin, for a better look. What I saw was a mound of infected pus that covered a deep cut in his flesh. His shoulder was black and blue, and swollen to twice its normal size. It looked painful and smelled awful.

Gently, I ran my fingertip along the line of the weeping cut, and the boy cried out in pain. The others in the room gasped at his loud cry.

Suddenly, my finger touched something just under his skin. Moving the flame even closer, I tried again, and felt the faint outline of a sliver deep inside the gash. As I did this, the boy moaned loudly, and I knew that whatever was under his skin had to be removed.

"Do you have anything for pain?" I asked Marcus.

"Aye." He searched quickly inside his pouch, then pulled out a dried leaf and handed it to me. "He chew. Soon no pain."

Standing, I handed the leaf to Woodpecker, while motioning with my mouth to indicate that the boy should chew it.

Woodpecker tasted it with her tongue, then nodded her head 'yes.' As she told the boy what to do, I moved through the gawking braves who filled the doorway, making my way outside.

Walking the shoreline with a faint heart, I thought, *What the hell do I do now?* I knew the boy would die from the infection if that sliver – whatever it was – wasn't removed. But what would happen if I removed it and he died anyway? This savage meant nothing to me, especially as he was one of the reasons why we were marooned here... But he was just a boy, and I didn't want to face damnation again. God had guided me here, and I needed to believe in Him, and in myself.

On the shore, I found two pieces of dry driftwood that were thin and long. I could use these sticks as a torch. I also searched out a smooth, porous rock that I could use as a sharpening stone.

Returning to the hut, I put the sticks close to the fire, then asked Woodpecker for animal lard and a wet cloth. As the boy's wife searched for the lard, I removed the sea knife from my pouch. The watching braves let out a gasp when they saw my shiny blade. After the wife handed me the lard and a wet cloth, I knelt back down, next to the boy's head. Looking down at his face, I noticed that his eyes were upward and he seemed to be resting quietly.

"How's he doing?" I asked Marcus.

"Feel no pain," Marcus answered.

Taking my knife, I smeared it with lard and then began rubbing the blade across the sharpening stone. I checked its edge several times, before burning off the lard in the flames of the fire. The knife sizzled in the heat. Thrusting both sticks into the fire embers, I positioned myself just above his shoulder, with my hot blade poised just above his wound. The room went silent; all I could hear was the crackling fire. Taking the sticks from the flames, I dug the torches deep into the sand at an angle, just over the boy's shoulder.

Turning to Marcus, I quietly directed, "Hold him down."

Marcus placed his hands firmly on the boy's chest and nodded.

With sweat rolling down my face, I took my blade and quickly cut into the pus and infection, peeling the skin along the line of the gash. The boy let out a soft moan but did not flinch. With my knife, I made the same cut again, only deeper, and that's when the blade hit the sliver.

Instantly, the gash turned bloody, and I wiped it with the cloth. With my fingertips, I probed under his skin. Finally, feeling the sliver, I stuck my blade alongside my index finger, pinching the fragment.

With a combination of a gentle pull and a little luck, the sliver slid out of his shoulder. Looking at it under the torch light, I saw that it was a small, jagged piece of iron from the grapeshot fired from our swivel guns. The rusty metal had festered under his skin for over ten days; no wonder he had developed a painful infection.

Carefully, I felt my way along the wound, alert for any other iron fragments, but I found none. Removing one of the torches, I pushed the flaming end into the sand until the fire was out. Then, pulling it back, I blew on the end until the embers were red again. After cleaning the wound once last time with the cloth, I laid the red hot torch directly on the gash. It seared for a second filling the room with the smell of burning flesh, and I quickly pulled it back.

The boy let out a loud cry and then passed out. But within a few moments the boy was breathing normally again, and I found no fresh blood around his wound…thank God.

Collapsing to the sand on my butt, I looked around the stunned, silent hut. All of the Indians stood shocked, their faces filled with disbelief.

Marcus removed his hands from the boy's chest. "He okay, Joe?"

"Aye."

"You okay, Joe?"

"Aye."

As I got to my wobbly feet, Woodpecker and Bright Cloud started chanting. Soon the other braves joined in. Taking the iron sliver, Marcus and I went outside. In the overcast light, we examined the fragment, and then I threw it into the bay. It seemed only fitting that some of our ship's iron had been removed by members of her crew. What a strange twist of fate.

When a gentle rain started, Marcus and I retrieved our still-damp coats from the rocks. As we were putting them on, Marcus asked, "Where you learn that?"

"My brother Fredric had such a wound once. My father cut the sliver out and then slapped hot iron on the cut. Fredric screamed out from the pain… What kind of leaf was it that you gave the boy?"

"Come from coco plant. Very good for pain."

While I was putting my knife on my belt, Hawk pranced from the lodge like a rutting animal and started yelling angry words. Soon, other Indians gathered around watching. As Hawk continued his rampage, he held up two fingers.

Staring back at him, I kept shaking my head and saying, "No understand."

His fuming face was distorted with anger as he screamed more gibberish, his eyes ablaze with hate.

"No understand," I said again.

Then, of all things, he kicked sand at me. The crowd let out a gasp.

I started laughing. "What are you?" I asked. "A little boy?"

My delight made him angrier than ever. Then one of the braves from the canoe offered him a stone tomahawk. Grunting, he took the weapon and twisted to confront me.

Instantly, the smile on my face was replaced with the knife in my hand. Like roosters, we stood facing each other, waiting for the first thrust. Neither of us backed down or showed any fear. Crouching, we began circling in the sand, waiting for an opening.

Just then, I heard loud yelling coming from the lodge. Glancing that way, I saw Bright Cloud rushing towards us. Holding up both arms, he stepped between Hawk and me, screaming out unrecognizable words.

With his intervention, the scuffle was defused.

Later, I learned that two Indians from the village had been killed in the skirmish with the ship, and three others wounded. Hawk held me responsible for the deaths and was seeking revenge, even though I had helped save the boy's life. I also learned that kicking sand at another warrior was an Indian challenge of honor. Had I refused to fight, I would have been branded a coward. But there was no shame that the fight had been stopped by an elder, as that was the Indian way.

After the scuffle, with the weather souring, Hawk and his braves returned to Tillamook Bay in the canoe. They didn't ask if we wanted a ride back; they just left. Looking out at the sea's condition as they crossed the bar, I was relieved that they were gone and that we were safe on shore.

We waited outside of the lodge as the boy's young wife and the two shamans provided him with care. By the afternoon, he was sitting up and doing better. Even the swelling around his shoulder had improved.

After an evening meal of dried venison and root greens, the boy's wife showed us to a small mat house behind the lodge. Here, Marcus and I would sleep. It turned out to be a miserable stay, because it rained all night and the roof leaked.

The next morning, with the weather improving, I asked Woodpecker if I could return to Tillamook. She agreed, but said that Marcus would remain with her until the boy had more fully recovered.

Finishing a meager meal of oily fish gruel and bread cakes called *wapato*, I started walking south on the hard beach sand. With a cool breeze on my face, my mind filled with thoughts of Hawk and how I might dissuade him of his belief in my complicity with the ship's skirmish. If left to fester, I feared that his hatred for me could doom our future.

Lost in these thoughts, it took a while before I became aware of an object floating in the surf. At first, the small bobbing item scarcely registered, but then I realized that it looked much like a cheese wheel from a ship.

Moving into the shallow water, I soon had the block in my grasp. It weighed a good ten pounds, with a hard crust that was faded red. With much excitement, I carried it to shore. Once I cut into it, however, I found only a hard substance that looked and tasted much like beeswax. Where the devil had it come from? Disappointed, I almost threw the wheel back into the sea, but decided to take it back to the village.

Schemes

With the day overcast and cool, I returned to the village and used a pistol flint to get a lodge fire going. With the flames established, I returned the gun to its hiding place.

Returning to the main room, I was surprised to find one of the chiefs from the ship standing in the doorway. His name was Hunting Fox; the week before, I had sharpened two chisels for him. Now he stood in the door, holding, of all things, the brass lantern he had stolen from the ship. Walking into the lodge, he held the light up to my face and shook it. "No work."

Taking the lantern from him, I opened the little door and found the inside candle burned to the base. "No candle," I answered back, but Hunting Fox didn't understand. That's when the idea hit me like a winter storm: make candles from the wax. Surely the Indians would marvel over my light-sticks and trade for them. Blimey... what a great prospect!

After assuring Hunting Fox that I couldn't fix the light, I reluctantly offered him my pipe and remaining tobacco in trade for one chisel and the lantern. Tobacco being so highly prized, he cheerfully accepted, and rushed back to his lodge for the chisel.

With our trade complete, I started searching the lodge for anything that I could use as a wick. I tried some straw, but it burned too fast. Then I found some animal sinew, but it was hard to light. Finally, I came across a thin strip of dry cedar that I sliced into strands. Using these slim fibers, I tightly braided them together to form a wick.

After making a dozen two-foot wicks, I moved the iron pot outside to melt the wax. With a good fire going in the pit, I placed the pot on the flames and threw in some chunks of wax. Slowly, I stirred the melting wax until the pot was almost full. Then, hanging some of the wicks from a stick, I started dipping the strands into the wax.

As I worked by the pot, many of the neighbors came by to see what I was cooking. Once they had touched my candles and tasted the wax, they soon walked away, obviously thinking me crazy. But I was confident that my scheme would be rewarded and enrich my standing with the tribe.

When I finished, that evening, I had forty eighteen-inch candles hanging from the lodge ceiling to dry. I also had a devil of a time cleaning the waxy residue from Woodpecker's cooking pot.

Walking the bay's shore, the next morning, I found a handful of flat rocks that I could use as candle holders. Returning to the lodge, I cut all the dried candles in half and placed them in two large baskets. Surly, once the Indians saw the value of light in the dark, they would want many candles. This labor gave me a feeling of pride, as working with my hands always had.

Late that afternoon, Woodpecker and Marcus returned from Nehalem. With my candles hidden under some animal hides, I waited for the right time to show them my invention. After a cold meal of greens and dried fish, the old woman filled the cooking pot and put some spices into the water. Soon, Timber Wolf and Raven appeared to hear the news from the north.

Marcus and I were delighted to see Raven again, as she could answer the many questions we had about the Nehalem people. But as the conversation unfolded, I learned other things, as well. Woodpecker heaped great praise on Marcus for saving the Nehalem boy's life with his potion that stopped pain. She did say that I helped, but she insisted that it was Marcus who had driven out the evil spirit. She went on to tell Timber Wolf that Marcus was a great medicine man, one who would someday replace her as the healer shaman. Marcus translated her testament without protest, so I guessed he agreed with her notions. *Good for him*, I thought. *His potions were big tonics.*

Eventually, I told them of finding the wheel of wax floating in the surf. They told me that this was not unusual; the villagers had been finding these useless blocks for years. That's when I told them of my new invention, light-sticks. Then I revealed my baskets of candles and lit a few candles so that Woodpecker and the others could see how they worked. Melting a candle to a rock, I moved it to a black corner of the room so they could see the light it produced.

They seemed unimpressed.

As they looked at my sticks in the basket and talked, I retrieved the brass lantern and lit the short candle inside. Standing by the door, I told them that now I could walk in the night and see my way. Sitting back down, I handed the lantern to Timber Wolf, while telling them that I would trade my candles with the villagers for food and other goods.

Timber Wolf examined the lantern carefully and then asked how many 'shiny lights' I had.

When I answered just one, he shook his head and said, "Light-sticks no good outside, wind blow out."

"But light-sticks good inside," I replied.

Placing the lantern on the sand he said, "No, people use torch from fire to see inside. Light-sticks no wampum… fire-sticks big wampum."

Even the old woman agreed with him and said people would not use my candles. As they talked, I could feel the wind being sucked from my sails.

Later that night, as they were leaving, Raven told me she liked my idea, but that new ways were hard for the Indian people. With her brown eyes gazing at me earnestly, she said, "Some people like the dark."

In the end, they were right. I gave one free light-stick to each lodge in the village, but no one asked for more. Another prospect for respect had slipped away. Maybe Raven was right: people who lived in the dark liked the dark.

September was a beautiful month on the bay, and I continued working with Timber Wolf and Coyote to learn canoe-making. Meanwhile, Woodpecker taught Marcus the ways of a spirit healer. They were a good team, both searching the forest for more potions that could help the tribe.

It had become my habit to explore the bay in the early evening hours. The old woman had two canoes, both built by Timber Wolf, that I could use. The smaller one was just right for a lone paddler. With the dugout, I rowed the meandering shoreline, drawing every creek, river and bog. From these travels, I found all five of the southern villages and noted them on my map. After conversations with the locals, I even found out that there was a small bay to the south, with yet another village.

During these outings, I watched in awe as a great herd of elk grazed at the water's edge, without regard to me and my canoe. I found large flocks of ducks and geese on the bay, as well, and witnessed many fish rolling in the water. Tillamook Bay teamed with wildlife of all sizes and kinds. But of all the places I visited, it was the long, low sand spit to the west that I enjoyed the most. The bay side was shallow; at low tides, I dug many clams from the soft, wet sand.

The ocean side of the peninsula was long and straight as an arrow. Here I spent many hours walking the surf and watching the amber sun slip below the horizon. It was a beach that no other white man had ever seen, and I wondered if my footprints were the first to mark its sands.

It was on this stretch of surf, after a lengthy argument with myself, that I decided to read my mother's letter. I had resisted the urge for weeks, but now, with my fate uncertain, it was time. Perching myself atop some driftwood in the fading light, I reached into my pouch and removed the envelope that Father had given me, a year before. Seeing my mother's delicate handwriting filled my heart with memories of her sweet face and soft touch. Opening the parchment, I slowly read her epistle.

My dearest Joseph,

It is with a heavy heart that I speak to you from my grave, to tell you something that I should have told to you in life. Please forgive me for what I am about to say.

Soon after you father and I married, he went off to fight in the Indian wars. During his time away, I met a ship's officer from Holland. His name was Horace Clarke and he had come into my parents shop, buying provisions. He was a tall, dashing young man dressed in the blue uniform. Under his beautiful auburn hair was a face with a smile that could fill any room. He moved with grace and spoke with authority. The moment our eyes met, I felt something I had never felt before. I fought this strange emotion with all my strength, but to no avail. It was as if the Devil possessed me, filling my heart with a brash desire that was taboo. We had a short liaison that ended with his ship leaving and a seed growing inside of me. That seed was you.

When your father returned home, I was two months pregnant, and I told him the disgraceful truth, thinking that he would surely kill me or divorce me. Instead, with courage and devotion, he pledged to forgive me and raise you as his own. But I fear that my infidelity wounded him deeply, driving him to doom and drink.

I tell you this sad truth now so that you will better understand yourself and, I hope, find forgiveness in your heart for your father. It takes a great man to forgive such a sin. You were a child of love and the beacon of my life. I would not change any of that, not for all the wealth in Boston. Please forgive me, your devoted and loving mother.

Finishing the last word of the final sentence, I dropped her letter to the sand. With her words rolling around my head, I felt my birthright slipping away. Looking out to the crashing surf, with solitude on one shoulder and despair on the other, I cried like a baby. I had no future and my past had been a lie. The simple truth was that I was cursed and wasn't worth spit. Lord forgive me, I wanted to die.

Mother taught me that only God controlled our density, if that's true, why has he heaped so much misery on me? And why was I now questioning God and his motives? Should I accept the path he has placed me on…or was the pistol the best way?

These were the thoughts that weighed heavily on my soul. They were, of course, questions without clear answers. I could brood about my past and let depression control my future, or I could use the pistol, here and now. It was my choice.

After a few enduring days of reflection, I picked life. He who wanders the barren land with an empty heart is doomed. So the only salvation was to dig deeper and learn to trust in the glory of God.

Prospects Lost and Gained

Towards the end of September, Woodpecker and Marcus traveled to a village named *Netarts*, where a young squaw was having a difficult pregnancy and needed help. To get there, they took the small canoe to the southern end of our bay, then walked a well-traveled Indian trail to the village. I stayed behind, still working with Timber Wolf.

With their departure, a new scheme came to my mind. I remembered how, while standing a dog-watch aboard the Orphan, Mr. Haswell had told me about Captain Cook's crew making spruce beer when they first arrived in the Pacific Northwest. He said they had mixed fresh shoots from spruce tress with molasses and water, then fermented it to create a brew that was both tasty and potent. While I didn't have any molasses, I did have fields of ripe blackberries. If the Indians didn't like my candles, maybe they'd like my beer.

In the cooking pot, I crushed two gallons of over-ripe blackberries into syrup. Then I mixed in one gallon of tender young spruce shoots with roughly two and half gallons of water. After stirring the mixture well, I placed cedar planks on top of the pot. I guessed that the mixture would take a few days to brew, inside the warm lodge.

The very next morning, I awoke to the bitter-sweet smells of fermentation. Four days later, I strained the lumpy mixture through a series of baskets and cloths until I had almost three gallons of a dark, foamy liquid. Dipping a mug inside the bucket, I tasted my first batch of spruce beer.

Its flavor was bitter, with just a hint of berry and spruce. The brew was more like ale than beer, and I could detect the strong presence of the alcohol. Although it wasn't as potent as Mr. Gales *Green Thunder,* it had a good kick.

That evening, I let some of the neighbors sample my brew, and was soon trading bladders half-filled with beer for other goods. Before my bucket was empty, I had a deerskin, a bow with three arrows and a rusty hammer head. My spruce beer was a hit, and I dreamed of making new batches to trade for more goods.

But these dreams were thwarted when Woodpecker and Marcus returned from the south bay. The old woman became furious when she learned that I had made what she called *ishkodew aaboo* (firewater) for her people. While she acknowledged that liquor was a prized possession, she said it brought out the evil spirits in her people. Therefore, I was forbidden to make any more firewater in her lodge.

To not heed her wishes would have been disrespectful, and deep down, I knew she was right. But my spruce beer was another prospect lost.

By the end of September, the first big storms came blowing up from the south. The rains from these squalls raised the levels in the rivers and cooled off the bay with fresh water. The change in conditions would signal the salmon out in the ocean to return to their home rivers and spawn. This salmon migration happened twice each year, in the spring and the fall.

With this changing weather, the tribe busied themselves by making preparation for the salmon run. Raven told me the rituals for the first salmon of the season were the most sacred in the liturgy for all of the villages on the bay. The fish caught over the next few weeks would sustain the Indians over the winter, lasting until the next spring run. Since the salmon was the lifeblood of the natives, the first few days of harvesting the fish were steeped with superstition and village rituals.

After each storm, two canoes were floated just off shore, with cedar planks across the hulls. On this platform, the fish shaman would dance and chant. The villagers would build bonfires in front of the canoes and watch his performance. Sometimes, he was joined by the fishing chief, Hunting Fox, and the two men would dance together. This spectacle was colorful and mysterious. Both men dressed in buckskins and feathers, with their faces painted black and red. As they moved to the beat of a single drummer, the men shook long strands of sea shells while chanting to the salmon gods. The longer they danced, the more excited the villagers would become. This mesmerizing throb of the drum, and the chanting of the two men, reminded the people that only the fish shaman could see underwater and forecast the return of the salmon.

During this time, no one could fish in the bay or out in the ocean. The tribe believed that each river had its own god or master that would tell the fish when to return. Even after the salmon were in the rivers, no one could fish in the bay until the great flocks of pelicans returned. These rituals were as rigid as rock; if any of the rules were broken, the offender would be killed.

On the river next to our village, each family had a spot. These fishing holes had been passed down for generations. After her husband died, Woodpecker gave her family spot to Timber Wolf and his family. Although, for as long as she lived, Woodpecker could share in the fish caught from that spot. In fact, most of the fish taken each season were shared equally with all of the villagers, rich and poor alike.

As the men waited for the salmon to return, they honed their harpoons and fashioned more fishhooks out of bone. They also built fish traps across the narrow upper reaches of the river. These fish traps, made of sharpened cedar poles and netting, allowed fish to swim into shallow, restricted areas where they could be speared.

While the braves made these preparations, the woman built large wooden racks for smoking and cooking the fish. These racks would be held up over the fire pits by long poles dug into the sand. Everyone in the village worked toward the same goal: catching enough fish to live through the long winter.

After a third big storm, the first fish was killed in our river. This salmon was brought to the village and, with great ceremony, was cleaned and cooked in a fire pit next to the shore. With all the villagers watching, the fishing chief held the fish to the sky and prayed to the spirits of the ancestors. Then, with the help of the fish shaman, the salmon was placed on a wooden rack and suspended over the pit's flames.

As the fish cooked, the Indians danced around the fire, shouting out messages to their ancestors. As Marcus and I watched this ineffable ceremony, I noticed Hawk in the frenzied dance circle. He seemed to be shouting the loudest, and kept glaring at me. Finally, he broke away from the ring and approached me. With an odd grin on his ugly painted face, he demanded to see my knife.

I hesitated for a second…then relented.

"We had no part in your fight with ship," I said as he clasped my blade.

Holding the pointed end of the knife in my direction, with his eyes dancing in the firelight, he answered, "Promised spirits, after Woodpecker crosses over, you die."

"But why?" I demanded. "We are no threat."

"Fire-Head bad omen. You my coup!"

Flipping the blade, he extended the handle to me. Then, with a humorless smile on his savage face, he whooped and rejoined the bewitched circle.

His threat had been bold and public, but I was not frightened. As for some reason, fear had vanished from my soul.

After the fish was cooked, Hunting Fox ate the whole salmon, head and all. As the crowd watched, he threw the bones and guts from the fish into the fire. When he was finished, he also burned the wood rack on which it had been cooked. Then, with one last chant to the sky, he declared that the salmon had returned.

At this avowal, all the Indians rushed to their fishing grounds on the river – all except Marcus and me. We could watch them fish, and we could eat our share, but because we weren't Tillamook's, we couldn't fish until the pelicans returned.

At the end of the first week of the run, the pelicans arrived. Now, finally, Marcus and I could help the tribe harvest the fish. Over the next few weeks, the village took thousands of pounds of fish from the river and the bay. With Woodpecker's instruction, I soon became proficient at cleaning and filleting the salmon, and what fish they were! Some weighed thirty or forty pounds, and were as fat as my torso. Their shiny skin was bright silver, and their meat a deep, rich pink. Inside the females we found large quantities of red roe, a delicacy that the Indians ate right out of the carcass. They also consumed the salmon's cheeks and gills raw.

With my sharp knife cutting, we soon had long strings of skinned salmon hanging high in the lodge's ceiling, where they could soak up the smoke from the pit fire. We dried other fish in the sun, or cooked them fresh in the steam pit. All the bones were burned, while the innards and heads were returned to the bay for the crabs. Nothing was wasted; we even extracted fish oil from the carcasses. The wild, majestic salmon was the spiritual force and wealth of the Tillamook nation.

In late October, after a violent storm, I rowed across the bay and walked the ocean side of the spit. This had become my habit because, after big storms, unexpected items could often be found washed ashore. The week before, I had found a topsail spar floating in the surf. When I got it ashore, I discovered part of a sail tied to the pole, underneath the tangled rigging. It was a great find, and I wanted more.

This particular storm had produced extraordinary high tides that were receding as I walked the hard sand. I enjoyed the solitude and beauty of the walk, and the excitement of the search. However, on this day, although I walked several miles, I found nothing.

Turning, I headed back up the beach, walking in the soft sand close to the driftwood that littered the upper reaches of the beach. This route also proved unproductive…until I came to the path to cross the spit. There, under a pile of bleached logs, I found a ship's hatch cover, four feet square.

The cover was made of wood planks, six inches thick, and held together with three four-inch-wide metal strips bolted through the top.

The metal was rusty and the wood weathered. Just removing the hatch from the pile of logs was a big task, as the cover must have weighed over fifty pounds. Cart-wheeling it over the sand, I slowly moved the hatch down the path to the other side of the spit. There, I let it fall to the shore.

Why do I want this hatch? I asked myself. The wood was of no value, but the metal banding might be a different story. *Why? For what?*

Leaving the hatch behind, I rowed back towards the village. Halfway across the bay, the answer to '*for what?*' came to me. After the salmon season, I would build a forge to make arrow heads and chisels from the metal strapping. If that worked, it could improve my standing with the tribe.

The next day, I retuned to the shore and built a large bonfire on top of the hatch cover. Feeding the fire with driftwood, I let it burn for hours. Then, when the flames were almost out, I used long poles to fish through the embers for the three metal straps. Then I cooled this iron in the bay water. Each strap, if unbolted, would be ten foot long. If I could unscrew the nuts from the bolts, I would have nine seven-inch iron bolts and nuts. This prospect held great promise.

As the weeks of our stay at Tillamook Bay passed with the seasons, I began to notice the influence that Woodpecker and the tribe were exerting over Marcus. During salmon season, that clout started to turn him native. Soon, he discarded his western clothes for buckskins tailored by Woodpecker. He wore moccasins on his feet, and around his waist he sported a belt of sea-shells, along with a stone tomahawk.

He also took to painting a white line across both tops of his black cheeks. All this change bewildered me, and I reminded myself that he was just a boy and easily swayed. Marcus had taken to the Indians' ways far better than me, and he was now respected by the villagers as a healer with great powers. Indeed, without any extraordinary effort, he had gained precisely what I sought – their trust.

With a bitter wind blowing off the bay and the crimson leaves of fall swirling in the air, Marcus and I decided to try our luck one last time in Woodpecker's old fishing spot. As we walked up the deserted river path, carrying our harpoons, I talked to him about his new Indian ways.

"Why you dress in Indian garb?" I asked.

"These people much like my tribe," he answered without hesitation.

"Soon, Columbia or another ship will come for us. Is that what you want?"

He thought for a while as we walked, then stopped and twisted my way. "When ship comes, I will decide. If not, no woe."

"If Woodpecker dies, Hawk will kill us."

"Aye, but old squaw not die. I talk to her guardian spirit, and she live."

From these words, I realized that the boy was starting to believe this spirit nonsense, and that worried me more than I cared to admit.

The fishing hole, flanked with giant fir trees, was a deep gorge on the river, with tall boulders and a waterfall upstream, and another hole just downstream. In the middle of the ravine, the rushing current was strong as it tumbled over the falls, swirled around, and then dropped down to the next hole. On our side of the river, there was a small sandy beach where we could wade into the water. As I undressed in the chilly morning, I noted how much more water there was in the river. The last time I had fished here, the upstream waterfall had been narrow and gentle, now, with more rainwater, it was wide and wild. Removing my coat and trousers, I placed them on the beach alongside my poke and knife. Then I put my boots back on and waded into the cold water, armed with just my harpoon.

The boy did the same. Early in the season, we had fished in nearly hip-deep water, just in front of the waterfall. Now, that water was above my waist, and was as cold as winter snow. The idea was to harpoon the salmon in the pool just before they jumped in their effort to get over the falls, or to spear them as they lunged into the air. If I stood totally still, in the foaming white water, I could see them just under the surface. Marcus and I had caught many fish using these techniques.

Marcus was the first to snare a good-sized fish, which he dragged to the beach. After he returned to the falls, I speared a fifteen-pounder as it broke the water, jumping for the falls. With some effort, I got the still-flapping fish to the beach. As I turned to rejoin the boy, I saw a sight that made me doubt my own eyes.

There, standing at the top of the waterfall, was a big black bear. The creature was on his four legs just above Marcus, looking down at him. The boy, with his attention on the water, had no idea what loomed just above.

I shouted over the roar of the river, "Marcus, move back slowly."

He shifted his gaze to me, and I motioned with my head for him to look up. As he did, the bear reared up on his back legs and let out a growl that rolled through the gorge. This black monster had to be six feet tall and must have weighed close to five hundred pounds.

"Hold your harpoon up to him," I screamed, and rushed back into the water.

The boy raised his spear and started slowly stepping backwards.

The bear let out another roar.

I shook my harpoon at him, splashing towards Marcus. When I was within ten feet of the boy, he slipped on the rocky riverbed and fell backwards into the water. In the fall, he let go of his spear, which was quickly lost to the flow. I lunged across the water toward him, knowing full well that he couldn't swim. Just as the fast current was about to drag him under, I grabbed hold of his buckskins and pulled him against me.

By the time we regained our footing on the riverbed, we were thirty feet downriver from the falls. Just as I looked up, the bear jumped from his perch into our fishing hole in front of the falls, hitting the water with a splash that echoed off the boulders and enveloped the ravine.

Quickly, we splashed towards the beach area, with me pointing our only harpoon in the direction of the bear.

He roared again and charged towards the beach.

On shore, I reached down for one of the salmon and threw it directly at his face.

With one swipe of his powerful paws, he caught the fish, hesitated, then took a bite from the flesh.

Reaching for a second salmon, I repeated my throw. Dripping wet, with my heart racing, I watched the monster devour the first fish and go after the second. He was so close that I could smell his awful breath and see his yellow, rotting teeth. As he ate, the boy and I quickly gathered our belongings and ran off.

Half a mile down the trail, we finally stopped to get dressed. With my heart still pounding like the surf, I said, "I think the bear thought ya a sow."

"A sow?" the boy exclaimed. "Why?"

"Your black skin and those white marks on your cheeks."

Marcus's eyes widened. "You saved my life, Joe. I not forget."

"Aye."

That was the last time I ever saw Marcus wear war paint. Whatever else might befall us, he would never again be mistaken for a sow.

Later we found out that the bears always returned to the river at this time of the year. The Indians couldn't stop them with their crude weapons, so no one tried. The Indians just moved to fishing on the bay. I had been lucky not to have tried my harpoon, as I was told it was useless against the thick-pelted black monsters.

That evening, we told the old woman of our run-in with the bear, and about the threats from Hawk at the harvest ritual. She feared the first but not the latter, warning us to stay away from the rivers until the salmon were gone, and then assured us that she would speak to Hawk about his bullying. After that, the old woman said something that surprised me.

"Fire-Head, you and Raven always together. You desire on her?"

I wasn't sure about the word she used for 'desire.' Realizing this, she signed by humping her old hips. This made my face flush red, as I had never thought about Raven as a woman, only as our lifeline to the Indians. I had no idea how to answer Woodpecker's question.

"You desire her?" she asked again.

"She is Timber Wolf's slave. I have no right," I finally answered.

Nodding her wrinkled face, she added, "You trade for her, she become *your* slave."

"But I'm your buck. What would people say?"

"Sandpiper no like Raven in her lodge, but she okay with me. She give you what I can't. Papoose."

In the firelight, I could see Marcus's mouth drop open at the mention of a baby. It was a subject we had never talked about, and the thought of having a baby with a brown woman was unimaginable to me. Anyway, who in their right mind would bring a child into this savage wilderness? Besides, slavery was wrong. But if I did trade for Raven's freedom… she would be free to choose her own way.

"What would I trade?"

"He fancies your knife."

Woodpecker went on to tell me that I wouldn't have to beat Raven, as she was a good worker. And that, while Woodpecker considered her to be ugly, because her forehead didn't slope, she could cook and care for my needs.

The comment about 'ugly' made me smile; the Tillamooks had a distorted view of beauty. While Raven wasn't beautiful like my Becky, she was pleasing to my eyes. But trading my knife for her?

Bewildered, I replied, "I don't think so. My father's knife I can't give up."

Marcus had a suggestion. "You could make another knife from your iron scraps."

That I could do. It was time to build the forge.

My idea for the forge was simple enough. Build a three foot high rock pit about four feet across. Then fill the open pit almost full of rock rubble. On this debris I would work my fires and control the embers with a bellows made from cedar boards and the deer hide I had traded for. This big project could take weeks to complete, but I consoled myself with the thought that every good enterprise starts with sweat and ends the same way.

Carrying large stones from the bay's shoreline, I started two piles behind the lodge. On one heap, I placed flat stones for the walls of the pit. On the other, I made a stone pile of different sizes for the rubble. And as I worked, I kept a keen eye out for that special stone that would become my anvil.

While I was carrying stones from the shore, a young brave approached and asked what I was building. I recognized the lad as the runner who had called me back to the village when I was working with Timber Wolf. Talking by the rock pile, I noticed that the boy stuttered his words. His smile was wide and his yellowish eyes were bright, but this speech impediment made him talk very slowly. He was a strange-looking lad, with a large, fleshy nose, and a crooked, sloped head. He stood only about five feet tall and was dirty from head to toe.

"How old are you, boy?" I asked.

"Fourte-e-en seas-o-ons."

"What's your name?"

"Tribe call me-e-e Mole. I work fo-o-or you?"

What a great idea. Sliding my knife from my belt, I said, "If you help me build my forge, I'll make a knife like this one for you, and I'll pay you in food. What say you, lad?"

As he examined my blade, his face lit up like the summer sun, and he swiftly agreed.

Later, I learned that Mole was one of the poor people in the village. The tribe called him Mole because he dug the privies and did other kinds of dirty work. His mother had died giving birth to him, and his father had run off to live with the Clatsop Indians when the boy was just ten years old. Because the villagers thought him slow-witted, no one would take him in, so the boy lived in a mat house somewhere in forest, doing odd jobs to survive. He was an outcast in the village, just like me, and I took to him quickly.

Working with Mole proved to be a joy. He gave me ideas and taught me the Indian way of building a pit of stones. As we worked, he mixed bog mud with dried squaw grass, producing a mortar that held the stones firmly in place. Once the walls were done, he jumped inside the pit and smeared mud onto the interior. Then we built a fire inside the pit and dried the mortar to a hard bond. Finally, we filled the pit half-full of sand and placed the stone rubble on top.

At the end of each day, I gave the lad a basket of food, and he returned to the forest. An hour after sunrise, the next day, he would return with the empty basket.

As we worked, Mole helped me with my Indian words and asked questions about the pale man's ways. Through our conversations, I soon found that he had more wit than most of the tribe. He seemed to understand the concepts of yesterday and tomorrow, as well as those of right and wrong. Mole had an inner pride that evinced a story of survival.

When I finished with the forge, I went to work on building the tools I would need: long metal tongs to handle the molten iron, a file – coarse on one side, fine on the other – and a new handle for the hammer-head I had traded for. While I worked, Mole built a structure, open on three sides, with a shed roof over the forge to keep out the rain. Against the closed-in wall, we stacked our fire wood, safe from the weather. With the help of Mole, I selected the hottest-burning firewood, by trial and error. After only tens days, I was ready to begin making the knife that I hoped would free Raven.

Using my forge to heat the quarter-inch strapping, I cut off a ten inch strip. Then using a stone chisel, I split the four-inch-wide iron lengthways. Taking my long prongs, I placed this blank into the hot embers. Feeding the fire with air from my bellows, I began to hammer and shape the blade. With sparks flying, and the molten metal answering my sledge, a crude blade soon took shape.

As I worked the furnace, many of the villagers came by to gawk at my actions. They had never seen fire so scorching or molten sparks so big.

And when I placed the red-hot blade into a bucket of water to temper, they would jump back from the sizzle and steam. To them, my mysterious motions had something to do with the color of my hair and the glow of my embers.

My finished knife was seven inches long and just under two inches wide. At the top of the blade, I had forged a three inch long prong to receive a handle made from a piece of elk bone. The finished knife had good balance and, after hours of sharpening, an edge that was shaver-sharp. While my dagger was crude, compared to my father's steel blade, it was still a great improvement over the stone knives that the Indians used.

I was pleased with my work. Even Woodpecker liked the blade. She said the knife was good enough to trade for Raven's freedom. Marcus agreed…but this idea of trading something for another soul was troubling to me. Was I doing the right thing?

Chapter Six:
The Tillamook People

From San Francisco north to Nootka (Vancouver Island) and beyond, the coastal lands alongside the Pacific teemed with different Indian nations. Some of these nations were tiny, such as the Siuslaws, just south of the Tillamooks, while others were large, like the Chinooks that lived on the yet-undiscovered mighty river to the north that would be named Columbia. Within each nation there were tribes, and within these tribes there were bands, and within these bands there were different clans. Each nation lived to the dictates of the resources Mother Nature provided and their ability to hunt and gather food.

In the early 1800's, the Tillamook nation numbered roughly 2,200 natives. These people lived in nine different villages, from the Nestucca River in the south to the Nehalem Bay in the north. The largest Tillamook village was Kilharhurst, which occupied the land which is the present-day site of Garibaldi, Oregon. The river next to this village was called Kilharnar, and is known today as the Miami River. This village had about fifty lodges and five hundred inhabitants.

There are those who say that the word *Tillamook* means 'land of many rivers,' while others believe the word comes from the Chinooks and means 'people of the Nehalem.' In either meaning, the importance of water is emphasized. The Tillamooks always built their villages at the mouth of bays, rivers or creeks, and they were the only nation to use wood-framed cedar planks for their lodges, which always faced the water. This was understandable, given the importance of the salmon to each village.

Over time, the Tillamooks assumed most of the customs, habits and dress of their powerful neighbors to the north, the Chinooks. Although both nations spoke the Salish language, their dialects were so different that, when they talked, they had to sign. This was not unusual for coastal Indians, as each nation might speak a different tongue derived from the same general language.

The Killamucks, as some people called the Tillamooks, bore a likeness in looks, dress and manners to the other coastal nations. They were usually small in stature, with bowed legs and, thick, flat feet. These crooked legs were caused by the practice of squatting on their calves. Also, their women wore tight bandages of cloth and beads around their ankles that rendered their legs malformed and swollen.

Their skin tone was the usual copper-brown, and they had fleshy noses and wide mouths with thick lips. Their eyes were generally black, with stringy hair that was also matte-black. The men wore animal hides decorated with feathers, and adorned themselves with piercings of bones and sea shells. The woman wore grass-like skirts and tops made from cedar-bark strands, and they used their own urine as a shampoo.

The Tillamooks had no calendar, only a notion of the passing seasons. Indeed, they had only vague concepts of yesterday and tomorrow, and yet they understood the tides almost to the hour. As a people, they were peaceful and seldom went to war. Other nations, however, often raided their lands, killing and stealing. These actions were always met with quick and deadly retaliation. When necessary, the Killamucks could be savagely brutal.

The roots of the Tillamook nation grew deep in the sands and surf of the rugged Pacific Northwest wilderness. Their survival is a tribute to a culture of strong men and staunch woman. They were more like us than different, and they routinely faced and weathered human calamities we can barely imagine.

Winter Festival

WITH THE BAY BOILING AND THE WINDS howling, I stumbled through the village with my new blade in hand. The dark, overcast sky veiled the basin like a black cloth, and while it wasn't raining yet, there was a dampness in the air that seemed to soak into my bones. November had truly turned the seasons from fall into winter, and the outlook was gray, wet and dismal.

Arriving at the lodge, I scratched the door. Sandpiper answered and showed me into the hut, where I found Timber Wolf sitting on his haunches next to a large fire.

Surprised at my arrival, he looked up. "Fire-Head why you here?"

I knelt next to him and answered, over the swirling winds, "I've made something you might like."

Handing him the knife, I watched his eyes as he slowly examined the blade. Across the smoky room, I could see Sandpiper watching, as well.

"Good knife," he said at last. "Like handle. Very sharp." He held the blade out to me.

Stopping him, I said, "I want you to have the knife…in exchange for Raven."

His eyes widened as he looked again at the blade. Grunting a few times, he held the knife up to the fire light and checked its balance.

"See your knife?" he asked.

I handed my knife to him, and he held both, side-by-side.

Turning to me, he said bluntly, "I give you Raven for your knife, not new blade."

Across the room, Sandpiper smiled, then turned her back to us.

"Why my knife?"

"It shiny, like your light box."

"Then I'll trade the new knife and the light box for Raven."

Shaking his head, he answered, "No. Your knife."

Slowly taking both blades from him, I stood. "That I cannot do. My knife is special to me."

He got to his feet and nodded. "Fine."

As I left the lodge, I noticed the sour look on Sandpiper's face, and wondered what she would say to Timber Wolf after I was gone. As the old woman had told me many times that Sandpiper wanted Raven out of her lodge.

That evening, I confessed to Woodpecker and Marcus of my failed barter. They both agreed that my iron knife was practical, but not pretty, and so Marcus suggested that I cut his steel cutlass down into a shiny knife.

It was a good idea, if I could get my fire hot enough to forge steel.

Early the next morning, in a light, sticky rain, I got my fire going in the forge and searched out alder wood for fuel. Of all the wood in the forest, I had found alder to burn the hottest.

As I worked by the woodpile, Mole joined me. Before sending him out for more wood, I offered him the iron knife that Timber Wolf had rejected. "Here. This be for helping me build the forge."

His eyes lit up like embers, and a broad smile raced across his face as I handed him the blade.

With the knife in hand, he stammered, "Me b-b-big h-hunter n-now."

Then Mole walked into the forest, wearing his new blade on his belt. I felt a sense of pride for what I had crafted, and pleasure at helping this curious young man.

Working my furnace, I watched the color of the embers until I judged that the coals were hot enough to work steel. Then, taking the cutlass, I cut off the top of the sword, leaving only the handle and an eight-inch blade. Hammering the hot steel, I pounded the blade into a thin, wide edge. Then, using stone chisels, I serrated the top of the edge, while leaving the lower edge straight and tapered. When finished, the total length of the knife was just under a foot, with its steel blade sharp and its brass hilt shiny.

That day, I also started making arrowheads and lance tips out of my scrap iron. Mole was a big help. After the metal had cooled, I showed him how to use the file to sharpen and narrow the heads. We also replaced my arrowheads with the new iron tips, and they worked just great. Mole was pleased with the arrows' balance and their sharper impact; I, in turn, was impressed by his bow skills. Our little metal tips were lighter and flew farther than the stone-tipped shafts used by the tribe. Excited about our new invention, we agreed that soon we would go hunting together.

The next day marked the beginning of the winter festival. This was the most important social event of the year for the tribe. It was a time to renew old friendships and build new alliances. The salmon run was over, and the Indians braced themselves for the long, dark rainy season. The celebration was low-keyed and relaxed as the Tillamooks enjoyed dancing, food and telling tales inside their warm lodges.

Woodpecker hosted the first event for her extended clan. The day before the celebration, some braves came in and hung hollow cedar poles from the ceiling. Some of the poles were long and narrow, while others were short and stout. These braves also covered the sandy floor with mats, and stacked fresh firewood for the festivities.

Early the next morning, Woodpecker's invited relatives started to arrive. While Marcus welcomed them to the lodge, I watched the old woman making baskets of food. In one creel, there were strips of dried salmon; in another, strips of dried venison. The final basket was full of dried clams. All of this food would be dipped into small wooden bowls that contained a lumpy fish-oil paste. Earlier, Woodpecker had told me that this dip was made with special mushrooms she found in the forest. She said her guardian spirit had told her where to look.

Soon the lodge was filled with people. The women, adorned with sea shells, and dressed in bark skirts and tops, found their places on mats surrounding the fire. Meanwhile, the men, dressed in deerskins graced with bones and shells, squatted closest to the fire pit, holding long poles that reached to the ceiling. These staffs were called 'story poles,' and they were skillfully carved with symbols of fish and fowl. The braves holding the rods were all wearing colorful headdresses made of feathers and shells. There were no children in the lodge, as the opening day of the festivities was reserved for tribe members that had found their guardian spirit.

The dark room was stuffy, crowded and smoky. As Woodpecker's bucks, Marcus and I were allowed to watch and eat, but not participate in the rituals. Timber Wolf and Sandpiper were the last to arrive, while Raven remained behind, watching after their children. As they quietly found their places, the old woman passed out the baskets and bowls.

Then a hush fell over the room, and one man started punching the hollow log above his head with his story pole.

Thump...thump... thump...

Then he started chanting to the rhythm of his strokes.

Thump...thump... thump...

Another brave hit an opposing ceiling log with his pole, producing a differently pitched sound. He started chanting in cadence with the first brave. Soon, all eight warriors were banging the ceiling logs with their story poles, and chanting in unison. Then the women started humming in the background. Their pitch went from high to low and back again. The stale room filled with their slow rhythm, and the rafters shook from the pounding. This went on for the longest time...and then stopped, as quickly as it had begun.

With the room dead silent again, Woodpecker was the first to tell a story, in a firm, steady voice. As she talked, people ate the food. The myth she told was that of Thunderbird, one of the Tillamook gods, who flew over the ocean and found a giant whale eating all of the salmon. Quickly, he swooped down and attacked the whale. The battle was long and the struggle fierce, but finally Thunderbird prevailed. He lifted the dead whale out of the water and flew with the carcass to the shore. There, he dropped the whale from the sky, causing it to hit the ground with a loud 'clap,' shaking the land. The point of her tale was that when the Tillamooks heard thunder or felt the ground shake, it was Thunderbird dropping another whale, and that if a tribe found a dead whale in the surf, it was a gift from the gods and had to be shared.

Other Indians told different homilies, all of them about the salmon, their ancestors or the gods. But as these tales were told, they grew more violent and gruesome. Trying to understand the words, I listened carefully, all the while eating the dried food dipped into the paste, which was queerly bitter.

In between the stories, there was more drumming and chanting. Soon, the drummers picked up the beat, and the women began to dance around the room, with distorted faces and cries of woe. Their dancing bodies casting long, ghostly shadows on the walls. It was as if they were all drunk.

Glancing into the flames, I begin to see images of an eagle flying, and then the eerie face of my dead mother. These strange visions danced with the rhythm of the music and the shouts of the squaws. It was as if I had been transported to another level of being. My view was like peeking through the wrong end of a telescope.

These weird fancies unnerved me, and I begin to sweat. Trying to clear my head, I slowly pulled myself back from the abyss. Then I remembered the mushrooms, and I wondered if the paste had somehow clouded my mind. Pushing the food aside, I decided that I would eat no more.

Marcus sat next to me, moving his body to the beat of the drums. His eyes were empty, and he appeared to be in a trance. I told him not to eat the paste, but he paid me no heed. From our dim corner of the room, we continued witnessing this savage ceremony for hours. Soon, the men started brandishing spears and dabbing war paint on their faces, while the squaws rolled on the mats, screaming as if giving birth. It was a sight that reminded me just how desperately I wanted to leave this godforsaken bay.

In mid-afternoon, the rituals abruptly stopped. As the braves rested, the squaws got busy preparing the evening meal. Soon, the outside fire pit was burning, and then was filled with food. While the grub was cooking,

I noticed Timber Wolf leave the lodge for the slit trenches. Going outside, I waited next to my forge for his return.

When he came back down the trail, I called him to my furnace. There, standing under my shed roof in a light rain, I showed him the shiny new knife.

He liked its look and balance, even throwing the blade against the back wall several times.

Then I showed him my arrows with the iron tips.

These he shot into a nearby tree.

When I saw that he seemed pleased with both of my new weapons, I asked, "Do we have a trade for Raven?"

He thought for a moment. "Yes. Knife." He held up three fingers, "Arrow tips."

I quickly agreed, before he could reconsider.

When we returned to the lodge, Timber Wolf whispered something to Sandpiper, and she swiftly departed the hut with a large smile on her face.

Taking Woodpecker aside, I told her of my successful trade. She smiled and promptly went into the next room to prepare the fourth bed.

Just as the food was being served, Sandpiper returned with her children and Raven...but Raven's face looked sour, not happy. She carried a parfleche of her belongings, and she talked to Woodpecker with her back to me. Soon, both women went into the next room.

When they returned, Raven marched up to me and whispered, "So, you will have your way with me now." Her words were angry, her eyes sad.

"No, that is not true. I – "

Before I could say more she cut me off. "You traded for me. Is that not true?"

"Yes. But I release you. You are free!"

She glared at me for another moment, as if she didn't understand my words. Finally, she replied, "Free from what? Free to be taken by other braves? I was safe in Timber Wolf's lodge. Now I must tell children we friends no more."

Before I could say another word, she turned and joined the children on the other side of the room. Her anger caught me off-guard, but then I realized that I had never actually thought to ask her whether she wanted to be free.

During the meal, Marcus announced to the clan that, come spring, he would seek his guardian spirit. Amid great shouts of approval, some of the Indians looked my way, as well. But I said nothing. Marcus's edict surprised me, as he had not mentioned a word of this before. I feared that the old woman's influence was taking hold.

After the meal, I left the smoky hut for the damp, fresh air. The evening was dark and cool, and I wanted to walk the shore and ponder the day's events.

Soon, I came upon the embers of an abandoned bonfire. I stopped there and added more driftwood to the coals. Sitting on a damp log, I watched the flames take hold, and heard the heavy surf in the distance. Its sound seemed to echo my loneliness. I had traveled far and needed to travel farther, as life with the Indians was not for me. Under a starless sky, with a cold breeze on my face, I began to play my flute, dreaming of home.

My music was soft and lonely, my crackling fire tall and cozy. The barbaric stories and dancing had been harsh, confusing me. I needed softer memories.

As my music floated on the air, I felt someone watching from the shadows. Turning toward the darkness, I spotted Raven. When I put down my flute, she approached and sat next to me on the log.

"Don't stop. Music good."

"I didn't know you were there. Is the festival still going on?"

"Yes. Are you mad for what I say?"

In the firelight, I could see that her anger was gone. And now her brown eyes searched my face for answers.

"I had no notion you didn't want to leave Timber Wolf's lodge. I should have asked."

"Sandpiper good to me… I love her children. But I yours now. I be good to you."

Twisting my body towards her, I said earnestly, "You do not belong to me. You are not a slave. You are free to choose your own path."

In the flickering light, she turned her gaze from me to the flames. I watched as Raven tried to understand what I had just said. She seemed confused, as if unable to believe the truth at hand.

Finally, her gaze returned to me. "Then I choose you. You take me home?"

"Home?" Something about the intensity of her gaze told me that she wasn't just referring to Woodpecker's lodge. "Where would 'home' be?"

"The cove where the Tolowa people live. Where Mother is."

"How far away is this cove?"

"Many, many leagues," she said, pointing south. "There is a white man's store and a priest. I can show you trail."

Suddenly unsettled, I got up and placed more wood on the fire. Then, slowly, I turned and knelt in front of Raven, taking one of her hands into mine.

"A journey that long seems impossible…but if the chance comes, I'll take you home. Understand this, though – with the first ship that arrives, I am gone. If the ship goes north, then I will go with it. If the ship goes south, then I will see about getting you home. No promises, either way."

She considered my words for a moment, then grabbed my other hand, "Fair. Until white-bird comes, I take care of you." Squeezing my hands tightly, she continued, "Woodpecker say you want papoose. We start tonight?"

Quickly I pulled both of my hands away, and my mouth dropped open. Her carnal notions astounded me. Jumping to my feet, I looked her right in the eye and angrily answered, "I want no papoose, and we will not be that way."

She looked up at me, the firelight washing her pleasant olive face. "You no like me?"

"Not that way. We both want to go home. That's the way it will be."

Reaching to her right shoulder, she untied the top of her rawhide blouse and let it fall open. "I am soft. Touch me. I know how to please a man."

My face flushed. The desire that the sight of her bare torso awoke in my body annoyed me. Mother had explained to me that such lust was sinful.

Staring back at Raven, where she sat with the wind in her hair, I loudly protested, "Not this man. Cover yourself, girl. There will be no fondling between us."

She retied her blouse, then asked, "Have you been with girl?"

Just then, lighting and thunder roared across the sky, and it started to pour. Jumping to her feet, Raven said with a smile, "Thunderbird drop whale," and we both ran for the lodge to get out of the rain.

I never did answer her question.

That night, while trying to sleep, I realized that Raven had become a temptation that I feared more than I feared Hawk. Her provocative ways could doom my thoughts of home, unless I stayed on my guard. Come what may, loving an Indian woman was out of the question.

Early the next morning, Woodpecker and Marcus went to another lodge in the village for more festivities. I had had enough of the Winter Festival, and so I stayed behind, working with Mole, forging more weapons. Raven remained in the lodge, cleaning up from the activities of the day before.

Late in the morning, with the rain blowing sideways, she came out of the hut, dressed in a seal skin coat, with a basket hat tied over her head. She shouted over the wind that there was a low tide and that she was going to gather clams for dinner.

I nodded my approval and went back to work at my forge.

That day, I made two more knifes from the remaining steel from the sword blade. After the shanks cooled, Mole affixed bone handles to both and sharpened the edges. As he worked, I made another half-dozen arrow tips and three iron harpoon heads.

Soon, a neighbor came by and examined one of the shiny new knives, and we started to barter. I told him I would trade only for other iron goods, but he told me he had no such items. I didn't believe him. In the end, he relinquished an iron chisel from the ship, and two tanned deer hides for the blade. I was delighted.

In the early afternoon, as I was finishing up with my last tip, Raven returned, all excited. From inside her basket of clams, she proudly produced a canon ball she had found in the shore rocks of the receding tide. The six pound ball was about four inches around. It was made of pot iron, the easiest metal to forge, so I knew I could make something from it. The ship had fired many cannon shots, so if Raven could find one, I reasoned that I could find more. It was a great discovery and, without thinking, I thanked Raven with a hug, something I had never done before.

She seemed stunned by my touch, and gave me an odd look before rushing back to the lodge in the rain.

With the old woman and Marcus still away at the festivities, I invited Mole to stay for dinner. He gratefully accepted. There was a lot of hard bark about this boy, but he also had an inquisitive mind that I liked very much. This would be his first time inside the lodge; Woodpecker would never invite him in, as she felt his guardian spirit was evil.

That night, Raven served us planks of fresh clams, dried salmon and roasted tubers that tasted much like potatoes. Her cooking was good, and Mole couldn't stop praising her for the tasty meal. That's when I noticed that Mole didn't stutter as much when he relaxed. His words came more quickly, and his sentences were clearer. He was no dummy. The three of us had a delightful time, talking of the day's events.

After Mole went home, Raven asked to see my two deer hides. After examining the pelts closely, she stood up and held one hide in front of herself.

"Please... sailor coat off."

Her expression was serious as she moved to my side of the fire. I rose to my feet and unbuttoned my tattered coat, letting it drop to the mat.

Holding the hide against the front of my body, she proclaimed, "I make you winter coat."

As she touched me with the pelt, her fingers probed my body with an odd look on her face.

"You big man."

Then she moved the skin to my back and told me to hold it in place while she marked it. Using a sharp bone, she stood in front of me. After showing me exactly how to hold the hide high on my shoulders, she began marking the outline of my body on the pelt. As she worked with the marker, I noticed how soft her olive skin looked in the firelight. For the first time, her full lips seemed inviting. As she moved the bone around, I felt her tender touch. There was a strange, savage beauty about this girl. She was like a mountain that needed climbing, or a fish that needed catching. There was something...

Then a noise outside make me jump, and I realized that Woodpecker and Marcus were returning to the lodge.

Awakened

THE NEWS OF MY IRON TIPS AND shiny knives moved through the tribe like the wind. Over the next few days, I did a brisk trade, bartering with the Indians. One brave came from Nehalem with the chest plate from an old suit of Spanish armor. He told me that his grandmother had found it on a holy mountain, just north of the bay, many years before. While the armor was dented and tarnished, I knew I could forge more weapons from its steel. It cost me four iron arrow tips and two harpoon heads, but it was worth it.

Others came by, with axe and hammer heads, chisels and more hides. One brave showed up with a whipsaw blade that I remembered from the ship's barter. The cross-cut saw was four feet long, rusty and dull. But I knew that, with it and the others tools I owned, a cabin could be built. For that item, I traded the last of the shiny knives I had made from the sword.

Building a cabin was an idea that had been gnawing at me for weeks. If I remained on the shore by the bay, I couldn't watch for ships. My notion was to build a cabin on the high ground just north of the slit, which would give me a view of the ocean for miles. It was a scheme I could carry out if Woodpecker and the elders approved and if Mole and Raven would help. Besides, I looked forward to making a proper bed frame, or maybe a hammock; anything would be softer than those bloody cedar shelves.

Each evening, I watched as Raven worked on my winter coat. The bone needles she used weren't sharp enough to penetrate the thick hide, so she had to use a stone punch to make the holes. That gave me the idea of making an iron awl.

Another problem she faced was the cutting of the pelt. She used sharp stones, but it took hours to slice through the hide. Shears were needed, and so, out of the hard steel of the armor, I crafted a crude pair of scissors.

Raven seemed impressed by my simple sewing tools. In the back of my mind, however, I envisioned using these tools to make and mend sails. Somehow, someday, I was going to leave this place, even if I had to build my own sail boat to accomplish it.

As the last days of the Winter Festival began, Woodpecker and Marcus walked to Nehalem for the final rituals. The old woman said they would be gone two nights. Raven and I were invited, but we decided not to attend. I did ask Woodpecker to talk to the elders about my cabin on the point, and she agreed.

After their departure, I put Mole to work, cleaning and sharpening the saw blade. That's when I noticed the improving weather. It had stopped raining, and slivers of sunshine rolled across the bay. While it was still cool, the conditions were good enough for me to think about a visit to the river. It had been over a month since my last bath, and my dirty body offended even my own nostrils. Telling Mole and Raven where I was going, I started the walk to the river.

As I made my way, the morning weather kept improving. Looking out to the bay, I saw a few dugouts dragging lines for an ugly fish that the Indians called *sturgeon*. Watching them fish, I thought about making iron hooks which would be superior to the bone hooks they used.

Halfway up the trail, Raven caught up with me, carrying a basket of clothes that needed washing. We stopped at the soap tree, then proceeded to the rocky little cove that the old woman had showed to me, months before. The river was high and swift from all the rain, and looked cold as ice. Standing in the sunshine, I removed my boots and began to undress, handing my dirty clothes to Raven. That's when she started pointing out all the burn holes in my sea coat and my shirt from working at the forge.

The scorching from the sparks didn't surprise me, so I kept undressing. Finally, when I stood in front of Raven in only my smallclothes, she asked for my undershirt. I hesitated for a moment, then relented.

"White men wear many hides," she said with a grin.

When I removed the shirt, Raven saw all of the burn marks on my skin from the molten sparks. Touching some of the marks, she asked if they were painful. I told her that they weren't.

Then she touched the tattoo on my arm. With her soft fingertips, she felt the ink lines and gawked at the clumsy image. "You make eagle land on me?"

"Yours would not be an eagle. It would be a raven."

She smiled. "You make it land?"

Thinking a moment of the tools needed for a tattoo, I answered, "Maybe I could. We'll see."

As I bent to put my boots back on, Raven demanded my undershorts.

Smiling back at her, I said no, then proceeded into the water, with soap leaves in hand. *It was cold!*

As I bathed, Raven went to work, washing. By the time she was done, I was out of the water, shivering in the sunshine as I tried to dry myself with a small cloth. Then, with all of the clean clothes spread out on rocks, Raven went to the water's edge, turned her back to me, untied her buckskin and let it drop.

She wore nothing else. As she slipped into the cold water, I willfully gawked at her backside. Her legs were short and muscular, with narrow hips and a slender waist. Her upper back was shapely, with olive shoulders that caught her long black flowing hair. She eased into the deeper water and turned to me.

It was a vision I would never forget, the moment of my awakening.

"You like what you see?" she asked.

Quickly, I turned away. Feeling embarrassed, I did not answer her question.

"Fire-head, you so bashful."

During the long, silent walk back to village, I cursed myself for my shameful thoughts. My feelings reminded me of my mother's words: *It was as if the Devil possessed me, filling my heart with a desire that was taboo.* Why had this girl smitten me so?

I did not know. I only knew that she had.

That afternoon, Mole and I went into the forest and started cutting up downed alder trees. The long saw blade had a single handle at one end; after working it a few hours, I wondered if a second handle at the other end would make the saw more efficient. Other than that, the sharp blade worked wonderfully and we returned with a half cord of firewood.

That night, after our evening meal, Raven gave me the winter coat. With the fur side in, the coat was warm and well-sewn, with tight, straight stitches. There were pockets on the sides and a buckskin hood to keep the rain off. She had done a marvelous job.

Wearing the coat, I strutted around the lodge, praising her work. But there was more: she also gave me a pair of moccasins. She told me that, during the nights, she had used my boots for size, and had crafted the shoes while I slept.

The moccasins, adorned with small seashells, fit perfectly. They were beautiful and practical, something I had desperately needed. Holding the moccasins up to the fire light, I nearly cried.

Then Raven surprised me again, with a buckskin sleeping robe. Over the sounds of a whispering rain, she asked me to put it on so that she could check its fit.

Going into the next room, I removed my clothes and slipped the robe over my head. When I returned, there was a sweet smell in the room that Raven said came from burning soap leaves. I saw that she had placed an elk hide on the mats next to the fire. There she stood, waiting to see me in my new robe.

While I quietly stood in front of her, she moved her hands around my body, checking the fit. The robe was soft and supple, her touch gentle but firm. There was a look of pride on her face as she felt her stitches and probed the tailor of the hide against my body.

Overwhelmed by her kindness, I kissed her.

My awkward lips caught her off-guard for a moment, but then she answered with a kiss of her own. We held each other for a moment, then slipped to our knees on top of the soft elk skin. In the fire light, she slowly untied her buckskin and let it slip from her shoulders, exposing her soft, full body. Then, with that strange look on her face, she reached out and pulled the robe off of me. After a few embraces, I cradled her cheeks in both my hands and looked straight into her brown eyes.

"I've never done this before," I whispered over the pouring rain.

Placing her hands on mine, she softly answered, "We go slow. I show you."

Clinging together on the elk skin, we talked, chortled, and came together many times. Any fears I'd had about my sinful actions quickly vanished, replaced instead by a few bright moments of love. Raven's savage beauty awakened me, and I was surprised by how much appetite I had for her. Sometimes we just held each other, not saying a word. Other times, we quietly explored each other's bodies. Raven was the first woman – other than my mother – that I had ever kissed. I had no idea whether what we felt for each other was love or loneliness. What I did know was that I felt no shame at being with a brown woman. As for Raven, she knew no better. And while I might regret my actions tomorrow, on this night I would bask in the warm afterglow of love. With the winds swirling and the rain pouring, Raven became my guardian spirit that night, and I became hers.

Early the next morning, I awoke abruptly to the sound of Mole scratching on the door. Opening it a crack, I told him there would be no work that day. He glanced at my robe and sleepy face, then smiled and walked away.

Closing the door and turning back to the room, I saw that Raven was still asleep on the elk skin. Next to her on the mat was my folded sea coat and shirt. Both had been mended with bits of cloth to cover the many burn holes. While the fabric didn't match, I didn't care. The realization that, once again, Raven had cared for my needs while I slept reminded me of just how special she was.

We spent that day together. In some ways, it was if we had just met. She put on a seal slicker and basket hat, while I wore my new coat, and we rowed across the bay in weather only fit for fools. Then we walked the wind-swept beach, holding hands. She smelled of the soap tree, and her face was bright with a quiet air of satisfaction. I showed her where I had found the hatch cover, and talked about the topsail spar I had recovered. She told me more about her home and her people, and about how far away they lived. She talked about being violated by the Indians who had stolen her from her family, and how her faith had guided her. We also talked of the Tillamook people and their culture.

We waded through the shallow surf, kissing and hugging. Then, after hours of wandering the spit, we hurried back to the village to warm up and dry off.

That evening, I played my flute for her while she made me a leather apron to wear around my forge. The thick hide had two pockets and a place to hang my hammer. I was in awe of her craftsmanship and attention to detail. Then we came together again.

Afterward, Raven rolled her naked body towards the fire and shivered. Getting up, I retrieved a blanket and returned to her on the elk hide. Covering us both, I laid next to her, touching her bare back.

"When Woodpecker and Marcus return, we cannot be like this," she said, staring into the flames.

"Aye,"

"So we will need a mat house of our own."

"No, I am going to build us a log lodge. It will take a while, but it will keep us warm and dry."

"How we be together until then?"

"We have the beach and forest, the lakes and rivers. We will be together."

After a long pause, she added, "Until white-bird comes?"

"Aye," I whispered softly.

The next day, when the old woman returned, she told me that the elders had approved my building scheme, but I had to promise to alert the tribe if I saw a ship trying to enter the bay. They worried about another battle and wanted time to prepare.

I agreed.

For the next few weeks, Mole and I worked to clear some high ground, just north of the slit. The fir trees there were tall and straight, and I planned to nestle the cabin just inside the cleared opening, giving us protection from the wind on three sides. The work was dirty and hard, the weather awful, and the terrain rocky and dangerous. However, with lots of sweat and planning, we soon had a parcel of level bare ground, fourteen paces wide and twenty paces deep. This land looked out to the sea, with good views north and south. Behind the parcel, just over a hill, was a large fresh-water lake. We had the land cleared and logs cut; all we had to do now was build a lodge.

When we weren't working the land, we made more iron tips, and bartered them with the Indians. Mostly, I traded for items from the ship, other scrap iron, blankets, animal hides and occasionally food. One day, Hunting Fox, who was the chief of fishing, stopped by. He asked if I could make a large iron hook for dragging big fish into his canoe. Then he showed me the bone hook he had been using, which had broken in half. For payment, he promised me the first sturgeon he caught. Hunting Fox was a legendary fisherman, and I trusted his word. The next day, I crafted a sixteen-inch gaff hook made from the last of the armor steel. When I gave the hook to the chief, he seemed very pleased.

A few days later, he reappeared with two other braves, carrying a fish that was twelve foot long and must have weighed over two hundred pounds. Helping them, we strung it, tail first, from my shed's rafters. It was a bony, ugly fish that was shaped much like a shark. The chief told me its white meat was sweet, like no other fish, and that it was full of flavorful oils. Other than a whale, this fish was the biggest I had ever seen. I could only imagine how they had gotten the creature into their dugout.

Woodpecker and Raven cleaned and skinned the carcass, then traded half of the fresh meat for other food stuffs. They wanted to smoke the remaining filets, but I cut off a few steaks first. Being weary of dried fish, I wanted to pan fry some of the meat.

Taking the six-pound cannon ball that Raven had found, I melted it down and hammered out a two-foot-square griddle. The final skillet was so big that Mole put bone handles on two of its sides. Then we placed some flat rocks in my forge fire, and lifted the grill above the flames and rested it on the rocks. After adding fish oil to the pan, I placed two sturgeon steaks on the hot iron.

Minutes later, Mole and I dined on some of the tastiest fish I had ever eaten. Even Woodpecker and Raven joined us under the shed roof, feasting on the bounty. If my grill was this good with fish, I could well imagine what it would do for venison or elk.

It was time to go hunting.

The changing years weren't celebrated by the Indians, who had no written calendars, only a notion of the seasons. By watching the position of the sun, however, I had a reasonably good idea when 1788 ended and 1789 began. On that day, I thought of all the horrible events and passages of the previous year, and prayed for deliverance in the coming year. Somehow, this nightmare had to stop...but what then of Raven? Would I take her with me?

The weather improved, right after the first of the year. So it was with blue skies and a crisp breeze, Mole and I took our new weapons into the forest in search of game.

Before leaving, I had removed my pistol from its hiding place. Taking it to my shed, I cleaned, oiled and reloaded the gun. It would be my weapon of choice. Then, I gave my bow and arrows to Mole, as he was the much better archer. Carrying only my pistol and two lances, we headed out to hunt.

Mole told me that he had seen deer grazing on the mountainside, just a few miles up from his hut, so we started walking the forested trail behind the village. Soon, we passed the slit trenches, with their awful smell. A few minutes later, we came to Mole's mat house. As we walked past it, I noticed the squalor he lived in. His hut was built into the side of the mountain and looked like a mole hole with dirty grass mats. It was a shelter unfit for a beast, let alone a man, and its closeness to the trenches made it reek with an odor that brought tears to my eyes.

"Why you live like this?" I asked as we passed his hut.

"N-n-ooo place else t-tooo live."

I shook my head in disbelief, and we continued up the tree-lined trail.

After a few more miles, we came to a large clearing near the top of the mountain. Just below this opening, in the timberline, we found a small creek. As we walked its muddy shoreline, we came upon many deer tracks and found a well-traveled game trail. We guessed that the deer came down this way from the open mountainside to drink the water.

We moved back up to the clearing and found a fallen log snag which offered good cover, next to the trail. The clearing above us had no standing trees, but the ground was covered with rooting snags and tall underbrush that grew in and around the downed logs. All this forest must have been blown down in some winter gale many years before.

The morning was bright and cool, with the low winter sun and breeze on my right shoulder. Worried about our scent, I told Mole to move quietly to his left, up and around the clearing, until he came to the top of the mountain. Once he was there, I wanted him to start making noise as he walked the half-mile downhill to where I would be hiding. By doing so, I hoped he would flush some deer and herd them towards the game trail, where I would be waiting with pistol in hand.

Just before he started out, I gave him one of my spears. Mole seemed pleased with the plan and started creeping uphill to his left.

After clearing some underbrush, I climbed under the snag's upright stump for cover. The downed fir tree was about sixty feet long and six foot thick. The scrub growing in and around the dead tree made a good hiding place. Lying under the tree, I had a good view all the way up to the top of the mountain, and I knew I would have a clear shot at any animal that came down the game trail.

As I started the hunter's wait, my mind harkened back to the numerous times I had gone hunting with father. He had always been in charge and a good shot. Now it was my turn.

One daydream led to another; until I realized with a start that Mole had been gone for over an hour. Gazing up at the clearing, my eyes moved slowly, searching for any sign of the boy. By now, he should have reached the top and begun his noisy descent. But I saw or heard nothing.

Where the bloody hell is the kid?

The question kept racing though my mind, over and over, like a heartbeat.

Then I heard hooves moving down the trail to my right. Picking up my pistol, I fully cocked the hammer and checked my flash pan.

Moments later, a deer came into view, walking down the path. He had an uneven winter coat of splotchy brown fur, and his head held a rack of antlers with four spikes. He looked to be good-sized – I guessed about two hundred pounds, the four-legged equivalent of the chief's sturgeon. Quietly, I waited for him to get closer.

At one point, he seemed spooked, and he stopped several times to sniff the morning breeze. Finally, he moved to within twenty yards of me and stopped again. This time, when he raised his head and sniffed, his brown eyes looked directly my way.

Taking aim, I pulled the trigger.

Flash! Bang!

The ball struck the deer's chest, and he went down, kicking and spurting blood. But the pistol didn't have the velocity to kill the animal outright. As he tried to get up, I dropped the pistol and rushed towards him with my spear. Quickly, I thrust the lance into the wounded deer's chest and twisted the iron head. He let out a soft whimper, his sad eyes staring up at me, and died within seconds.

As a boy, when father killed a deer, I'd felt sorry for it. But now that I had killed my first, I found that there were no such feelings, for I viewed all animals only as sources of food or profit.

As I stood gazing down at my kill, I heard a hissing noise behind me. Twisting in that direction, I felt my heart falter. There, perched on top of the log snag, was a large hissing cat.

This was no ordinary wild cat. I had seen plenty of bobcats before. This cat, by contrast, was angry and gigantic. Backlit by the sun, the cougar's tawny-colored fur glistened, and I guessed it weighed more than I did. He snarled and hissed at me again, with the hair on his back standing on end. He had probably been hunting the same deer, and now I had become his prey.

Staring at the cat, I reached for my spear, which was still stuck in deer. I gave it a pull. Nothing happen. The iron tip was fouled on some inside bone.

I pulled again. Still nothing. My heart raced, and I began to sweat. My pistol was empty, on the ground over by the cougar, and my spear was useless. Reaching for the only other weapon I had, I pulled my knife. Crouching, I held the blade high in front of my body and, from pure nervous bravado, yelled, "You want me for dinner? Come and get me, you mangy devil."

My body shook with adrenaline. I knew it would be a fight to the death, most likely mine. My sea-knife would be no match for this muscle-bound monster, but what else could I do? I was alone. But <u>why</u> was I alone?

Where the bloody hell is that kid?

What happened next played out like a dream. The cougar hissed and growled one more time, showing off his gigantic yellow fangs. Then he sprang into the air, coming straight for me, his claws and jaw ready for the kill. When he was ten feet from landing on me, *whoop,* an arrow sliced through his neck in mid-air. The force from the blow threw him off track and he landed hard on the ground, not five feet to my right. He struggled to get up but, with my adrenalin pumping, I threw my knife into his chest with a *thump,* just as a second arrow found it's mark.

His thrashing stopped and the cougar went limp. He was dead and

I was safe, but I realized belatedly that, in the struggle, I had soiled myself.

Mole hurried to my side, his third arrow ready.

"Wh-why yoou talk to c-cat?"

Mole had saved my life!

The Cabin

We dressed out the animals there on the mountain. Mole wanted the cat's hide, fangs and claws. Then we hung what remained of the carcass in a tree, so other Indians could take what they wanted. Nothing would be wasted. From the deer, we got over a hundred pounds of meat, some innards and his beautiful pelt. As we worked at cutting up the venison, I kept thanking Mole and praising him for his marksmanship. I was in his debt and I would not forget.

When we got back to the lodge, I got my fire going and placed the skillet on the rocks. Soon, we were all feasting on fried venison. The deer had almost cost me my life, so I relished every bite.

That evening, after Mole had gone, I told the old woman and Marcus about the squalor in which the boy lived and how he had saved my life. Then I asked Woodpecker whether Mole could build a new mat house behind my forge shed, until the cabin was finished.

The old woman was hesitant, clearly still feeling that the boy was inferior and had an evil soul.

"He's a smart kid," I pleaded, "and his guardian spirit is good. It saved my life."

Finally, Woodpecker relented, but Mole was still banned from taking his meals in the lodge.

"Where he sleep after cabin done?" Raven asked, her troubled gaze betraying her fear that we wouldn't be alone.

"He will live behind the cabin and eat with us."

"Is he your slave now?" she asked, sounding angry.

"No. He is my mate, and I be in his debt."

When Mole returned the next morning, he was proudly wearing a necklace that bore one of the cat's yellow fangs and eight cougar claws. Reaching into his buckskin pouch, he produced a similar strand and handed it to me.

"We bloood brothers now," he said with pride.

Putting the necklace on, I beamed in agreement. We were blood brothers, and I would do my best to protect this strange little guy.

When I asked him if he wanted a new mat house behind the shed, and told him of Woodpecker rules, he jumped at the chance to get out of that stinky, damp forest. But he asked, with a sad look on his face, "Woodpecker still think me evil?"

"Aye. But I don't, brother."

We spent the rest of the day trading arrowheads for reed mats and other building materials. By that evening, Mole had a cozy little hut that was protected from the wind and the rain. He could cook and take his meals at the forge fire, while sleeping in the new mat house upon his cougar hide. He seemed delighted.

Before starting the cabin, I asked Marcus if he wanted to live there, with Raven and me. He could help with the construction and also keep a keen eye to the sea.

To my surprise, he wanted no part of it, and couldn't understand my obsession in wanting to be rescued. To him, living with the Tillamooks was a joy, and he even talked of taking a wife. Marcus had turned native, and was being groomed by Woodpecker to become the next great tribal shaman, a job he relished.

My plan for the cabin was simple enough. The overall size would be twenty feet long and twelve feet wide. The length included a six-foot covered porch that faced the sea; it would serve for firewood storage and be a place where I could sit as I watched for ships. As a result, the living area of the cabin was just fourteen by twelve feet. The sidewalls would be six feet high, with end walls and roof hip ten feet high. The porch end would include a single door to the cabin. At the other end, I planned a large rock fireplace for heat and cooking. The floor would be made of thick cedar planks, fastened to puncheons dug into the ground. I longed for a window, as I feared how dark and dreary the cabin would be without one, but I had no glass, so I resigned myself to doing without.

We would also have to move my forge and shed the two miles up to the clearing, so that the forge, too, would have a view of the ocean. My quest was to always keep a vigil for ships, and nothing would stay this fixation.

At the forge, I made splitting wedges, sledgehammer heads and a draw knife. Then Mole and I split two twenty-feet-long fir logs lengthwise. The four log halves were then dug into the soil, split side up, parallel to each other, as our puncheons. On top of these logs, we laid our cedar plank flooring, fastening the boards with crude iron nails that I forged. Then, on top of this finished deck, we began building the log walls.

The building process was slow, tedious and wet because of the miserable weather. But, while our tools were primitive, our resolution was joyful. Raven joined Mole and I almost every day, doing her share of the work and more. The building site was just a few hundred yards up from the rocky shoreline of the slit, so she carried baskets full of rocks for the fireplace. Mole had never seen a lodge with a wooden floor, but they both helped split the cedar planks, then used the draw knife to square and smooth the boards. At night, Raven braided long cedar strands into rope, which we then used to roll the logs into place. She was a hard worker, with the strength of a man, and she never grumbled. Soon, she and Mole were fast friends.

As the walls got higher, we needed more help. Working the forge, I made more tips and heads, and traded them for Indian labor. The day that we raised the twenty-foot ridge beam, we had a crew of seven helping. It was a joy to work with the other villagers, although they thought my log home looked funny and considered my wood floor impractical.

"Too hard for sitting on. Too many splinters for bare feet."

Once the ceiling beam and rafters were in place, the hardest work was over. Mole, Raven and I could easily finish the roof, build the fireplace and chink the walls with moss. But before saying goodbye to my crew, I had them dismantle my forge and move it and the shed to the building site.

On one particular bright, sunny February day, Mole asked if Raven and he could go down to the surf and play an Indian game he called '*shinny*.' We had all been working so hard, I thought it a good idea. After agreeing, I walked down to the wet sand with them to watch. On the beach, they asked me to keep score, and explained the rules to me. Lines were scratched in the sand, a few hundred yards apart. Then, standing between these lines, with Mole on one side of me, and Raven the other, I was to drop a cedar ball wrapped in rawhide to the ground. Using curved J-sticks made of vine-maple, they each tried to roll or kick the ball across their opponent's line. There were no rules as to how the players accomplished that. They could – and frequently did – kick, push, trip or tackle the opposing player.

As they played, I realized the game was much like British mob football.

I had watched Tories play this game many times, during the revolution. The keys were speed, brutality and agility.

For over an hour, Mole and Raven gleefully ran up and down the sand. When their score was tied at two each, I challenged them, thinking they were spent.

They smiled at each other and agreed.

I found a stick of driftwood, and Mole dropped the ball, laughing as the game started. With my fresh legs, I was soon charging their goal line, but Raven clipped me from behind, and I fell hard to the sand. As I scrambled up quickly, Mole tripped me with his stick and I went down again. By the time I got to my feet, Raven was crossing my goal line.

Cheerfully, Mole and Raven scored three more times before I dropped to my knees in the wet sand in surrender. Just as I did, a sinker wave rolled up my back, drenching me in cold sea water.

Giggling, both Mole and Raven piled onto my wet body.

"This is not fair," I shouted with a smile. "I need another player."

"Yes," Mole answered with a grin. "You need muuch help."

Getting up from the soggy sand, Raven pulled us both to our feet, saying, "We'd still win. Fire-Head too slow!"

It had been a long time since I'd laughed so hard or enjoyed myself to much. Indian football was a wonderful game that I looked forward to playing again.

With the cabin almost finished, I started to build wooden furniture. My first project was a bed frame, something I had thought about for months. Taking some thick cedar boards, I made a frame, four feet across and six feet long. To these planks, I attached four legs, each three feet high. Then, using a hand bore, I drilled holes into the side of the planks. Through these holes, I wove lengths of rope, securing each end with square knots. The woven rope gave good support with just a little give. On top of the rope, I placed my 'mattress,' an elk skin I had traded for.

I also made a proper table, with two benches and a chair for sitting in front of the fireplace.

Mole looked at my furniture with amazement, as he had never seen such odd objects before, but Raven had encountered such furniture at the white man's trading post. Both wondered out loud why such items were needed.

Once a week, I shaved the stubble from my chin. Raven loved to watch this weird activity while asking questions about how white people groomed themselves. I told her what I could, and taught her what I should. Soon, she was shaving me and trimming my hair. She relished both tasks because my 'fire-hair' symbolized one the Tolowa gods of love. She even kept a lock of my hair in a small pouch around her neck, next to her wooden cross.

When she asked to shave me, one stormy evening, I thought little of it. With Marcus and the old woman squatting across the lodge fire, I sat down for Raven. She placed a warm, wet cloth over my face, and I could hear her dragging my knife blade across a sharpening stone. Soon, she removed the fabric and started scraping my whiskers. As she worked, she rambled on about springtime and the new life it brought. She talked of bird eggs that would be found in the rocks, and the new seal pups in the sea. Then she babbled about fawns in the forest and the duck chicks on the bay. Her words went on and on, seeming pointless, much like the stories from the winter festival.

As she prepared to start on the other side of my face, I interrupted her. "What are you carrying on about, woman?"

She lifted the blade away, but did not answer. Then she started scraping me again.

From across the flames, Woodpecker said in a firm voice, "Raven tell you important stories. Squaw way to say papoose coming."

It took a moment for the old woman's words to sink in. When they did, I jerked in surprise, and felt the blade bite my chin.

Raven dropped the knife and reached for the damp cloth. Pressing it to my skin, she said, "You cut self."

I grabbed the cloth and turned to Raven, looking her in the eye. "Papoose? Child?"

"Yes," she answered with pride. "Seed growing inside me. Papoose come at salmon season."

"Is it mine?" I asked without thinking.

Raven looked instantly indignant. "Who else?"

With my mind reeling, I heard myself shout, "No, no, no… This cannot be! I want no half-breeds."

As Raven heard my angry words, her face twisted into a mask of sadness, and she started to weep. After a long moment of sobbing, she answered, "If you no want papoose, shaman take."

"Take?" I was bewildered. "Take how?"

"Use sharp willow stick, put inside me to kill seed."

This conversation was like a nightmare, filled with no good options.

With the old woman and Marcus glaring across the fire at me, and Raven crying, I could not believe the dilemma I was in. Then I heard my father's parting words: *'We live by accident or we live by purpose.'*

With the winds swirling and the rain rattling the rafters, I finally answered, "Nay, witchcraft or willow sticks will not touch my baby. This child is of God's making, and I will care for it always."

Reaching out, I embraced Raven, wiping her tears with my bloody chin-cloth. My first reaction was that fatherhood would be much like the outside weather: unwanted, unexpected and unpredictable.

But I could not – would not – forsake my own blood.

Chapter Seven: Tillamook Culture

Most of the coastal Indians living north of the great Columbia River developed societies where arts and crafts played a key role in the culture. These nations carved tall, beautiful totem poles, drew colorful images on hides and sewed elaborate ritual clothing.

The Tillamook culture was different. The men were renowned craftsmen of wood, and built canoes that were both durable and beautiful. They were also great sailors, traveling long distances by sea, and superb fisherman. The women were brilliant basket-makers who could weave creels that were strong, flexible and capable of containing liquids. The squaws also made superb textiles out of tree bark, and they crafted garments of animal hides.

Over the centuries, the Tillamooks developed a detailed oral mythology about their nation. These stories were told and retold by the elders during the long winter months. Their folklore told tales of the past and made predictions about the future. All these narratives spoke of their gods, their ancestors' spirits or the animals they fished or hunted. Spiritually, the tribe believed in life after death, and that a soul within each person could endure independently in trances, dreams, curses and sickness. This soul-spirit existed not only in the Indians but in all living things.

Such spirits demanded certain courtesies and affirmations. Therefore, when a brave killed an elk, he would speak with its spirit, and would do the same if a salmon was caught. These primitive beliefs were just as meaningful to the Tillamooks as any religion is to a devout man today.

Most of the tribes practiced polygamy and slavery, and both were considered to be signs of wealth. Before the white man, the natives had a simple monetary system of small white dentalium shells that were strung together. After contact with white traders, the natives added animal hides as another mode of currency. However, though the Tillamooks were a wealth-oriented society, they also were given to *potlatch*, a practice of ceremonial festivals at which gifts were bestowed upon guests, sometimes to the point of poverty for the giver.

Childbirth was steeped in customs and rituals which were faithfully performed to assure a healthy, beautiful infant. Among the Tillamooks, it was believed that a pregnant mother-to-be could not eat the foot or knee of the elk, or else the baby would be born with feet like an elk. Similarly, neither parent could eat sturgeon, or the infant would have small eyes and a tiny nose. Clams were also forbidden, or the child would be born with a large mouth. After the birth, the baby's cut umbilical cord was given to the grandmother, who would wear it around her neck. It was believed that failure to do so would result in the child being sickly or feeble-minded. The delivery was followed by ten days of rituals and feasting, after which the shaman would give the grandparents a cradle in the shape of a canoe. This oblong box, lined with dry moss, was fitted with a flat cedar board that was tied to the baby's head each night, to start the practice of head-flattening. The reason for deforming the infant's skull was both practical and spiritual. The Indians believed that a sloping forehead was a sign of beauty, and that the parents would be rewarded, in the next world, for following this practice. Indians with unflattened heads were considered ugly, and were usually put into slavery.

The valley Indians, on the other side of the mountains, were nomadic and traveled on horse back, which was considered a great sign of wealth. The horses increased their ability to hunt land animals, provided the tribes with greater mobility, and eventually lead the nations into a more war-oriented economy. The coastal Indians, meanwhile, had few horses and traveled in dugouts, always searching for salmon and other seafood. The rugged west-coast wilderness was like a mother to the Tillamooks, and she was bountiful; therefore, they prospered and developed a more trade-oriented economy.

Over the centuries, the Tillamook nation faced many dangers: from the sea, from the land and from within. But on that fateful August day of 1788 when the *Lady Washington* slipped across the bar into Tillamook Bay, no one could envision the dark consequences that would follow. At the time that first bower took hold, the Pacific Coast Indians had survived for almost 500 generations. But in a single generation from that first contact with the white man, the Tillamook nation would lose their lands, by treaty, to the white settlers and homesteaders. A proud nation would be conquered by the white man's encroachment, diseases and guns, and would simply fade from history.

New Challenges

As I walked the rain-swept beach north of my almost-completed cabin, my guts twisted like the swaying trees. With my legacy gone, and marooned in this godforsaken wilderness, I had compounded my plight through my lust for Raven. What the hell had I been thinking? Now my life wasn't worth cougar piss, and I was about to become father to a half-breed baby, three thousand miles from home. Was this just a quirk of fate or an abject reminder of my stupidity? In my pocket, I clutched Becky's locket and cursed the gloom for my weakness.

With the raindrops rolling down my cheeks, I glanced up to the black overcast and sought succor. "Forgive me, God. I know not the path I am on. Please, oh Lord, help me find myself again... and please stop this wretched weather."

Since the first of the year, there had been only three clear days, and a cold wind had blown from the south almost constantly. Boston had been stormy and sometimes rainy, but never in my life had I experienced such wet and wind for so long. With the black clouds clasp in the trees, my prospects seemed as dismal as the weather.

Before moving into the finished cabin, Woodpecker released me from being her buck and volunteered to be one of Raven's midwifes. We were pleased with her offer and humbly accepted. The old woman had been good to us, and we valued her friendship and experience, but we wanted no other birthing rituals from the Tillamooks. Raven and I had secretly decided that our baby would be born and raised in the Christian way, but we did not share this decision with the tribe.

When we had the fireplace completed, a sturdy door in place and reed mats on the floor, we moved into the cabin at the end of February. The plan had been that Mole would sleep behind the forge shed, in his mat house, but the weather was so deplorable that Raven and I invited him into the cabin. Building a ladder and laying some planks in the rafters, Mole soon fashioned a cozy sleeping loft. Since my new wood-framed bed was just under his loft, Raven draped blankets around our area for privacy. Here we could enjoy the fire and each other, with the comfort of knowing that Mole was safe and out of the elements. He had saved my life and helped build the cabin, so we were happy to accept him into our lodge. And now he could be another pair of eyes in my continuing vigil for a ship – and freedom.

After our move, some of the villagers came by with gifts, curious to see the lodge where a white man lived. Their presents were practical; breech cloths for the baby, a tiny hide sleeping robe, small woven blankets and, from the old woman, a cradleboard she had carried her own children in. All these gifts were appreciated and so, in the spirit of potlatch, I gave away many iron heads and a few knifes.

One of the most unusual offerings came from Marcus – a small pouch full of dry leaves and bark. Sitting at our table, he carefully explained to Raven how to use his medicine before and after the birth of our baby. After his instruction, he squatted on the mats in front of the new fireplace, and we talked.

Dressed in buckskins, with a large shell dangling from a pierced earlobe, he looked at me and said, "I Marcus no more... me take Indian name, *Lnoli*."

It took me a moment to translate. "Black Fox?"

"Aye," he answered with pride.

"Why an Indian name? Don't you want to go home?"

Without hesitation, he flashed his bone-white teeth at me and answered, "Me stay with Tillamooks, someday be chief."

"How many seasons you live, Marcus?"

He thought a moment, counting on his fingers. "When find guardian spirit this spring, I be three hands."

"You're the same age as Mole. He hasn't found his spirit yet, either. Will you take him with you on your search? I'd feel better, knowing you two were together. He is very good with the bow."

He thought for a moment, gazing at the flames, his black skin glistening. Then he turned my way again. "Yes, I take... Fire-Head, elders worry many whites come to this land. What say you?"

"I think they are right. In a few generations, there will be homes and industry all around this bay. Just look at what it has to offer... Yes, many people will come."

"What of the Tillamooks?" he asked with a bitter face.

"They will do what the Indians did in Boston – adapt to the white man's ways."

His eyes flashed with anger. "We no give land to whites. We fight. We need weapons and braves to drive away ships before they land. You see ship, you alert us."

I sighed. "War is not the answer. That would be a hopeless enterprise. But I have agreed to alert the village if I see a ship trying to cross the spit. If that happens, the tribe should trade pelts, not arrows, as the wooden ships are sailed by iron men, and the Tillamooks are no match for them."

Marcus glared at me for a moment and then stood. As he turned to leave, he stopped and said in a stern voice, "Remember your friends, Joe. They took us in and saved our lives. Don't turn your back on them now. It could be dangerous."

Black Fox's parting comment reminded me to tread lightly with the tribe. I was still only a stranger in a strange land.

With the improving spring weather, Mole and I started building dugouts, down by the estuary. My notion was to build one large canoe, twenty-two feet long, and one small canoe, sixteen feet long. The big dugout would be deep and wide and sail-powered, while the smaller dugout would be narrow and powered by paddles. If we took long sea journeys, the two dugouts could be connected together, much like the outrigger canoes I had seen at Cape Verde. A double-hulled sailboat is more stable in rough seas and can be very fast, with a good breeze, yet can be paddled when needed. The locals in Africa had called these kinds of boats *proa* and praised their seaworthiness.

For the mainmast, I would use the topsail spar I had found in the surf. It was made of oak and was eighteen feet long and six inches thick. The problem would be finding enough canvas to make a proper sail. The canvas I had found with the spar was torn and tattered, and was quite small, so I would have to find more or make a new sail out of natural materials. Reeds might work, or maybe cedar bark strands.

Using the knowledge I had acquired from Timber Wolf, Mole and I started shaping the outer hull of the large canoe. As we worked, I told Mole that Marcus had agreed to take him along on his quest for a guardian spirit.

He became very excited. "I find goood spirit… Woodpecker no think me evil."

"Aye, you will find your spirit and all will be forgiven."

Turning to me with a serious face, he asked, "You come, too, Fire-Head?"

I shook my head and answered, "No, I found my spirit many years ago."

"Which spirit yoou find? Beaaver?"

I stopped my chisel for a moment, then pointed to the sun. "I found the true spirit. Light."

Turning to the sun, then back to me, Mole looked confused. "I nooo understand."

"It's the white man's God. Maybe someday I'll explain."

He nodded and went back to work. Watching him scrape away some bark, I worried about his soul. However, knowing that it was a taboo subject with the tribe, I resolved to tell Mole only what he needed to know.

The lake behind the cabin was only a short walk up a slight hill, then down a gentle path. Raven used this trail every day to fetch water and sometimes bring back fresh fish. The pond was long and narrow but deep, teeming with freshwater trout, bass and perch. The green lagoon was surrounded with tall fir trees that protected the lake from harsh winds. Growing in and around the shoreline was tall golden grass that sometimes danced in a pleasant breeze. It was a placid lake that reminded me of lazy summer days back home, when I was just a boy.

As the weather improved and the days got longer, I began joining Raven at the water's edge after our evening meal. Here we could talk and be together in the privacy of tall blades. Raven had a lot of grit about her, full of determination and always carrying her own load. But there was a tender side, as well; this softness was like a spring day, warm and alluring. On a soft bed of grass we would talk of our yesterdays and tomorrows. Raven was full of curiosity about the eastern women, my world and my family. She was in awe of the white man's cabin, my pistol and the boats we sailed, but could not picture simple things like a woman's spring bonnet or eastern ladies' dresses. So I would sketch these items on pieces of parchment from my pouch. Studying my charcoal drawings, she seemed to grasp the notions.

"You want me to wear big dress with funny hat?" she asked with an enormous smile.

Shaking my head, I answered, "No, but that is how squaws dress, back home."

"You take me home with you?" she asked, her face full of eagerness.

Looking into her sweet brown eyes, I answered, "If I could… I would.

Therefore, our child will speak English and learn the white man's ways. He or she will not be raised as a half-breed."

"Our child is a boy. The spirits have told me so." Then she lifted her rawhide dress, exposing her plump tummy, and put my hand on it. "Feel your son. He will be powerful warrior and lead the tribe for many seasons."

With my hand on her warm honey stomach, I kissed her and whispered, "Let him be hardy and wise. That's all I ask."

"Soon we be family… just like yours back home."

I wanted to believe her. I could even envision her, decked out in a yellow spring bonnet and a white lace dress, walking the cobbles of Boston. She would be a beautiful woman in all her eastern finery. But I feared that this was just an amorous delusion, as our reality was this wilderness and the dangers that lurked from within.

I named our lake *Hope*, and prayed that someday our daydreams might come true.

With the improving spring weather came calmer seas. One sunny morning, Woodpecker stopped by and asked us to join her and Black Fox on an egg hunt. After Raven explained the hunt to me, we quickly agreed and gathered up some baskets and rope.

As we walked back towards the old woman's lodge, I noticed how tired she looked. Her walk was more of a stumble, and her back looked more hunched than I had noticed before.

"Woodpecker, how many seasons you live?" I asked as we moved down the trail.

Without breaking stride, she held up two fingers and replied, "After two around my fingers and toes, I stop counting. That was many years ago. Why you ask?"

"You look tired this morning."

At this, she stopped and turned to me, with fire in her eyes, "Squaw's work never done. Braves have easy lives." Then a grin crossed her wrinkled face. "Me still like eagle… never give up."

Was this another clue for my riddle? One thing was for sure; this old woman had more grit than most, and demanded my respect.

When we got to Woodpecker's lodge, we found Marcus waiting on shore next to the big canoe, which was filled with baskets and a net. The old woman told me to take the stern while Black Fox would take the bow.

Then she placed Mole in the middle, with the squaw's front and back to him. As we pushed off, she told us how we would paddle across the bar and turn south for *her* rock. She made it sound quite simple, but just the thought of crossing that slit again brought a knot to my throat.

The day was bright and cool, with calm winds, but once we got to the estuary, I could see breakers rolling across the slit. As we got closer to the bar, the waves got bigger and louder. With paddles working, the old woman shouted instructions: *Pull to the right – pull to the left – faster – deeper.* We took the first breaker head-on, paddling up its face and down its brow. The next one was curling with white water as our boat slipped over its crest. The third wave almost caught us sideways, drenching us with cold sea water, but we corrected our angle and got over its enormous peak. Slicing down the ridge, we faced smaller breakers, and I felt a warm conviction that I was finally learning the mood of the bar.

A few minutes later, we were floating on an open sea with gentle, rolling swells. Here we stopped and bailed out the dugout before turning south. After an hour of hard rowing, we came to a large cove that sported many rocks protruding from the green ocean floor. These boulders were hundreds of feet high and had thousands of birds flying around their craggy tops. I recognized some of the birds as a type of murre that I had seen back in Boston.

The screaming birds were like a swarm of bees after a honey hole. On the shore, the cove was ringed with tall, rocky cliffs that met the sea, dropping almost straight down to the pounding surf. On top of these cliffs were rolling hills with giant trees for as far as the eye could see. It was the most savage and beautiful vista I had ever witnessed.

Woodpecker directed us to a large pillar a few hundred yards from shore. Once we got close, she pointed out the rocky ledge where she wanted to be. As we paddled closer, she replaced herself with Black Fox at the bow and tossed a coil of rope over her shoulder. The sea swells were about six feet high, but rolling long and agreeably. As we positioned the dugout's bow close to the rocky shelf, Woodpecker timed the swells and, on the high roll, leaped from the canoe onto the ledge, some few feet away. As the dugout moved down with the wave, the old woman grabbed some rocks and pulled herself onto the monolith.

Quickly getting to her feet, she moved barefoot up a steep path. Her way was wet and slippery, covered with bird droppings. As she climbed higher up the rock, we held our position, while birds screeched all around us. Once at the top, Woodpecker secured the rope to the outcropping, then threw the other end down to us.

Raven quickly tied the baskets and the net to the rope. After these items were pulled to the top, she took up a position at the bow of the boat.

As we maneuvered the canoe back to the ledge, I yelled, "You are with child woman. Do you want one of us to take your place?"

She glared back at me from the bow. "This be squaw work. You just get me close."

Carefully, we again positioned the boat just in front of the ledge. On the next up-roll, Raven jumped across, but almost lost her grip.

My heart was in my mouth. The boat moved down with the surf, while she scrambled to regain her footing. Finally she did, and moved quickly up the monolith, shouting for us to move away from the pillar until she and Woodpecker were done.

With my hands still shaking from Raven's near mishap, we paddled a few hundred yards out from the rock. From here we could look up and watch Raven crawling the last few feet to the top of the monolith. What gutsy squaws these Indians were! They were putting their lives at risk, while here we sat, floating on calm seas.

"Can you believe what we just witnessed?" I shouted over the squawking birds. "I'm not sure I have the guts to do what those squaws just did."

Mole turned to me to say something but, before he could, I noticed more dugouts coming into the cove.

Pointing in their direction, I asked, "Are they coming for eggs, too?"

Mole watched them for a moment and then answered, "Somme, yes. But some come to kill seeals."

Mole was right. Looking again, I noticed seal heads in the water around the base of the boulders. They must have been after eggs, as well. Bobbing on the ocean, we watched as more boats moved to different pillars. Soon, we could see other squaws jumping to the rocks.

"What a bizarre way to hunt for eggs," I yelled.

Marcus turned to me with a serious look and yelled back, "It be Tillamook way."

Half hour later, Woodpecker waved us in from atop the rock. As we approached the ledge, the first basket was carefully lowered down to us. Inside the creel we found dozens of brown and blue oblong eggs resting in straw. These eggs were larger than chicken eggs and had black spots and squiggly marks on them. Soon a second basket of eggs was lowered, and then the net, containing dozens of dead birds. These birds were a sort I had seen before, diving in the bay; they had white bodies with dark brown tops and pointed black beaks. They were big, plump birds with fat chests.

Raven was the first to descend the rock, using the rope. As I positioned the boat for her jump, Mole and Marcus went forward to help her, if needed. Once she was safely aboard, the old woman climbed down the monolith with the rope around her shoulders. Arriving at the ledge, she tossed the rope to the boat and turned to watch the swells. On the next high wave, she leapt from the rocky outcropping and was carefully recovered.

With both women safely aboard, we paddled away from the pillar and headed for home.

As we moved across the water, the old woman twisted my way and proudly shouted, "Not bad for a *tired* old woman. What say you now, Fire-Head?"

"You are an amazing squaw," I yelled back humbly.

By the time we crossed the bar into Tillamook Bay, the women had cut and cleaned the dead birds. They even kept a few colorful feathers for future adornments. It had been a fruitful but fearful journey, one that reaped us food that would be enjoyed for many days to come. Later, I learned that these egg hunts happened every year and had to be timed perfectly with the mating habits of different types of birds. For a people without a calendar, this seemed to me to be a remarkable achievement.

We finished the dugouts in the first week of June.

Our boats were different from the canoes already on the bay. The big dugout had a tapered stern and bow with a rudder station on both ends. In the center of the hull was a thick cedar block, with a deep hole to receive my spar mast. Front and back to this mast were cedar planks for seats, wide enough for two paddlers. The hull was deep and thick, sturdy enough for long sea journeys. The smaller boat was narrow and shallow, with a pointed bow and stern, and it had three small planks for single paddlers. The large dugout could be connected to the small canoe as an outrigger by using cedar timbers and the bolts from the old hatch cover. The day we launched the dugouts, Timber Wolf came by, giving us pointers and praise. He had never seen an outrigger canoe before and was very curious as to its purpose and construction.

Mole and I tested the boats for the next few days. We found, when we used the small boat as the outrigger, that the big boat was hard for just two people to paddle, but using the small canoe alone with just two paddlers worked just fine. The big dugout required three or four paddlers, and it needed a sail.

It was time to look for some canvas.

Mole and Marcus went on their guardian spirit search in the middle of June. With Raven's belly now as big as a watermelon, I turned my attentions to her and the needs of the cabin. As I was sawing firewood, one afternoon, Hunting Fox stopped by to trade for a harpoon tip. As we talked, I told him of my need for canvas. At first, he said he knew of none, but then he remembered an old brave's lodge at Netarts that had a cloth roof made from materials he had found in the surf. Hunting Fox wasn't sure what kind of cloth, but the old man had used it to stop some leaks.

The next morning, Raven and I took the small dugout and paddled to the south end of the bay. There we walked the few miles to the Netarts village. This was a difficult journey for Raven, but she insisted on coming along.

We found the old brave's lodge and saw, on his roof, a large section of a dirty old sail. I tried to trade for it, but the old man didn't want any of my iron wares. Changing my approach, I offered him a new roof, and he eagerly agreed.

Two days later, we paddled the stained canvas back home and started working with it. When we pieced the remnants of the two sails together, we used elk sinew in the seams and double-stitched the canvas, to give it strength. And I made iron grommets, mast rings and rudder hardware at the forge. In the end, we had a triangle sail, fourteen high and fourteen feet wide. It wasn't pretty, with all the seams and shades, but I reckoned it was practical.

That evening, with a light breeze and clear skies, we rigged the sail to the mast and took the longboat for a cruise on the bay. With the Indians gawking from both bay and shore, we gave her the wind and sailed the length of the inlet and back again. She handled like a Boston catboat: quick on the move and smooth on the ride. As we sliced through the water with the wind at our backs, I was pleased and proud at what we had built, and I knew this boat could be our passage home.

With the sun setting and the tiller in my hand, Raven looked my way from her seat next to me, "Never see white-bird before, and now I ride one. What a wonderful season this is."

Reaching over, I kissed her on the cheek. "I will name this boat *Thunderbird,* and she will fly us home."

Cries of Life

Mole and Marcus returned from their spirit search after only five days. Of course, Black Fox proclaimed that he had seen a gigantic snake that had given him the spirit of a powerful shaman. Mole's vision was a simple timber wolf, which meant that he would become a mighty hunter. But something strange and remarkable had also happened on their quest. Black Fox told the story of seeing his snake on the first day, and said that, while using the serpent powers, he put Mole into a trance and healed him from his stutter. At first I could not believe this tale, but then I heard Mole speak without any repetitions. How Marcus had accomplished this marvel, I did not know. Was it the power of the snake's spirit or the power of Mole's mind? Or maybe Marcus was indeed a great magical healer; all I knew was that Mole no longer stuttered.

Woodpecker held a gathering to celebrate the wonderment of their quest, and Mole, for the very first time, was allowed into her lodge when she was there. Because of his new guardian spirit and the healing from Black Fox, the tribe elevated him from poor to middle class. This rise in social status was quite rare, among the Tillamooks, so both men talked with pride of their exploits, swaggering around the lodge like roosters on the prowl.

During the festivities, many of the elders approached me and asked again about when another ship might come. I assured them that I did not know, and that I would remain on vigil for the tribe. Then they asked if I was about to sail away in my new white bird. I told them no, that I was only planning a few short trading trips with some of the other coastal tribes. This seemed to appease them, although there was still a great deal of concern on their faces. They were genuinely worried about the future of their nation.

The day after my birthday, what I believed was the fourth of July, I built a small raft, down by the bay. On top of this float, I stacked firewood and kindling. Then I took an extra piece of tattered canvas and cut a three-by-five-foot length. Using charcoal, I drew the America flag with thirteen stars and stripes on both sides. While I sat on the front porch, working on the jack, Raven came out of the cabin, holding her belly.

"What you make?" she asked with an inquisitive look.

"My tribe's flag," I answered without looking up.

"What is flag?" she asked, squatting next to me.

Looking at her curious face, I smiled. "It's a symbol that tells friends and foes what tribe you are from. You will see it tonight, when we celebrate my nation's birth."

Shaking her head, she stood. "Food ready soon."

When I had finished fashioning my crude-looking ensign, I attached it to a tall pole. Then, taking the flag to the small dugout, I fastened the pole to the boat. Tonight, the stars and stripes would fly again over Tillamook Bay.

At dusk that evening, Raven, Mole and I went to the water's edge and lit the fire on the raft. Then, towing the float with a rope, we paddled the small canoe toward the village. It was a perfect evening on the bay, with the sun setting in a clear sky, and the breeze warm and gentle. As we positioned the burning raft a few hundred feet from the village shore, I untied the tow rope, and we moved a few feet from the flames. Then with my flag flying, I fired my pistol into the air.

The loud sound of the shot echoed across the water and bounded back again. Soon, the beach was filled with gawking, pointing Indians. Then, taking my flute in hand, I began my serenade with *Yankee Doodle.* With my music floating on the air, the tribe caught the idea of my gaiety, and begin shouting and whooping their approval. My next song was *Lady Hope's Reel,* and I finished with *Washington's March.*

With the burning raft about to sink into the bay, I reloaded my pistol and finished the celebration with one last shot into the air. The blast from the barrel lit the sky with sparks, and when I looked up, I spotted a shooting star falling across the clear sky. The Indians on shore let out a cheer as if I had just shot it down. It was a wonderful finale for a spectacular evening, one that the tribe would talk about for many seasons to come. And while they never grasped the notion of my celebration, I did, and was once again proud to be an American.

"Joe, wake up!" Raven said, poking me, and I could hear fear in her voice.

I was lost in a dream, standing on a ship's deck, with Becky at my side. The day was bright and the seas calm…

"Joe, wake up! Baby come!" she shouted while shaking my shoulders.

When I heard the word 'baby,' my eyes popped open like a dandelion in the sun, and my mind reeled back to reality. Leaping from the bed, I almost collided with Raven, who was standing over me, illumined by the firelight.

"Baby…too soon. This just August," I stammered, looking into her pinched face.

She pressed both of her hands to her robe, where it covered her plump tummy. With a groan, she closed her eyes and shook her head.

Grabbing her arms, I lead her over to the chair in front of the fireplace and helped her sit down.

"Mole, wake up," I shouted, once Raven was safely settled. "Wake up!" I shouted again, this time throwing a chunk of firewood up at his sleeping boards.

I heard him move. Then, in a sleepy voice, he asked, "What go on?"

"You run and fetch Woodpecker. Tell her it's time for the baby, then hurry back," I yelled up to him.

"Yes, me get dressed."

Turning back to Raven, I asked softly, "Are you sure?"

In the dim light, she grabbed onto my hands. "Yes. My water break and baby move."

"You should be in bed. I'll help you."

She shook her head without letting go of my hands. "No. Get me a wet cloth and put me on floor."

As I moved to the water bucket, Mole clambered down the ladder and ran out the front door. As he did so, I noticed that it was still dark outside. I returned to Raven and handed her the cool cloth, then placed an elk pelt on the floor next to the bed. She nodded, and I helped her onto the hide, with her back resting against the bed frame.

"Wouldn't bed be more comfortable?"

"Bed too soft for birth." She paused as another pain rolled through her body. "Soon, your son comes. You get many cloths wet."

Returning to the water bucket, I did just that.

As I worked, Raven asked in a weak voice, "What name you want for son?"

Twisting her way while wringing out the fabric, I admitted, "I haven't thought about that. What say you?"

In the dim firelight, I watched her carefully as she fought off another sharp pain. Returning to her with two candles and more wet cloths, I knelt by her side.

"Me always want to have boy named *Tejon*. In Spanish, it means Badger."

"Why Badger?"

With both hands on her tummy, she forced a smile "Badger quick. Live with no fear. And it is my brother's name."

There was determination on her face, and I knew this name was important to her.

"And what is Badger in Tillamook tongue?"

She thought a moment, then answered, "*Dutcu*"

Taking one of her hands, I smiled. "Sounds like Dutch to me. That is good European name. Our son, if it's a boy, will be named Badger." Then I wiped her face with a damp cloth and kissed her cheek, wondering, *where the hell are they?*

Moments later, Mole, Woodpecker and Sandpiper burst through the door. Instantly, the midwives took over the cabin and ordered Mole and I outside. As I was putting on my togs, Raven cried out once again, and I could see the anguish on her face.

With panic in my voice, I said to the old woman, "Take good care of her. Soon I take her home."

Woodpecker pointed towards the open door. "Indian woman have babies for many seasons. You leave now."

She was right, and so, like a frighten doe, I turned and fled into the night. This was squaw work and I wanted no more of it.

Mole and I silently walked the beach in front of the cabin and soon noticed the coming sun in the east. My innards were twisted because of Raven's agony, and my head was spinning with thoughts of doom. There was so much that could go wrong. There was so much that *had* gone wrong.

With the first rays of sunshine on my face, I stopped and dropped to my knees in the wet sand, looking up towards the sun. Then I said, out loud, "Oh Lord, protect Raven and keep her and the baby safe."

Mole dropped to his knees next to me and asked, "Can you see your spirit?"

"No," I answered, shaking my head, "but I can feel him."

"Your God name is Lord?"

Getting to my feet, I answered softly, "He is called many names by many people. He created the sun and the earth and sea we fish. He watches over all of us, all the time."

"Why then you remind him of Raven and baby if he so powerful?"

I thought a moment, for it was a good question. Looking down at

Mole, still on his knees, I finally answered, "For the same reason that you speak to your ancestor's spirits – out of respect."

Reaching down, I gave Mole a hand up.

As he got to his feet, I noticed a satisfied look on his face. The notion of my God had made sense to him, and he had no more questions.

As the beach warmed in the hot summer sun, Mole and I retreated to the shade of the front porch. Here we could be close and, if needed, we could help. With the front door shut, we couldn't hear any sounds from inside, so we quietly sat on the cedar boards, each lost in our own thoughts.

About mid-morning, the door finally opened, and the old woman came out and asked me to fetch more water. Then she turned to Mole and told him to run back to her lodge and bring back Marcus with his special mushroom potions. Woodpecker looked weary, with a face full of concern.

"Is everything alright?" I asked.

Turning to me, she looked at me straight in the eye, "Baby not turned right. Black Fox make Raven feel no pain and we turn baby right. Then baby come. You get water."

Half an hour later, Marcus came and gave Raven some dried mushrooms for her pain. After taking the potion, she made a few loud whimpers but then nothing more. Soon, I could hear Marcus chanting through the partly opened door. This went on for hours, and it rattled my nerves to my core. The droning, the waiting, the uncertainty was paralyzing, and all of it was compounded by the hottest day of the year.

With sweat pouring down my face, I finally heard silence fall, and then some mumbling. Moments later came the loud crying of an infant. It was a wonderful song!

Sitting next to me on the planks, Mole twisted my way with a big grin. "You have new baby."

Grabbing his right hand, I shook it – a custom he did not understand. With his hand pumped in mine, I smile and answered, "Aye."

Just then, the old woman came through the doorway with a bloody umbilical cord wrapped around her neck. She looked exhausted, but on her wrinkled face was a smile.

Jumping to my feet, I turned to her. "How is Raven? How is the baby? Can I see them?"

"You have a baby boy who is strong and noisy, much like a Badger," she said, her eyes dancing. "But Raven lose much strength and she not with milk yet. Black Fox go to village for wet-nurse. After baby feed, you can come in."

As Marcus came out through the doorway, he stopped and said, to no one in particular, "A hot day is a good sign, when the baby's father is Fire-Head." Then, turning to me, he continued, "Congratulations... *Dutcu* is fine Tillamook name. I get wet-nurse fast."

With my head full of thoughts of the baby, and my heart full of concerns for Raven, I had to get off the porch and do something while I waited. So I ran to the beach, stripped off my clothes and jumped into the ocean to cool off. It was refreshing, it was cold, and it made me think of the wonders of nature and the power of God.

When I got out, I lay in the warm sand to dry myself, and thanked the Lord for the blessing of life.

In the late afternoon, I was summoned back to the cabin. Inside, in the dim doorway light, I found Raven on the bed, holding our baby, while Woodpecker and the wet nurse stood and watched from the shadows. Ravens eyes were half-closed, and she looked spent.

Kneeling next to her, I reached out and gently grabbed one of her hands.

At my touch, her eyes opened and she turned my way. "You see your son," she whispered in a weak voice.

"Aye, he be a fine lad… but how are you?"

From the shadows, the old woman spoke. "She needs much rest, have very hard time. You and Mole sleep outside for the next few nights. We care for them."

Raven squeezed my hand with a small smile. "I be fine, just need sleep. Woodpecker… right," and her eyes closed again.

Raven's milk flowed a few days later, and she started to regain her strength. While we waited, Mole and I busied ourselves with cutting firewood, fishing down on the lake and sleeping in his mat house. Even though salmon season was coming, the days were so hot that I didn't work my forge. Those tasks would have to wait.

In short visits over the next few days, I got to know my son. He was tiny and red and as helpless as hope. There is innocence to a new child that can melt your heart and lift your spirits. And while I wanted cooler weather, my soft bed and my cabin back, I wanted Raven's recovery and the baby's safety more. Therefore, Mole and I followed Woodpeckers instructions and slept outside for almost a week.

When the old woman finally returned to her lodge, Raven was strong enough to care for herself and the baby, but still shaky on her feet. So I took over all the duties of a cabin squaw, which included fetching water and cooking all the meals. I didn't mind, as it was such a joy to watch Raven and that squirmy little guy. He had a full head of auburn hair, a honey complexion much like his mother's, and a set of lungs that could raise the roof. Once he found his mother's tit, that's where he wanted to be, and we didn't mind, as it kept him quiet.

One evening, after our meal, while Raven was feeding the baby on the bed, I pulled the stool alongside.

"I have a surprise for you."

"And what would that be?" she asked, with the baby suckling and her face aglow.

"Timber Wolf showed me how to make color stains for my boat bows. We made blue and red ink, and they are good enough colors for a tattoo. Would you like one?"

An enormous smile raced across her face. "You make bird land on my shoulder?"

"Aye. But it will take some time, and it might hurt a little."

Instantly, she pulled her robe aside to expose her left shoulder. "How sweet you are… with baby and now tattoo, I just like eastern squaw."

Using a drawing that I had made of a raven, some sewing needles and my ink, I went to work on her shoulder. She did not flinch when I pressed the inked points below her skin, she just beamed.

While I worked, Raven and I talked of the agony of the birth, the beauty of the baby and our plans for the future. Then she asked a strange question, with a suddenly doleful eye, "Do you have squaw back home?"

Glancing at her concerned face, I answered the best I could, "No… not in the Indian way. There is a girl that said she would wait for me, but I fear she will not."

"What is her name?" Raven asked, looking at my face for the truth.

I thought a long moment, as this was a conversation I did not want. "It doesn't matter. She is the past. Our baby is the future. I will teach our son to be a great hunter and builder of sturdy boats. And I will teach him the white man's ways, and how to read and write."

"Me think squaw wait." Raven expression turned inquisitive. "I no understand *read and write*."

I had never talked of this before. "Words are written in books and these words are read."

"I know not of books."

"When priest christened you, did he hold a black book in his hands?"

"Aye, he say it held his spirit."

"Black book had words inside. I will write a word below your tattoo. It will say 'Raven' for those who can read."

She thought a moment, then asked shyly, "You teach me, too?"

New Horizons

Ten days after the birth, Woodpecker held a small gathering to celebrate the baby's infant spirit. Neither Raven nor I wanted to attend but, after all that Woodpecker had done for us, we couldn't say no.

On the day of the party, Mole and I paddled Raven and the baby, bound in tiny blanket, in the small dugout to the village.

The people attending the festivities were mostly of the old woman's clan, along with a sprinkling of elders who had a few chosen words to say about birth and life. They were all friendly enough, and some of the people gave us more gifts for the baby. One of these offerings was from Woodpecker, a cradle in the shape of a small canoe that was lined with moss. And inside was a small plank for head flatting. The old woman told us that she had rocked her own children in that very crib. Then she asked us if we knew how to use the plank each night.

"Make sure the board is tied tight to the baby's head. He will cry a little, but soon he will get use to it," she said while holding the plank to her flat wrinkled forehead. "In a few months, your baby will have beautiful sloping head and you will be rewarded by the spirits."

Raven and I looked at each other. It sounded dreadful, but we thanked the old woman and all the other Indians for their advice and gifts.

Before leaving the celebration that day, I told Timber Wolf and his brother Coyote about my plans to sail north to trade with the Clatsop nation. They volunteered to come along and provide the introductions, as they had traveled north many times before. Also, they were interested in learning how to build and sail a white-bird canoe of their own. They were excited about wind power and saw it as the future.

Pleased with their offer, I eagerly accepted.

With August came the silent reminder that I had been marooned with the tribe for one year. It was an anniversary that I spent in solitude walking the beach. Reflecting on my fate, I thought of my fears, my doubts, and my genuine love for the Indian woman who had brought forth my child. While Becky's face was still etched vividly in my mind, and I truly missed my family, the importance of those people seemed to have vanished like the fog in the night. There was something about fatherhood that changed my purpose forever.

Raven slowly recovered during the austere summer days. By the end of the month, I was confident that she could care for herself and the baby. She wanted to go with us on the trading trip, but I thought this a bad notion, given that the baby was so tiny. She finally agreed, so I filled my poke with iron tips and departed for the north, right after the first of September.

Carrying the sail wrapped around the mast, Mole and I met Timber Wolf and his brother, down by the shore of the estuary. As we worked, loading the rigging into the big dugout and connecting the small canoe, I explained to Timber Wolf that this was the first time that I had tried to cross the bar with the outrigger, and that I didn't know if I should use the sail or the paddles. Because we had four people, he suggested paddling so we could be more maneuverable. After checking the wind direction and studying the bar conditions, I agreed.

The day was warm and bright and as we approached the first towering gray breaker, I held my breath and paddled with all my strength. Up we went and down we dashed, cutting through the boiling sea at a great speed. I was surprised by how stable the dugouts were when joined together.

The second wave was bigger and curling. We climbed the ocean wall straight on and sliced through to the other side without a drop of water falling into the boat. After three smaller waves, we had crossed the surf line and were bobbing on a calm sea.

It was the easiest passage of the bar I had ever made. Even Timber Wolf and Coyote commented about the agreeable crossing. The *Thunderbird* had proven herself in surf; now it was time to see what she could do under sail.

It only took Mole and me a few moments to rig the mast and put the tiller in place. Then, while I kept my hands on the rudder, Mole pulled up the sail. It filled with a southerly breeze, and he tied the line off. Instantly, the dugouts answered the sail's power and begin moving quickly and silently north.

The two brothers, with paddles in hand, sat next to each other with their mouths open and eyes wide. Gliding through the swells at five or six knots, they could not believe how fast we were moving or how effortless it made the ride.

Turning to me with a face full of excitement, Coyote asked, "How long white man use white birds for their canoes?"

I thought a moment, then replied, "This power was given to us by our spirits, many seasons ago."

As we passed the slit for the Nehalem Bay, I began questioning Timber Wolf about different landmarks, like the tall craggy mountain just north of the bay. He said it was a holy place called *Neahkannee* (place of supreme deity), and that many ancestor spirits lived there. He also said the mountain had great elk herds, and that one day he would take me there so we could hunt.

Moving farther up the coast, with the warm sun on my face and my eyes ablaze with glory, I continued my queries. Timber Wolf had stories and names for all the major landmarks. There were coves and cliffs, jagged outcroppings and more haystack rocks. He knew this coast like the lines in his palms, and was a great help navigating the route. But when I asked him how much farther we had to travel, he answered in the normal Tillamook way: "Sun go little more."

Some hours later, we passed a mountainous point that reached almost a mile straight out into the sea. Timber Wolf told me that north of this head was the land of the Clatsop Indians. He said their nation sprawled all the way up the coast to a mighty river he called *Wimahl*, which meant Big River. When I asked if we could sail into this river, he shook his head and answered, "No, it too violent."

With a corrected heading of north-by-northwest, we sailed past the peak and all the shore rocks that protruded from the sea. The last rock west of the head was as big as an island, and it towered from the ocean hundreds of feet into the sky. This blue-granite pillar had a rough rocky top, stained with dirty white bird droppings, and it reeked of ammonia as we sailed passed it. It was an ominous looking island, fit only for the sea birds that inhabited its summit.

Once we had passed this monolith, I turned east and we sailed into a small cove, then turning north again, I followed the surf line. By now, the craggy coastline was giving way to rolling sand dunes covered with golden sea grass. Behind this plain were tall green mountains capped by puffy white clouds. A few miles farther up the beach, Timber Wolf pointed to a scant opening in the dunes. Just north of this gap, we brought the sail down and paddled towards the surf, making for a sandy, shallow slit that Timber Wolf said would take us into a bay.

Sure enough, once over a few waves, we could see a channel of quiet green water that flowed from the south-east. Paddling farther down the slit, we turned east into an inlet and sighted a river from the south and another coming from the east. On the high ground, just north of this confluence, we saw the smoke of an Indian encampment. Turning the outrigger in that direction, we paddled for the northern shore of what Timber Wolf called the *Necanicum Bay.*

As we approached, I noticed over a dozen sojourn shanties with many Indians rushing to the water's edge to witness our strange-looking boat. Once in shallow water, Mole leapt out of the boat and helped drag the bows to the land. By the time we waded ashore, over twenty braves had assembled, gawking and talking. Soon, pushing through this crowd came an older man with a stoic face and a basket hat. His jaw was square, his hairline mostly gray, and he had a wrinkled, dirty face that looked much like weathered leather. He walked with authority and stopped in front of me.

I tucked my head to him. Then Timber Wolf introduced me as Fire-Head, the great boat builder of the Tillamooks, and he flashed an open palm across his chest. I did the same, out of respect and as a symbol of our friendship. The old man gave me a good look, eyed our boat, and finally twisted his palm.

His name was Wasp, and he was the fishing chief of his tribe. We talked a few moments, but the Clatsop tongue was so different from ours that we had to use hand signs for many of the words. The Indians I faced looked much like the Tillamooks, in both body features and dress. They were friendly enough and kept staring at my red hair. This conversation went on for a few minutes. Then I returned to the boat and removed a harpoon I had crafted with an iron tip. On the shaft of this weapon, I had carved symbols of whales and colored them with my lacquers. This spear I gave to the chief as a gift. He beamed with pleasure at the present, and passed it around so the others could hold it. Then, of all things, he asked me if I was a Spaniard. I told him no, that I was an American, but this he did not understand. Opening my pouch, I showed him my iron tips and explained that I wanted to trade them for other iron goods or otter pelts. With the braves watching, he examined my wares and looked at Mole's arrows with the iron points. Then, using his bow, he shot a few arrows into a nearby tree.

Once he heard the twang of the arrows' powerful blow, a smile crossed his sober face, and he agreed that we could barter. He went on to tell us that his village was far up a creek, and that a canoe would be sent to bring back trade goods. Since this boat could not return until the next day, he invited us into his fishing wickiup.

That afternoon, Wasp cooked a fish for us that I had not eaten before. He called it Indian Salmon, but while the fish was big, it looked and tasted much like trout. He told us that the river just across the bay was full of such fish, and that they came each spring and fall. For his tribe, this fat silver fish was a staple that was consumed year-round. He also served a root green I had never tasted before; its flavor was much like a sweet potato with stringy fibers. To round out the meal, we ate huckleberries and drank a warm, greasy clam broth.

After this meal, with the tide rising, Mole and I took the chief and a few Clatsops for a ride in our dugouts. As we paddled the bay, Wasp pointed to an emerald creek, framed with lush vegetation that flowed from the north. He told me that up this stream was his village. I asked what was beyond.

"Broken trail to *Netul* River that drains to big bay and *Wimahl*... trade with Spaniards."

His words astonished me. With excitement, I asked, "White man's trading post on big river?"

"No...come many seasons ago in white bird, trade for otter hides."

With the sun low in the sky and a fresh breeze from the south, we turned from the creek and paddled down the river from the south. It was a wide, rocky estuary nestled between white rolling sand dunes with tall green foliage. As we came to where the tidal waters ended, I turned the boat; on my signal, Mole raised the sail. With the wind at our backs and the last rays of the warm sunshine on our faces, we raced across the water for the bay. Our new friends being speechless leaned over to drag their hands in the fast flowing river water. It was an amazing ride, as we were flying so fast that even the seagulls couldn't catch us.

That evening, in the red glow of the setting sun, we squatted around a bonfire and smoked Indian tobacco. I had learned many things this day about the waters north of my cabin, the character of the Clatsops and the power of my boat. My mind needed to hold these notions close for future use and my dreams of a passage home.

The next morning, we traded with the Indians, and by the afternoon all my tips were gone. In the small outrigger, I stowed my bartered goods: one rusty iron chain almost ten feet in length, a dented armor chest plate, and two large hammer heads. These items I could forge into many iron tips and other goods. I also traded for three beaver pelts and one otter pelt. These I hoped to sell in the future, when I returned to civilization.

With the sun moving lower in the sky, I walked the sand to the slit and checked the sea and tides. The winds had freshened from the south, with a wind chop across the ocean as far as I could see, and the rising tide had made the bar boil. With the sea against us, as well as the tides, I asked Wasp if we could spend another night. He cheerfully agreed, and that afternoon we drifted the river to the south, catching many Indian Salmon, which we cleaned for the journey home.

Early the next morning, with wind and sea conditions improved, we said farewell to the Clatsops and paddled out of their bay and over some curling surf. Once into the ocean, I turned the boat south-west, almost directly into the onshore west winds, and we continued rowing into deep water for the next three hours. Then, just as the land was slipping from view, I changed course to the south-east and we raised the sail. With moderate seas and rolling swells, we bounced across the water for over two hours. As we approached land again, with Neahkannee Mountain just off our bow, I turn south and we lowered the sail. An hour later, we crossed the Tillamook bar and slipped into the estuary, just down from my cabin. It had been a smooth sail up and back, and the weather had been with us all the way. The boat had preformed agreeably and, while she needed a bigger sail, I knew I would feel safe, taking her on sea journeys.

As we turned for shore, I noticed Raven at the water's edge holding Dutch in her arms.

As the bow touched land and Mole jumped out, I shouted to her, "How's my little guy?"

Beaming, she answered, "He missed his father and has been looking for you all day."

While Timber Wolf and Coyote removed their gear from the boat, I jumped out and kissed the boys amber colored locks.

Then, proudly twisting to Raven, I said, "He's a handsome-looking lad and destined to be a fine jack-tar."

Resting against the bow of the boat, Mole said, "Black Fox come."

Turning, I looked down the path to the village and found Marcus running at full speed, directly for us.

Moments later, out of breath and with sweat rolling off his brow, he stopped in front of us. His face was full of sadness and his eyes were puffy and red from crying.

"What's wrong?" I asked.

Taking a deep breath, he said softly, "Woodpecker is dead."

Chapter Eight: Fading Footprints

Captain Robert Gray made a second historic trip to the Pacific Northwest in 1792. On that voyage, he discovered and named the mighty Columbia River. Many believe that it was this event that set in motion the demise of the coastal Indian nations. Soon, other 'Boston' men came to the Oregon Country, to search for furs and to trade goods with the natives. Iron blades replaced stone adzes, copper kettles took the place of stone bowls, and glass beads became favored over sea shells. Even the salmon gods were pushed back into the sea by the power of the crucifix.

Prior to this time, the Tillamooks had been protected from the outside world, and from most other Indian tribes, by the harsh environment that surrounded their villages. With the coming of pale faces, however, the Salish language began to change to a jargon of English, French, and the Chinook tongues. These traffickers also influenced the native culture, and soon 'trade goods' were coveted in all of the Indian lodges. Gradually, the coastal Indians lost their faith, their rituals and many of their traditional ways. Worse yet, an invisible import lurked in the hulls of these trading ships, for the white man also brought with him European epidemics. Before long, smallpox and venereal disease would loom over the inhabitants of Tillamook Bay like a black shroud.

Over the centuries, death had come easily and often to the Tillamook nation, and the tribe had developed religious practices and superstitions to deal with the passing of their loved ones. Tillamook burial methods varied widely from those of most other tribes, as their rituals focused on both the living and the dead. Burials took place four to six days after death. The interim time was allotted to efforts by the shamans and relatives to bring the newly deceased person back from the spirit world. Chanting, blood-letting, self-inflicted wounds and fasting all played a part in these ceremonies. When the body was finally removed from the lodge, it exited through an opening other than the front door, usually through the roof. This was done to confuse and trick the ghost of the deceased from visiting any people still living in the lodge.

On the sixth day, fasting ended with the eating of fresh fish or game. Then the lodge and all the belongings of the deceased were spiritually purified by the shaman. Sometimes, the death lodge was set ablaze, especially if the person had died of a mysterious disease which the Tillamooks feared was contagious or had been caused by an evil spirit. This practice of fire purification only increased after the arrival of the white traders and settlers.

After removing the deceased from the lodge and performing the pre-burial rituals, villagers took the body to a river and cleansed it thoroughly with fresh water, then wrapped it in mats and robes. The personal canoe of the deceased became their crypt, to carry them to the after-life. The inside of the dugout was painted red, and a hole was drilled in the bottom to release any rainwater that might accumulate. Then the body was placed in an oblong cedar box, and this casket was placed in the canoe, along with the deceased's paddles and personal effects. Planks were secured over the top of the burial canoe to keep out predators. The canoe was then placed in its final resting spot – in a tree, on a rocky ledge or on the ground. This placement always faced west and had cedar posts driven into the earth, where the Indians could hang the fishing and eating implements of the deceased, in the belief that these items would be needed for the long journey to the spirit world.

This practice of canoe burials continued until the arrival of the settlers. With the large influx of the whites came the clearing of land, and the pioneers burned most of the burial canoes, partly because of the odor but mostly because they were in the way. Some settlers, needing boats for travel, would dump out the bodies, plug the hole in the bottom, and paddle off. Naturally, this practice was an affront to the Tillamooks, who soon resorted to burying their dead in unmarked graves.

In 1856, the Tillamooks and twenty other tribes were placed on the Siletz Indian Reservation. At that time, fewer than 200 Tillamook Indians remained. The last full-blooded Tillamook Indian, Ellen Center, died in 1959, at the age of ninety-seven. She had been born in 1862, when the Indians still had one active village on the bay. With her demise came the end of the great Tillamook nation.

Spirit Journey

In some strange way, Woodpecker had been like a grandmother to me. She had shown me her anger, over my spruce beer, but I had also felt her kindness after she rescued us from Hawk. She taught me the Indian ways and, with great patience, even their language. Therefore, her death brought a knot to my stomach and tears to my eyes. I cursed myself that, in life, I had not told her how strongly I felt about her. She was by far the most resourceful, trusted and respected elder and shaman in the entire nation. Her death cast a long dark shadow across the waters of the bay.

Marcus told me that she had died painlessly in the middle of the night. When he found her the next morning, he tried to revive her, but her spirit told him that she wanted to join her husband and children and wander the land of the spirits forever. He said that, at one point, he watched her soul leave her body and float mysteriously about the room. Then her spirit spoke to him and said he would soon become the chief and shaman of the tribe but, before that could happen, he would have to show the elders and other chiefs his powers. He was to seek their wisdom with fire and light, and then gain their confidence with a vision of Woodpecker and her family together again in the spirit world. After that pronouncement, her phantom soul vanished through the walls of the lodge.

As Marcus related these events, the expression on his face frightened me; the lad believed this spirit nonsense, and nothing I could say or do would sway those notions. Black Fox was determined to become the boy chief.

Our clan attended the first few days of the mourning rituals. Inside the death lodge, we found Woodpecker laid out on some mats next to the fire pit. Squatting by her dead body was Marcus. His face was distorted with grief, and his eyes wept with tears as big as dew drops. He sat there for hours, fasting, chanting and moaning while stroking the old woman's gray hair. He seemed lost in her spirit world.

The lodge was dark and warm, while the gathering was large and somber. With others from the village filing in with long faces, some of her clan knelt beside the body, chanting and poking her flesh with needles and sharp rocks. When she failed to move or cry out, these relatives would shout out to her spirit and mumble the old woman's name. I found this brutality to her body morally despicable, and I had to bite my tongue so as not to cry out in protest. It was a cruel wont that served to remind me how primitive these Indians were. After the second day of the rituals we stopped attending, as the body was becoming deformed, and the smell of death filled the cramped, stuffy lodge. We had seen enough, we had heard enough, and we now wished to remember Woodpecker as she had been: alive and full of life.

On the morning of the fourth day, a few braves gathered to remove her body through the roof. Then some of the squaws took her to the river, to clean and prepare her for the long journey to the afterlife. As they worked, Timber Wolf and Coyote built a cedar box and painted the inside of Woodpecker's small canoe red. When the squaws returned to the village with Woodpecker's body, it was rolled inside a robe and some mats. Only her head could be seen, and her white hair had also been painted red. It was a gruesome sight.

With lots of chanting and wailing from the villagers, the old woman's body was placed inside her wooden coffin. Next, Timber Wolf placed her paddles on top of her robes. Then the box was lifted into the canoe, and her clan filed by, dropping food and trinkets inside the casket. Black Fox was the last in line. While throwing dried flower petals onto the canoe, he chanted, then turned to the crowd and announced, in a loud, firm voice, "Woodpecker was a great healer and seer, and the true leader of this nation. Last night, her spirit came to me and told me what to do. We will take her to the gathering place, overlooking her rock. There she will rest beside her husband for all time. I will speak her name no more."

When he finished, her boat was gently pushed into the water, and a tow line was passed to the largest war canoe on the bay. Marcus sat at the bow of that dugout as thirty warriors slowly started rowing across the inlet. We followed in my small canoe, along with forty other boats, in a procession that headed southwest across the bay. It was an easy row for Mole and me, with Raven in the middle, carrying our baby in the cradleboard that Woodpecker had given us. The day was clear and bright, with beautiful puffball clouds on the horizon. The breeze out of the north was warm, and the glinting green waters were placid. Soon, we were joined by other dugouts from the south and north villages. Then, just as the boats reached the middle of the bay, a flock of geese flew overhead, heading south in a V-shaped formation. As they flew over, with their loud honks screaming, I marveled at their timing and beauty.

When we reached the far shoreline, more people from Netarts village were waiting. After helping Raven and the baby ashore, Mole pulled our dugout high onto a rocky, sandy beach. As he was doing this, I turned and saw a row of resting boats almost a half mile long. Rising from this line was a horde of what I guessed must be a thousand Indians. *What a wonderful tribute to the old woman*, I thought, my heart aglow.

Six braves, dressed in their finest buckskins, lifted Woodpecker's canoe out of the water and onto their shoulders, then started walking up a rough trail toward a scant mountain. Marcus walked grimly behind the dugout, and we followed behind him.

The trail moved up a few hills and crossed many creeks and rills. At one point, I turned to view a somber line of black heads behind us, almost a mile long. As we moved, the Indians began to chant out a cadence to the march. Soon, the trail meandered into a forest of towering fir trees, and up some steep rocky raises. Finally, we reached the top of the peak, where I could taste the sea air and hear the crashing of waves. Here the trail turned south and, a few hundred yards farther along, down a slight slope. Before long, we came to a large clearing that was the Tillamooks' gathering place.

The unburdened area faced west, looking over cliffs and down onto the cove where we had hunted eggs. There, in the middle of that vista, was the old woman's rock, glistening in the sunlight. For me, the sight of her pillar brought back a rush of memories of better times.

Up from this view, in the center of the clearing, was a tree like none I had seen before. The tree trunk, at its base, was wide and fat, but the young spruce limbs didn't simply grow up, they grew straight out and then bent up. The shape of these limbs reminded me of spider legs; and, resting inside these horizontal legs, were other burial canoes. As the crowd silently gathered around this tree, I counted the remains of five other dugouts. The Tillamooks called this place *Octopus Point,* and said that their gods had provided it solely for the powerful chiefs and shamans. This was holy ground, filled with the spirits of the Tillamook nation.

Before Woodpecker's dugout was lifted into the tree, two holes were drilled in the bottom, to drain the rainwater. Then, with more chanting, the dugout was lashed to a lower limb next to her husband's canoe. After it was secured, Timber Wolf and Coyote climbed up the tree and fastened cedar planks to the top of her canoe to keep out any predators. Once they had finished and returned to the crowd, Bright Cloud, the shaman from Nehalem, said a few words. He talked of the great supremacy of this land,

and how the spirits that resided here were as powerful in death as they had been in life. He named all the chiefs buried in the tree and told of all their coups in life. As he spoke to the enthralled crowd, I noticed how peaceful and beautiful this gathering place was, the way the sun filled the clearing and the grace of the tall fir trees that grew like sentinels around the spruce burial tree. Other than Bright Cloud's words, I heard only the sound of the surf and the rustling of a breeze with the songs of some birds. Octopus Point was a majestic resting place, and I silently prayed for Woodpecker's soul and thanked the Lord for her wisdom and foresight. She would be missed and always remembered.

Once Bright Cloud was done, the Indians filed by the tree, hanging trinkets on the limbs. Their gifts were baskets, fishing lines, strips of cloth, wooden cups and bowls, all the items that would be needed in the spirit world. With the ceremony over, the murmuring crowd then started walking back down the trail toward the bay.

As they departed, Marcus perched himself on the cliff overlooking the old woman's cove. Here, with the sun on his face and tears in his eyes, he chanted and blessed the sea. We lingered behind to give him comfort, and then walked back with him.

We were the last to leave the point, and we found that Bright Cloud had waited to join us in the long, solemn walk down the mountainside. As we made our way, I commented on how beautiful the ceremony had been, and Marcus shook his head in agreement. Other than that, no one said a word. Then suddenly, just before we were out of the forest, we were set upon by a band of three howling braves. They came at us from behind some fir trees and ferns, with their faces painted and war axes in hand. The first one was Hawk, and he rushed past me with a glancing body blow from his shoulder. The other two Indians were his brother Sea Lion and a cousin named Frog. They only taunted our group with their tomahawks.

As I stumbled to regain my footing, I reached for my knife. Angrily, Hawk screamed, "Woodpecker dead. Today you die with her!" But the braves simply turned and ran off down the trail, whooping. Their quick, brazen attack had startled us all, and the baby started crying. Raven's face filled with fear, and it took me a few moments to get everyone calmed before we started moving again.

"What was that all about?" Bright Cloud asked as we stumbled along.

Slipping my blade back into its scabbard, I answered, "In life, the old woman protected Marcus and me from Hawk. Now I fear that protection is gone. He is seeking vengeance for the battle with our ship. No good will come from this."

"I will intervene with the council," the shaman said. "Revenge is for the elders to decide. Steer clear of Hawk until his crazy spirit is quiet."

"Aye...we will try."

With each twist of the trail and each rill we crossed, I wondered and feared if Hawk and his band might be lurking, but they did not approach us again. By the time we reached the bay, most of the dugouts had departed. Of the few Indians that remained on the shore, I only recognized Timber Wolf and Coyote, talking to a group from Netarts Bay. As we approached our canoe, however, we heard a wail from behind a sand dune just up the shoreline. Twisting that way, I saw Hawk, Sea Lion and Frog howling while rushing over the grassy crown of the dune straight for us. As they drew near, I noticed that Hawk carried a stone tomahawk and lance, while the other two still brandished only war axes. Instantly, I reached for my knife, positioning my body in front of Raven and the baby. Mole rushed to my side with his blade in hand, but Bright Cloud stepped forward and raised his hands into the air, shouting to the approaching band to stop.

They finally did, only a few paces in front of us.

"There will be no blood-letting, this day," the shaman angrily roared.

Hawk glared at me from behind his war paint and replied, "Today, Fire-Head dies! This is my pledge to the spirits of my ancestors. Let no one try to stop me."

"This day is to remember and mourn Woodpecker, not to fight," Bright Cloud sharply responded.

"Step away, old man, or you will feel the sting of my stone," Hawk answered, gesturing with his tomahawk.

No one had ever talked to Bright Cloud in such a way before, and the few Indians watching let out a gasp. As Hawk spun his angry face toward me, I felt anger rush up my gut, and I knew that this was the day I had dreaded for so many months. In the end, Hawk would die or I would; there could be no other result.

In a firm, angry voice, I asked, "Am I to fight all three of you dogs?"

Hawk glared at me, then kicked sand in my direction, causing another gasp to rise from the watching crowd. "I kill you alone and slow," he said. "You will cry for the mercy of death."

Kicking sand back at him, I moved slowly to my left and up the beach.

Bright Cloud protested our moves, but the crowd let out another huff and formed a big circle around us. Never taking my eyes off Hawk, I spotted a stout stick in the sand that I could use as a club. Stooping, I picked up the short rod with my left hand. As I rose again, now with club and knife in hand, Hawk and I faced each other, some twenty feet apart.

With the sun on his ugly face, Hawk raised his spear high over his head, making motions of throwing, while moving the war club in front of his body.

Crouching low to the sand, I crept in a circle more to my right. When water was at my back, I started slowly moving towards Hawk, alert to his spear. He waited, all the while mocking me loudly. Then, just as he was about to throw the lance, Black Fox stepped between us, with his hands outstretched.

"This stops now," he yelled. "I am the shaman of the tribe, and I demand your obedience." Turning his sweating black face to me, he continued, "Joe, I ask this for me and in the memory of Woodpecker." Then, twisting to Hawk, he bellowed, "If you don't stop, I will drive out your guardian spirit and curse your lodge with a plague. This I can and will do!"

The threat of witchcraft caught Hawk off guard. His face seemed to turn to stone as he gawked back at the boy who was well admired as having such powers. Most of the tribe believed that Black Fox walked with the midnight gods, and that death would never find him. In a few short heartbeats, terror took hold of Hawk, and he slowly lowered his spear and axe to the side of his body.

Then Marcus slowly turned again to me. "Joe, I pledge you my protection."

The look in Black Fox's eyes told me that this was the truth, so I dropped the club to the sand. Marcus had defused the fight with fear and friendship; maybe he would make a wise leader, after all.

Sliding my blade back into its sheath, I stepped closer to Marcus and whispered, "This will not end with Hawk until one of us is dead."

The boy heard my words of caution, and nodded.

I turned my back on the Indians and walked towards Raven and Mole at the canoe. After a few paces, I heard a loud gasp and, before I could turn again to face the crowd, something pierced my back with a loud *swish-thump*. As the lance went through my body, I felt something snap, and my right arm went limp. In an instant, I buckled to the wet sand, clutching my shoulder.

When my eyes focused again, I found one of my rusty iron tips, at the point of Hawk's spear, poking out the flesh of my right shoulder. Then came the pain – appalling pain that rushed through my body. I let out a cry and twisted my head towards the crowd, to find Marcus, Timber Wolf and Coyote wrestling Hawk to the ground, with the other Indians holding Sea Lion and Frog.

By the time Mole and Raven reached me, Hawk had been subdued.

They gently got me sitting up again, with the long shaft of the spear dangling from my back. I was surprised by how little blood was visible around the protruding tip. But the excruciating pain throbbed all the way down my right side, and I feared that I would soon pass out.

"Should I break the shaft off?" Mole asked, his brown eyes flashing fear.

"How long is the shaft?" I weakly answered.

"Three arms," he replied.

"Break it off… but leave two fists to the shaft," I answered, my head spinning.

When Mole grabbed onto the spear and broke it, everything went black.

The next thing I was aware of was a wet, cool cloth being wiped across my sweating forehead. When my eyes finally opened, I found Raven sitting by my side, in the old woman's lodge. I was bare from the waist up, positioned so that I was sitting on the ground, with my back resting against the log in front of the fire pit. The pain seemed more bearable, and the wet fabric was refreshing.

"He's awake," Raven said loudly.

Quickly, Mole and Marcus came to kneel at my side.

"Joe, that shaft has to be pulled out of your shoulder," Marcus said. "I'll give you a tonic for the pain and then we pull it out."

For some reason, I was having trouble finding my words. Stammering a few times, I finally whispered, "No… We must singe the inside of my shoulder or I will die from blood poisoning."

"How do we do that?" Mole asked.

Slowly, I reached for my knife and handed it to Raven. Looking into her frightened face, I said, "Cut a deep V in the shaft that protrudes from my back." Then, turning to Mole, I continued, "You, run to the cabin and get my powder horn, a hammer and a flat iron rod."

"Why?" Marcus asked, looking confused.

With a dry mouth and a lump in my throat, I mumbled as best I could, "Put the gunpowder in the V of the shaft, light it, and hammer the spear through my body while it's on fire. Then slap a red hot iron against my skin, front and back, to stop the bleeding. It's the only way to block any infection."

"That's makes no sense," Black Fox blurted. "You could die from the pain."

"Aye… or die from the poison."

"How you know this?" Marcus asked.

"From books. It was the French way, during the Indians Wars. Even if I pass out again, this must be done or I'll surely die."

With great looks of concern on their faces, they all agreed. Then Mole quickly departed for the cabin while Marcus fed me some dried leaves for the pain and Raven cut the groove in the shaft. With each move of her blade, unbearable pain racked my body, but I didn't cry out, as she had to complete the notch.

By the time she was done, I was only half-conscious. What happened next remains only in short spurts of memory. I remember hearing the hiss of the gunpowder, and smelling my scorching flesh as the shaft was driven through my body, searing my innards. I heard my own screams, and the horrible smells that rose from my burning flesh from the hot iron…and then, mercifully, I passed out again.

When I awoke next, I could feel the hard planks of the old woman's bedchamber through an elk skin. It took me a few moments to gather my thoughts and recall the events that had placed me here. The chamber was dark, with a small fire burning in the pit, and I seemed to be alone. My shoulder was still on fire, but it seemed somewhat more bearable. Looking at the front of my chest, I could see a black-burned wound, mostly covered by a pitch-cloth. My back felt much the same. But I still could not feel anything in my right arm; it seemed to be detached from my body and totally immobile. When I tried to move it, the only answer was a shooting pain in my shoulder, and I gasped, desperate for relief.

Out of nowhere, Raven's face was looking down at me.

"Are you awake?" she asked in a near-whisper.

"Aye… How long have I been out?"

"Two days. Do you want some water or broth?"

"Maybe. Where is the baby? Is it night or day?"

Taking a damp cloth, she wiped my brow while answering. "It is just night, and Mole is with the baby, back at our cabin. You must heal before we take you home."

"Let me see if I can sit up," I whispered, trying to pull myself up with my left hand. Raven helped me position my upright body on the planks.

That's when I became aware of the mumbling coming from the next room. Looking towards the elk-covered doorway, I asked, "What's going on?"

"Council powwow. The elders come at sunset. Soon, Black Fox becomes chief."

This was a bold move by Marcus, as Woodpecker had been dead for only a few days. I knew the lad was determined to become chief, but surely the elders would think him too young.

"This I would like to see… Help me to the doorway."

"Joe, you too weak. No start bleeding."

With my left hand, I touched her sweet face and looked directly into her brown eyes. "Please, give me a hand."

She did, and we quietly stumbled to the doorway. Bracing my left shoulder against the wall, Raven held back part of the elk hide so we could peer in.

Almost a dozen elders and chiefs sat around the fire pit. They were all dressed in their finest buckskins, with feathers and shell adornments. I recognized almost all of their faces, for they had visited the old woman's lodge many times before. In the dim firelight, they seemed to be asking Marcus questions about his powers, his coups and how he would lead. Each time Black Fox answered, the council grunted and shook their heads in agreement. This went on a few minutes; then Bright Cloud asked what the punishment would be for Hawk, his brother and his cousin. For the answer, Marcus stood, holding out two fists above the fire. Opening one fist, he sprinkled gunpowder onto the flames and, at its *flash*, said angrily, "Hawk will be marked with fire." Opening the other fist, he did the same, causing another burst of flames. *Flash!* "Hawk and his clan will be banished forever from the tribe." With no understanding of gunpowder, the council was wide-eyed at the sight of the white glow of fire, which they believed was a manifestation of Black Fox's spiritual power, and they quickly grunted their agreement.

"Is that my gunpowder he's using?" I whispered to Raven, my head spinning.

"Yes, he keep your horn," she whispered back.

"I've seen enough. Help me back to bed and I'll try some broth."

A few hours later, after much chanting and pounding of the drums, Black Fox was declared chief of the Tillamook tribe. The council proclaimed him to be a midnight spirit that would guide the nation to a bright and shining future.

In the excitement of this proclamation, Black Fox invited Raven and me into the council room. Before leaving the bedchamber, I had Raven drape a cloth around my neck, as a sling for my dead arm. Then, still nude from the waist up, I stumbled into the next room with Raven's help. Once there, she slowly lowered me down on a log stump, next to a wall that I could lean on. The dim, smoky room was stuffy and smelt of gunpowder and fish.

As I was coming to rest, all the elders and chiefs twisted my way, staring with glossy eyes at my scarred, wounded shoulder.

"Fire-Head has joined us so you can see the damage Hawk has done. Had it not been for my powers with fire, he would be dead now," Marcus proclaimed.

As usual, he was taking the coup for my recovery. The boldness of this lad, and the stupidity of the elders and chiefs, surprised me. Then I noticed the bowls of red, intoxicating mushroom that they had all eaten. No wonder! With those mushrooms, the boy could have convinced even me that he was divine. This council meeting had been nothing more than Black Fox's phony show. I felt sorry for the Indians; they were too innocent to understand that Marcus was a charlatan!

Squatting by the fire while sprinkling gunpowder into a bowl of warm pitch, Black Fox said, "I have summoned Hawk and his clan so they might know their fate."

The council grunted their approval and then talked amongst themselves. Some moments later, there came a scratch at the door, and Hawk entered the lodge, flanked by his brother and cousin. He looked angry, glancing around the room suspiciously.

"Why wasn't I told of this council meeting?" Hawk demanded.

Standing, Marcus moved to confront Hawk, face to face. In a firm, fluent voice, Black Fox said, "You are here to learn your fate."

Waving his hand, Hawk replied, "My fate is not in your midnight hands, boy." Then, turning to the elders, he said angrily, "I am the tribal war chief, and I serve only this council."

With a wet cloth in his hand, Marcus held out his wooden bowl of pitch and put a punk to it. In an instant, the crock was aflame with smoke, hissing loudly.

The elders gasped at the burning bowl, and Hawk's expression turned to stone.

As the white smoke dissipated, Marcus said, "This council has made me chief of the Tillamook nation. You have threatened Bright Cloud, the shaman of the Nehalem people, and you displayed your cowardice by striking Fire-Head with your lance when he was under my protection. For these actions, you will be marked with fire." A hush fell over the room as Black Fox turned to Sea Lion and Frog and commanded, "Hold his arms tightly, or his fate will be yours."

As they grabbed onto Hawk's arms, Marcus moved to the fire pit and, with the wet cloth, pulled my flat iron from the coals.

Holding the glowing red iron, Marcus turned to me. "Fire-Head, you have the right to mark this brave."

Hawk's eyes bulged with fear as he struggled to free himself from his captors. Revenge could be mine…

But I had no stomach for such actions. "No, vengeance is for the foolish," I said in a weak voice.

"Very well." Black Fox turned to Hawk. "My spirit will mark him." He ripped off the hide covering Hawk's chest. Then, blowing on the hot poker, he said, "You and your clan are banished from our lands. If you are not gone from our shores by sunset tomorrow, you all will be killed." Then he pressed the flat iron at an angle on Hawks chest.

Hawk squirmed and screamed under the hot tip. It scorched his skin, and the room smelt of burning flesh.

After removing the poker for an instant, Black Fox did it again at a different angle, forming a burning X on Hawk's upper chest.

Hawk bellowed again. Then his eyes rolled up into their sockets and he fainted.

Finally withdrawing the iron, Black Fox looked at Sea Lion and Frog. "Be gone by sunset tomorrow or all will be lost."

As Hawk was being dragged out the door, I stared at Marcus, who was still holding the hot iron. What had happened to the harmless young lad who'd been Captain Gray's cabin boy? Now he was a boy chief, full of brutality, revenge and tricks. He saddened me, and I yearned for home.

The Lost Year

The next day, Black Fox gave my powder horn and flat iron back to me.

When I shook the horn, I found it was empty. All of my gunpowder had been wasted on his deception, and now my pistol was as useless as my right arm.

From the hard planks of my bed, I let Marcus know how I felt about his shameful performance with the council, but he didn't care. He was the chief now, and no Indian would dare doubt his spirit powers. He told me that he would be a great prophet for the tribe and would teach them better ways, his African ways.

I reminded him that the Tillamooks had done very well with their old ways, and advised him not to interfere. He scoffed at my plea and reminded me of what the white man had done to the Indians in the colonies…and sadly I knew he was right.

His final words would stay with me over the coming winter: "Mend your body and mind, Joe, or you will be useless to your chief."

Late that afternoon, Mole came by the lodge to take me home. He helped me to the small dugout and then paddled us towards the estuary.

As we moved slowly across the water, two war canoes passed us. Inside those dugouts was Hawk's clan – about twenty squaws, children and braves, in all. They were a shabby bunch, with all their worldly possessions lashed to the boats. As they slipped by us, I noticed Hawk slumped at the stern in the last canoe. His upper body was bare, showing the scars of the red, weeping burn that had been singed into his chest. He glared at me across the moving water with eyes of hate that told me that our struggle had not ended. He might be marked and banished, but he still sought satisfaction.

"I wonder where they'll go," I murmured out loud as they rowed by.

"I hear live with the Clatsops," Mole answered.

Blimey, I thought at the news, *escaping north is now out of the question.*

Raven was waiting onshore for our return, and she and Mole helped me up the slope to the cabin. It was good to be back in my own bed, surrounded by my people. Now all I had to do was heal.

I didn't make a good patient, and brooded for the first few weeks. My right leg tingled all the time and could barely hold my weight, and my right arm was as dead as the old woman. I was a useless figure of a man. Mole and Raven cared for me as best they could, but I would lash out with anger at their hovering concern. I couldn't put on my own trousers, fasten my buckskins, work at the forge or do any chores. And my scars were ugly, offending even my eyes. But in time these problems improved. After a few weeks, I could once again feel my toes and walk without a crutch or crouch. Then the fingers on my right hand began moving again. After that, I started moving my wrist, and then my elbow. At the end of three miserable months, my dead arm was coming alive again. But it wasn't strong, and I still couldn't control all of my muscles.

During my recovery, the salmon season came and went without much help from me. It was Mole and Raven, with the baby on her back, who fished rivers, filleted the fish and dried them for the winter. It was they who hunted the forest, killing two deer before the winter, and it was they who gathered the roots and clams in the shallow, brackish bogs. They did this work without complaint and only showed me love and care. And, while I was proud of my family and did all I could to pitch in, I was also deeply depressed over my fate. Therefore, I spent hours walking the beaches, pondering my lot. Oh, how intoxicating self-pity can be! You blame everyone but yourself for your station in life. It was never my fault for the fight, being marooned, losing my birthright or fathering a child in the wilderness. No, everyone else stood guilty of the troubles that plagued me.

But soon, with a fresh determination, I reckoned that these thoughts of self-pity served no purpose. Feeling sorry for myself was a luxury I couldn't afford. From my earliest days, I had lived my life in a passive way, always accepting my fate. That had to stop. You cannot find life if you avoid to live. It was my vision that was small… and it was time to take control of my own life.

By the early spring, I was back working my forge with a mending arm. There was a seed of a plan in the back of my mind that drove me to make as many iron tips as I could. I would trade those tips with the Indians for the only currency I knew: animal pelts. Raven had told me many times about the half-moon bay, many leagues south, where her family lived, and about the Spanish trading post. There, I hoped to trade my pelts for gunpowder, provisions and maybe even passage home. But getting that far south would require a harrowing sea journey, so I began by planning shorter trips down the coast to trade with other tribes. Those voyages would be made in the summer, when the weather was better; by autumn, if we had found our sea legs, I would take Raven home. And while my plan was full of pitfalls and danger, at least I was starting to control my own fate.

We had few visitors, the winter I was stove-up. The cabin was remote from the village, with a long path that was always windswept and wet. But with the improving weather came our first visitors of the season, Timber Wolf and Sandpiper with their imps. And they brought with them the hind-quarter of an elk. Raven was delighted to have another woman to talk with, and to see the children she had helped care for. So with the squaws gathering roots outside, and the children playing with the baby, Timber Wolf squatted by the fireplace and we talked.

"I hear you work with iron again."

"Aye."

"This spring, brother and I build boat for white-wing. You help?"

"Aye, but you will need canvas for the sail, and there is no more."

"Maybe other tribes have cloth."

"Perhaps. Soon, we will be sailing down the coast to trade with other Indians. How far to the next tribe?"

"One day… hard paddle. I have been there many times. It be the tribe where I won Raven."

"What are they called?"

"*Siletz*, brothers to Tillamooks. Maybe they have cloth."

"Do you and your brother want to come with us?"

Timber Wolf thought a moment and then, with a sheepish look on his face, shook his head. "No, I promise Sandpiper no more gamble. No more squaw slaves in our lodge."

He went on to tell me that the main village for the Siletz tribe was close to a bay just inside a small slit in the breakers, much like the bar at Tillamook Bay. There were no rocks guarding the entrance, he said, and I could find the slit by looking for a narrow opening in the green sand dunes that were on either side of it.

"At low tide, bar very shallow, but once over the surf you will find channel to big bay and river to village."

"What language do they speak?"

"Much like ours. Raven live there, she can help. You find me canvas."

"Aye."

We had a delightful time, that evening, feasting on elk meat that I grilled over an open flame, with roots and young greens. The conversation was pleasant, and the friendly faces were appreciated, after almost seven months of constant foul weather. But they also expressed concerns about Black Fox's cruelty to Hawk and the fact our baby wasn't using the head-flatting board. We tried to quiet their worries and assure them that all would be well. From the looks on their faces, however, I was afraid our words fell on deaf ears.

They stayed until near dark and then departed. After they were gone, I told Raven and Mole that, come June, we would sail to the land of the Siletz to trade for furs and search out canvas for Timber Wolf. Mole was excited about the trip, while Raven had a bitter face.

"What is wrong?" I asked while she fed the baby.

"Those flatheads enslave me. They snatched me from my cocoon like a butterfly, then beat me and rape me. Now you wish me to forgive these Siletz dogs!" she answered in an angry tone.

"You are my squaw now, and no one will dare touch you!"

She thought a moment and then, with a slight smile, replied, "Aye. I am *your* squaw now."

The first few weeks of June were wet and miserable, with rough seas and an almost constant wind from the south. During the third week, the weather improved, but the breeze was still out of the south and the ocean choppy. While we waited on the weather, Raven packed panniers with our traveling provisions. We took winter coats, sleeping robes, blankets, basket hats, extra moccasins, grass mats and seal-skin jackets. For food, we packed dried fish, venison jerky and a paste made out of crushed lean meat and animal fat that the Indians called pemmican. Raven also loaded some baskets of dried camas and berries. The last of our provisions were two animal bladders of fresh water. The weapons we carried were two spears, one harpoon, two iron tomahawks, Mole's bow with six arrows, our knives and, just for show, my empty pistol. Stowed aboard the dugout were two fishing lines with assorted hooks, a gaff hook, ropes and a net for catching birds. We had no compass, no maps, no telescope and no extra sails. With our provisions finally ready, I wondered if we were good enough sailors to find that tiny slit to Siletz Bay.

Just before departing for our trip, we told Timber Wolf that we planned to return in seven to ten suns. Then, with a warm breeze out of the north, we shoved off in the early morning hours of the last week of June.

It was good to be on the water again, to taste the salt and feel the sun. But with my right arm still not fully recovered, and with Raven carrying the baby on her back, I worried about only three of us paddling the big canoe across the bar with the outrigger. So, as we approached the slit, I had Mole raise the sail, and we rode over the bar with the power of the wind. Fortunately, the tide was right, with scant breakers, and we cut through the curling green sea under a blue dome with wispy clouds. I was pleased how well the Thunderbird answered the helm and handled in the turbulent surf. She was a good, sturdy boat and I had great confidence in her. In a few short moments, we were outside the bay and moving south down the coastline, riding long green gentle swells.

Timber Wolf had told me that it took him one full day of hard paddling to reach the slit, so I guessed the bay was about fifty miles down the coast. At our current speed, I reckoned we would be there in about five hours. All we had to do now was enjoy the quick passage and fill our eyes with some of the most rugged and beautiful vistas I had ever seen.

With birds squawking overhead, we soon slipped by the old woman's cove and spotted her rock. Above the little lagoon, I could see the opening in the tree line that was her final resting place, and I gave her a silent prayer. As we moved further south, we found more coves, more cliffs, more haystack rocks and more beauty. With calm seas and a warm breeze, I steered the boat a few hundred yards off the surf line, but we still had to maneuver around a few off-shore pillars.

Just before noon, I spotted a narrow gap in the shoreline, with rolling verdure dunes on each side. This had to be the place, so we came about and dropped the sail. With the tide ebbing, we approached the surf line with caution while searching for a slit in the breakers. Then, just north of the gap, I saw some quiet surf.

We paddled in that direction. Once I was confident that this was the channel, we turned the boat into it. With some hard rowing, we moved towards the bar and, while we scraped the shallow bottom a few times, we always kept moving with the rushing surf. Soon we had crossed the bar and were in the deeper waters of an estuary. We paddled this channel south and around the gap until we came to a large bay. Looking east, we saw what looked to be a native village, a mile across the lagoon.

Turning in that direction, we raised the sail again. Mole tested the depth of the water with our harpoon as we slowly glided across the bay towards the site.

By the time we approached the shoreline, a cluster of curious Indians awaited our arrival. Lowering the sail and paddling to the beach, we went ashore. The Siletz stood in silence, gaping at our boat and at the three of us standing before them.

"We are from the Tillamook tribe," I said while taking off my basket hat, and the crowd let out a gasp at the sight of my red hair. "Timber Wolf sends his best wishes to the Siletz people. We come in peace, trade for hides."

These Indians looked much the same, in dress, skin color and stature, as the Clatsops and Tillamooks. The group was mostly braves, but there were a few squaws and some children.

"What is your name?" someone in the crowd finally asked.

Smiling while pointing to my hair, I replied, "They call me Fire-Head." Turning to the others, I continued. "This is Mole. He is my brother. The squaw is Raven. She is my woman, and the baby on her back is Dutch, my son."

"I remember your woman," one burly brave yelled, while stepping forward with a threatening look. "Timber Wolf cheat me for her. She was my slave."

Staring at the man's sour face, I placed my hand on the handle of my knife and replied, "Aye, and now she is my woman and none of your concern."

The Indian glared at me for a moment until an older brave stepped forward and placed his hand on the man's shoulder. "Everyone cheats you, Bull Frog...You are so easy!"

The crowd chuckled, and the tension was broken. Their tongue was much like ours, and we had no problems understanding what they said. The older man was the fishing chief, and he explained that the hamlet we were at was just a temporary fishing camp. The main village was down the bay and up a river, in a small valley. He offered to take us there and introduce us to the tribal chief, and we agreed.

We spent a week with the Siletz and, after I showed them the power of our iron tips, and letting them touch my hair, their chief, Running Fox, couldn't have been friendlier. He gave us food, offered us an empty lodge, and introduced us to all the other chiefs and shamans. We fished and hunted with them, ate with them and gave most of them rides in our sailboat. They were a joyful bunch, very much like the Tillamooks in both rituals and beliefs. But they were different in one aspect: they weren't a seagoing tribe like the northern nations. They had dugouts and they fished the rivers and the bay; sometimes they even went across the bar to fish the sea. But they never traveled far on the open ocean. And while they didn't have any horses, they seemed to prefer traveling cross-country.

Before we started trading, I let it be known that the only furs we were interested in were beaver and otter pelts, but that I would also consider iron items and trade goods. When we finally started bartering with the tribe, I was surprised by what they brought. One brave had an old, rusty Spanish blunderbuss with a bent barrel and a broken stock. That iron was worth a few tips from me. Another person offered two trade blankets made out of hemp. The fabric was tight, strong and lightweight; I guessed that the cloths could be sewn together for a small sail. The blankets cost me four tips. One squaw offered a handful of iron spikes that she had found in the sand after burning some wreckage from a ship, and there were other trinkets of iron, as well, but mostly we traded for pelts. By the time we departed, we had seven beaver and five otter hides, and I had no more tips in my pouch. It had been quite a profitable enterprise.

After saying farewell to the tribe, we sailed up the bay and crossed the bar without incident. The day was bright and warm, with a fresh breeze from the south.

Once we had turned for home, Raven moved from her center seat and sat next to me at the tiller. After she started feeding Dutch, she twisted my way and said angrily, "I spit on the Siletz. They are dogs."

Smiling at her, I replied, "They be good people. Our outrigger is full of their pelts, our bellies full of their food, and you're still my woman."

"Aye," she replied, "but spirit sad. Never take me there again."

Journey to the Southlands

We learned many things from our trading trip with the Siletz. We had a good boat and we knew how to sail her, but we would need to take more food and water for our longer trip south. Moreover, the wicker panniers that we had used to store our goods were too big for the outrigger, and too open to the weather. Our clothes were always damp and the food tasted of sea salt. Therefore, we would have to craft seal-skin pouches that were weather-tight and could be stored flat in the small dugout. Also, we needed more rope, and the two canoe hulls needed a few coats of Timber Wolf's lacquer, to help prevent sea seepage through the wood.

With that in mind, Mole and I emptied out the dugouts and removed the sail and mast. Then we paddled the boats to where Timber Wolf was building his first sailing canoe. This work site was just east of the village, on the banks of the bay. When we arrived, Timber Wolf and Coyote warmly greeted us and helped secure our boat to the shore. The shaping of the hull of his new boat was completed, so now they were working on digging out the inside.

Taking some tools in hand, Mole and I began to help them with the work. As we did, I told them of our trading trip and showed them the hemp blankets. Pointing out the tight weave and light weight, I spread the cloths, side by side, on the ground. Then I paced out the size, while explaining to them that the two blankets, sewn together, could become a sail large enough for the dugout they were working on.

"And what blankets cost me?" Timber Wolf asked.

"I was thinking about that," I answered, picking up the cloths. "I'll have Raven do the mending. She has done it before. And Mole and I will make the mast and spar and do the rigging. For this, you will paint three coats of your varnish on *Thunderbird*."

Timber Wolf twisted his scruffy head towards where my boats bobbed on the water. As he did, the sun caught his face, accenting his profile with its big crooked nose and sloping forehead.

Turning back to me, he nodded and said, "This be big job, take many suns."

"That will be fine," I answered. He was a great craftsman, and I was pleased with our accord.

Before we returned to the cabin that day, we all went to the bay and carried the dugouts ashore. After Mole and I unbolted the struts to the outrigger, we turned the hulls upside down.

As we were finishing, I said, "I'll forge all the hardware needed for your new boat, but before you lacquer my big dugout, will you carve a raven on both sides of the bows?"

"Yes," Timber Wolf said, then grinned. "She must be good squaw."

We all worked on our different projects during the next few weeks. Raven made seal-skin pouches and sewed the sail. Mole crafted both a cedar mast and spar while I worked at my furnace making more tips to trade for more seal-skins. Over each evening's meal, we shared our progress and talked about our journey south. There was a twinkle in Raven's eyes as she relished the thought of being reunited with her family. Mole was also excited, as he looked forward to living in a warmer climate and learning the ways of Raven's tribe. As for me, I couldn't work fast enough at forging out my tips and making plans for the voyage. After being marooned on Tillamook Bay for almost two years, nothing could stop me.

Towards the end of July, I had a surprise visit from Marcus. He looked tired and grim as he stumbled up the hill to the cabin, carrying the old woman's iron pot. His black face was sweaty, with droopy eyes, as he set the heavy kettle down next to my forge.

"We need to talk," he said, with perspiration pouring off his brow.

Taking a red hot iron out of the coals with my iron grips, I pounded it with my hammer and yelled, "Give me a minute."

He watched as the sparks flew with the ringing of the mallet. Then, with the poker still hot, I slid it into a bucket of water that sizzled. Once the metal had cooled, I pulled it out and turned to Black Fox, with it still smoking in my grips.

"What can I do for you, Marcus?" I asked.

He stared into my whiskered face for a moment and then said, "I be Black Fox. I want you to make special warrior spear tips out of Woodpecker's pot. I want them long and thin, sharp and serrated, and strong and straight."

"Are you going to war?" I asked.

He scowled at me for a moment. "Old woman came to me in vision. She tell me burn down lodges and fight white man in forest."

"The old woman was for peace. Everyone knows that," I said with a chuckle while placing the iron back into the furnace. "You have no enemies, and there are no signs of the white men coming. Don't tell this vision to the elders. They will think you young and dumb. Rule with hope, not fear."

My harsh words caught Marcus off guard, and he looked at me with contempt, "I am your chief, so tread carefully, Joe. What happened to Hawk can happen to you."

His threat surprised me, but then he believed all this spirit poppycock. "I will soon banish myself from these waters," I told him. "We sail south to a Spanish outpost and then home. You are welcome to come."

My news shocked him, and he mused over my words for a while. "You need my permission to leave this bay, and I don't give it."

Feeling anger swell up inside of me, I asked, "Why are you so determined to make me your enemy? I saved your life at the falls, and you repay me like this? Your voodoo doesn't frighten me. If you interfere with my plans, I'll show the council your fire tricks."

With a nervous twitch of his face, he answered, "You have no powder."

"I have a single load in the pistol. Just enough for one good show."

He frowned at me, not sure if I was lying, and then calmly said, "I will stay here with my people. You make me spear heads or not?"

Shrugging, I answered, "Aye…but this will take some time, and my iron tips will be no match for cannons and muskets. War is not the answer. The people will lose."

He turned to leave, then spun back again. "Victory belongs to those who want it the most. And, Joe, when you leave…never come back. You are the last white eye to walk these shores, and you no longer have my protection."

As he stumbled down the slight hill, I was disheartened. The tribe had given this boy chief too much power, and he was leading them down a war path. This I could not change, but his threats told me that this place was no longer safe.

That evening, I told Mole and Raven of my run-in with Marcus. I told them of his threats to me and his plans to burn down the villages and fight his fictitious war from the forest. They were disturbed by my news and wondered aloud whether we should tell the elders. I thought not, and told them we should simply depart the bay with all due haste.

"We will row when we have to, and sail when we can. Along the way, we will put into bays and coves and trade with the locals until we reach Raven's half-moon bay."

"What of the old woman's pot?" Mole asked.

"We will take the kettle with us, and destroy the forge before we go."

"What of the cabin?" Raven asked with a concerned look.

"We will take what we can and leave what we must," I answered.

"We should burn it down," Mole said with a sour face.

"No that would alert them that we are gone, and they might come after us. How and when we leave is our secret. We say nothing to anybody."

They agreed, and we spent the next few hours making plans for the voyage.

The next week, Mole and I walked through the village, carrying Timber Wolf's new mast and sail. As we walked by Black Fox's lodge, he came out and asked about his spearheads. When I told him they would be ready in the next few days, he seemed pleased; without another comment, he turned back into his home. I knew this would be the last time I would ever see the lad, but I could say nothing. Instead, I silently prayed for his soul and hoped he would gain some wisdom. He and Woodpecker would never be far from my mind.

When we got to the work site, we found the new boat floating in the bay. And there on the shore, right side up, were our two dugouts, gleaming in the sun. Timber Wolf had done a remarkable job, applying a shiny burnt-red varnish to the boats, and his carving of the raven on the bows was outstanding. As we walked around the boats, rubbing our hands over the finish, he explained that there were three coats of lacquer on the hulls but only two coats on the inside. He asked for another few days to complete the job. I was more than satisfied, and told him we needed the boats for another trading trip, so his job was done.

A little later, Mole and Coyote began bolting the struts to the outrigger, while Timber Wolf and I went to the bay and rigged the mast for his new boat. Once all the hardware and cloth was installed, we took the canoe for a test ride on the bay. After paddling out to deep water, Timber Wolf raised the hemp sail, with me at the tiller. A fresh breeze filled the cloth, and the boat lurched forward, cutting through the placid green waters. As we moved effortlessly over the lagoon, Timber Wolf's face filled with pride and his lips curled with a grin.

When we got to the middle of the bay, he took the helm, and I gave him his first sailing lesson. He worked the boat like an old jack-tar, and soon we were coming about at the southern end of the bay. After showing him how to position the boat to catch the wind for the north, we started moving again.

As we quietly sailed along, I told him of my run-in with Black Fox, and of his vision to burn the villages and move to the forest to fight his phony war.

The look on Timber Wolf's face changed from pride to fear and then to anger. Gripping the tiller firmly, he listened to my words and then said, "You must tell the elders of his crazy plan."

"You are a chief and respected by the tribe. *You* must tell them. We leave in two suns to trade with the Clatsops, so tell them after we are gone. I want no part of a fight with Marcus."

Timber Wolf thought a moment and then agreed with a grunt. As he turned the boat for shore, I wanted to say farewell to him and his family, but I could not. Our secret had to be kept.

Early that afternoon, we paddled our newly varnished canoes to the shore in front of the cabin. But before we started loading the dugouts, I blindfolded Raven and walked her down to where the boats rested. When I removed the cloth from her eyes, she got her first look at the glistening dugouts. Then I pointed to the bows and showed her the carvings.

"Oh Joe," she said joyfully, "just like the bird on my shoulder. What beautiful canoes we have!" Then she kissed me and whispered, "Thank you for taking me home."

Looking into her sweet brown eyes, I replied, "We aren't there yet. We will see what King Neptune has to say."

"Who is King Neptune?" she asked with a puzzled face.

"He is the sea spirit for my tribe," I answered with a grin.

We shoved off just before daybreak the next morning. The outrigger was packed to the gunnels with all our provisions and possessions, and on top we fastened a seal-skin tarp to help keep the water out. The big hull was also loaded, but not so cluttered that we couldn't move around. As we paddled away from the shore, I looked up at the faint outline of my cabin and felt sad about leaving our first home. Then, twisting to view the bay, I saw the silhouette of the rocks that protected the lagoon that had been my home for two years. I would miss the Tillamooks; they were more similar to me than dissimilar. They had survived for thousands of years on wits and grit, and I wished them well.

As we approached the slit, in the dim morning light, I could see and hear the pounding surf. I knew this long voyage would be fraught with risks. Just before the first line of breakers, I shouted to Mole to raise the sail. As the wind took hold, I felt the boat's heavy weight tug at the sluggish tiller, but we were committed; there was no turning back. We sailed through the first few rows of surf, with the spray crashing over our bows and cold sea water rolling down our faces.

Once we had crossed the last line of waves at the bar, I looked towards the western sky, seeking hope and a rhythm in the ocean, with a warm gentle breeze that would blow us safely south. What I found instead was thunderheads on the horizon and a violent green sea, with cold swirling winds that could block our passage. We were riding the beast of the sea now, where anything could happen.

Chapter Nine: Reunited

Following the Lady Washington's daring escape from Tillamook Bay in August of 1788, Captain Gray moved slowly north, up the rugged coastline, looking for other tribes to trade with. But the tragic events at 'Murderer's Harbor' would taint the crew's attitude about the Indians for the remaining voyage. No longer would groups of natives be allowed aboard his ship, nor would crewmembers be sent ashore unless they were heavily armed. Captain Gray was determined never to lose another sailor or skirmish to the savages.

Almost a month later, after brisk trading with the coastal tribes, the sea-battered Orphan limped into Nootka Sound on September 17, 1788. Soon after arriving at Friendly Cove, she completed her much-needed overhaul, and brought fresh supplies aboard. But just as the *Lady Washington* was preparing to get underway, the *Columbia*, under the command of Captain Kendrick, entered Friendly Cove, as well. His ship had been delayed for months in the Juan Fernandez Islands, making repairs to storm damage. The commodore had been fortunate to find a Spanish-controlled port where such repairs and resupply were granted. But now, after 110 days of sailing from South American, she, too, was in a desperate need of a refit.

At long last, the two ships were reunited and safely moored at their destination. This event was a cause for a jubilant celebration, with fine foods and strong spirits.

These ships, along with other British fur traders, wintered at Nootka Sound. While the *Columbia* was being refitted, Captain Gray traded up and down the coastline, doing a brisk business in otter pelts. He also explored and charted many bays and inland waters around the sound.

In May of 1789, the Spanish Crown sent two warships to the area, as a show of its sovereignty over the fur trade. These Spaniards seized a number of British merchant ships, causing the Nootka Crisis, which almost resulted in war between the two nations. But because of the quick thinking by the Yankee captains, the Spanish believed that the *Columbia* and *Lady Washington* were owned by the American Congress, and therefore the ships were not seized.

In July of 1789, the two American ships departed Friendly Cove after all the pelts had been transferred to the *Columbia* and all the remaining trade goods loaded onto the Orphan. The original plan was that the flagship would sail for China, via the Sandwich Islands, while the *Lady Washington* would remain in the waters, trading for more skins. But the quirky Captain Kendrick had a different idea: he would trade commands with Gray. Therefore, it was Captain Robert Gray and the *Columbia* that departed, with over 1300 prime pelts, for China and home. Why the commodore made such a last-minute decision is not known.

Gray arrived in Canton in early 1790 and traded his cargo for large amounts of tea and other goods. He then continued west, sailing through the Indian Ocean, around the Cape of Good Hope, and across the Atlantic, arriving back in Boston on August 9, 1790. As such, the *Columbia* became the first American ship to circumnavigate the globe. The black-eye-patched Captain Gray was paraded through Boston for this accomplishment, and attended a reception held in his honor by Governor John Hancock. And, while the commercial value of that first voyage was disappointing, due to damaged tea from sea seepage, Captain Gray and the *Columbia* would depart for a second historic voyage to the northwest in just six short weeks. On this trip, he would discover and name, after his ship, the mighty Columbia River.

Dark Passage

Hidden deep within every soul is the fear of the unknown, so the Lord gave us hope, which is fear's best enemy. All day, I had been searching for something, a glimpse of ship or maybe just some relief from feeling hopeless. The seas had been choppy, and we had been sailing for hours. Then, finally, land came back into view. As we approached it, I looked to the south and found, in the distance, the rocky mountain headland that marked the beginning of the Clatsop nation. With this landmark, I knew where we were – just north of the slit for Necanicum Bay. That's when I remembered hearing the Indians talk about a river named Wimahl. Could the ship I sought have slipped into this river? Could we follow her?

As we reached the surf line, I turned the boat north, in quest of this river. The land here was straight like an arrow, with rolling green sand dunes and dancing blonde sea grass that stretched for miles inland. Above these verdant mounds were the foothills and mountains of a lush rainforest that shaped a long, broken horizon with hues of green. The vast richness and beauty of this land took my breath away.

Suddenly, with his arm outstretched, Mole shouted back to me, "Smoke."

Turning to his point, I too saw the dark smoke from a fire. As we came closer, we could see an Indian sitting next to a bonfire on the beach.

"Let's talk to him," I yelled to Mole.

He agreed with a nod of his head. So, with the surf slight and the breakers manageable, we came about and dropped the sail. Then, with paddles in hand, we rowed across the surf line and came to rest on some wet sand, a few hundred yards down the from the stranger.

Jumping out of the canoe, I told Mole to stay with Raven and the baby while I parleyed with the man. Then, turning, I walked toward the fire.

The deserted beach was wide, and stretched for miles in either direction. Up from the wet sand, the shore was littered with bleached-white logs that had rolled in from the sea over the many years. These snags formed a pale ribbon down the beach for as far as I could see. The bonfire was on dry sand, up from the shore and close to the rubble. As I advanced the fire, I saw the Indian resting on a beach log, cooking a fish over the flames.

He looked up from his food, and waved me into camp.

As I got closer, I noticed that he was a very old brave, with long, straggly gray hair under a strange-looking basket hat. His buckskins were tattered and without adornment, and he wore no moccasins. The fish he was cooking was a salmon that he held above the fire by the tip of his spear. Other than that, he had no weapons. As I closed on this scruffy Indian, I wondered what tongue I should use to address him.

But before I could say a thing, he turned to me and called, in English, "The ship you seek rests on a quiet bay in the mighty river."

His language and the look on his face startled me. His ghostly eyes glowed with a blue haze, and he had a vacant gaze. Was this old man blind? What Indian spoke my language?

Approaching his camp, I asked, "How do you know what I seek?" Then, carefully, I watched his hollow stare as it left me and turned toward the sea.

"I watched you come. I know your heart."

"So you can see?"

"Aye, Joe, I see many things."

By now, I was standing over the man, looking down on him. He looked up at me and rolled his eyes inward, then slowly back again, and they were suddenly brown and normal.

Disturb by his changing glare and unsettling words, I demanded, "How do you know my name and tongue?"

He stood, still holding the fish over the flames, and we came face to face. He was a tall, thin man with a bony, fragile figure, and again his eyes glowed.

"I am your guardian spirit."

His look and words frightened me, and I jumped back from him. Was this some kind of evil spirit that Marcus had conjured up? For a fleeting moment, I had a notion to run back to the boat.

Finally, though, I gathered my courage and said in a strong voice, "I sought no guardian spirit. I am a Christian."

He smiled. "Yes, I know... It is your mother who sent me, not Marcus. The ship you seek has golden wings and will take you home."

His glowing eyes probed my soul with a fixed stare, and suddenly I had a sense of warmth and well-being. My fears vanished and my racing heart calmed.

"How will I find this river?"

"Look for a white feather and listen to your head. I will guide you. For now, you and your family should join me and eat this fish I have prepared."

With my head spinning with questions, I heard myself ask, "Are you an Indian spirit?"

He crouched down again, still holding the fish over the embers. "I am called many things, by many people. Your mother calls me a guardian angel, but I came to you in the form you would understand." Then, motioning his head towards my boat, he continued, "Gather your clan so we can eat."

Turning, I ran back across the wet sand to the dugout. This stranger seemed to possess me – not with fear, but with excitement and hope. Could my mother really be watching over me? Was this scruffy Indian truly my guardian angel? If he was, he could answer so many questions!

Reaching the boat, I told Mole and Raven that we had nothing to fear, and that the man had offered us food. They were pleased at the thought of a hot meal, and we pulled the boat farther up the beach.

As we gathered some of our belongings from the dugout, Mole asked, "What kind of Indian is he?"

"He is a great seer and chief," I answered.

"Is he a Clatsop?" Raven asked.

Looking into their curious faces, I didn't know how to answer. "No, he is from a different nation."

Then we turned from the canoe and walked towards the smoke. But what our eyes gazed upon was a fire without the stranger. The Indian and his fish had vanished from the beach in a whirl of blowing sand.

He was not real. He could not save me. He was just a dream…

…squawk…squawk…

The loud squeal of a crying bird woke me.

With my mind still cloudy, I snapped open my eyes to find a fat seagull resting on the canoe's gunnels. As I moved my cramped body, the bird squawked again and then flew off.

Pulling back my robe, I quietly brought myself to a sitting position in the bottom of the bobbing dugout. It was morning, early morning, and thick blankets of gray still engulfed us. This fog had been with us for days, and we had spent two restless nights sleeping on the open ocean. And, each night, I had the same recurring dream about my guardian spirit. We were lucky be alive and still I dreamt of more divine guidance.

Glancing down the boat, I could see the broken struts that had once connected to our outrigger. Those sticks had snapped like twigs in a nightmare gale, three days ago.

Twisting my head, I saw Raven and the baby still sleeping under the tattered sail at the bottom of the hull. Next to them, curled up by what remained of our mast, was Mole in his sleeping robe. King Neptune had mauled us badly, and now we were hopelessly adrift, so I would not disturb them. They needed their rest.

With our departure from Tillamook Bay, we had sailed directly into a summer storm with precipitous seas and contrary winds. Turning the boat south, and lowering the sail, we paddled for hours straight into the curling ocean. The boat took the weather well, pounding through waves as the cold wind blew seawater across our hulls. With all of our strength, we worked the paddles to keep control of the boat. While inside the hull, we were bounced around like sticks in the surf.

Then, just before noon, the skies brightened and the winds abated. Stopping to bale out the boat, I noticed the swells were softening, and that we had lost sight of the coastline. So, with a fresh onshore flow, we raised the sail and changed course for the southeast.

By the time we raised land again, I had no notion of where we were. We must have passed the opening to Siletz Bay many miles before. What we sought now was another gap in the shoreline, another tribe to trade with, and a place to dry out and rest. Turning the boat south, we followed the coastline with the help of light and variable winds. A few hours later, we came to a large rocky headland, after which the land was straight, with rolling green sand dunes. A few miles south of the promontory, a narrow slit in the land came into view.

Lowering the sail, we paddled closer to the slit and found a small river flowing into the sea. Here we crossed the bar, with little difficulty. Once inside the limpid estuary, we raised the sail again and began to move upstream. Around the first bend in the river, not far from the bar, we came upon the first of many Indians villages that dotted the shoreline of this green and placid river.

The Indians here were called *Siuslaw,* and their looks and language were quite different from the northern tribes. The first thing I noticed was that they didn't practice head flattening, and their skin color was more bronze. At first, they were a little alarmed by our sailboat and by my red hair, but they warmed after we showed them my iron tips and knives. Then, using sign language, I told them we wanted to trade for otter pelts, and they agreed.

With night approaching, they offered us sleeping planks in their lodge, but I told them we would camp across the river. Their homes were dug deep into the ground and built with cedar planks. Passage in and out of the lodges was by ladder. Their headman explained, with signs, that each village was really just a large family compound, with an entire extended family living in one large room.

The men of the tribe didn't wear much, just a buckskin breechcloth and a strange-looking hat made of an animal hide. Most of the braves and the squaws had their hair braided and neither had any eyebrows. The woman wore capes and skirts of hides and maple bark. They also adorned themselves with strings of shells and colorful feathers. Both the men and woman had tattoo marks on their upper arms.

Seeing that, I showed them Raven's tattoo. They were stunned to see a bird on her shoulder, and many of them touched Raven's arm to see if the bird would fly away. Then I showed them my eagle, and they did the same with my tattoo. Soon, everyone was giggling and laughing. It was a wonderful way to break the tension. The Siuslaw's were a curious people but, because of the language barrier, we didn't get to know them well.

We camped on a sand spit, across the river, for two nights. Because of their unfamiliar tongue, I hadn't felt comfortable mingling with the Indians at night. But as we got to know them better, over the next few days, I found my fears were unwarranted. The Siuslaw's were an agreeable people, although they had some strange customs. The tribe wasn't a wealth-orientated society like the Tillamooks. When a man needed to cross the river, he would build a dugout and then just leave it on the shore, once he was on the other side. And when they went to war with the tribes upriver, the women would paddle the war canoes while the braves stood, using spears and clubs. And if any of these warriors fell into the water, they would likely die, as none of the Indians knew how to swim. But the people were a happy tribe, where the social unit – or what they called *the talking circle* – was the most important thing. For this and their friendly ways, I held them in high regard.

Less than a day's sail south of the Siuslaw tribe, we found another slit in the land. Flowing from this opening was the strong current of a major river. We tried to cross the bar twice, but were driven back each time by challenging currents and contrary winds. Finally, we retreated seaward to wait out the tide.

A few hours later, with an ebbing flow, we were able to paddle across the bar and into a large estuary that looked to be the confluence of two rivers. The tranquil watershed was vast and beautiful, teaming with fowl of countless sorts. The northern canal was wide and long, while the southern tributary looked narrow and slow, so we turned the boat north and raised the sail.

Not far up the river we came to a few dugouts fishing. Reefing the sail and coming abeam, we talked to the wide-eyed Indians. They told us that their tribe was called *Coquille* (pronounced Ko-Kel), and that the river was named *Coos*. As we signed with the trepid braves, Raven became excited as she recognized some Tolowa words mixed into their local language. She said this proved that we were getting close to her village. Also, she told me that 'Coos' was a Spanish word that meant *speak softly*. With the wary Indians glaring at my red whiskers, I told them we were from the Tillamook tribe and had come to the river to make trade. After some hesitation, they offered to take us to their main village, which was just below the mouth of the southern river.

We spent a few days trading with the Coquilles. They were much like the Siuslaw tribe in both dress and stature and, while their languages were similar, with a few added Tolowa words, we still had great difficulty understanding their tongue. But they were a friendly lot, and I gave the village chief a ride in our sailboat and the gift of an iron blade. In return, he gave us the use of a lean-to shed made of planks, and we shared all of our meals with his clan. As we got to know these people, they told me with signs that I was the first pale face to visit their tribe…but then I noticed that some villagers had scars on their faces from small pox. From these marks a differed story was told. One brave asked me, playfully, if all white men had red hair. I answered no, and told him it was a sign of great wisdom.

That first evening with the tribe, Mole gave a demonstration of his prowess with the bow and iron-tipped shafts, while I obliged by throwing my iron blades into tree trunks. Right away, the Indians realized the power of our weapons, and were eager to barter. In the end, they proved to be skilled traders and soon exhausted my wares. But as we sailed away, we had nine prime otter pelts and three beaver furs stowed in the bow of the big canoe. Trading with the Coquilles had been a profitable enterprise, and we made many new friends with the people who lived on the Coos River.

We had been forewarned of the river's undertows and contrary currents when crossing the bar on a flood tide. So, approaching the slit, we paddled hard in a northwest direction to avoid the rocky escarpment just south of the opening.

Once we were a mile seaward, we turned south and raised the sail. The blue ocean swells were long and shallow, and the weather cool but clear. As we sailed past a few deepwater rocks, I noticed they were without any birds. That seemed strange. Then the morning sky turned almost orange, and clouds in the south began to stack like firewood. That was stranger yet.

Soon the ocean turned sloppy, with the swells building and their tops curling. Then the wind died out to nothing. With a knot in my stomach,

I knew what was coming. We needed to find a harbor, or at least a cove, but the coastline we followed was tall, craggy cliffs with a shoreline of dangerous rocks. If a storm pushed us towards the shore, we might perish. Therefore, with our limp sail flapping, we paddled for the relative safety of deep water.

Just before noon, the variable winds shifted from the south, and the ocean began to boil. Turning the boat, we lowered the sail and drifted with the swells, which were pushing us north. Soon, black thunderclouds blocked the sun, turning day into night. Lightning flashes crackled across the horizon with deafening roars. These quick bolts of light pierced the murk and hurt my eyes. With a bitter cold tempest howling overhead, it started to rain big, cold raindrops that blew sideways, directly onto our faces.

This miserable weather reminded me of Cape Horn, and I feared the worst. At one point, I looked around to find us lost inside a dark haze of a squall. Straining my eyes, I looked for the distant coastline, but could not find it.

"Keep an eye out," I yelled into the wind. But I wasn't sure anyone could hear my words of caution over the clamorous gale. At the next flash of lightening and clap of thunder, I searched the boiling sea again for our position. That's when a tall sneaker wave crashed over the dugout on the port side, breaking apart the mast and snapping off the outrigger.

In that split second of being drenched with icy sea water, I saw Mole being catapulted into the ocean with the mast and sail. Then, with the powerful flow of crashing water, I let go of the tiller, and the boat nearly capsized. Quickly, I struggled to gain control again, and gazed with fear at Mole, who was thrashing about in the sea, entangled in the sail and floating masthead. Yelling for Raven to take the rudder, I ripped off my soaked buckskin shirt. Then, as she rushed to the tiller, I dove into the water and came up, gasping, just a few feet from the struggling lad.

Holding to the wreckage, with his brown round face full of fear, he yelled frantically, "Brother, my leg is tangled."

Looking around, I saw a rope still connecting the debris to the boat. Putting my knife in my mouth, I dove under water again and cut the rope holding his foot.

Once he was free, he grabbed onto the floating masthead, and I helped him to the dugout. As he swiftly pulled himself into the canoe, I pushed his wet butt aboard. Then, with my knife still in my mouth, I pushed off and cut the canvas from the masthead, and then pulled the cloth to the boat.

As I pulled myself aboard, I glanced out over the sea and caught my last distressing glimpse of our outrigger, bouncing on a distant gray swell. She was still floating upright, but too faraway for me to swim. The small boat was gone, along with almost all of our worldly possessions, and there wasn't a bloody thing I could do about it!

Our boat was full of water, and we were all soaked to our skins. So with daylight bright thunder still rolling across the sea, we quickly started to bale out the hull.

With the ocean leaping up at us, Raven and the baby got under the sail canvas for protection from the rain. While they shivered under the cloth, Mole and I steered and paddled the boat as best we could. As we bounced along, both of us squeezed out the sea water from our clothes and put on the seal skins to help keep dry. This had been a frightening event for all of us, and all we could do now was pray and try to keep control of the dugout.

For hours, we rode the swells deep into their gray valleys, only to be pushed by the winds and currents to their curling crests. Each time we reached the top of the swells, I twisted around, watching for another sneaker wave and trying to find land. But because of the rain squalls my view was bleak. Then, in the afternoon, the rain stopped and the skies brightened. Soon, the winds abated and the swells flattened. Finally, a warming sun darted from behind the clouds, and steam from our damp clothes began to fill the air. It was a wonderful feeling, as we were all soaked to the bone and weary of rowing.

With the improving weather, we stopped and searched the sea for any sign of land or our outrigger. We found neither, so we pulled out our sleeping robes and spread them in the sun to dry. We were exhausted, so we spent that first night watching the sunset, eating a cold meal and sleeping on the open ocean. When we arose, the next morning, the storm had been replaced by calm seas and a heavy shroud of dense fog. We made no progress on that second day, as we had no notion of which way to paddle. We were adrift and lost.

Slowly, I pulled myself to the seat next to the tiller and stretched out my legs. My mood was as gloomy as the fog, and I knew we had to get moving. But, without a compass, which way should we row? Glancing out to the vacant gray sea, I spotted a small leaf floating near the boat.

Using my paddle, I pulled the stern closer to the leaf, and then snatched it out of the water. It was just an ordinary leaf, but the sight of it had given me an idea. Looking up from my prize, I watched Mole shed his robe and then stand at the bow to relieve himself.

Once he was done, I asked, "How much drinking water do we have?"

Pulling back part of the canvas, he answered, "Half a bladder."

"Bring the bag and a small bowl to me."

As Mole moved down the boat with the bladder and bowl, Raven poked her head out from under the canvas and asked what was going on. I told her I had an idea and would need her help. With Mole sitting next to me at the tiller, I poured the bowl half-full of water and placed it on the bottom of the hull. Then I floated the leaf in the bowl. When Raven squatted next to us with the baby in her arms, I asked her if she still had a sail needle, and she nodded yes. Removing it from the inside of her buckskin top, she handed me a two-inch-long iron pin, which I rubbed in my dirty hair. Then, gently, I dropped the needle onto the floating leaf, and told Raven and Mole to be still. We all stared at the bowl with wide eyes, as if magic was about to happen.

And it did. With the needle resting on the leaf, it slowly twisted to a different position in the water. Then it stopped.

Pointing in the direction of the needle, I said, "That is north." Then I pointed my other hand 90 degrees away. "And that is east. We will row in that direction."

They both gazed up at me with strange looks on their faces, but then, without questioning my 'magic,' they agreed. So, after a quick meal of elk jerky, we started to paddle, using the leaf and needle as our compass. Long ago, my mother had taught me about this simple compass after reading an article by Benjamin Franklin about magnetic poles. I silently thanked my guardian angel for bringing it back to my mind just when I needed it most.

We rowed for hours in a fog so thick we couldn't see much beyond the boat. The only sounds we heard were our oars in the water and our own heavy breathing. It was an eerie paddle, as if we weren't moving at all. Every few hours, we would take a break and listen carefully for any distant sounds. During these respites, we talked of many things: the provisions we had lost, the damage to our boat, and how we had escaped death from an unforgiving sea. At one point, Mole thanked me again for pulling him out of the water, and said he was still having dreams about drowning. I told him that, once we got to dry land, I would teach him and Raven how to swim. Something I should have done many months before.

At another stop, he asked a curious question. "If your bewitched needle tells you which direction to row, why can't you use your powers to blow away this mist?"

I remembered posing a question like that to Sandy, aboard the Orphan, and I used his answer. "A sailor can use the wind, but not make it blow."

As we got underway again, I asked Raven how the baby was doing.

Twisting back to me, with a paddle in her hand, she answered, "Your son born with sea legs. He say almost nothing in big wind."

"He'll be an old salt after this passage," I said, pulling back on my scull.

"Aye," she answered, "soon we be home."

A few hours later, we heard the faint sounds of lapping waves.

Stopping the boat, I tried to judge the distance and direction of the sounds, and then proceeded with caution. After a few hundred yards of rowing, through the gloom appeared the ghostly outline of a gigantic rock. With waves curling at its jagged base, the monolith looked threatening, and we stopped again.

"I know that rock!" Raven shouted. "It guards our bay."

"Are you sure? Which way should we row?" I asked with excitement.

Pointing south, wearing a grin from ear to ear, she said gleefully, "Short row that way and then turn inland."

Some moments later, I turned the boat east. Within a few paddles, the fog slowly started lifting, eventually revealing a clear blue sky, a sandy shore and the gentle green waters of a crescent bay. With a single white feather floating down from the sky and landing next to me at the tiller, I knew Raven was home, and we were safe. God bless my guardian angel!

Bittersweet

Entering the lagoon beneath a warm, bright sun, I noticed a narrow wooden pier built out from the shore. Up from this wharf was a log fort. Across a dusty lane stood two buildings; one was made of logs, and the other looked to be wood-framed. The Tolowa village was situated on the other side of the garrison, next to a river that drained into the bay. It was a picturesque hamlet of about fifty lodges, built on a verdant terrace with tall, green mountains as a backdrop. Resting on the shoreline were many large, flat-bottomed canoes that were square at both ends, made from a wood that was almost blood red.

As we beached our boat near the hamlet, a few curious onlookers gathered, but no large crowds. I jumped from the canoe, asking Mole to stay with the boat and watch Dutch while Raven and I walked to her village.

Along our path there were a few children playing, and we heard some barking dogs. Behind the village, I could see a grassy knoll, with a few hobbled horses grazing. It was a charming native setting. The Indian huts were built of split planks of the same redwood as the canoes, and were octagonal in construction. The Indians themselves were not flat heads, and both the men and the woman wore little clothing. They were tall in stature, with bronze skin, but their black hair was not as shiny as Raven's.

As we walked through the village, Raven stopped and talked to a few people she recognized. She was warmly received and hugged by many. Finally, we were joined by what I guessed was the chief, as he had woodpecker feathers in his hair and wore a necklace of whale teeth. He was an old brave with a wrinkled face, and his black hair was braided with streaks of gray. Raven greeted him cordially, and they talked for a few minutes in words I could not understand. Then, suddenly, Raven started weeping and dropped to her knees. Instantly, I came to her side and helped her to her feet.

With tears running down her cheeks, she sobbed, "My mother is dead!"

"What of your brother?" I asked.

Turning to the chief, she asked my question in a broken voice. After his answer, she turned to me, shaking her head. "He in mountains with renegades."

Putting my arms around her, I looked into her sad face. "We will search him out."

The chief invited us to his lodge, where his squaw served us a meal of fish and greens. His house was one room, with a large fire pit and a hole in the roof for the smoke. As we ate, Raven and the chief talked, and she translated their words for me. First, she told him of how she had been taken and enslaved by the Siletz, and how I had rescued her, many years later, from the Tillamooks. He listened quietly but never looked my way.

The chief's name was Black Crow, and I could tell from his body language that something was wrong. After Raven had completed her story, the old man told us that he had been chief for many moons, and had seen many things. Raven's mother had died two seasons back, after being mauled by a bear while gathering berries. Raven's brother, Badger, had taken the news of his mother's death badly and had become rebellious. He started stealing and getting into fights with other young braves. Finally, the chief stepped in and banished him from the tribe. At that, Badger set fire to his mother's lodge and went away. Black Crow had heard he was running with a band of renegades up on a mountain named Buzzard Peak. He said this group was bad medicine.

During this story, the old chief didn't look my way once. Finally, through Raven, I asked him about the Spanish fort and the trading post.

At that, he scowled at me over the small fire in the pit, and asked why my hair was bloody.

As a surprised Raven told me his question, she reached over and rubbed her hands in my dirty hair, then showed the chief her bloodless palms. He grunted, still staring at me with an annoyed look. Then he told us that the Spaniards were the masters of the land, and that soldiers had long ago tamed the Indians with their fire-sticks. These days, everyone lived in peace, so the soldiers were no longer needed. The trading post was for all the tribes, a place to trade hides for iron goods and blankets, food and spirits. He said the Spanish had even brought their god to his people, in the stories told by a priest named Mendez. Now, most all of the Tolowa people had become Christians, and everyone was happy. But when I asked if we could stay amongst his people, he abruptly said no, and that we should move on. Raven tried to find out why he felt that way, but he would not say. He simply made it clear that we were not welcome.

When we left the chief's lodge, I knew our long journey had been in vain. Now, all we could do was move farther south, down the coast. To do that, however, we would have to make repairs to the boat, and trade for fresh supplies.

We walked back to our dugout to get the only trade goods we had, the pelts from the Coquilles. Reaching the boat, we talked of our cold reception and decided to move the canoe away from the village, to the other side of the pier. Here we would be closer to the Spanish compound and could camp on the beach while searching for Badger. In the warm sun, we paddled down the bay, past the dock, and carried the dugout to a grassy knoll. Then we all worked at emptying the boat and turning it sideways as a lean-to, with our paddles holding it up. After Raven had fed the baby, we walked towards the trading post with our pelts, while Mole remained behind to finish the camp and look after Dutch.

The fort was in bad disrepair. Most of the vertical log walls tilted from the winds, and the main gate had fallen to the ground. Its size was large, and I could see a few cabins inside the ramparts, but we didn't go in.

Across from the fort was a white-washed, wood-framed church, with one window above the front door and a small steeple on the roof ridge. It glistened in the sun and was in good repair. Next to the parish was a large log building with a narrow front porch and hitching post. There were no windows in the cabin, and no sign outside saying whether it was a trading post. It was a shabby looking structure, with a damaged roof and log walls that had not been chinked.

As we approached, I noticed a horse and a mule tied to the hitch. A few moments later, a squaw came out, carrying supplies. She was a chunky Indian, dressed in dirty, tattered buckskins. We walked by as she was loading the mule, and I saw that her face was full of sweat and sadness.

Climbing the porch, I opened the door and we entered the cabin. The inside was dark and dusty, and it smelt sour. The only light came from the many cracks in log walls. At the far end of the dim room was a tall counter made of planks resting on large wooden barrels.

Standing at this make-shift table were two men. The one on our side looked to be a mountain man, as he was big and burly, with a head full of brown hair. He was drinking from a pewter mug.

Across from him was a rawboned man, dressed in a dirty white apron. He had short, black, curly hair and a swarthy complexion. Both men twisted our way as we walked in. When we got to the counter, I took our bundle of pelts and put them on the planks.

Then, turning to Raven I said, "Tell them in Spanish that we are here to trade for supplies."

Instantly, the skinny fellow moved down the counter to our pelts. "I be Virgil, and I speak some English."

"Give the breed some rum first, so he won't faint from your prices," the burly trapper chuckled with a French accent.

With the clerk now standing in front of me, I got a better look at his face, and saw that he was part Negroid.

"Where ye get these pelts?" the shopkeeper asked while looking through my pile.

"From the Coquilles, up the coast," I answered.

"Never heard of them redskins," the mountain man slurred, and drank some more from his mug.

"They are fine pelts," the clerk replied. "What are your needs?"

"Food, some tools and gunpowder," I answered quickly.

The room fell silent for a moment. Then both men started laughing loudly.

Gleefully, the trapper said, "I told you he would need some rum."

"What did I say?" I asked.

The skinny clerk looked at me with a big grin. "We don't trade gunpowder with Indians. It's against the law."

"I'm no Indian," I shot back, "I'm an American, and my woman here is half Spanish."

The clerk's face turned serious. "You come in here dressed like a breed… then you are a breed."

We were a shabby-looking couple, with my cougar tooth necklace, our filthy buckskins, stained white with dried sea salt. And our faces were dirty, and my unkempt whiskers and hair were long and tangled. But I was no breed.

"Have you ever seen an Indian with red hair? Or one that speaks English?" I demanded, with eyes afire and anger in my voice.

The clerk slowly reached under his side of the table, brought out a pistol and set it on my pile of pelts.

"If you're no breed, then you have no rights to these hides. The Spanish Crown controls all the fur trade around here, so I'm confiscating your pelts, in the name of King Carlos."

My gut flared up with ire, and I put my hand on the empty pistol in my belt. As I did so, the mountain man quickly reached to his side, pulled up his musket and pointed it at me.

"No need to die for a few skins, lad," the man said, with a fixed glare.

"The padre will be here soon," the clerk added. "He will decide the fate of your pelts. Until then, they will be safe with me."

Raven put her hand on my shoulder and whispered, "Let's go, Joe. I know Father Mendez. He be a fair man. No fight for furs."

The walk back to the canoe was slow and quiet. The Tolowa chief had rejected us, and now the Spaniards had stolen my pelts. Bringing Raven home had been a disastrous notion, and my heart was full of fury.

That afternoon, we walked to a creek behind the Spanish compound, where we took baths and washed our clothes. Then Raven cut my hair and trimmed my beard with the hunting knife. I would not be thought of as a breed again.

It was late afternoon by the time we retuned to camp. With the skies clear and the offshore fog burnt off, Mole built a fire and rolled some log snags around our pit. Then we ate a meal of elk jerky, greens and dried berries. We were all exhausted, after two nights on the open ocean, and soon our sleeping robes were on. We talked awhile and watched the setting sun light up a brilliant crimson sky.

Mole was the first to slip under the canoe and sleep upon the sail, quickly followed by Raven and the baby. With my body tired but my mind racing, I awaited a star-studded sky by putting more wood on the fire. Soon, I had Becky's locket in hand. Snapping open the cover, I looked at her likeness in the flicking firelight. I'd been gone for over three years now, and I still had nothing. Over fifty prime pelts and all my tools had been lost in gale, so I had only anger and frustration to show for my years of labor.

Just as those thoughts swept through my mind, Raven stirred under the canoe. Looking her way, I realized that the gloom of self-pity had raised its ugly head again. I had a son, a good woman and a blood-brother that I loved very much. I wasn't poor. No, I was rich! With all due haste, we would find Raven's brother and leave this place with supplies or my pelts, even if I had to steal them back.

Skunk Creek

The next morning, I was awakened by a shake from an Indian boy. As soon as I opened my eyes, he started talking in words I couldn't understand. Getting to my feet, I found my robe covered with heavy dew and the sun already up behind the mountains. I had slept all night with my back resting on a snag next to the fire pit. Looking around the camp, with the boy still chattering, I found it empty, and guessed that Mole and Raven had gone in search of food. Finally, the boy reached out and pulled at my hand while saying, "Father Mendez," over and over. He wanted me to come with him. Quickly getting dressed, I kept shaking my head *yes* to the lad.

The boy led me to the church, and we went in. The inside of the parish was murky, with the only light coming from a small, round window above the front door. The room held a dozen rows of short bench-seats on each side of a center aisle. At the far end of the room was the altar, behind which was a large log cross, hanging on the back wall. The boy pointed for me to take a front bench and then disappeared through a small door at the rear of the room.

Taking the seat, I smelt a sweet fragrance, and then noticed all the unlit candles behind the altar. The wooden cross on the wall was beautiful, as it had graceful lines and was wonderfully carved. *This might be just a wilderness church*, I thought, *but it is also inspiring.*

Then the rear door opened and a tall, large man dressed in a brown monk's flock with a white rope belt walked through.

As he came towards me, I stood up and said angrily, "What right has the Spanish government to confiscate my skins?"

He said nothing, and we came face to face.

When we had looked at each other for a moment, he said in a gentle tone, "Good morning, my son. Please forgive my English. It has been years since I spoke it last. I'm Father Mendez. And you would be…?"

Still angry, I replied, "I would be Joe Blackwell from Boston, and I demand that my furs be returned."

He grinned. "I can see you're a determined young lad, Joe, but I'm not your enemy. How did you come by these pelts?"

The Father had a stoic face with a chiseled chin, but there was kindness in his eyes. His hair was brown, cut close to his scalp, and I guessed he was middle aged. He had a huge, muscular body and wore a small silver cross around his thick neck. His giant size and the tiny crucifix seemed at odds with each other.

"I traded for them with the Coquille Indians, up the coast." I quickly answered.

"This is a tribe I haven't heard of. How many leagues north from here?"

Shaking my head with frustration, I harshly answered, "I don't know. A hundred or more. What difference does it make?"

His hazel eyes softened as he smiled. "A big difference. My sovereign King Carlos III has claim to all of the lands and people, including the fur trade, north of San Francisco. But that sovereignty stops forty leagues north of here. So, my son, you may have your skins back. The crown has no lien on them."

Just like that, the incident was over, and my rage slipped away. Then Father Mendez disarmed me further by inviting me to join him for a morning meal.

We ate at a table on the back porch of the church. He had a squaw who cared for his needs, and she served us hot coffee, biscuits and blackberry jam. To be eating bread and tasting coffee again after two years… I could not believe my good fortune. I devoured both, much to the delight of the watchful padre.

Over our meal, I told him of my ordeal at Tillamook Bay, the gale that had taken our supplies, and the recurring vision of my guardian angel. He listened carefully and asked many questions. Then he asked of my family, both white and Indian. When I told him about Raven and the baby, his face lit up like a candle, and he said he remembered baptizing her. When I told him about the death of Raven's mother and how the brother had ran off to be a renegade, he offered to send a runner in search of him. Then he told me not to worry about Black Crow and my cold reception, as the chief hated all *gringos*, including the Spanish.

Farther Mendez was much like Captain Gray, easy to talk with and a man that demanded respect. As I finished my third biscuit, I asked about the supplies, including gunpowder, that I could trade my pelts for.

"I will give instructions to Virgil. He will trade you one horn of gunpowder for one prime pelt. You'll have to haggle with him for the rest of your needs. But once you have your goods and tools, what are your intentions?"

"Sail for San Francisco," I replied. "Then find a ship and passage home."

The monk looked at me with doleful eyes, and shook his head. "That would be unwise, as my government would slap you in irons and ship you to Madrid as a Yankee spy. And then they would enslave your family, as well. No, Joe, politically your timing is wrong."

We talked of this problem and of the world news for a while, without any real resolution. Then, changing the subject, he told me to take the remaining four biscuits back to camp for my family. As I gathered them up, he also invited my family to come for a meal after his evening mass. I quickly accepted.

Finally, he asked a strange question. "Do you play chess, Joe?"

Standing with the biscuits in my pouch, I answered, "My mother taught me many years ago, so I remember the game poorly."

"Good." He smiled. "I love to win."

We attended Catholic mass, late that afternoon – something I had never done before. I sat next to Raven, holding our baby, and marveled at the glee on her face, while Mole waited outside, fearful of coming into the Spanish church. Father Mendez was a forceful speaker, filling the crowded room with his booming voice. Because of the Latin and Tolowa language used throughout, it was a ceremony as alien to me as most of the Tillamook rituals. Still, I was pleased that it had such a deep meaning for Raven.

After the mass, the padre and my family rounded to the rear of the church, where we were served foods that had been long lost to my taste. His squaw made a rich onion soup in a tasty broth, and she passed around platters of pork, apples, cheese and bread. The meal reminded me of our farewell dinner aboard the Columbia; the only thing missing was the spirits. As we ate, Father Mendez held Dutch in his arms, and talked with Raven in Spanish for the longest time. He seemed to be a genuine man with a caring soul, and I was pleased we had found him.

After thanking the padre for the delightful meal, my clan returned to camp with the setting sun, but I stayed behind. Knowing that darkness would soon be upon us, Father Mendez lit an oil lamp on the porch table and asked me to set up the hand-carved wooden chess set he brought out. While I scratched my head, trying to remember the rules of this long-forgotten game, he disappeared into his sleeping quarters and returned with a box of cigars and a clay jug. Sitting down across from me, he smiled his approval of the board and then offered me a cigar. While I lit the tobacco in the chimney of the oil lamp, he made his first move with a pawn.

In the harsh light of the lamp, we played chess for hours, and the padre won every game. Over our play, we talked politics and religion, with the conversation well-oiled by cigars and brandy from his jug. I told him more of my plight with Captain Gray, and my deep desire to find a ship home. He was surprised to learn that I wanted to blend my Indian family with my Boston clan, and he worried about the outcome. And, again, he expressed his concern about us moving farther down the coast.

"Your timing just isn't right, Joe. My government and yours are at odds over this land and the fur trade. If you move south, you'll endanger your family."

Then Father Mendez told me a little more about himself. He had been a Franciscan monk for over fifteen years, serving three coastal Indian villages and trading posts. His monastery was in San Francisco, and he traveled north to his villages every few months with a pack train of mules carrying trade goods and returning with pelts. These skins were collected from all over the area and then shipped from San Francisco to the Philippines. The pelts were then traded to the Chinese for tea and other goods that were shipped back to Spain. This trade was big business for King Carlos, and the local monks were the enforcers to keep the supply of skins flowing.

"I thought a priest saved souls, not pelts," I said, lighting my second cigar.

He grinned at me in the flickering light. "Honestly, I care more for the Indians than the skins. But without this trade, we couldn't bring the savages to Christ."

His English was good, with a little Tory twang, so I asked where he learned the language. He said his father had been the Spanish ambassador to the English Crown for many years, and that he had been educated there. After his eighteenth birthday, he had joined the Spanish navy and become a ship's officer.

"It's a big leap from stripes to a monk's frock," I said with curiosity.

"Aye. I spent many years in the fleet, and watched in horror the brutality of the admirals. Then I was sent to South America, where my government enslaved the natives in gold mines under such horrible conditions that thousands died. This treatment was unacceptable to me, and so, much to the chagrin of my family, I resigned my commission and returned to Madrid, where I joined the Franciscans. Then, as an act of retribution, the crown sent me out here. This is my penance, and here I will die."

The priest's story enthralled me and answered many questions. Farther Mendez was a gentle giant with a sharp wit and a nimble mind.

Just as he check-mated my king for the third time, he said, "It's getting late, Joe, and you're getting better with every game, so it's time to quit."

Standing, I stretched out my hand. "Thanks for your kindness, Father. It was a wonderful evening. Now all I have to do is figure out our future."

Grasping my hand, he replied, "Tonight, I learned you're a bright lad, and your woman tells me that you're a good man, so maybe I can help. Come by again, late tomorrow, and we'll talk of it."

The next day, I went back to the trading post and exchanged one prime pelt for a horn of gunpowder. The skinny clerk's attitude towards me had greatly warmed; he offered me rum, and we talked. Virgil turned out to be a Cajun from New Orleans who had worked for the Spanish on the Mississippi River. He told me that there were many Indian tribes in the area, along with a few white trappers and prospectors. "There is gold in the streams and silver in the mountains. This wilderness may be raw, but it has riches for the taking," Virgil told me with a Creole accent. Then, pouring a little more rum into my mug, he tried to trade for the balance of my furs. Instead, I took my pelts back to camp, not yet knowing our destiny.

When I arrived back at the boat, Mole told me that the runner Father Mendez sent out had returned with Badger. The brother and sister had been having a tearful reunion while I retrieved our skins, and now they were walking together on the shoreline.

An hour later, when they returned, Raven introduced me to Badger. He was a young brave, about the same age as Mole, and his body was lean, tall and muscularly built. He wore only a breechcloth, moccasins, and a feather in his hair. His chin was square and his brown eyes deep set and close together. And, much like his sister, Badger was honey-fleshed. The lad was an unusually handsome Indian.

With Raven translating, we talked while sitting around the camp fire. Badger's body language was dour, much like that of Black Crow, and he seldom looked me in the eye. He asked about where we had come from and where we were going. When I told him we might return north to live with the Coquilles, he angrily demanded that Raven remain with him.

"What of our papoose?" I asked.

After my question was translated, he spoke his answer to Raven, but she hesitated telling me.

"What did he say?" I inquired.

With sadness in her face, she turned to me and said, "He say, 'Gringo baby half-breed, but he can stay with mother."

With his rude answer, I glared at him across the flames, trying to hold down my rage. All I could think was, *He sits in my camp and insults my family? This will not stand.*

Turning to Raven, I said sharply, "You telling him this, word for word. If he ever calls my son a half-breed again, I will kill him where he stands. Dutch is our child, and the only 'breed' in him comes from your family!"

Then, jumping up from fire, I stomped out of camp. A few minutes later, Raven caught up with me, walking the beach. With tearful eyes, she apologized for her brother's cruel words, and begged me to take Badger with us.

This was a bitter notion, one that I would have to ponder.

Late that afternoon, I rounded the rear of the church to find Father

Mendez reading his bible at the table. He greeted me warmly and invited me to join him. As I climbed the porch, I could see two half-full panniers, a long rife and a pack saddle resting on the planks. When I took a seat across from the padre, he closed the bible and fixed his gaze on me.

"I want to tell you a story, Joseph," the padre said in a strong voice. "It's about a man named Jeremiah Jacobson. He came from your land, a place called St. Louis, many years ago. He lived with the Plains Indians for a few seasons and took a woman. Soon after, they traveled west, until they came to a range of snow-capped mountains that were as tall as the sky, stretching for as long as they could see. There, they turned south, in an autumn of warm days and cool nights. Months later, in a bitter-cold blizzard, a local trapper found them, near frozen to death, and brought them to me. I nursed them back to health with prayers, broth, and strong spirits. They were good people who had trekked across the continent in search of the same thing you now seek – a future. Once they were on their feet again, Jeremiah built a fine cabin up on Skunk Creek, and he taught himself to trap. They prospered for many years here, hunting the mountains and trading skins. I baptized both of them and married them in my church. Then, two years ago, his wife died of the pox. Jeremiah took her death poorly, and I traveled many times to his cabin to console him. Slowly, he recovered, but it was if a candle had been snuffed out inside of him, and I never got it lit again. Then, this spring, as Jeremiah was riding out with his winter pelts, he was ambushed by some renegades. As he galloped away, the Indians gave chase, and he was shot by a few arrows. When he arrived here, he was near death. Virgil did the best he could for him, but by the time I arrived from San Francisco, he had died. After giving him a Christian burial, I gave his horses to the Indians and took his pelts back for the church. What remains here," he gestured toward the baskets, "is his kit. I want you to have his trappings. Maybe you and your family can make a life here, where you will be safe."

The tragic story – and his kindness – caught me off guard, and I felt my mouth hanging open. Quickly getting to my feet, I knelt by the panniers and looked at the contents. One held clothes, blankets and a canvas tarp, while the other had camping supplies, two hunting knifes, and a pistol with two horns of gunpowder. Lifting the resting rifle, I noticed its heavy weight and felt its long barrel.

"Jeremiah told me that the rifle had been specially built for mountain men, and that it could drop a buck from a great distance," the padre added, as I ran my hands down the barrel.

A chance to possess a rifle and another pistol? I could not believe my good luck.

Father Mendez went on to say he would draw a map to Jeremiah's cabin for me, and that he would sell me a mule for ten pelts that I could pay next spring.

Sitting back down at the table, still holding the rifle, I asked, "Why are you doing this for me, Father?"

He lit a stub of a cigar, and answered through blue smoke. "If you're close, I can tell you when it's safe to travel to San Francisco. And I want to marry you and Raven, next year, so your son will not be called a bastard." Then, sliding his black book to me, he continued, "But first I want you to read Jeremiah's bible. It will enlighten you on the spirit of life and marriage. I gave him this testament, many years ago, and I've written about his life and death inside the cover. It's printed in English, so you can read it to your family."

The notion of living in a moderate climate, in a cabin already built, was appealing beyond belief, and no one would ever call *my* son a bastard, so I quickly agreed. Then we prayed together, with our hands on Jeremiah's bible. After that, over a few spirits, we talked a long while about finding Skunk Creek and surviving this harsh wilderness. Stunned by my good fortune, I had to wonder whether mother had somehow sent this priest to me.

A few days later, my family and I were trekking up a path like pilgrims alongside the crooked river that flowed next to the Tolowa village. The mule that Father Mendez had sold to us was loaded with the two now-full panniers as well as some other supplies for which we had traded our pelts. Walking with the mule, each of us also carried rawhide packs containing the balance of our goods. We had been told that the distance to Jeremiah's cabin was two days on foot, so we kept up a brisk march. The trail we trudged had a gentle uphill slope, next to the lazy green river with tall fir trees on each side. The weather was warm and bright, and the trail was well-marked, so we were making good time.

I had surrendered to Raven's pleas, so Badger was with us, but only after we'd had another powwow and he fully understood that I was the headman. He was a troubled lad, with his life just blowing in the breeze, and I wasn't sure I trusted him. Therefore, Mole carried the extra pistol, while I had the rifle and the other flintlock.

Along our way, we forded many creeks and rills, and by noon we came to the fork in the river that we had been looking for. Here we turned down the southern tributary and soon found ourselves in a forest of the biggest, tallest redwood trees I had ever seen. We had been forewarned that the forest was the perfect place for a renegade ambush, so we moved quietly with our weapons at ready. Silently walking across the forest floor, I kept bending my gaze upward to where the crowns of the redwood trees blocked the sunlight into an eerie emerald haze. I had thought the firs of the Tillamooks were giants, but these redwoods dwarfed them, many times over. These towering, magnificent sentinels reminded me of the power of Mother Nature, and of how insignificant man truly was.

Late in the afternoon, we came out of the forest to find a long blue lake, nestled between two mountains, which was the headwater of the creek we had followed. Here we spent the night, eating fresh lake fish and wild berries while watching a light show of shadows from the setting sun dance across the tall, rocky cliffs of the far mountain.

The next morning, we walked the southern shore of the lake for miles, until we came to a fast-moving creek from the southeast. This was Skunk Creek. Here we turned up the flow and followed the stream for another few miles. As the stream narrowed into a granite gorge, we came around a bend…and there before us was the cabin, resting on a grassy, elevated terrace just above the creek.

Stopping in our tracks, with an eagle soaring high above the vista, we surveyed the beauty of this perfect setting. The cabin was built of fir logs and was oblong in shape, with a rock chimney at the far end. The wall facing the creek had a door made of wooden planks, with windows on either side that were closed with shutters. The shingled hip roof was tall and looked to be weather-tight. Behind the cabin was a large grove of maple trees, their colorful autumn leaves rustling in a breeze. On the far side of the house, we could see a corral and a small stable for the animals.

With the afternoon sun glistening off the fast-flowing creek and the gold and crimson backdrop of the maple leaves, it was an extraordinary sight to behold. We had found Jeremiah's cabin and maybe, in time, our own future.

Moving to Raven, I gave her and Dutch an embrace and simply said, "Our family is home."

Chapter Ten: Five Cents an Acre

FAR FROM THE RUGGED BEAUTY OF THE Pacific coast, many mighty nations jockeyed for control of the Indian lands and all their great resources. Russia laid claim to the far northern territories; Great Britain sought sovereignty over the northwest coast. Spain protected her lands north of Mexico, on a large swath of land that would become known as California. On the eastern continent, the American states and territories stretched from the Atlantic Ocean to the Mississippi River while, just across the shores of that mighty river, was an expansive area known as the Louisiana Territory. This large region of land – owned first by France, then by Spain, then by France again – extended from the Mississippi River to the Rocky Mountains. This land blocked America's westward expansion and, because Spain also owned New Orleans, they controlled the commerce on the vital Mississippi River.

The United States didn't appreciate having European powers on its western flank. It wanted to acquire New Orleans, primarily to guarantee its right of commerce down the Mississippi River, through Spanish territory, and its right to unload goods at New Orleans for shipment to the Atlantic coast and Europe. Moreover, the United States wanted to open the entire territory of Louisiana, both because so many American settlers and merchants were already living in the domain and because of its vital geographic position.

Through a secret treaty in 1800, Spain ceded Louisiana to France once again. Napoleon Bonaparte, the future Emperor, envisioned a great French empire in the New World, and he hoped to use the Mississippi Valley as a center of food and trade in order to supply the island of Hispaniola, which was to be the heart of this new empire. First, however, he had to restore French control of Hispaniola, where Haitian slaves had seized power. In 1802, Napoleon sent a large army to suppress the Haitian rebellion. However, despite some military successes, the French lost thousands of soldiers, mainly to yellow fever, and Napoleon soon realized that Hispaniola would have to be abandoned. Without that island nation, he had little use for Louisiana. Facing a renewed war with Great Britain, he could not spare troops to defend the Louisiana Territory, and he needed funds to support his military ventures in Europe. Accordingly, in April 1803, he offered to sell all of Louisiana to the United States.

Concerned about French intentions, President Thomas Jefferson (the third American president) had already sent James Monroe and Robert R. Livingston to Paris to attempt to negotiate the purchase of New Orleans and the surrounding land on the lower Mississippi or, at least, a guarantee of free navigation on the river. Surprised and delighted by the French offer of the entire territory, the U.S. immediately negotiated a treaty.

That treaty was ratified on Apr. 30, 1803, enabling the United States to purchase from France the Louisiana Territory, which encompassed more than 800,000 square miles. The price was 60 million francs, or about 15 million dollars.

The Louisiana Territory, purchased for less than 5 cents an acre, was one of Thomas Jefferson's greatest contributions to his young country. Louisiana doubled the size of the United States literally overnight, without a war or the loss of a single American life. It set a precedent for future purchases of territories, and opened the way for the eventual expansion of the United States across the entire continent to the Pacific. First, however, these newly purchased lands had to be explored and mapped, and so Congress organized and funded the Lewis and Clark Expedition, an overland journey to the Pacific. After this expedition, opportunity after opportunity opened for the fledgling American nation. The Louisiana Purchase proved to be the crowning achievement for this young republic and its soon-to-be-famous president, Thomas Jefferson.

Seasons

As a young jack-tar aboard the Orphan, one of my watch duties was to monitor the time glass that swung beneath the compass head. Just as the sands ran out, I would twist the glass again and ring the ship's bell so that all would know the time. In those rolling, lonely waters, this passage of time always seemed to slip slowly by like the vastness of the sea itself. But now, as I look back, those sands raced through the glass with no regard for my longevity. Time was much like the Continental Dollar given to me by Captain Gray; only I could spend it wisely.

We had learned from Father Mendez that the local Indians avoided Skunk Creek, as they believed it was a place with evil spirits. Many years before, a local chief and three braves had hunted up the creek's gorge and were lost forever. The local tribes searched for their bodies, but they were never found. Now, all the Indians told stories of an evil, flesh-eating creature that lived on the creek, devouring anyone foolish enough to hunt the ravine. Because of this myth, Jeremiah had selected Skunk Creek for his home, so that he and his wife would be safe from the Indians.

His cabin was strongly built and full of unexpected treasures. The padre had told me of his tools, but there was much, much more. His pantry was stocked with abundant staples, as well as pans, plates, mugs and eating utensils. And then there were his clothes and his wife's garments. We found blankets and robes and even a buffalo-fur mattress on a large, sturdy, wood-framed bed. He had snowshoes, waterproof moccasins and a buffalo coat that weighed heavily on my shoulders. Going through the dead trapper's things was a little macabre, but I reconciled those feelings by knowing that all his abundance would be put to good use.

The biggest prize we found was a written journal about his trap lines, complete with crude maps and tips for luring his prey. With the help of that account, and the sharp jaws of his iron traps, we were soon collecting beaver and otter pelts.

That first winter on Skunk Creek was a learning experience for us all. I taught myself and the lads, Mole and Badger, how to trap and hunt in a wilderness that was foreign to us, and how to survive the brutally cold weather. As we men toiled in the forest, Raven got the dirty squaw jobs of curing the pelts, watching over our child and cooking stout meals.

Then there was the language problem. Early on, I let it be known that only English would be spoken inside the cabin. This meant that the always irritable Badger was silent for the first few months, but soon he came around to my notion and began talking in my tongue. There was a reason for this: I wanted my two-year-old son to learn his language first and relate it to his culture.

During that first snowy season, life wasn't always gloomy. On many evenings, I would read aloud from Jeremiah's Bible and embellish the stories. Raven and the boys loved this oral pastime, as storytelling was deep rooted in their tradition. They asked many gleeful questions about my tales: What is a camel? Where did Adam and Eve come from? Why was the apple forbidden? My Bible readings were always enjoyable. And, to be honest, I learned many things from this long-forgotten book.

In the evenings, after the lads had gone to their loft and Dutch was asleep, Raven and I would sit next to the fire and spend time together. It was during these moments, over mugs of coffee, that I started teaching her to read and write.

My first lesson was her name and how to draw the individual letters. She worked hard, learning how to hold the charcoal and form her characters. Her first tries were splotchy and crude, but finally she got her letters right and showed me her parchment.

"I write just like you, under bird tattoo," she said proudly.

"Aye, and now the power of the word will tell people of you."

She thought for a moment, gazing upon the crackling fire, and then turned to me. "Why is this needed?"

Smiling, I replied, "So that, someday, people will tell stories about you from books."

"So I will be in black book you read?" she asked with a curious innocence.

"Yes, something like that," I answered with a grin. "But you'll need more than just your name for a story."

Raven's face lit up with a smile as she dreamt of great stories being told about her life.

In the middle of April, we trekked out of the mountains with twenty-two pelts on the back of the mule. My plan was to pay off Father Mendez and then acquire enough supplies for the coming summer. Over the winter, I had also decided that repairing the boat was an imperative task because, if the Spanish sent soldiers again, we would then have a way to flee.

When we arrived at the compound, Virgil informed me that Father Mendez did not plan to be back until the end of the month. So I traded my pelts with Virgil, and then we all began to work on the canoe, enjoying the warm spring sunshine.

By the end of the month, the boat had been scraped and sealed with three fresh coats of lacquer, and we had made a new mast from redwood. While the boys and I accomplished these tasks, Raven sewed a new lug sail, made of canvas from the trading post. When she was done, we rigged the sail with a new yard, boom, ropes and pulleys. Then, with Badger sitting next to me at the tiller, I gave the lad his first sailing lesson while we cruised around the crescent bay. When the new, bigger sail filled with a fresh breeze, the Thunderbird responded quickly by gliding across the placid waters at a greater speed than ever before.

With wind in his hair, Badger turned to me with a rare smile and gleefully said, "Your gringo bird fast. I become fine Indian sailor."

"Aye," I replied, "but first you will learn to swim. This, I will teach you at the lake this summer."

Badger had proven his worth in hunting and trapping, but his moods were always as dark as rain squalls. Maybe teaching him to sail and swim would help me forge a bond with this gloomy lad.

The padre arrived the next day and, over a few mugs of rum, we had a sobering reunion talking politics. He told me that Spain and England might soon be at war because of the fur trade and what he called the *Nootka Crisis.* He warned me that, if his government reopened the fort, I should take my family north.

"The soldiers won't care if you're a Yank or a Brit. The outcome will be the same. I'll warn you if I can, but you should stay alert."

Because of this looming crisis, Father Mendez married Raven and I the next day in his wilderness church. It was a simple ceremony, performed both in Latin and English. Raven was beautiful, in her sun bleached deerskin skirt adorned with colorful trade beads and a pure white satin blouse given to her by the padre. During the service, she beamed with joy and squeezed my hands tightly.

At the end of the wedding, when we kissed, she whispered, "We be like geese, bonded forever that no one can divide."

After the ceremony, the padre took Jeremiah's bible and wrote in it:

Joseph Blackwell of Boston and Raven of the Tolowa Indians
Were married in a Christian church on May 2nd 1792
By Father Mendez, Franciscan Monk

Handing the book back to us, he said, "This is proof to all mankind that you have a Christian union and family. Let no man ever doubt these words."

That evening, the padre held a small reception for us behind the church, with delicious foods and strong spirits. Our guests included Virgil from the trading post, Black Crow, his squaw and a few friends from the village. After the meal, I played my flute and we all had a delightful evening, dancing around the fire pit. Then, with the last rays of sun slipping over the horizon, the old chief surprised Raven and me by inviting us to spend our wedding night in a special wigwam that the tribe had set up for us on the shore. It was a grand gesture, coming from Black Crow, and we humbly accepted, thanking him with a gift of colorful feathers. After our soiree, Raven, Dutch and I snuggled into our special lodge and enjoyed the sweet choir of the lapping waves.

Early the next morning, after turning the canoe upside down next to the church, we prepared to return to Skunk Creek. When we had loaded the last of our supplies onto the mule, Father Mendez appeared from the church and gave me two clay jugs of Franciscan brandy.

"This is my wedding present, Joe, for those cold winter nights. I'll be back here when the leaves turn color. Until then, stay alert. God speed, son."

Embracing the padre, I thanked him again for his blessing. Then we slowly moved up the trail toward our mountain retreat.

That summer, I taught my clan to swim. Even Dutch learned not to fear the water, and how to tread it like a dog. In the hot sun, we spent many enjoyable days, swimming together and playing Tory football on the lakeshore. Even Badger and I found some mutual respect, although he always held that undertow of hostility toward me for being a gringo.

That autumn, we built a small bunkhouse for the lads, behind the cabin. We constructed it much like a Tillamook lodge, using redwood planks with a pole frame. In the center of the room, there was a large fire pit, with an opening in the shed roof for the smoke. Here, Mole and Badger each had their own sleeping shelf, covered with animal pelts. The lads still took their meals in the big cabin but, with the cold winter nights coming, Raven and I were pleased to have the cabin to ourselves.

Early the next spring, while working our trap lines, I caught a lucky glimpse of a large gold nugget. Had it not been for the angle of the sun, I would have never noticed the shining lump beneath the fast-flowing surface of the creek. Quickly, I snatched the thumb-sized nugget from the water, and wondered its worth. Search as I did, around the many other rocks in the creek, I could find no more. But then, gold is always elusive and normally not worth the time of the search.

In May, we returned to the Spanish compound with our pelts and my nugget. When we arrived, I was disappointed to learn that we had missed the padre by only a few days. But he had left me a note that simply read:

War clouds still brewing. Will return in July. Please join me for summer celebration. God bless. Father Mendez.

The other news, which I learned from Virgil, was that a Spanish warship had recently anchored off-shore for fresh provisions and then sailed north in search of British fur traders. This was disturbing news, and I didn't want to dally long in the village, for fear that the ship might return. Therefore, I traded our pelts for supplies, and exchanged my gold nugget for a young horse and saddle that Virgil had out back.

We spent but one night in the village and then returned to Skunk Creek. The new mare was named Amber, because of her color, and she was a wonderful addition to our band. With Raven and Dutch riding her back, I took the point jogging, while Badger and Mole nudged the mule along from the rear. Now we could make the journey from village to home in a single long day.

We came down from the mountains once more that year, in July, and had an enjoyable reunion with the padre. He had no good news, only a few special trinkets from San Francisco that he gave to Raven and Dutch. As for our chess games, he won every match.

That autumn, Badger ran off with a squaw from the nearby Yurok tribe. The impulsive lad told us his plans one night, and the next morning he was gone. Raven and Mole were sad to see him go, but deep down we all knew that having a family would be good for him. Then, suddenly in the spring, Badger returned. His woman had run off with another brave, leaving him living with a tribe he didn't know.

We were pleased with his return, but I was confident he would leave again. With Mole also of age, I talked to him about taking a squaw. He was quite shy about the subject, and would only tell me that women were still a mystery to him.

"If I find woman, she live here with my family. I no leave you and Raven."

Over the years, Dutch grew like a weed. In the blink of an eye, he was six years old and wanting to go hunting with the men. Raven was hesitant about this young desire, so I convinced him that at age eight, I would take him along. In the meantime, he would learn the skills of the bow from Mole, and from me he would learn how to fire our flintlocks.

Dutch was a strong lad who was sprouting straight, like the redwoods, with a nimble and inquiring mind. When he was but five, he found an abandoned baby skunk behind the cabin. He brought the animal into the house, wanting to keep it as a pet, and he became red-faced and furious when Raven and I forced him to release the creature back to the forest. At seven, he disturbed a bee hive and got stung so many times that his face puffed up like a sea urchin. He couldn't understand why the bees were so mad; all he'd wanted to do was hold a few in his hand. And the lad was full of questions that always started with the word 'why.' He was a delightful child in both body and spirit, and he explored the wilderness with an innocent curiosity.

Raven and I tried for years to have more babies, but were never so blessed. Therefore, we did all we could to make sure that Dutch's childhood was not rushed. He would learn to read and write, to obey God's laws and, most importantly, to have confidence in himself. I taught him, as my mother had taught me, with love and patience.

Life comes fast, on the frontier, and bad things can happen to good people. When Dutch was ten and we were hunting, one winter day, I slipped on an icy rock and fell into a narrow, deep ravine. Hitting the bottom hard, I felt my right leg snap, and a terrible pain rush through my body. Instantly, I screamed out for Dutch, but he didn't respond. Slowly pulling myself to a sitting position, with a boulder at my back, I looked up the steep rock walls and cried out again.

Then from the top of the gorge, out of sight, I heard my son's voice.

"I am here, Father. I have Amber and I've tied a rope to her saddle. I'm coming down."

"Careful, lad. The rocks are icy," I shouted back up to him.

Dutch moved slowly down the rope, causing small stones to rain down on me. Covering my head with my arms, I prayed for relief from the pain. Once my son was at my side, he helped me stand on my one good leg.

Then, with the rope secured around my waist, we both started to creep up the rocky ledge. I pulled myself with the rope, while Dutch pushed me up from below. It was a slow, painful journey up the rocks, with me crying out all the way. When we were nearly at the top, I was exhausted and dizzy and could move no more, so Dutch climbed around me and used the power of the horse and his own ninety-pound body to pull me to flat ground.

"Where's your rifle, Father?" Dutch asked as he dragged me closer to the horse.

"I don't know," I answered, panting. "It was with me when I fell."

Dutch moved back to the cliff edge and looked down. "I can see it. I'll get it."

Holding on to my leg, with pain rippling through my body, I muttered, "Forget it. Take me home."

Dutch knelt in front of me and looked me in the eye. "You taught me the power and value of that rifle. I'll get it first. Then we will go."

So that's what the lad did, and he was right. Our only rifle was our lifeline, and without it we might be lost. As Dutch scrambled back down the ravine to retrieve it, my pride for him overtook my pain. At ten years old, he had stayed calm and used his wits to save the day. God, I was proud him!

With me riding Amber, we got back to the cabin just before sunset. That evening, Mole and Raven set my broken leg, but not before I drank two cups of the Franciscan brandy. Because of that accident, I was stove-up for six months. During this time, Dutch and the lads worked the trap lines and did the hunting, while Raven had me and my black book to teach her more of the white man's ways.

In the wilderness, survival is all-consuming, so being with Raven during this respite was special for me. Listening to the murmur of the creek at our front door, we shared our love and renewed our respect for each other. Each morning, I would wake at dawn with my heart aglow, and give thanks for another day with my wife. It was a fabulous time to just be alive.

A month after my mishap, Father Mendez rode out in the middle of a snowstorm to check on my family. The gossip back at the village was that I had died from the accident, so the padre was relieved to find me hobbling around on a bum leg. He stayed with us for two nights, and we celebrated his friendship with good food and spirits. As for the world news, he told me that Spain and England had resolved the *Nootka Crisis* and were standing down from near-war.

"Maybe this summer, after your leg mends, you can travel to San Francisco with me, and we'll see if your timing is better," the padre ventured.

"Would we take my family?" I asked.

"No," Father Mendez answered. "Not until we know what sort of reception you'll receive. They wouldn't be safe."

As for our chess games, he won them all, except for the last match. But even then, my victory was hollow, as the padre had over-enjoyed the brandy and was not on top of his game.

That next summer came and went without any trips south. By the time I saw Father Mendez next, he told me that Spain had ceded back the Louisiana Territory to France, in exchange for the European country of Italy. The only remaining land that Spain owned north of Mexico was the territory where we lived and what they now called California, so the crown was determined to hold this land, at all cost. No outsiders would be tolerated. Therefore, any dream I had of returning home by way of San Francisco had vanished when France took control of Louisiana. My only remaining option was to stay in the remote mountains, growing my family and hoping for the best.

In many ways, my son's mind grew even faster than his strong, straight body. He had an appetite for words and read Jeremiah's Bible, cover to cover, three times. Father Mendez was delighted with his love of letters, and brought him a few books from the monastery library. One was about Captain Cook's third and final passage to the northwest, and another was on the American Revolution. Both these volumes were printed in English, and the padre gave them outright to Dutch. All the other books he brought were printed in Spanish, so Father Mendez taught Dutch how to read and speak that language, as well. Raven was excited that her son's second language was Spanish; then his third tongue became Tolowa, while from Mole he picked up many Tillamook words. But this gift didn't stop with just words; Dutch had a warming personality that could melt snow. He was inquisitive, smart and showed respect for people of all races.

In the summer of 1803, Badger married a Tolowa woman in a ceremony preformed by Black Crow himself. This non-Christian ritual was steeped in the pure Indian tradition of days of dancing and nights of feasting. Even Father Mendez and Virgil enjoyed witnessing the colorful pagan celebration. Badger had always been a handsome breed, and his new wife, Morning Glory, was an attractive young maiden who also was the granddaughter to the chief. After days of festivities, we wished them well and told them they were always welcome at our camp.

Sadly, almost a year later, Morning Glory died of the pox, which was decimating many villages. This tragic event turned an already gloomy Badger into an angry and depressed brave – emotions which then turned him to self-pity and rum. For over a month, he went wild around the Tolowa village, until Black Crow banished him once again from the tribe. At that point, Badger had returned to Skunk Creek, and became our problem once again.

After his return, I tried to find words of comfort, but they all seemed shallow. The death of a loved one, especially a wife, is an unimaginable tragedy that few could understand. After some days of moping about the camp, Badger announced that he was going into the redwoods to find Morning Glory's spirit. Then he picked up a spear and a knife, and told us not to worry. He was gone out the door before we could stop him or ask any questions.

Raven feared that he would take his own life, while I feared he would return to his renegade ways. But we were both wrong. A few weeks later, he returned, a changed man, wearing a bear skin around his shoulders.

Standing by a crackling fire, he told us a fascinating story of his adventure in the forest. On the first day, while walking a trail under the giant redwoods, he came upon a talking rabbit. This hare told him that a bear had stolen his wife's spirit, and that he should find the bear and take it back. A few days later, while searching for this bear, a talking owl landed nearby and told him that the bear he sought lived on the other side the mountain with the white hat. He walked many days and nights to find this monolith and cross it. Once he did, he came upon a large blue lake with granite peaks on one side and a vast pine forest on the other. Here he rested for a few days, talking to the mountain gods. Finally, a beaver swam by and told him that the bear he hunted would come to drink from the lake the next morning. When he did, Badger was to kill him and take his pelt, because it held his wife's spirit. All that night, Badger worried about fighting this bear with just a spear and knife, but deep inside he knew it had to be done. The next day at first light, the brown bear appeared, and they confronted each other on the lakeshore. The bear was tall and powerful, but Badger was quick and fearless. As he attacked the bear at the water's edge, he noticed that the bear had no claws on its paws. They fought for hours, in and out of the lake, up into the forest and back again. Finally, the exhausted bear told Badger that he had traded his claws for Morning Glory's spirit, but it had been a bad trade, and he wanted his claws back. Badger refused the barter and killed the bear with his spear. Now the lad had the bear's pelt and would wear it forever, as he believed it contained his dead wife's spirit.

As Badger told us this parable, he showed the paws of the skin, and they were indeed without any claws. Like most Indian folklore, there was always verity in their stories. Whatever the truth might be, Badger *was* a changed man thereafter, as he had lost his grief and found his grit.

Shifting Sands

In September of 1805, we came to the Spanish compound to trade for winter supplies. When we arrived, we found a small group of strangers working on the log fort. They gave us a curious look as we passed, but we didn't stop to talk. Once at our upside-down canoe, Badger and Mole went to work on setting up camp, while Raven, Dutch and I walked to the trading post. As we came inside, Virgil greeted me with a mug of rum and some hot tea for Raven and Dutch.

"Who are those men outside?" I asked while tasting my grog.

"Came up from the south a few days ago, sent by the crown to repair the fort," Virgil answered.

"Is the padre here?"

"Na, but I expect him any time."

Soon, our conversation turned to trade goods. Then we heard horses ride up to the post. Moments later, the door opened, and there stood a dusty Father Mendez, along with a porky man dressed in dirty city clothes and a tricorne hat. The padre's eyes flashed me a warning as he crossed the room while calling in Spanish to Virgil. The men came to rest at the far end of the counter, where Virgil poured them some rum.

As he did so, I glanced to the still open front door to see a woman and a young boy standing in the shade, drinking water from a canteen. They, too, were covered with trail dust. Also I could see a few tired and hard ridden horses tied to the hitching post.

When I turned back to the counter, the padre introduced me to the stranger, and told him that I was named Fire-Head. From what I could make out from his Spanish words, he also told the man that I was an Indian from the Tillamook tribe. The surprised visitor, Mr. Garcia, said something about my red hair, but the padre answered that many of the

Tillamooks had red hair. He didn't look convinced, and I could see from Father Mendez's expression that something was wrong, so we finished our drinks and quickly departed the post.

A few hours later, the padre came by our camp, and we strolled along the shore talking. He had disturbing news. Mr. Garcia was a government land agent, sent to survey the surrounding area for settlement. Then, in a few months, a ship would arrive with settlers and a detachment of soldiers. The crown had decided to open up parts of California by issuing Spanish Land Grants to Mexican immigrants. The king, worried about American encroachment, and wanted to flood the land with Spanish subjects before the Yanks could gain any footholds.

With an expression full of concern, Father Mendez said, "It is a bad idea. The Indians will become hostile because of the new settlers, and the Mexican tenderfoots will surly perish in this harsh wilderness. Trouble is coming, Joe, and I'm not sure your family will be safe."

Stunned by the news, I asked, "How much time do we have?"

"A month or so. That is, if Mr. Garcia doesn't realize that you're a Yankee."

"That's not much time," I answered, my mind racing.

"There is more. A recent Spanish newspaper told of your Captain Gray discovering a great river in the north that the Indians called Wimahl. He renamed it the Columbia River and has claimed it for your nation. The crown is not happy with these actions, so tensions are brewing again between our countries."

The news that the Captain might still be in northern waters lifted my spirits. If America now owned the mighty river, maybe there was a settlement there that could provide a way home.

"How long ago did he make this discovery?" I asked, with hope in my heart.

The padre shook his head. "The paper did not say."

That evening, around our fire, I told my family the grim news, then announced that Raven, Dutch and I would flee north in the canoe, making for the Columbia River. There I hoped we would find a settlement and maybe passage home. Turning to Mole and Badger, I explained that they didn't have to cast their lot with us. They could remain at the cabin, trapping, as the padre felt confident that the government would not interfere with them.

Mole reacted right away by telling everyone that he was going with us. Badger, on the other hand, hesitated, but by the next morning he also agreed to sail with us.

Over the next few weeks, we made two trips up and back to Skunk Creek, packing out what we would need for our trip. Closing up the cabin for the last time made for a sad morning, as we had spent so many wonderful years in this home. Raven was weepy, and Dutch reflected on his many memories of the cabin and the land where he had taken root. Even Mole and Badger had some joyful memories that they shared. Then we sadly said good-by to log house that Jeremiah had built.

Returning to the compound, I went to the Tolowa boat builder and traded six skins for a stocky, narrow, flat-bottomed dugout as our new outrigger. Then the lads went to work on crafting the redwood struts that would connect the two hulls.

While they worked, Raven and I walked Amber and the mule to the trading post. As we climbed the porch, I saw that the work on the fort was almost complete and that Mr. Garcia and his family had moved inside the stockade. This sight reminded me of our pending danger.

Virgil welcomed us warmly with tea and rum. Then we started trading for supplies. It was my notion to trade half our pelts for trade goods that we could use as barter, while the remaining pelts would be traded for food and our personal needs. The trade goods we selected were simple enough: blankets, blue and white glass beads, iron tips, iron tools and what the Indians loved the most – anything made of shiny metal. For our personal needs, we took flour, beans, molasses, coffee, bacon, cigars and four jugs of rum. In trade for our last two skins, Virgil suggested we take a canvas tarp that could be used as a shelter from the weather or as a replacement sail if we lost the one we had. It was a good idea, and we agreed.

"What of my animals" I asked the Creole

He answered with a small grin. "Father Mendez has an interest in them. Put them in the rear corral so he can look them over."

That evening, with the padre preparing to leave the next morning, Raven, Dutch and I stopped by the back of church to say farewell. He greeted us warmly, and his squaw served us tea on his porch table.

The first words from the padre were of caution. "I'm sorry we couldn't have a farewell party but, with all the strangers in camp, I didn't think it wise."

We agreed with him and then, over the brew, we talked of the years gone by. With great affection, we told Father Mendez that he was not only our spiritual leader, but also a dear friend.

With a warm look, the padre listened to our praise and then talked of his love for us. "I know we will not meet again, but I will always carry your souls close to my heart. You are special to me. When your out on that ocean and fearful of the sea, remember that life isn't about a destination, it's about the journey. So keep your love strong and your faith stronger."

Before Raven and Dutch left, that evening, Father Mendez gave them each a gift of a silver cross necklace just like he wore.

"Wear this crucifix with my blessing. May you always be safe," the padre said, his eyes tearful.

Then, just before my family departed for camp, the padre said a short prayer and embraced my wife and son. Watching them hug this gentle brown giant for the last time made me choke up and thank the Lord for his deliverance.

After my family had gone, Father Mendez and I sat down for one last chess game, armed with a fresh jug of brandy and a box of cigars. As we played, he talked of my animals.

"I want to trade you for the mule," the padre said, getting up from the table. "Excuse me for a moment."

When he returned from his sleeping room, he handed me a long, beaded rawhide sheath. Opening it, I found another rifle.

"I traded ten prime pelts for this, with a sea captain in San Francisco. He told me it was a Kentucky Long Rifle, with a range of over 250 meters. The crown won't miss the skins, and you'll need another rifle, now that Dutch is of age."

The musket was in excellent condition, with a barrel six inches longer than Jeremiah's rifle. Inside the sheath, I also found two horns of powder, a supply of flints and a pouch of balls.

"The captain told me the balls are called *peas* because of their .52 caliber size. The sheath is made of buffalo hide, and the beads are from the Cherokee Indian nation."

This was a generous trade, as the mule wasn't worth half the hides. Touched, I quickly thanked the padre and accepted his offer.

"Now, as to the Amber," he continued, "she's a fine mare, and I plan to keep her for myself. So I was thinking about what you would need in exchange for her." As the padre talked, he reached into his frock pocket and brought up a closed hand. "I'm sure the folks back in Boston don't trade in hides, so you're going to need money. Here are five gold doubloons for your horse," he said, opening up his hand. "In your money, that's about seventy dollars."

The sight of the gold coins made my jaw drop.

"You're overpaying, Father," I blurted, still staring at the coins.

Handing the gold across the table to me, the padre smiled. "Over the years, you've made the crown much money, so they won't miss a few small coins."

Small coins? Gazing at the gold in my hand, I knew that it was the most money I'd seen in one place in all my life.

The grinning padre kept a keen eye on my face as I studied the doubloons more closely.

Putting the coins in my pouch, I said, "Thank you. Please, give Jeremiah's cabin to some worthy settlers. Most of what we found is still there, and it's a wonderful place to raise a family."

Some time later, Father Mendez checkmated me for the last time, and stood from his chair. Holding out his mug, he said, "It's time to say farewell, but not before one last salute."

I stood with my mug high, and for a brief moment we just gazed at each other.

Then he said, with a sober face, "May a gentle sea rise up to meet you, and the winds forever be at your back. And may God hold your family always in the palm of his loving hands."

Then we both drained our cups and, with teary eyes, embraced. This brown monster of a man had turned out to be a giant friend, and I would surely miss him for the rest of my life.

The next morning, I gave Jeremiah's musket to Dutch, and the pistols to Mole and Badger. Then we walked behind the camp for one last lesson on how to use the weapons. My new Kentucky Long Rifle was a wonderful flintlock that could drop an elk from over 200 yards.

We departed the Spanish compound on October 2, 1805. As we paddled west across a peaceful sea I noticed a white feather resting on my bench, then turning from the tiller I watched the harbor slip away. The bright, sandy beaches glistened in the sunlight, and the tall mountains stood like sentinels, guarding the crescent bay. We had spent fifteen years on the California frontier, and now that part of our life was gone. And while our future was still in doubt, I had great hopes of finding a settlement on the Columbia River, and then a way home.

Once we were in deep water, I turned the boat north while Mole and Badger raised the sail. Instantly, the canvas filled with a fresh southerly breeze, and we started moving up the coast toward our first destination, the Coquille tribe.

Late in the afternoon, we came to the large slit in the land that was Coos River. Here we crossed the bar on an incoming tide without incident. Once inside the estuary, we lowered the sail and paddled for the main Indian village on the southern river.

As we glided across the water, I yelled out, "Keep your hands on your flintlocks and your eyes on our goods. There may be thieves among these Indians."

As we came ashore, a small crowd welcomed us, and I recognized a few faces. Pulling the canoe to high ground, a brave with a smiling face stepped forward, shouting, "Fire-Head!"

Touching my hair, I grinned and nodded yes, introducing my clan in both words and sign language to the assembled group. As I was doing this, the village chief appeared, wearing a colorful feathered headdress. He was a young, tall chief, with a pocked moon-face. With signs, I asked him about the headman of many seasons ago. He signed back that he was a new chief, called Many Feathers, and sadly, while making signs of tears, that the old chief had made the final journey. He seemed friendly enough, and told me that he remembered my last visit. Giving him a knife made of bronze, I asked if we could make trade with the tribe, and he quickly agreed. Pleased with my tribute, the chief invited us to sleep in a shed next to his lodge and to take our meals with his clan.

This being Dutch's first trading trip, he wandered around the village, wide-eyed, watching as some squaws prepared the evening meal, while others sat around a small fire, weaving beautiful baskets. Kneeling near this circle, he seemed amazed by their craftsmanship, and how they used warm pitch to make the creels watertight. At one point, one of the younger squaws gave Dutch a small basket she had finished, then flashed him an alluring look. I had taught my son about the dangers of the forest, but not of camp. This, I realized, I would soon have to do.

After an evening meal of fish, camas cakes and berries, Mole and I gave the braves a demonstration of our rifles. None had ever seen a musket before, and they almost jumped out of their skin when we fired our weapons. Mole shot at a nearby tree, while I shot a seagull as it rested on a log across the river. The Indians were bewildered and fearful of our fire-sticks, as they realized that the rifle was the future.

As it was late in the season, we spent only a week with the Coquilles. Keeping a keen eye on the always changing weather, we sailed across the bar on a cloudy day with calm seas. Packed inside our outrigger were a dozen fine skins and some fresh venison from a buck we had shot the day before. Once outside the bar of the Coos River, we turned the boat north.

We sailed all day, searching for the tiny slit to the Siuslaw tribe, but never found it. The weather was with us all the way north, with only a few sticky rain showers. But with darkness coming on, we moved closer to shore, hoping to find a place to camp.

As we rounded a large, rocky headland, Mole shouted that he could see a sandy cove that was protected on all sides. Reefing the sail, we paddled in that direction, dodging a few sea rocks. The onshore breakers looked manageable, and we crossed the narrow surf line without any problems.

Once ashore, we pulled the boat to high ground and tied it to a log snag. The cove was only a few hundred feet wide and backed by a sheer, mossy cliff with a shallow beach. Taking the canvas tarp and sail from the large dugout, we made a tent, using some of the many log snags that littered the upper reaches of the beach, and hunkered down for the night.

And what a night it was! By midnight, the first storm rolled in, with winds and rain that blew sideways through our little nook. All night long, we worked at keeping the flapping canvas overhead and the howling winds out of our shelter.

The next day was no better, as one storm after another rolled up from the south. For three days and nights, we huddled in our wind-blown tent, staring at each other and watching the pounding surf creep in. I thanked God for our venison and the dry driftwood we found.

Finally, the morning of the fourth day broke clear, with only a slight breeze from the south, but the dirty green breakers in the cove were still curling high and looked too dangerous to cross. By midday, with a slack tide, the surge moderated and we were able to escape from what we now called 'Cold Cove.'

Late that afternoon, with another gale on our wake, we crossed the bar and paddled into the shallow gray Siletz Bay. The stormy season had come early, and I feared being caught out at sea again. Therefore, I decided that we would winter with the Siletz Indians, and seek the Columbia River in the spring.

After I shouted this decision from the tiller, Raven twisted her head and flashed me a red-faced look of anger.

"Not to worry," I said in answer to her glare. "You're still my woman."

Clark's House

Running Fox was still headman of the Siletz, and he remembered me from my visit of many years before. At first, when I asked if we could winter with his tribe, he was hesitant. Sensing this reluctance, we gave him a demonstration of our rifles and told him that the muskets could bring down elk. Watching, and hearing about the power of our fire-sticks, he started to warm to my notion. When we also pledged to hunt and share all of our kills with the tribe, he quickly agreed. Elk was coveted in all of the villages, for its meat and soft pelt. However, because of its large size, few native hunters could bring one down with just arrows. With our rifles, we could now supply elk to the tribe, all winter long.

In the next few weeks, we built a small one-room cedar lodge, just down the river from the village. I purposely selected this location as it had protection from the southern storms, and was far enough away from the tribe so as not to be a temptation to any thieving natives. When it was completed, we moved in and prepared for the long, dark, stormy winter.

The elk were plentiful and the bay abundant. Raven cooked hot and hearty meals, while the lads and I hunted and fished. In the evenings, just like on Skunk Creek, Dutch read aloud from his books, regaling us with stories of Captain Cook and General Washington. Often I talked to them of Boston, the Orphan, my old shipmates and the passage to Tillamook Bay. Sometimes, Raven would talk of her tribe, her sad journey north and how I had rescued her. But Mole and Badger were of few words, and usually only spoke with questions. Long ago, the Tillamooks had taught me that lodge life could be enjoyable, even in the dreary winter months, if it was passed with a good fire, good food and good yarns. These we had aplenty.

With skies that were dark and gloomy, and air damp and raw, the winter storms blew through my body and into my soul. For four straight months, it rained sideways with little relief or time to dry out. Finally, March roared in with the last of the really big storms. By the end of the month, I could finally smell spring in the air.

About this time, I learned that a Siletz brave had returned home after wintering with the tribe on Netarts Bay. I was sure he would have news of the Tillamooks, so I sought him out at his father's lodge.

What he told me was astounding: two moons before, a group of white men had come to Tillamook Bay in search of seal oil and whale blubber. They stayed a few days and then returned to a village they had built in the land of the Clatsops. He said that they carried fire-sticks much like mine, and that their chief was named Clark. My heart jumped with the news, as this confirmed that there was a white settlement somewhere to the north. But when I asked him about Marcus, the chief of the Tillamooks, he shook his head no. He had only been with the tribe a few moons, and had never been to the main village. I thanked him for the news with some fishhooks, and departed for camp with great excitement.

We said farewell to Running Fox and his tribe, and departed on March 28th. I had kept a keen eye on the weather, so we found only blue skies and calm seas as we sailed across the bar. Once outside the surf line, I set my course north for Tillamook Bay. We were fearful of what our reception might be, but I hoped we could get more information about Clark and his village. Surely, after fifteen years, Marcus wouldn't begrudge us a brief visit.

On this day, King Neptune was with us, and we made good speed with a fresh breeze from the south. With Dutch sitting next to me at the tiller, we soon sailed past Woodpecker's rock, with thousands of birds flying around, and I told him the story of our egg hunt. Then I pointed to the opening in the tree line, above the cove's cliffs, and spoke of her final resting place. The lad asked many questions about the old woman, and was awestruck at the beauty of the setting.

As we approached the slit to Tillamook Bay, we lowered our sail and paddled across a lumpy bar. Once in quieter waters, Raven twisted to me, with sadness on her face, and said, "Our home is gone."

Looking in that direction, I could see that she was right. The log cabin was no more, and the opening in the forest showed only dead and scorched trees. Now weeds grew around charred logs where our cabin had once stood. I turned away, not wanting to see any more.

We paddled across the estuary and down the north shore toward the main village. The few people we passed on the water paid us no heed. Arriving at the hamlet, we pulled the boat to high ground, with only a few heads twisting our way. Handing a surprised Mole my rifle, I said, "We came for answers, not a fight." Then I told my family to stay with the canoe while I parleyed with Marcus.

As I walked towards the old woman's lodge, I recognized a few faces, and desperately worried about my welcome. Once in front of the closed planked door, I scratched it loudly, as the Tillamooks did.

Soon, the door opened – and, of all people, Timber Wolf stood before me.

He and I were bewildered to see each other, and it took a moment for us to find our words. Quickly, he invited me in, where I was warmly welcomed by his surprised wife, Sandpiper.

"Where's the chief?" I asked.

Sandpiper smiled, as did Timber Wolf. "I'm chief now," my old friend answered. "Marcus was deposed many years ago."

It took a moment for his words to sink in. Then I smiled back. "How wonderful, I pay you tribute chief."

Our old friends offered us their lodge, and we spent that night enjoying old memories and catching up on tribal gossip. Raven and Sandpiper were delighted to see each other, and spent hours talking of family. While the squaws chattered away, I broke out a jug of rum and, over the cups, learned the news.

After we had departed, fifteen years before, Marcus, in a fit of anger, had gone to our cabin and set it ablaze. In the process, he almost started a forest fire that could have burnt down the village. The elders were not happy with his actions. Marcus proved to be a brutal chief, and had many more run-ins with the elders. Finally, just three years after we had gone, the council stripped him of his powers and removed him as chief. He now lived with the Nehalem tribe, and had a wife and three children.

"Do you want to sail up and see him?" Timber Wolf asked.

I thought about this question for moment, and then answered, "No." Marcus had chosen his fate, and now I was searching for my own destiny. "What have you heard of this white man Clark?"

He replied that this man and his band, with their fire-sticks, had been to the village, and that Timber Wolf had signed with him. Then they had visited some of the other villages on the bay, before returning to the land of Clatsops. There had been no trouble, and no Indians had died.

"Do you know where their settlement is?" I asked with great hope.

"Clark say they live on Netul River that flows into Wimahl. They have many canoes and many warriors."

This was great news. "How long ago was he here? How might we find his lodge?"

"He here two moons ago. Ask any Clatsop where he lives."

Timber Wolf was right; any northern Indian would know where the white man settlement was.

Then, thinking of my old adversary, I asked, "What of Hawk? Is he still with the Clatsops?"

"He lives across the great river with Chinook people."

This, too, was good news. Now I was confident that we could safely find Clark. For this evening, however, we would enjoy our friendship, along with a warm fire, good food and bold spirits.

We departed Tillamook Bay early in the morning of April 1st, 1806. We had cool, clear weather and a moderate bar. Once outside surf line, I turned the boat north and we raised our sail. As the slit to bay faded from our wake, something told me that I wouldn't see this place again. These feelings saddened me, as the Tillamook people had proven to be much the same as me, full of faith and spunk, with a deep connection to the land.

A few hours later, we sailed past the headland to the Clatsops, and I turned the boat closer to the shore. As we moved north up the straight line of curling breakers, we looked for any Indians that might be on shore. We found none. Finally, we came to the narrow slit for Necanicum Bay and lowered the sail. Then, with paddles in hand, we crossed the shallow bar with an incoming tide.

Once inside the bay, we saw in the distance a lone fisherman in a small dugout. He waved from across the water, so we headed in his direction. As we approached, I noticed he looked very much like my visionary guardian angel. His basket hat, his gray hair, even his plain buckskins looked the same. As we came alongside his boat, however, he spoke only Clatsop, and his eyes didn't glow.

We talked awhile. Yes, he knew where Clark lived, and he gave us detailed directions on how to find his settlement. There was a nearby creek called Neacoxie that flowed into the bay; up this creek was a Clatsop village. Beyond the village was what he called a 'finger lake.' Using one of his fingers, he explained how three narrow lakes were connected together. Once we at the top of the top lake, we would find a well-traveled path leading towards the sunrise. Down this path, we would come to the Netul River that flowed into Wimahl. Walking downstream, we would come to the 'white man's house.'

"You will smell it first," he said, with his fingers pinching his nose. "White-man makes no trenches and stinks up the forest."

"Can we get there before dark?" I asked the old man.

"Maybe, but you must stop and pay tribute to Clatsops before you pass their village."

"Where is this Neacoxie Creek?" I asked.

The old man pointed to a slight opening, just up from where we floated. "Creek narrow and shallow. Your dugout too fat."

I thanked the old man with some fishing hooks and offered him a few iron arrow tips in exchange for the large basket of crabs inside his canoe. But he wasn't interested, so we paddled away.

As we approached the stream, I could see that the old man had been right about the size of our canoe, so we went ashore and removed the outrigger. After a meal of dried fish, we launched the big dugout again, towing our small flat bottom canoe. Then, with the sun high in the sky, we paddled up the creek.

The shallow green stream rambled north, cutting through a thick forest of tall trees. As we paddled up the creek, it was like moving in an emerald tunnel, with the crown of the tress blocking the sky. The narrow brook was only a few yards wide, and we dodged many snags that protruded from the water. After hitting the bottom a few times, I tried to keep the boat in the center of the rivulet.

"Are we stopping at the village?" Mole twisted to ask.

"No," I answered, "time is too short. I want to be with Clark tonight."

A few miles from the bay, we came to a grassy landing with many canoes resting on dry land. Up from these boats, nestled in the trees, I could see a few lodges with smoke coming from their roofs. I heard a barking dog and some children playing, but we saw no one.

"Everyone quiet," I whispered to those in the boat.

The only sound we made was that of our paddles in the water as we gently glided past the village. Once beyond the hamlet, we dug our paddles deeper into the water and increased our speed.

Soon thereafter, I heard a commotion from shore, then noticed some Indians rushing down to the stream and looking our way. Moments later, a dugout pushed off, with eight braves rowing. They had seen us and were giving chase.

"We need more speed," I shouted to my clan.

Looking up to the trees, I could see there was a breeze from the south, but the tall forest blocked that wind on the creek. Our sail was useless; paddling was all we could do. Quickly, I had Raven take the tiller, while I took her scull. We had a good quarter-mile lead on the braves, but we had only four oars, while they had eight. Soon, they would catch up with us.

I started calling out a cadence to the boat. "Row, one-two! Row, one-two!"

Just as my beat started, we heard a single drum from the Indian dugout, pounding out the same. We rowed hard, but they were gaining on us at every slender turn of the stream.

As their drum got closer, the land opened up and became less burdened with trees. Looking towards shore, I saw the blonde sea grass now dancing in a slight breeze. Finally, with sweat rolling off our brows, we glided through a narrow gap in the land and emerged onto a long, slender blue lake surrounded with rolling sand dunes.

We stopped to raise the sail. As Mole scrambled with the lines, I stood, and noticed that the approaching canoe had two standing braves, with bows in hand. Quickly, I bent for my rifle. When I stood again, there were two arrows in the air. One hit the stern of our dugout, making a *"swish-thump"* sound as it stuck into the wood. The other arrow flew past Raven, missing her by only inches.

I raised my rifle and yelled, "Dutch, take a shot at their boat." Then I fired.

Bang!

The loud report from my weapon rolled off the water, and my well-aimed pea splintered a hole in the bow of the Indian dugout.

As my smoke cleared, our boat lurched forward with a full sail. Then Dutch stood and fired his rifle. His ball blew a bigger hole, also in the bow of the dugout. The Indians looked stunned by our gunfire as they glided through the narrow gap into the lake. In fact, once on open water, they stopped rowing and pounding their drum. The power of our rifles had scared them off and, thank God, no one was hurt. In a few short moments, they faded from our wake and we were safely heading north.

The calm, blue lake we sailed upon was about two miles long and a few hundred yards wide. Most of the shoreline was sandy dunes covered with thick, green brush. There were a few small stands of windswept alder and pine trees dotting the lake shore but, for the most part, the land was open. The waters around the lake teemed with countless types of fowl, all of them feeding or fishing. As we sailed past a small, peaceful cove, I watched a skinny legged blue heron on the shoreline catch a bass with its long sharp beak. Then, still holding the fish in its mouth, it took off flying above the lake.

Just as the heron passed overhead, a colorful bald eagle swooped down out of nowhere, with outstretched talons, and snatched the fish from the heron's mouth. This splendid, savage spectacle lasted but a few heartbeats, but it embodied the order of things in this primitive land.

At the top of the first lake, we lowered the sail and paddled through a short narrow, shallow channel to the second lake. This pond was only a mile long but, once inside deep water, we raised the sail again and continued north. With geese flying in formation overhead, we watched the tranquil waters pass.

The abundance of this area surprised me. Approaching the top of the lake, we stopped the boat again and took our paddles in hand. But before we could dip them into the water, a herd of elk appeared in front of us, crossing the shallows of the final channel. There were more than thirty animals in the intrepid mob. As they splashed across the water, I counted six bulls, some weighing over a thousand pounds. Many of the local Indians called this type of elk 'white deer,' because of their light-colored bodies, but to me what made these animals magnificent were their gigantic size and the almost-black fur of their necks and heads. For a fleeting moment, I thought about shooting one, but it would have taken hours to dress the animal and pack the meat away – time we did not have.

After the elk herd passed, we rowed through the long, narrow channel and into the deep water of the third lake. Raising the sail again, we moved north for about three miles, to the top of the reservoir. There we found a raised terrace, with signs of other canoes and muddy footprints from many moccasins. Up from this dune was the clear path of a trail leading east.

Our boats were too heavy to portage full of supplies, so we removed what we needed, and then hid the dugouts in some heavy brush. Our plan was to return for the canoes after we found Clark.

With a warm afternoon sun in the sky, we packed our needs into rawhide pokes and began our trek. The first few miles were easy, as the path was in the open and snaked over hilly sand dunes. Soon we came to a slow-moving creek that was treed on both sides. We forded the water and picked up the trail again. Then our path stiffened, as we moved uphill into forested foothills.

An hour later, we came to the brow of the trail in an open clearing. From this high ground, we could look west and see, in the distance, the ocean stretching from the Clatsop headland all the way north. It was a spectacular vista of hues of blue. Once over this brow, the trail moved downhill at a gentle slope and through a forest of tall fir trees, with many rills and creeks.

Finally, late in the afternoon, we came to the Netul River, which flowed north towards the Columbia River. We turned with the trail and walked the high banks of this beautiful deep waterway. An hour later, through the shadows of the tall trees, just up the bank from the river, we spied a large, square, log blockhouse with small gun ports cut into the timbered walls. Clark's settlement was at hand!

My heart was pounding like a drum as we approached the fortification. Raising my voice, I shouted, "Hello in the fort. I'm a white man. We come in peace."

As I walked closer to the walls, I heard no response. I tried yelling again, but still received no answer. Finally, standing in front of the massive log gate, I reached out and found that I could pull the heavy door open.

Moving inside, I saw cabins on each side of a dusty courtyard that featured an empty flagpole. Scattered on the ground were some old clothes, rotting pelts and discarded moccasins. The place stank and was devoid of any living soul, red or white. The settlement was deserted.

As my clan joined me inside, I walked around the compound with a heavy heart, looking into the seven abandoned log rooms. One room included a large fireplace, while five others had only stone fire pits, all had only dirt floors. There were signs everywhere that many people had lived here, but how long ago?

Then, outside one of the rooms, I noticed a carving on the log wall. It simply said: *Fort Clatsop, Lewis & Clark winter camp, 12-10-1805 to 3-23-1806.*

We had missed Clark by only one week!

I began to laugh out loud, and found that I could not control myself.

"Why are you laughing, Father?" Dutch asked with a serious face.

"Do you know what day it is, boy?" I asked him.

"Yes. It's April the first."

"All Fools Day… and I am the biggest fool of them all, for thinking that Clark would be here!"

Chapter Eleven: Encroachment

SHIP-BOUND CARGOS OF ANIMAL PELTS TAKEN FROM the natives of the Pacific Northwest Coast and Alaska were called the 'maritime' fur trade, to distinguish them from the land-based fur trade in areas such as the Great Lakes and the Rocky Mountains. These maritime skins were mostly bartered in China in exchange for tea, silks, porcelain and other goods. This type of trading was pioneered by the Russians, who sailed east from their homeland, across the Aleutian Islands and down the southern coast of Alaska. British and American ships entered the trade in the 1780's, focusing on what is now the coast of British Columbia, and the American states of Washington and Oregon.

With trade goods such as axe heads, knives, awls, fishhooks, cloth, woolen blankets, linen shirts, kettles, jewelry, glass beads, mirrors and even muskets and gunpowder, the coastal Indians saw a rapid increase in their wealth. Unfortunately, along with these new riches came an increase in tribal warfare, slavery and deaths from Euro-American diseases. However, the Indian culture was not overwhelmed by these problems, and flourished with the maritime trade for many years. The use of the Chinook jargon arose during this era, and remains a part of the distinctive history of the Pacific Northwest culture. As for New England, the maritime fur trade, with all its profits, helped revitalize the region from farming to an industrial society.

This fur trade, both maritime and land-based, forged many alliances and helped maintain good relations between natives and nations. Many a white trapper ventured into North America, as young single men, and used marriage as a currency to form ties and accords between tribes and the competing nations for purposes of trade. These trappers often married or cohabited with the daughters of high-ranking chiefs, and had many children that developed not only their own language, but their own culture, as well. These descendants of fur traders and chiefs formed a society that is still recognized today as a separate ethnic group called Métis.

Because so much wealth was at stake, various nations competed for control of the fur trade and the various native tribes. The British encroached on the lands controlled by the Americans, while the Russians moved south down the coastline, encroaching on the British. After the Lewis and Clark expedition, however, the Americans started gaining an upper hand in the fur trade both in the Rocky Mountains and on the Pacific Northwest coast. With these successes came the formation of foreign trading companies that sought to stifle American ambitions and win back control of the trading and trapping of pelts. Soon, there were enterprises such as the British Hudson Bay Company and the Russian-American Company, charted by his Majesty Tsar Paul, who would challenge the Yankee control. To fight back against these monopolies, John Jacob Astor created the Pacific Fur Company, which would soon become the largest American fur trading company.

The long period of decline for the maritime fur trade started in the early 1800's, as the sea otter population began its slow depletion. Then the trade diversified by offering beaver, elk and other animal skins as new commodities, while continuing to focus on the Northwest Coast and trade with China. This new trade lasted until the middle of the 19th century. Soon, with expanding American and British settlements in the Pacific Northwest the local natives were displaced from the best hunting and fishing grounds, leaving the Indian culture in decline. Then, as the demand for pelts subsided because fashion trends had shifted from furs to felt, the Native Americans' lifestyles were again altered by the decline of trade goods. To continue obtaining those goods, on which the Indians had become dependent, the natives were often compelled to sell their land to the newly arriving settlers. Their resentment of these forced sales contributed to the many future wars with the homesteaders. In the end, most of the natives were thrust onto government reservations, where they lingered for decades in poverty. During this dark period, the culture and fabric of entire Indian nations were lost forever.

Fort Clatsop

With twilight fast approaching, my family set up camp inside the fort, while I walked to the river shore to look for signs in the soft mud. From the canoe indentations and the footprints, I guessed Clark had six or seven canoes, with over thirty men.

Walking a couple of miles farther downstream, I came to where the Netul emptied into a large bay. Just up from that spot was a raised unburdened terrace of land. I climbed up onto it. From that vantage point, I could see that the bay was open on the north to the mighty river – and what a river the Columbia was! This blue-gray estuary looked to be ten miles wide, and stretched to the northwest and east for as far as I could see. With all this open water, Clark's group should be easy to spot, if I had any notion as to their direction. Had they paddled out to meet a ship? Had they crossed the river to explore the northern lands, or maybe rowed up stream heading east?

The cove before me looked to be a natural harbor where ships could anchor for protection from the river's fast-moving currents. In the future, I would remember this point of land, as we would be able to see ships or canoes coming from any direction. As I stumbled back to the fort in darkness, I tried to convince myself that Clark might return, or that a ship would soon appear.

The next day, in a soaking rain, we retrieved our dugouts from the lake by making two long, heavy treks of over tens miles each. The portage of the big canoe was the worst, as I'm sure it weighed over five hundred pounds, even without the mast and sail. By the time both dugouts were floating on the Netul, we were exhausted and swiftly took relief inside the fort to dry out and eat a hot meal.

Just like Jeremiah's cabin, the stockade built by Clark was full of useable treasures. Most of the seven rooms were furnished with wooden bed frames, tables and chairs. All of the rooms had dirt floors, and the smallest of the seven was a meat locker, complete with iron hooks for hanging the game. Outside, the cabins were connected by a long gable roof that sloped down to the center courtyard. There were four rooms on one side of the stockade and three rooms on the other side. The fort itself was about fifty feet square, with walls built of horizontal logs over ten feet high. At one end of the quad, vertical logs were dug into the ground; at the other end stood a narrow gate, also made of standing timbers. Outside of the walls, land had been cleared all the way to the river and was open in every direction for almost fifty feet. Fort Clatsop was a well-thought-out stronghold that could keep us safe from mammal or man. And it was, by far, the biggest lodging I had enjoyed in my almost twenty years on the frontier.

Late that evening, with the boys sleeping in the next room, Raven and I settled in front of a warming fire and talked of our situation.

"We stay here, Joe?" my wife asked with a curious face. "This be a fine lodge."

"Aye, until a ship comes or Clark returns. Something will happen soon. I can feel it in my bones," I answered, and sipped from my mug of rum.

Raven reached across the table and put one of her hands on my red stubble. "Maybe we meant to stay here... Maybe Boston just a fancy memory."

"You may be right," I answered sadly, and finished my grog. "It's late now, and everything looks better in the morning sun."

"Joe, fix stink tomorrow. Then this place be good lodge."

At first light the next day, with the weather improving, I sent Dutch and Badger out to hunt, while Mole and I searched out the source of the rancid smell.

It wasn't hard to find. We just let our noses lead us to an open garbage pit in a shallow ravine not sixty feet behind the fort. There we found the bones and offal of well over a hundred elk and deer, along with other foul items, rotting in the spring sun.

You can tell much about a people by their dregs, and I was surprised to see how much game Clark's men had consumed in just three short months. And why had they not buried this stinking pile of carcasses? The open pit was a noxious place, full of flies and varmints, and it took us all morning to cover it with a thick layer of dirt. After we finished, we moved farther into the forest and dug a new, deep hole for our refuse. Then, a few hundred yards beyond, we added a new slit trench that we could use as a commode. It was dirty work, but a task that had to be done if our new lodge was to be livable.

Just after we returned to the fort, Badger and Dutch appeared, carrying a dead buck deer on a long pole. They had gutted and cleaned the animal in the field, so we hung the animal in the meat locker and removed its fur. This was a fine kill that would feed us for many days. As we worked, the boys told me that they had seen many tracks of elk and deer, and thought the area looked rich in game. Then I told them of all the animal remains we had found in the old garbage pit, and we agreed that we wouldn't starve at Fort Clatsop.

After finishing our work in the meat locker, we walked back into the bright courtyard – and found an Indian and his squaw standing just inside of the open gate. The brave wore a breechcloth with leggings and a buckskin top, and he had an iron knife on his waist. Under his basket hat, he had a large, bent nose and long, black, braided hair. From his sloping head and his manner of dress, I could tell he was a Clatsop. His woman wore a beaded deerskin frock with a seashell belt, and she carried a covered basket.

It was clear that they were as surprised to see us and we them, so our conversation started slowly and with great caution, but the brave appeared pleased with my Tillamook tongue, and he seemed to understand me clearly. His jargon was much the same as mine, with a few added Chinook words that I soon came to appreciate.

His name was Coboway and he was the chief of a nearby village. Later, I learned that this hamlet was only seven miles due west of the fort. His squaw's name was Ona, or Razor Clam, and the basket she carried was full of food for trade. I identified myself as Fire-Head and introduced the rest of my clan to them. Then we squatted and talked in the spring sun.

The chief told me that a runner had come from the Neacoxie village, with news of a man with bright hair moving into the white man's fort. Coboway said that he had come to welcome us, and to see if the flag flew down the pole. I didn't understand the pole part, so he explained that when Clark wanted to trade with the Indians, he would lower his flag halfway so the locals knew to come. So when the chief came, this day, and saw no flag, he wasn't sure if he would be welcome.

I told Coboway that Clark's way was good, and that I'd do the same in the future.

Then the chief told me that Clark had given him the fort, just before he departed with his men. "I no want this lodge, far from the sea, and elk too big to kill with arrow."

My hopes rose. "Do you know which way Clark went?"

"Yes, up Wimahl. Then walk home with Indian friends."

This cannot be, I thought. *The walk would be over three thousands miles!* Nevertheless, I silently wondered if we could catch up with them. No… we would wait for a ship.

Soon we moved out of the bright sun, and I invited the chief and his squaw inside the main cabin. There we sat on the dirt floor by the fireplace, and I poured him a cup of rum, while Raven made tea for Ona. Coboway had never tasted rum before, and enjoyed it with broad smiles and good banter. Over this grog, we talked for a good while, and I learned many things.

There were only a few Clatsop villages in the area, although the chief said that many Chinooks lived across and down the Wimahl. Most everyone was at peace, and the Indians always wanted to trade for white man's goods.

I asked him about the Columbia River and its bar to the sea. He told me that one of the Clatsop villages was located on a spit of land where the river met the sea. He said it was a poor place, because the weather was horrible and the ocean unforgiving. "Wind blow sand so hard, it buries lodges. People hunt for deer, but they are tiny. Only salmon good." Then, with the tip of his hunting knife, he drew a crude map of the mouth of the river on the dirt floor and warned me against trying to cross the bar in our dugouts. "Waves big, many shoals, much wind and strong currents," he said, pointing at the bar.

"Can ships with wings get across?" I asked, knowing full well that Captain Gray had done so.

"Yes. I see many try. Three have crossed... but no dugouts." Then, moving his point to the land just south of the bar, he continued, "If you need to go to ocean, cross sand spit by village. Only short walk carrying canoes."

As we talked, the chief wanted more rum. Long ago, I had learned that Indians and rum did not mix well, so I hesitated pouring any more.

He glared at me for a moment, then smiled and said, "I trade my food for more firewater." Then he took the cover off his basket and showed me that it was filled with cured anchovies and wapato roots. This I could not refuse.

Over his second cup of rum, we talked more of Lewis and Clark and what they had done at Fort Clatsop. He also told me about the best hunting grounds and what kind of fish we would find in the rivers. He was a friendly fellow, full of valuable information, and I enjoyed our powwow.

Somewhat later, Coboway staggered out of the fort, held erect by his squaw. At his departure, I rummaged through my things and found my old fourth-of-July flag. With the help of Dutch and Mole, we flew this pennant high from our flagpole. Fort Clatsop could be a profitable place if I had more strong spirits. Maybe – even if Woodpecker would frown on such a notion – it was time to think about making some spruce beer.

Over the next few days, we hunted, fished and explored the bay and the mighty river. Just as Coboway had said, the land was rich with game, and the waters full of fish and fowl. We even paddled the big canoe down the Columbia towards the bar. But when we got to within a few miles from the mouth of the river, the fast-moving current began to take control of the dugout, so we had to turn into the small inlet the chief had told me about. There we visited a Clatsop village of only a dozen lodges. They were friendly enough, after I told them that we were friends of Coboway, and they showed us their spit of land. Where the village stood, the pounding surf of the ocean was only a few hundred yards across from the river.

With the wind howling and my hair flapping, we walked to a long, narrow, sandy point, with the sea on one side and the river on the other. At the end of this spur, we could look out and see the terrifying bar of the Columbia River. The way across to a cloud-covered rocky headland on the north shore looked to be over a dozen miles of roaring, wind-swept waves some fifty feet high. And the depth of this curling surf stretched a mile inland and a mile out to sea. It was by far the most dangerous crossing I had ever seen. To me, the Columbia River bar looked like a widow-maker.

A few hours later, with an incoming tide, we sailed back down the river for home. While staring at the vastness of the Columbia River and watching its steel-gray water slip by, I marveled that Captain Gray had made it across that horrifying bar and into this smoky-blue gorge of land. God bless his seamanship.

With five bellies to feed, my clan was always on the move, hunting or gathering food. During our first month at the fort, we killed two elk and a deer, and traded some of the meat with the Clatsops for baskets of crabs and roots. We also found that the rivers and creeks were teeming with salmon, steelhead and trout.

Then there were the otter and beaver pelts that we still sought. We had brought with us ten iron traps from Skunk Creek, and Jeremiah's notes on snaring our prey. But first we had to explore the many creeks, lakes and rivers to find the most productive spots to set our traps. This took us most of the first month.

On the morning of the last day of April, Dutch with his musket and

Mole with his bow departed in the big canoe to go hunting across the bay. The day was bright and sunny, with a slight westerly breeze, so the lads used the sail to move down the river. From the fort shoreline, I watched, drinking a cup of coffee, as their sail disappeared onto the bay. Then, some moments later, as Badger and I were preparing to walk up the Netul River to check our trap lines, I noticed the big dugout returning upriver, with the sail lowered and the lads paddling hard.

As soon as the boat came into hailing range, Dutch shouted, "There's a tall ship anchored just inside the bay!"

This surprising news made my heart skip. Moments later, we pulled the big canoe ashore and I rushed back to the fort to tell Raven and to gather our pelts for trading. She was as excited as I, and wanted to go with us to meet the ship. This I quickly agreed to.

Some minutes later, all five of us were in the big dugout, sailing with the wind down the river and into the bay. Once we had cleared the last terrace of land, I got my first glimpse of the ship a few miles away. There, glistening in the sunlight, was a big square-rigged brigantine with a raised forecastle and quarter deck. She was painted brown and black with white gunwales, and looked to be over 200 tons. All of her sails were furled, and as she pulled at her bower, her stern floated our way on the incoming tide. After all my years in the wilderness, she was the most beautiful ship I had ever seen.

Then, as we got closer, my heart sank, for I saw that her flag was the Union Jack. Moments later, I could finally read her name, scrolled across the stern: *Sea Witch, Liverpool England*. Bloody hell. Of all the ships we might have found out here, why did it have to belong to the arrogant British? Damn!

As we approached the *Sea Witch*, we spilled the wind from our sail and maneuvered the *Thunderbird* near her starboard side. Looking up at her painted gunnels, I counted six closed gun ports. This Brit had a sting, and I would have to walk softly.

Just as we came to rest next to the ship, an officer appeared on deck, accompanied by two armed sailors. "Stay clear there! What be your business?" he called out from the planks. As he spoke, I noticed more armed jack-tars climbing the shrouds, fore and aft.

"We have furs to trade," I answered in a strong voice.

The three men on deck looked astonished when they heard my tongue. "What kind of Indian speaks the King's English?" the officer called, moving closer to the rail for a better look.

Taking off my basket hat to expose my red hair, I answered, "A Yankee from Boston. I have skins to trade. May I come aboard?"

In the down roll of the bay swell, the officer turned from the rail, looking puzzled, and disappeared from my view.

We bobbed in the waters for a few more moments. Then an older officer appeared, wearing a blue waistcoat, white britches and a bicorn hat. "Aye, mate, come aboard – but only you and your pelts, no weapons."

I nodded my agreement, and we paddled our dugout next to the ship's boarding ladder. There, I climbed aboard, along with two bundles of skins.

Once standing on the *Sea Witch*'s deck, I was surprised to see her armament; there were a dozen six-pound cannons, port and starboard, and four swivels fore and aft. And there were well over twenty sailors on deck, most of them armed.

"What are you staring at, mate?" the surly Captain asked.

Turning my gaze to him, I asked, "Are ye a man-of-war?"

"Nay, we be a merchant. But we are at war with the French."

Gazing around the ship again, I could feel the tension on deck. "This I did not know… but then, news comes slow, out here."

"And what would be yer name, Yank?" the gruff skipper asked with a deep British accent.

Watching his crew, I could see fear on some faces, but all of them had their ears and eyes on me. Looking back at the Captain, I cleared my throat. "I'm Joseph Blackwell, a sailor from the sloop *Lady Washington*, under the command of Captain Robert Gray. We sailed from Boston harbor in the autumn of '87, and arrived here during the summer of '88. After a skirmish with some Indians forced the hasty departure of my ship, I found myself marooned here, and I have been so ever since."

At my remarks, a quiet hush fell upon the deck.

The Captain had gray, bushy sideburns and the weather-beaten face of a mariner. He was a stout fellow, with hazel eyes that never left my gaze. "Your story is truly astounding, mate," he answered. "Almost twenty years of life wasted. I'm sure my crew can pity your plight."

Slowly twisting to face the crew again, I answered in a full voice, "I found my way on my own, and my life wasn't wasted." Then turning back to the skipper I asked, "And what would be your name, sir?"

"I am Captain Simon Harrison out of London. And who are those Indians in your canoe?" he asked, while staring at my cougar necklace.

"They would be my family, sir. And I wish to trade my pelts for our passage home."

There was loud snickering from the crew, and the Captain quickly put one of his hands in the air, "Enough," he shouted at them, then return his attention to me. "Your family… You took a squaw and raised breeds as your own children?"

"My Christian wife is half Spanish, and my son is all Yankee. The other two Indians are my brothers by blood and family," I answered sharply.

The Captain must have heard my resentment of his words, as he replied calmly, "How many pelts do you have, mate?"

"Thirty-one prime skins. And we can help you gather more from the Indians. We speak their language and know their ways. That is… if you be a fur trader."

"Aye, we are in that business," he answered, and stooped to examine my pelts where they lay on the planks. "This be our first voyage to these waters. We crossed your miserable bar on the morning tide and will leave for Nootka this evening." Harrison straightened and stared again at my necklace. "We only stopped for fresh water and to hunt some game."

"We have plenty of both around here. What of my furs?"

"They are fine and well-cured," he conceded, "and we will give you trade goods for them."

"I don't want trade goods. I want passage home," I answered, glaring eye to eye with the Captain.

He chuckled and shook his head "It would cost you far more than thirty pelts for passage. And having five savages aboard my ship is not a notion I relish. No, Joseph, you will need to wait for another ship."

My face flushed with anger. After twenty years of waiting, this arrogant Brit buzzard was rebuking a marooned sailor. I hated the British!

"So, how many pelts *would* it cost?" I finally asked, trying to keep my angry tongue in check.

The skipper swaggered to the rail and looked down at my clan in the dugout, then twisted my way once again. "Fifty per head, and everyone works. But that only gets you to England."

"That's a large sum," I answered, stunned.

"Aye, a sum you do not have. So trade your pelts with us and let us go about our business."

Stooping, I pick up my two bundles of furs, walked to the rail and tossed the pelts down to Dutch. Then, turning again to the skipper and crew, I said in a firm voice, "Thank you for your kindness, Brits, but I'll keep my pelts for the next ship. If you wish, Captain, my brothers can guide your hunters to herds of elk. And there is a fresh water spring next to my fort."

Now it was Harrison's turn to look surprised. "You have a fort?"

"Aye, built by Yankees and on American land. But we will allow you British to take some fresh meat and water. It's the least we can do for fellow mariners."

From the look on the Captain's face, he was well aware of my displeasure. "I would be obliged for your help," he said carefully. "And I would like to see your fort, if that is alright with you, Joseph."

I offered him a humorless smile. "Aye, you and your men will have my protection. No *savages* will do you harm."

Later that morning, the Captain and a few of his crew arrived at the fort shore in their longboat. Swiftly, I dispatched Mole and three of the ship's hunters up the river trail to hunt in the open plains by the lakes. For a second team, I sent Badger and two other crewmembers across the river in the big dugout to hunt the open meadows of the foothills there. Then, as the remaining crew started filling the water casks from the ship, I showed Fort Clatsop to the Captain and told him the story of Lewis and Clark.

He was clearly impressed by the stockade's construction and size. And when I told of the use of my crude flag and pole to communicate with the Indians, he smiled and grunted. After we had walked and talked for awhile, I took him into the main cabin and introduced him to Raven and Dutch. We drank some coffee, and I showed him what remained of my trade goods from the Spanish trading post. As he looked at the items, Dutch told him what the goods were worth when trading for furs. The Captain asked many questions, mostly about the Indians themselves and how he should deal with them. We told him of our experiences and how we always started trading by giving a gift to the local chief. He listened carefully and made many comments.

As the time slipped by, the Captain warmed to my family and seemed truly surprised by our education and the many languages we spoke. Then Raven served us some cured anchovies and Spanish brandy, and we talked of the world news.

By the time the water casks were filled and the longboat was ready to return, Captain Harrison and I had found some common ground. As he was leaving the cabin, he thanked Raven for her hospitality by reaching out and kissing the top of her right hand. His action caught her off-guard;

quickly, she pulled her hand back and twisted my way, her eyes wide. This was a custom I had never told her about, and she was horrified by it.

Not seeming to notice her reaction, the Captain thanked Dutch and shook his hand, then walked out of the cabin.

As I moved to follow, Raven whispered to me, "Why he kiss my hand?"

Turning to her, I whispered back, "He meant no harm. I will explain later."

As we walked down the path leading to his longboat, the skipper stopped suddenly and turned my way. "I am afraid I frightened your wife," he confessed. "For that, I am sorry. She is a lovely woman, and your son is a fine young lad with a good level head." He squared his shoulders. "So, Joseph, I have a notion. Why don't you trade your furs with me, and I will fill up that longboat with trading goods before it returns for the hunters. Then you could open a trading post in your fort and collect as many furs as possible from the Indians, this summer. When autumn comes, I will return and carry your family and furs out of here."

"And that passage will cost me fifty skins per head?"

Captain Harrison smiled. "No. We will share in whatever the furs are worth. But you will have to work your way back, as well. And I can still only get you to England."

Looking into the skipper's hazel eyes, I wondered whether I could trust him. After all, he was a Brit. Would England be any better a place for my family than here on the Columbia River?

"I've long feared that I would die out here," I heard myself say heavily. "And so I will agree…but I'll need a few other supplies."

"And what would those be?" Harrison asked.

Promptly, I replied, "Five gallons of molasses and of rum, three wheels of cheese, 10 pounds of coffee, two horns of gunpowder, and a wooden cask filled with as many empty earthen jugs and glass jars as you can spare."

The skipper grinned at my strange request. "I presume that is all?"

"No, sir. I would also like a spyglass. The Spanish trading post never had one, and I could use it out here on this open water."

"Very well, Joseph. I'll send everything you've requested back with the longboat when they come to pick up the hunters. Then, in September or October, we will return for your family and the furs. I'll use my signal cannon so you will know we are here. But understand this – we will wait but one tide."

"Aye, sir," I said, and extended my hand for him to shake, sealing the deal.

Later in the afternoon, the hunters returned. Mole and his group carried one elk and a fat buck back to the fort, while Badger returned with another large elk. Soon, the longboat also returned, loaded with my new trade goods and supplies. As we worked at unloading the boat, I noticed that everything promised was there, and that the wooden barrel I had requested contained over thirty empty gallon and quart jugs. Captain Harrison had even surprised me by sending out a real American flag from the ship's pennant locker. But when I unfolded it, I was startled to find fifteen stripes and stars, not the count of thirteen to which I was accustomed. Apparently, American had grown while I had been in the wilderness, and this astounded me.

Even the telescope that Captain Harrison had sent was of the finest quality, with good, clear optics, and made from brass. These gestures delighted me, and my opinion of Harrison improved. After helping load the game into the skiff, we bid a hearty farewell to the crew members, then went about organizing all our new treasures. It had been a fine, fine day.

Over our evening meal, I told everyone of the deal I had struck with Captain Harrison and how we were going to open a trading post in the fort. They listened closely and asked a few questions, but no one expressed any concerns.

Later that night, with the winds swirling and the rain dancing off our roof, Raven and I talked alone by the fire. "Will England be like Boston?" she asked while pouring more coffee for me.

"No," I answered quickly. "It is a place full of Brits, and they are a tribe I do not like. But it's close to my nation, so we will sail from England to Boston."

"Why did the Englishman kiss my hand?"

"In my world, it's a custom that gentleman perform, to show respect for beautiful ladies."

She thought a long moment, then asked, "Why you never kiss my hand? Me not beautiful to you?"

With a grin, I reached out, grasped one of her hands and kissed it. "It is something I will start to do when we are back in polite society."

She quickly pulled her hand away and, with the firelight washing over her pretty face, said, "If we get to your home and you kiss only my hand, I will no like this polite society."

The Trading Post

Choosing one of the empty rooms of the fort, we placed all of our trading goods on long tables. We had tools, knives, fishing hooks, copper kettles, clothes, fabric, blankets and shiny trinkets of many sorts. I knew that all of our items would be highly valued by the Indians.

In another room, we placed the wooden cask with all of our jugs, then set about making a batch of spruce beer. First we half-filled the fifty-gallon barrel with spring water. Next, I added two gallons of molasses and a jug of rum. On top of this mixture, we stirred in young spruce buds and needles until the cask was full. Then we covered the barrel with cedar planks and built a fire in the pit to keep the room warm.

Two weeks later, after the mixture had thoroughly fermented, we strained off the buds and needles, then filled our jugs. The beer had a good flavor, with a bold punch of alcohol – something I knew the Indians would like.

As we prepared to open the trading post, we settled upon some rules. The post would only be open a few hours a day, and we would use the flag to signal this fact. There would always be at least two of us, armed with pistols, inside the fort while trading was in progress. If the Indians wanted our spruce beer, it would cost one pelt per quart or two skins for a gallon jug, and they were not allowed to drink the beer inside the fort. If there was a disturbance, the Indians would be asked to leave, the flag would be raised and the fort's gate would be closed and secured. We wanted furs, not trouble.

Our first few days with the flag at half-staff were quite barren, as no one came to trade. Finally, Coboway and his squaw appeared and traded a fine beaver pelt for two woolen blankets and some glass beads. As I talked with the chief, I gave him a jug of our beer and told him the rules of trading post. Then, as we walked outside the fort, he sampled my brew and beamed from ear to ear. Even his squaw got a taste. Then, taking a second swig, he assured me that he would tell the other Clatsops of my beer, the trading post and the rules.

"Soon, many will come," he said as they started back along the river trail.

And come they did. Over the next few months, we traded with many Clatsops and Tillamooks, and even a few Chinooks from the north. Then, in the late summer, we were visited by some Multnomah and Yakima

Indians from far up the Columbia River. How they heard about our little trading post, I will never know. They simply appeared, prepared to barter for the goods and beer. We had no trouble with any of the Indians and, while a few drove hard bargains, everyone was treated fairly. Soon, our trade goods dwindled and our stack of pelts increased to over a hundred. By any reasonable standard, the fort trading post was a big success.

With the flag at half-staff, Raven, Mole and Badger manned the post while I took my son fishing on his seventeenth birthday. It was one of those rare, hot August days when nary a breeze blew across the water, and so, with paddles in hand, it took us almost an hour to get the big canoe to the incoming tide of the Columbia River. There we drifted in the current, using fishing lines made of elk muscle, and iron hooks with fish heads as bait.

It was a magical time, as the mighty river was as quiet as a lake, and the tall green-blue mountains on either side of the gorge rose up and kissed a cobalt-blue sky. There was a vast beauty here that about took my breath away. How lucky I was to be sharing this with my son.

Soon, in the hot sun, both Dutch and I had our shirts off, splashing ourselves with the cool river water as we fished.

"Father, will Mother be happy in Boston?"

"Aye," I answered quickly, "she will flourish with my people."

"And will I flourish?"

Dutch had a serious look on his face, as if this was something he had pondered upon quite seriously.

"Aye," I replied with a broad smile. "You will do very well in Boston. There is a whole other world out there, one you haven't yet seen. A world where people walk on golden cobblestones, eat food they haven't killed, and live in houses that are warm in the winter and cool in the summer. It is a place where young men control their own destiny."

"And how will I live? Will I be a hunter, a builder of things, or a war chief?"

My son's mind was like his body, lean and quick. He was a handsome young man with broad shoulders, olive skin, auburn hair and a strong chin with a deep cleft. Dutch also had eyes so blue that they about glowed, which always reminded me of my guardian angel.

"You will be whatever you want to be. That is the greatness of America – no borders, only horizons. Maybe you will be a sea captain, or a merchant, or even a politician. Whatever your enterprise, do it as best you can. Then success will seek you out."

Dutch thought a moment, with a somber face. "Did success seek you out, Father?"

I smiled. "Aye, and it's sitting in front of me."

Splash!

Out of nowhere, we were drenched with cold river water as something jumped alongside our boat. Then came a loud bark.

Instantly, Dutch leapt to his feet and looked in the direction of the sounds.

"Father, it's a ghost sea-lion," he shouted, pointing.

Standing next to my son, I saw what he was talking about. There in the river water was something I had never seen before, a pure white sea-lion. Then a second one appeared, also white in color, with flecks of brown. They were big and sleek, and they barked a loud call that echoed across the water.

"Blimey! White sea-lions – and look at their size," Dutch exclaimed.

They had been attracted to us by our fishing bait, and now they were rolling in and out of the water, not twenty feet from our boat.

"Let's kill 'em for their fur and oil," I shouted.

Dutch twisted my way, looking shocked by my comment. "Leave them be, Father. They are magnificent creatures."

"Those sea-lions are just like you, my son – a gift from above. We can sell their pelts in China and use the money to sail from England to Boston. It's your family's future swimming out there. So, what say ye now, lad?"

He looked at me for the longest moment. Then, with a reluctant grimace, he mumbled, "Kill 'em."

The taking of the white sea-lions was a great life lesson on a seventeenth birthday, as it reminded Dutch of the first rule of survival: take what Mother Nature offers. Life is cruel, and in the wilderness only the strong endure. We shot both lions in the head and got ropes quickly around their carcasses before they could sink deep into the water.

After lashing them to the boat, we paddled to a nearby island, where we gutted and skinned both animals. After a few hours of that slimy work, with sweat pouring off our brows, we loaded the blubber and skins aboard our canoe. Then, with a slight breeze from the east to aid us, we sailed for home.

"How much do you think the pelts will fetch?" Dutch asked with a solemn face.

"Hard to say," I answered from the tiller. "These are rare white skins. After your mother has cured them, they could fetch maybe a hundred dollars – more than enough for our passage home."

My son stared at me with sad blues eyes. "Sorry, Father. I just don't have your bloodlust. My heart cries from killing those fine creatures. Maybe someday I'll find your strength."

"Killing comes easy to some and hard to others," I answered thoughtfully. "I once thought as you, but this wilderness and my family changed that notion."

As we approached the fort, I saw that the flag was still down, and then noticed Mole cooling off in the water, just up-river.

Pulling the canoe to high ground, I shouted to him, "Is Badger with Raven?"

"No, Badger go to village to see squaw," Mole shouted back. "It too hot to make trade. We have just one Chinook all day."

"If Raven is alone, why is the flag still down?" I asked, starting briskly up the path to the fort.

"We forget to raise flag," he shouted back, moving out of the water.

As I got to the gate, I heard muffled noises coming from inside. Promptly, I pulled open the door to the courtyard and, to my shock, saw an Indian holding Raven down on top of a trading table. He wore only a loincloth, and had one hand over her mouth and the other up her dress. Raven was fighting him off the best she could, but the brave was young and strong. There was fear on her face as she twisted and moved, trying to scream through his powerful hand covering her mouth.

The Indian had his back to me as I rushed through the yard to the table. Reaching them, I pulled him off my wife, spun him around, and punched him hard with both of my closed fists.

At my blows, he let out a groan and dropped to the ground.

I picked him up again and threw him hard against the log walls. I was about to punch him again, but I heard my wife sobbing. Turning her way, I saw her roll off the table, pulling down her frock.

Turning back to the Indian, I put my left forearm hard across his throat and reached for my knife with my right hand. The Chinook brave was groggy and smelt of beer. His eyes were glassy, and his sweating face was not familiar. By the time I had my blade raised, Dutch was standing with his mother and Mole was running through the gate. The scuffle had lasted only a few seconds, but my anger still raged.

Finally, the brave's eyes seemed to come alive, and he started to struggle under my powerful forearm.

"I going to spoil your guts, you dumb buck. No one touches my wife," I shouted into his young face.

At my words, Raven moved quickly closer to me, whimpering, and said, "Don't kill him Joe. He not hurt me, he just drunk."

Then Dutch added, "Don't do it, Father. Killing him is wrong."

By now, the brave's eyes were wide. He knew from the look on my face that death was near. He mumbled something I could not understand.

Putting my blade closer to his nose, I looked him right in the eye and growled, "I should cut off your manhood…but I won't. Still, if I ever see you around here again, I will surely kill you."

Then, with a lightning-fast hand, I cut off the tip of his nose, and it fell to the dirt. Instantly, blood filled the slice, and I removed my forearm from his neck. With fear on his face, the Indian grabbed onto his bleeding nose. Turning back to the trading table, I ripped a piece of cloth from a shirt and handed it to the stunned brave.

"Get out of here, before I change my mind," I shouted, and kicked his backside towards the gate.

Once he was gone, Raven told me that the brave had traded for a jug of beer, earlier in the morning. Then, hours later, he had slipped back into the fort, looking for more. He had caught Raven off-guard, as she thought the flag was up.

At her words, I swallowed my rage, but not before I took Mole to task for leaving the flag down. And I did the same to Badger, when he returned. Luckily, Raven had not been violated, but the incident was a sobering warning to us all.

A few weeks later, Raven finished curing the white sea-lion skins, and I could tell from their touch and smell that we had something special. I was certain, because of their color and condition, that they were valuable furs. With that thought, I told my family that we would hide the skins in our pokes when we boarded the ship. That way, we could get them ashore and sell the skins ourselves when we reached China.

Final Passage

With the coming of the autumn colors, I set up a watch on the point of land where our river met the bay. From there, each morning and evening, we searched the waters with our telescope, watching for the return of the *Sea Witch*, or any other movement.

By the end of September, most of our trade goods were gone, and only a few jugs of beer remained. As for the pelts, we had one hundred and sixty-two furs, stacked skin to skin, and bundled with rawhide in one of the cabins. Now we waited anxiously for the return of Captain Harrison and our escape for home.

On the last day of the month, I was sitting by the morning fire, talking with Raven, when Mole burst through the door with news that two native war-canoes were coming our way. He had seen them from our lookout point and run the two miles back to alert us.

"Are you sure they are coming here?" I asked.

Out of breath, he answered that the canoes had crossed the Columbia from the north shore and then turned into our bay. Just before he started his run back to the fort, he had counted nineteen braves in the two dugouts, with no squaws or papoose.

This was disturbing news, as nearly all trading parties contained woman and children. Hurriedly, I grabbed my rifle, and we all rushed out to the courtyard, where I yelled for Dutch and Badger. As soon as everyone had gathered around, we talked of the news and of what actions to take. We weren't sure the Indians were hostile, but we wanted no trouble.

After some planning, we opened the gate, and I positioned Badger and Dutch on either side of the entrance, armed with rifles. Raven, carrying one of the pistols, stood in the cabin shadows, next to the trade tables. Finally, I sent Mole and his bow to the cabin roof, overlooking the path from the river.

My final actions were to lower the flag halfway down and then walk toward the water, with our remaining pistol tucked in my belt. By the time I got to the river's edge, I could see the two canoes, half a mile downstream. Standing in the sun, I used the telescope to watch the approaching boats. Focusing on the lead canoe, I was surprised to see a youthful, skinny white man in buckskins, with a black oddly braided beard. He wore a red derby hat adorned with a protruding black feather. He looked so out of place that I had to chuckle to myself.

Paddling just behind this man were eight Chinook braves, a few of whom had muskets resting next to them. This was the first time I had ever seen Indians with flit-locks, and it was a nightmare come true.

Then my view turned to panic, as I spotted Hawk in the second dugout. He was the lead paddler and wore no shirt; the ruby scar across his chest was clearly visible. Looking carefully, I also saw the faces of his brother Sea Lion and cousin Frog.

Slowly, I lowered the glass from my eye. Trouble was upon us.

As the lead canoe slid to shore, the man in the red hat stepped off, with his hand outstretched. "Would ye be Fire-Head?" he asked in crude English while approaching.

"Aye, I'm known as Fire-Head, but my Christian name is Joseph," I answered as I grasped his hand.

The young man's eyes were black, but they never focused directly on me. Instead, they scanned the fort behind.

"And you would be?" I asked removing my hand from his limp grip.

"I am Count Ivan, a nobleman in the royal Russian family."

I snickered to myself at the suggestion that this rawboned man was royalty. "And what would be your business, sir?" I asked, and glanced at the braves resting in their canoes, half of whom were armed with rifles.

"I have heard about your trading post and wanted to see it first-hand. Are we welcome?"

There was treachery written all over this man's black, hairy face, and his eyes still had not yet met mine. "You are welcome, Count, but we only allow two Indians at a time inside the fort's walls, without weapons."

"Aye," he answered with parted lips and a sly smile, "that would be wise. It is only I who wishes to see your fort. My men will stay here in their canoes."

"Very well," I answered, and turned up the path.

The Count asked many questions about the fort as we walked in its direction, wanting to know who had built it, when it had been built and why. I responded to all of his queries with vague answers. As we passed the gate, his gaze darted from Dutch to Badger, then – once we were inside – to Mole on the roof, and then Raven, who waited by the trade tables. "This be a big place. Is this all of your band?"

He was sizing us up, and I didn't like. "No," I answered. "We have more out hunting."

He smiled at Raven, as we came to the tables, but she only looked my way, and I didn't introduce Ivan to her.

After handling some of the items on the table, he asked, "Your stores seem small. Do ye have more trade goods?"

"The season is about over, sir, and we have enough to finish it."

The Count then picked up a jug of beer and shook it, close to his ear.

"Sounds like firewater. No wonder the Indians talk of your post. But really, mate, what fool gives Indians alcohol?"

His superior tone was much like that of the English, and it chafed me. "Hopefully not the same fool that gives them rifles."

His eyes finally met mine, and he frowned at me. "That be a good point, Joseph. Can ye show me your furs?"

"Why would I do that, sir?"

"Maybe I wish to buy them. Or maybe you wish to be polite."

"My pelts are already sold sir, and I wish you no rudeness."

The Russian now gave me a really good look, as if he were searching for my weakness. After slowly putting the jug down on the table, he turned back to me. "The facts be, Joseph, that this land and all of its furs belong to his Majesty Tsar Paul of Mother Russia. I be his representative and I come to collect his property."

His words hung in the air, and again I knew trouble had rowed ashore. "You are mistaken, sir. Long ago, this land was claimed for America by Captain Robert Gray. And this fort was Yankee built, on American land. We wish no trouble, but we will not relinquish what is rightfully ours."

"I am afraid we disagree, Joseph, but I wish no bloodshed. So pay the Tsar a tribute of half your skins and we will paddle away and bother ye no more."

By now, sweat was rolling down his forehead from the hot sun. His gaze was determined, and he had one hand on the butt of the pistol that hung from his belt.

"I must refuse your offer, sir. Our furs are not for tribute," I answered, scowling at him.

Hostility filled the air, shimmering like the heat. Even the birds had stopped singing.

His eyes darted again to Dutch, then Badger, then Mole. It was his move… his decision.

Slowly, he pulled back his hand from the pistol butt and forced a smile. "I will give ye some time to consider my offer. Soon, we will return – for your tribute or your blood, whichever you decide."

He then turned and strolled for the gate. I nodded for Dutch and Badger to let him pass. Then, after he reached the river, we closed the gates. Soon from the rooftop, Mole told us that the boats were paddling back down the river.

After the renegade's departure, we all gathered around and discussed our visitors. It had taken a lot of grit for him to stand in our fort and make such outrageous demands. His actions told me that he did not fear us, and that wasn't good. Our only hope now was to stay within the safety of the fort's walls, and pray that the *Sea Witch* would soon arrive.

As a precaution, we carried the large dugout into the fort, as we worried that it might be damaged if the Chinooks returned. Then we filled the empty beer barrel with drinking water, and I sent Dutch and Mole out for a nearby hunt. As soon as our meat locker was restocked, I knew we would have enough provisions for a long wait.

For over a week, we stayed within the fort's walls, with a lookout always perched on the roof. But we saw no one, and heard nothing, so soon we came to believe that the Count and his band had moved on.

When Coboway and his squaw appeared again, with two pelts to trade, we opened the fort for them, and traded the last of our blankets, an iron cooking pot and handfuls of trinkets for the skins. He was surprised with my generosity, but I thought it was only fitting, as he had been our first customer and now, more than likely, was our last. In a final gesture of potlatch, I offered the chief a cup of rum, and he joyfully accepted.

As we moved into the big room, he asked if we were going to winter at the fort.

"No," I answered, "we soon leave this land." Then, pouring the grog, I told him of the Chinooks and my fears.

"Will the Russian take over the fort?"

"You know of this Russian man?" I asked with amazement.

"Aye, he and his band come to village five suns ago. He say you have no right to skins, only him. But I trade with you. We are friends."

"Do you know where he is camped?"

"Aye, he camp on bay shore, just down Netul River."

Squatting to the ground, I used my knife in the dirt to draw out a rough map of the bay and the rivers. Then I asked him to point out where the Russian camp was.

The chief joined me on his heels and showed me, with his finger, a spot just the other side of the point where our river met the bay. There, the Russian would have the high ground on the terrace land we had used as our lookout point.

I was pleased to know where he was, but disappointed that he hadn't moved on. As we got to our feet, I asked Coboway if some of his braves would help us, if we had trouble with the Russian.

He shook his head quickly. "No, we at peace with Chinooks, and man with red hat want same with Clatsops."

I was dismayed, but fully understood. Most coastal Indians hated conflicts and would avoid them at all costs.

After we finished our rum, I bid farewell Coboway and Ona. I knew full well we would never see them again, because soon we would be gone… or dead.

All that restless night, I worried about where the renegades were camped. When we departed for the ship, we would have to paddle right past that point. And with them holding the high ground, they would be in a perfect position for an ambush. Our only hope was to have good wind at our backs so that we could swiftly sail past them and reach the open bay. A few miles after that, we would be at the ship. That was our only hope.

Early the next morning, Mole rushed into the big room, carrying Badger's bear cape.

"Badger gone. He go to village to see squaw, last night, and no return. He leave behind his wife's spirit blanket and now I fear for him."

"That bloody fool," I fumed. "He puts us all in danger."

Bang!

I heard a rifle shot from outside the walls. Quickly, I grabbed my weapon, and we all ran out into the courtyard.

Dutch was standing by the closed gates with his rifle at the ready. As we moved towards him, Mole climbed the ladder to the roof. Then we heard a loud knock on the log gates.

As we approached the entrance, I saw through the timber cracks that Count Ivan was standing in the shadows, with his rifle resting across his arms.

"Let me in, Joseph. I come for my king's tribute," he shouted.

"No such tribute will be made," I barked back.

"Then we will take some of your blood, this fine morning. If your roof watcher looks downriver, he will see one of your braves by a tall tree… about to die."

From the rooftop, Mole spun that way, then looked down to me. With a sad face, he nodded.

Raven grabbed my arm and whispered, "Don't let them kill my brother."

"Yes, Father," Dutch added in a low voice. "Give him what he wants."

Their fear was a blindfold and I felt their worries. But we hadn't come this far to be set upon by pirates. "What he wants," I said in a fierce whisperer, "is all our furs, the fort itself, and to kill us all. That I cannot allow." Holding up my hand, I silenced any further pleas. Then, in a loud, firm voice, I shouted, "I will give you half our pelts for my brother's life. But you must bring him onto the open ground before I come out with the skins."

The Count beamed. "Very well. I'll wait for you next to your brother, on the open ground. No weapons, Joseph, or he will die."

Swiftly, I moved to the fur room and grabbed a bundle of skins. Then, rushing back outside, I handed my rifle to Mole and took his pistol, which I checked to be certain that was loaded and primed. Half-cocking the gun, I slipped it carefully between the two top skins.

"Both of you, get onto the roof, and keep a keen eye on the bushes behind the Russian. That is where the danger will lurk," I told Mole and Dutch.

They scrambled up the ladder and got into position. As they did, I removed my sea knife and handed it to Raven.

Dutch peered over the roofline, and whispered down that only Badger and the Count stood on the open ground.

"What of you?" Raven asked as I moved for the gates.

"I will trade these pelts for Badger, but I fear that the Russian wants me, as well."

Anguish raced across my wife's face. "You no go. Send me. He not hurt me."

My eyes spoke a thousand words to her as I shook my head, opened the gates and walked outside. Raven had no notion of the deception this greedy Russian was capable of, and I hoped she wouldn't learn it, this day.

The morning was bright and clear, with the distant mountains peaks holding firm to a few wispy clouds. There was a slight, cool breeze on my face, and I heard the call of an eagle flying high above. I needed his strength today.

Walking around the corner of the fort, I held my bundle of furs high so that the Russian could see that I wasn't armed. Fear dragged at my footsteps, while determination held my heart.

As I moved closer to the two men in the open, I noticed that Badger's hands were bound with rawhide, and that the Count had a pistol in his belt.

Still with my bundle high, I approached them and challenged, "You said no weapons, but you are armed."

"Just for my protection," the Count answered, and raised his hand. "That is far enough, Joseph."

Stopping a good ten feet from the men, I carefully scanned the tree line behind them, hoping that Dutch or Mole would have a clear shots. Then I slowly lowered my bundle of furs to waist level, and slyly slipped one hand inside the skins to grasp the pistol.

The Russian and I just stared at each other, for the longest moment. He was nervous and twitchy, while Badger stood, stoic, with a fearful face.

"How many skins, Joseph?" the Count finally asked.

"Twenty-four. That's half our poke," I lied without blinking.

"Not enough, Joseph. It will cost another bundle."

With my hand now firmly on the pistol butt, I prayed that my aim would be true and my reflexes swift. "Take this bundle and go on your way. There will be no more."

The Count, glaring, went for his pistol.

Instantly, I dropped my fur bundle, revealing the pistol in my hand as I quickly cocked it all the way. Then I pulled the trigger.

Bang!

Smoke exploded from the barrel, and my lead ball hit Ivan's right shoulder hard. The Russian fell to the ground, still gripping his unfired gun. Through the gun smoke, I jumped for Badger and knocked him down.

Bang, bang!

Shots rang out from the bushes behind us, but the bullets missed us.

Bang, bang!

Two answering shots from the fort rang out. I heard one Indian scream, but I didn't see him. With Badger now on the ground, I rolled across the dirt and wrestled the loaded pistol from the hand of the groggy and bleeding Count. Then I sat the wounded Russian up in the dirt, using him as a human shield, and placed the barrel of his pistol against his head.

Two arrows whizzed by me, while a third found its mark, with a loud *thump,* in Badger's ribs as he foolishly tried to stand. He let out a loud moan, looked my way, rolled his eyes upward, and collapsed onto the dirt once again.

"I'll shoot this Russian dog if there is any more fighting," I yelled out in my best Tillamook tongue.

No answer came from the tree line. After a few heart beats of silence, I yelled for Raven to come out. Next, holding the back of the Count's rawhide shirt with one hand and the gun to his head with other, I pulled him, scooting on my butt, across the ground to the corner of the fort's walls, then propped him up so the Indians could see him.

When Raven stood next to me, I gave her the pistol and yelled loudly, "Shoot him if there is trouble."

Again, there was no response from the tree line, and so, with Raven standing over the Russian, I walked quickly back and lifted Badger onto my shoulders.

From the limpness of his body, I feared he was dead. Stooping, I picked up the bundle of furs, as well, and returned to the fort.

"What of this Russian?" Raven asked, pistol in hand, as I stumbled by.

"Leave him," I answered, scowling at the dazed look on Ivan's face.

With Raven close behind me, we went back inside the fort and secured the gate. Then I laid Badger on one of the tables in the fur room. With Raven now wailing, I checked for any signs of life, but found none.

I covered him with his bear skin. Now his wife's spirit would be close.

A few minutes later, with Dutch and Mole by my side, I said a short prayer and wished him well in the spirit world.

Sometime in the middle of the night, with Raven still sobbing over her brother's body, the Russian was carried away. We found the moccasin tracks the next day, at first light, but we didn't give chase. The Indians were gone, and we had the Russian's pistol. We were safe, for now.

Later that day, we buried Badger, wearing his bear cape, just outside the fort walls. His death had been a tragedy, and he would be sorely missed.

In the forenoon, two days later, we heard what we believed was thunder roll across the land. But the sky had but a few clouds and the temperature was mild. Therefore, with great caution, I conclude that the big bang had, in fact, been the loud report of the *Sea Witch*'s signal cannon. Our escape was finally at hand.

Since the shooting of the Russian, I had made a plan for our hasty departure. First, we carried the big canoe back to the river's edge and rigged it with our mast and sail. Next, we loaded the dugout with our furs, seven bundles in all, placed along the port side of the boat. Then I showed everyone how we could use the bundles as a shield if we came under attack from arrows.

"These furs won't stop lead balls," Mole commented.

"No," I answered soberly, "but they are better than nothing."

Finally, we loaded the boat with panniers that contained our personal belongings, the white sea-lion skins, our sleeping robes, blankets, and a few extra knives and war axes.

When we had done so, I put into action the last part of my plan – a diversion.

With everyone gathered around the dugout, I said, "And now we will burn down the fort."

Raven's mouth dropped open, "Burn down the fort! You don't even know for sure if the ship is on the bay. Everything else we own is still inside the walls."

"Aye," I answered, "and the Russians will not get this fort or our kits. It is Yankee-built, on American land."

"But, Father," Dutch pleaded, "if the ship isn't there, we can make our way back to the safety of the stockade."

"The ship is there, and I want the Chinooks to see our smoke and come running to investigate. Then we can safely sail past them and out into the bay."

"That's a bloody big gamble," Dutch said, looking grimly concerned.

"Aye, but I'm right. The ship is there, and we need the Indians off the high ground. It's the only way for our family to survive. Do I have your support?"

The others looked at each other for a brief moment, then nodded. Once again, I was putting my family in jeopardy, and I prayed that I *was* indeed right.

Walking from room to room in the fort, we used the last of sea-lion oil to soak the timbers. Then, just before setting the stronghold ablaze, I ran down the flag and placed it in my pouch. Moments later, with the furniture torched in each room, we quickly moved through the gates as the flames took hold.

Standing in the heat of the roaring fire, I sadly watched the gray fortress burn like the devil itself. Soon, black smoke filled the sky. Looking above the tree tops, I saw the haze floating northeast on a slight southerly breeze. This was as planned; soon, the Chinooks would see and smell the smoke, and come running upriver.

Turning our backs on the fire, we quickly moved down the path to the canoe and shoved off.

We paddled a half-mile down the river and put in at a small eddy on the other side of the tributary. Here we could conceal the dugout in some reeds and watch the trail that led to the fort.

A few minutes later, five braves ran up the river path. I was disappointed that there weren't more, but then, this was five we wouldn't have to face downstream.

As soon as the Indians disappeared from view, we paddled the canoe out into the river's current. There we raised the sail into a slight breeze and continued down river. Half a mile farther, we came to tidal water, and I felt the boat slow on the incoming tide. We reached for our paddles and dug them deep into the river.

As we got closer to the bay, I steered the dugout toward the eastern bank. Then, with the smoke of the fort fire filtering the sunlight, we came abreast of the terrace of ground that overlooked the bay. At first, we saw only geese squabbling on the shoreline, and I hoped we might sail right by. But just as we slipped by this point, a group of Indians appeared and opened fire upon us.

At their first salvo of arrows and bullets, Raven took the tiller, crouching low in the hull to guide the boat. Standing, Dutch and I returned fire on the group a hundred yards across the water. Our first shots missed, as did those of the Indians. After reloading, we fired again, and this time I hit a brave just as he shot a flaming arrow into the sky. He collapsed, but his burning arrow found its mark in our sail cloth.

As Dutch stood with his second shot, I grabbed our bailing bucket and filled it with river water. Then, getting to my feet, I threw the water onto the burning sail.

Just as I did, Mole leapt across the canoe and knocked me to the hull. As we hit the bottom of the boat, he let out a groan and then went limp on top of me.

Stunned, I rolled him off of me…and found his lifeless blank eyes gazing back at me.

Mole was dead. He had taken a lead ball in the back of his head, lead that had been meant for me. He had saved my life.

With tears rolling down my cheeks, I pulled my brother's body down the hull and placed him close to the masthead. Then, weeping like squaw, I reloaded my rifle and stood for another shot at the Indians.

Bang.

Through my tears and the drifting gun smoke, I watched as another Chinook dropped with his rifle in his hand. Then I felt Dutch and Raven pulling me down to the hull.

"Father, they are almost out of range," Dutch said, his face streaked with tears.

Peering back over the stern gunnels, I could see that he was right. Then, twisting to face the bow, I saw that we were inside the gray bay. And there, like a mirage in the distance, was the *Sea Witch* at anchor. Thank God! We only had to cover about three miles of open water to safety.

As Raven lifted herself back to the tiller seat, I crawled to my brother's body. There, with Dutch at my side, I closed Mole's dead eyes with my finger tips. Then I removed his cougar necklace and lowered it over my son's head. "He would want you to have this," I said, with weeping eyes.

Dutch reached out to gently touch Mole's face, and sadly shook his head. Then, turning to me, he said, "There is a hole our sail. Mole is dead, and we should be paddling."

My son was right.

With the scorched hole nearly the size of a bucket in our sail, the boat's speed was reduced. Dutch and I grabbed our paddles and dug them deep into the water.

We had barely started to row when Raven called out from the tiller, "The Russian comes after us."

I looked to our wake and saw that a war canoe had just shoved off from shore. Using the telescope, I counted the paddlers.

"They have nine paddles to our three," I shouted, with the glass still at my eye.

"How far, Father?" Dutch asked, with his scull digging into the water.

"Half a mile and closing," I answered, taking back my paddle. "We must row like the wind!"

Raven tied the tiller off and frantically helped us row. We had some advantage with the sail, but the breeze was slight and the hole spilled much of the wind. With my arms working the scull, I looked out towards the resting ship, and guessed we had over two miles to go. With our bow slicing though the calm waters of the bay, I felt the warmth of the afternoon sun on my back. Twisting to look astern, I found that I could still see the smoke from the fort fire drifting in the air.

We rowed hard for many minutes before I stood again with the glass to my eye. Our pursuers had closed much of the gap, and now I could see the Russian, his shoulder in a sling, sitting in the bow of his canoe. Next to him, standing, was Hawk. He carried a rifle at the ready, and his face was colored with war paint.

Hastily, I returned to my paddle.

A few moments later, we heard the roar of a flint-lock, and turned to watch smoke rising from the war canoe. The ball fell short, hitting the water in our wake.

Looking back out to the *Sea Witch*, I guessed we were only a mile out. But, at our speed, Hawk and the Russian would soon be upon us.

"We are going to have to fight," I yelled while working my scull. "I'll fire first and then row, while Raven reloads. Dutch, you do the same. If we can shoot a few rowers, we'll have a chance."

I stood and fired my rife, but the ball hit the water just short of the war canoe. Then, with Raven reloading and me paddling, Dutch stood and fired his rifle. His ball, too, fell short.

After a few more strokes, with my gun now reloaded, I stood again and took aim. Just as I did, Hawk pulled his trigger.

Bang.

The sound of his shot rolled across the water, and his ball hit our stern, splintering some wood.

Bang.

My shot answered, and I watched through my smoke as a Chinook paddler buckled from my ball. Then, as Dutch stood, two shots rang out from the war canoe, and he quickly ducked back behind the gunnels. Both balls hit our dugout, but they caused little damage. Swiftly, Dutch stood and fired again, then dropped to the hull.

Twisting from my scull, I watch his ball hit the Russian. Ivan grabbed onto his chest for a split second, then collapsed backwards.

"You killed that lousy Russian. Good shooting, Son!" I yelled over my scull.

When I stood again, I noticed four Indians with their bows bent to the sky. "Arrows," I yelled, and I fell back to the hull, reaching for a bundle of furs.

Swish- thump!

Arrows rained from the sky. Two stuck in the wood of the boat, while a third hit the top of the bundle of furs that Raven held over her head. Her frightened gaze darted my way for an instant, from under the shield of skins. Then she dropped the bundle and went back to reloading her son's rifle.

Standing again, I saw that the war-canoe was now only fifty yards away. Quickly, I took aim and fired my rifle, then ducked behind the gunnels. As the gun smoke cleared, I heard moaning from a brave. Then the Chinooks returned fire with a salvo of their own. Bullets ripped into our boat, followed by two fire arrows, one of which lodged in our canvas again, setting it ablaze.

Quickly, I scrambled for the bailing bucket, while Dutch stood and fired. Dipping the bucket into the bay water, I noticed the *Sea Witch's* longboat rowing our way, filled with armed sailors. Help was at hand!

Boom! *Boom!*

Two swivel guns opened fire from the *Sea Witch*. Their canon balls fell just short of the war canoe, throwing plumes of water high into the air.

I stood and swiftly drenched the sail with my bucket of water. Then, as I turned from the sail, I saw a puff of smoke from Hawk's rifle and felt his hot lead tear open my guts.

Dropping the bucket, I stumbled to the stern and fell to the tiller seat, my belly on fire. Raven rushed to me, while Dutch turned to stare at my bleeding stomach. Then, with fury on his face, he pulled the two pistols in his belt and fired them both across the water.

Bang. Bang.

Through the smoke, I watched Hawk get hit directly in his eye. His face exploded with black blood, and he collapsed, slumping over the bow and, into the water.

As Dutch ducked from his shot, I blinked and nodded my head. With our rescue within reach, my son had killed my nemesis and he had killed me. How destructive hate can be. God forgive his savage soul.

With my guts boiling and my head spinning, I heard two more *booms* from the swivel guns. This time, they blew the war canoe in half, throwing Chinook bodies into the bay.

Raising my eyes to the blue sky, I spotted a white feather slowly floating toward our canoe. My guardian spirit was with me, and oh sweet Jesus my mother waited...

With the battle over, Raven hovered above me, and I felt her tears drip onto my cheeks. "You no die," she yelled frantically.

Mustering the last of my voice, I whispered, "We are like geese… always together."

Joseph Blackwell, my father, died of wounds inflected by Chinook renegades on October the tenth, 1806. His death occurred within the shadow of his deliverance. With the help of the ship's company and Captain Harrison, he and my brother Mole were buried together, next to a big boulder on a gentle knoll overlooking the bay.

Before my beloved father was laid to rest, I took from him his cougar necklace, pouch, long rifle and sea knife. Then I spread the scorched sail over their bodies, and the Captain read from his Bible as dirt was shoveled in. My mother was in such a state that she had not spoken a single word since Father died in her arms.

After the burial, I helped Mother aboard the ship. Then, as the *Sea Witch* prepared to get underway, she quietly made an appeal to Captain Harrison and me. She asked that our dugout, the *Thunderbird*, be set ablaze and allowed to drift on the bay as a tribute to her husband.

Without hesitation, we agreed. Moments later, after soaking the dugout with whale oil and pushing it away from the ship, I used one of my brother's arrows, lit with fire, and shot it into the canoe.

Then, as the *Sea Witch* slowly departed, Mother and I stood at the stern rail, watching the burning *Thunderbird* and the Columbia River gorge slip away. This land had claimed my father and brother in a single day like no other. During that day, I had tasted my Father's bloodlust and it was bitter sweet. As I knew the sight of Hawk's exploding eye would haunt me forever.

Turning to my mother's sad face, I said simply, "We shouldn't have tried to leave this land."

She looked up at me with tears in her eyes and softly replied, "Never let fear rob your future. This land swallowed your father and gave him only dreams of home. Follow his legacy, you can do no better."

Turning from mother, I gazed upon the distant burning canoe. "Aye… we will find father's tribe and thrive in his land."

Chapter Twelve: Outward Bound

WITH SHRIEKING SEA BIRDS SOARING HIGH ABOVE the ship's wake, the *Sea Witch* crossed the Columbia Bar in the near-perfect conditions of a slack tide. For that, all hands rejoiced, as earlier that morning they had crossed in sloppy waters and towering waves. Once past the mountainous northern headlands, Captain Harrison turned the ship southwest and ordered all sails to the wind.

As the ship pitched and rolled towards the setting sun, the third mate gave Raven and Dutch a tour of the massive brigantine. As they silently walked the unfamiliar decks of the ship, they were greeted with smiles and tipped hats from officers and crew. After the tragic events of getting their furs aboard, the ship's company couldn't have been more agreeable. When finally finished, they joined the skipper on the quarterdeck, where he offered them the use of the first mate's cabin. Raven sadly shook her head no, telling the Captain that she would prefer sleeping on the open deck, where she could be closer to her husband's spirit. She looked so forlorn that neither Dutch nor the skipper had the heart to refuse her request.

In the fading light, they rolled out their buffalo skins on the forecastle deck and did their best not to be under the boot of the working crew. Raven was quiet and withdrawn, her face puffy from tears. After the bedrolls were in place, she stood stoically at the bowsprit and gazed upon the brilliant sunset until the sky was black and studded with stars. Soon the cook sent out some food, but she ate very little and refused all offerings of wine or rum. She seemed to be in her own world, pondering her own demons. And, while Dutch was constantly by her side, he could give her little comfort.

Before they fell asleep that night, Raven whispered to her son, "I be melancholy for my husband. Do not worry of me. He will embrace me soon." Then she kissed him on his cheek and, with a strange smile on her lips, pulled a blanket over herself and gazed upon the stars. Raven's mood frightened Dutch, and he prayed for his father's soul and his mother's relief.

Over the next few weeks, Raven's attitude changed very little. She was quiet and listless, spending hours at the rail, watching the view of glory and all beyond. Most of her son's time was spent seeing to her needs and carefully exploring the items he found inside his father's pouch. Sometimes, Dutch showed his father's drawing to his mother, then read to her what he had written on the back of the parchments. She seemed to enjoy her husband's art and hearing his words. Most of time, however, she could only weep, which added to her misery.

Dutch also found a few items in the pouch that he didn't share: strange gold coins, a locket with another woman's image inside of it, and a letter from his father's mother, written on her deathbed. These items were too private, and he felt instinctively that they needed to be kept secret.

The ship sailed southwesterly across long, rolling ocean swells that slowly turned from blue to green.

After four weeks of sailing, and with the air smelling of sweetness, the Sandwich Islands finally came into view. The ship was soon greeted by several outrigger canoes paddled by natives who wore only grass girdles around their waists and flower chokers around their necks. These people came alongside, singing a joyful welcome and offering curious foods. Raven and Dutch watched this event from the rail and pondered the natives. They looked to be the true children of the sun, as their bodies shone like polished cedar. They were colorful in garb and friendly to a fault.

Soon, the ship bore away from the outriggers and, some miles later, anchored in a harbor on an island called Maui. Here, joining several other ships at moorage, Captain Harrison spent three warm tropical days taking on fresh provisions.

On the second day, a few of the crew took Raven and Dutch ashore, where they explored a small village called Rainai. This beautiful land was just like Dutch's father had told him, full of strange sights, new smells and people as colorful as a rainbow. To his surprise, the native Hawaiians were much the same as the coastal Indians. While their culture was different, their stature and skin tone seemed much the same. The locals were a friendly lot, and mother and son enjoyed sampling delicious fruits and tasting a sweet seed called a cocoanut. The islanders wore light clothing made of fabrics as colorful as a butterfly, and the little village bustled with people of all nationalities, working together. Dutch mused that Rainai might be a shining example of what could happen to the Indian villages on the Pacific coast. This, he decided, would be a good notion.

On one of the side streets, Raven found a small, white stucco church, and they went inside. The sanctuary was dark and cool, with a stone floor and colorful window glass. As they sat on a wooden bench in front of the altar, they were joined by a missionary man dressed in black. His tongue was English and they talked awhile. Raven showed him the silver cross she wore around her neck, as did Dutch. Then she told him of her sorrow, and they all prayed together. When they finished, the pastor whispered something in Raven's ear. Then mother and son walked out of the church, into the bright sunlight. Soon they found themselves strolling on the warm sands of the harbor shore, and finally they talked.

"Preacher man say death is part of life. But he no tell me why God takes my husband."

In the warm, sweet air, Dutch noticed how weary and gaunt his mother had become, and it frightened him. "Mother, you need to eat better, and your heartache must stop. It's not good for you."

"I wish Father Mendez was here. He would comfort me."

"You are my family. I will care for you, but you must end this mourning. Father is dead. This we cannot change, so please stop your suffering."

Raven came to a halt in the sand and turned to her son, placing both of her hands upon his face and gazing into his blue eyes. "It is a squaw's way to suffer," she said with a slight smile.

"Mother, we have a long journey ahead, and I need you well."

She squeezed his cheeks gently. "I fear that, in your father's land, Indians will not be welcome. I have seen this in the eyes of the pale faces, and I know it to be true."

Dutch raised his hands to hers. "We will both flourish in father's land. But it's a long journey. Will you be by my side?"

"Aye," she answered. "I will always be with you."

On the third morning outward bound from Maui, Raven died.

The evening before, she had spoken to her son from her buffalo skins, wishing him a good night. Then she rolled her back to the planks and gazed upon the stars, saying, "I will sit with your father this night."

Dutch thought nothing of her comment, thinking she meant simply being close to his spirit. But the next morning, when he went to wake her, she was gone. Her spirit was indeed with his father forever. Her death caused such despair in Dutch that he crumpled to the deck, unable to do anything but weep.

Captain Harrison looked for any signs of what might have caused her death, but found none. Therefore, he logged her death as resulting from a broken heart. Then, with most of the crew watching, the sail maker stitched her body inside a canvas shroud, weighed with stones. Just before he was finished, Dutch roused enough from his grief to remove the silver cross from her neck and say a tearful farewell. Then, when the sail maker had sewn the final stitches, Dutch stood and lifted her slight body to a wooden plank that rested on the gunnels.

Out of respect, the Captain ordered her shroud covered with the British flag, but Dutch stopped him. Instead, he took from his father's pouch the American flag from Fort Clatsop. This he carefully draped over his mother's canvas shroud. Then, with a warm, fresh breeze pushing the ship along, the sad-faced crew gathered around the Captain while he read aloud from his Bible.

When he was done, everyone came to attention and watched as Raven's body slid off the tilted plank into a coral-green sea. Her shroud made a splash and then sank into the depths.

Dutch stood silently at the rail, his expression bitter. He had never seen a burial at sea before, and thought the ritual was horrifying. His mind filled with foggy images of his brothers, his father and, now, his mother. How could God, in a few short weeks, rob him of his entire family? He could discern no reason for it, no mercy in it, nor any hope in it. Dutch, lost in his misery, cursed the sea and sky.

Shortly after the ceremony, he was summoned to Captain Harrison's cabin. There he was given a mug of rum, along with words of concern from the skipper.

"Grief isn't welcome aboard my ship. I tolerated it in your mother, and she died from it. But this I will not allow for you. No, Dutch, the best way to deal with trouble is to work through it. So, beginning today, you will move to the forecastle and learn the ways of a sailor. A busy mind and a tired body make for peaceful nights. Finish your grog, lad. Ye be a jack-tar now."

The newest crewmember to the spars wasn't happy about his abrupt servitude. But after a few days of swallowing his fury, he reckoned that death was much like life: given and taken only by God. Therefore, he stored the fond memories of his family in a special place within his mind, a place so deep inside that only he could retrieve them.

Dutch's strong, nimble body fit into the shrouds like a hand to a glove as the crew taught him the ways of the ropes. The work was hard, the days hot, the nights long. Quickly, his sorrow dissolved in sweat, as his mind filled with thoughts of a future in his father's land. And, always, the ship plowed due west in crystal-clear seas.

After they sailed across the Pacific, and then the China Sea, the Asiatic mainland came into view. Soon, the ship came under the lee of a large island, where pilot sampans awaited all arriving vessels. Once a Chinese pilot had come aboard, the *Sea Witch* sailed for the Portuguese port of Macao. There, she anchored for boarding by Chinese port officials.

The passage from the Sandwich Islands to the Celestial Kingdom had taken ten weeks. After receiving their pratique, the ship sailed up the Pearl River to Whampoa Roads, a deep-water moorage for foreign merchant ships. Here they anchored again, awaiting Chinese permission to sell their cargo. In the harbor where they now rested, over sixty other ships pulled at their bowers. Dutch stood at the rail, wide-eyed, looking out at those tall ships, most of which were twice the size of his brigantine. He had never seen a white-winged ship before the *Sea Witch,* and now he marveled at the site of this strange harbor filled with them. His father had been right: he had much to learn about the white man's world.

After the ship's cargo had been again inspected and all taxes and fees paid, a license was granted to sell the furs. Soon, shallow draft sampans arrived from Canton, some twelve miles upriver. These boats brought in over a thousand chests of Chinese tea as payment for the furs that were uploaded to them. Other sampans arrived, loaded with fresh foodstuffs, livestock, water, firewood and spirits.

For over two weeks, the crew labored at unloading their wares and loading the new cargo. To Dutch's young eyes, these Chinese boats and the yellow people who sailed them looked to have stepped right out of the pages of a book. The coolies were a hard-working lot, always on the move, babbling in their local tongue. So far, however, Dutch's only view of China had been from the deck of the *Sea Witch*. Then, on the last day of loading the return cargo, Captain Harrison released a few crewmembers for a longboat visit upriver to the city of Canton.

When Dutch stepped to the wharf with a sea-bag over his shoulder, he found himself walking through an exotic place like no other. The city was vast and busy as an anthill. It bustled with colorful, narrow-eyed Chinese who chattered in a jargon totally unfamiliar to him. These people wore robes made of shiny fabrics, and wore basket hats with no brims. The women were small and slight, while the men were large and, in many cases, fat. The most common mode of transportation was the rickshaw, small two-wheeled wagons pulled by people, not horses. Canton was an extraordinary city of smells and sights that were as fascinating as they were frightening.

Dutch walked the crowded, noisy streets with a keen eye, looking for a furrier where he could sell his white skins. When he finally, spotted a shop that displayed fur coats and capes in its window, he entered the storefront. Once inside, he was greeted by a brawny Chinese proprietor who spoke no English. Dutch tried Spanish and, much to his surprise, the man understood some of that jargon.

Soon, Dutch's white sea-lion pelts were spread on the counter top, and he and the man started haggling in a clumsy Spanish tongue. The proprietor wanted the fine furs and began by offering trade goods in exchange for the pelts. Dutch kept shaking his head no, while holding up one finger and saying, "Hundred Yankee gold." To this, the proprietor shook *his* head no. Then the shopkeeper showed Dutch a stack of Chinese paper money and tried to offer that in payment. "No," Dutch replied, still with a single finger up, "Hundred Yankee gold."

The bartering went on for almost an hour, but when Dutch noticed the approach of darkness, he picked up his furs decisively and began to stow them back inside his sea bag. Once the proprietor saw this, he reached for his purse. Moments later, a stack of American gold coins gleamed on the countertop.

As Dutch counted the money, he realized that the proprietor had paid him a hundred dollars...per pelt! Oh, the value of that single finger in the air. His father would be proud.

The next morning, after a pilot came aboard, the *Sea Witch* slipped her moorings and proceeded back down the Pearl River. Once the river pilot was dropped off at Macao, the ship bore south into the China Sea. With sharp lookouts aloft, Captain Harrison's course took him well west of the low-lying Asian islands and reefs where local privates roamed.

In four weeks' time, with Indo-China and Malaya in the ship's wake, the *Sea Witch* crossed the Equator and sailed the Strait of Sunda. Halfway through the strait, Captain Harrison put in at North Island. Here the crew watered, wooded and laid in provisions. Then the skipper set his track across the Indian Ocean.

With Asia now well behind the ship, the men started to relax and become more joyful. On some evenings, Dutch would play his father's flute, then tell the crew stories of living on the frontier. All hands enjoyed these tales and, over mugs of rum, they asked many questions about his father's Tillamook passage. Even the officers took an interest in his narratives, and on several occasions Dutch was invited to dine with them. Over one such meal, Captain Harrison offered Dutch a berth on the ship's next voyage. But the lad declined, telling the skipper that only his father's land held his future.

Six weeks later, the *Sea Witch* rounded the Cape of Good Hope in fine weather. Once in the South Atlantic on a northerly course, Captain Harrison bore for the British-controlled island of St. Helena. There he made port in Jamestown for fresh provisions. Two days later, the ship departed the island on limpid emerald waters, embarking on the final leg of her passage to England.

On July 2, 1807 the *Sea Witch* entered the Liverpool harbor and came to rest next to a stone wharf. Their passage from the Columbia River had taken just over nine months. Quickly, the crew cleared the deck and opened the hatches so that they could begin unloading the tea to the waiting wagons. Within seventy-two hours, the cargo was gone and the crew turned-to on the quarterdeck to be paid off for their two-year voyage.

Dutch watched from the shadows as nineteen sailors stood patiently in line, waiting to take leave of the ship. These jack-tars had been fair to Dutch, and had shown him the ways of a sailor. For this, he silently thanked them. Then, just as the third officer started pay call, Dutch was summoned to the Captain's cabin.

In the stateroom, Dutch found the skipper seated behind his desk, its surface stacked with papers. The two aft windows of the cabin were open to the harbor, but still the cramped quarters smelled of stale cigars and brandy.

Harrison smiled, looking up from his papers. "Come on in, lad, and have a seat."

Once Dutch had settled into a chair across from the skipper, he was poured a flagon of rum. As he accepted the drink, the Captain sat back in his chair, with a crooked grin on his lips. "Pay call is important to all sailors. It's when they forget all those sea days of misery, and look to shore for hope." He paused and leaned forward in his seat. "I sent ye into the shrouds, just out of Maui, and you have pulled your share ever since. Therefore," he said, and reached into his desk drawer for a small pouch, which he then tossed to Dutch, "you have earned some pay, as well."

With a surprised look and quick reflexes, Dutch caught the pouch and shook it. The sound and heft told him that it was full of coins.

"You'll find about forty U.S. inside. And listen, Dutch. Come October, the *Sea Witch* will return to the Northwest Coast, and I'm offering ye a berth as our furrier. You know the Indians and how to trade with 'em. For that, you'd be paid thirty pounds sterling for the voyage and two percent of the ship's profits. What say ye?"

Dutch was gratified by the offer, as it made him feel his worth. But he had no desire to sail back across that vast, unforgiving ocean again.

"I'll think on your offer…but what of my father's skins?" he asked the skipper.

"Aye," the Captain said, "there is money due from them, as well." Harrison shuffled through his papers and selected a small envelope. This he pushed across his desk to Dutch. "Here is an accounting of your father's pelts. After all the costs, his share be seventy-two-pounds. It's all written out, along with the money inside."

"What costs?" Dutch asked warily.

Captain Harrison nodded at his tone of concern. "Be assured, I have no wish to cheat you. The trade goods we sent out to the fort had a cost. Then we sailed the pelts over six-thousand miles to China. We also paid all of the taxes and fees required to sell the skins in Canton, and carried you home, as well. No one is trying to deceive you, lad. It's the way the fur trade works."

"My father and mother died for those skins, and this isn't home," Dutch replied angrily.

"Aye," the Captain conceded, "no skins are worth what you have lost. But seventy-two sterling is a sizable sum. And, as for home…there's a schooner, the *Mary-Beth,* two wharfs over. She sails this evening for Boston. Her skipper is a friend of mine, and I've already paid him for your berth."

"So I'll work his shrouds?" Dutch asked carefully.

"Nay, she be a passenger ship. And I'll make bold enough to suggest that you use your time aboard to write out your father's story. He's a sailor's hero, and his life should not be forgotten."

The Captain's words rang true, and Dutch felt proud. It *was* a story worthy of telling. Dutch stood and extended his hand. "Thank you Captain. You've treated me fairly. I'll consider your offer, after I've sampled my father's land. But for now, I'll get my sea bag packed."

The two men shook hands, and Dutch turned to leave.

"And, Dutch…?" the skipper said.

Dutch turned back to face him.

"Before you sail, buy some new togs and get a shave. People in Boston don't live like mountain men."

"Aye," Dutch answered with a shy smile. "That I will."

Boston

THE SCHOONER MARY-BETH REACHED BOSTON HARBOR FIFTEEN days later. During the voyage, Dutch had indeed written a brief account of his father's Tillamook passage. Now he stood at the rail as the boat docked, gazing in wonderment at a large sprawling city. The harbor was full of tall ships of all sizes and descriptions, and the city buildings rose up from the piers to form a skyline that looked to be many miles long. In the early morning summer light, America looked to be a golden place.

For his arrival, Dutch wore shiny new boots, brown britches, a white linen shirt, his cougar necklace, and a dark beaver hat that had been made by his mother. And, at his midriff, he sported a brilliant beaded Indian leather belt with his father's sea knife. A waistcoat had come with his new togs, but on this day it was too hot for him to wear it. He felt funny in the English clothes, but he knew they would help him blend in as he ventured forth in his father's land.

After the schooner came to rest, Dutch rushed down the gangway with his sea bag over his shoulder, in search of a street named Fulton. He remembered, from long ago, how his father had said his family lived above a blacksmith shop just off Fulton. After stopping and asking directions from a dockworker, Dutch learned that the street he sought could be found just three blocks away.

Standing on the cobblestones of that busy avenue, he found it crowded, much like the streets of Canton, and with a clamor that was almost deafening. Tall brick buildings stood on each side of the road, with street-level storefronts facing a broad sidewalk that was also made of stones. The boulevard was wide and filled with wagons and carriages of all shapes and sizes, pulled by hordes of high-stepping horses. The people of Boston wore clothes much like the British, and they all seemed to be in a hurry, with little regard for one another. The city's smells filled his nostrils with an odor that reminded him of the first days at Fort Clatsop. This was a strange place for a breed to be, and he doubted that these streets were filled with glory or gold.

Dutch turned south on Fulton and walked through the noisy crowd. As he did, heads turned and people gaped at him impolitely. Dutch felt uncomfortable beneath the passing stares, and he kept up a brisk pace down the stone way. Every few blocks, he stopped and asked a local merchant if he could supply directions to the blacksmith shop of Samuel Blackwell, but no one seemed to know of it.

Finally, he came upon a delivery man with a cart full of spirits. The man said he knew of only one blacksmith shop in the neighborhood, and that it was just down the road, where Fulton and North Street came together.

Dutch thanked the teamster and hurried farther down the avenue.

He found the shop, but the sign above it proclaimed that John Cornwall was the proprietor.

Walking through the wide open gates, Dutch spotted a robust man working the forge. He was dressed in dirty overalls, along with a leather apron covered with scorch marks. As Dutch approached the furnace, the blacksmith turned his way, hammer in hand.

"What be your business?" the man asked, while ringing the sledge to hot iron.

Dutch raised his voice to be heard above the din. "I'm searching for the smithy of Samuel Blackwell. Would you know where his shop is?"

Plunging the iron back into the forge, the smith pumped the bellows, fanning the flames. "Why do you seek Samuel?"

His question caught Dutch off guard, and he stared for a long moment at the dirty face of the smithy. Finally, he answered, "He be my grandfather, and his son, Frederic, is my uncle."

The blacksmith's face turned somber, and he stopped his pumping. Then he reached for a stained cloth and wiped his soiled hands. "Sorry to tell you this, lad, but Samuel died, a few years back. I bought this shop from his son Frederic."

The news struck like a thunderbolt, and Dutch felt sorrow well up within him. How could this be? Had God forsaken the entire Blackwell family?

With his face softened by concern, the smithy asked, "You alright, lad?"

"Aye," Dutch answered quietly, unable to hide his sadness. "But I've traveled far to find my grandfather…and now he is gone. What of Frederic? Where is he?"

Shaking his head slowly, the blacksmith replied, "He said something about going west in search of a lost brother. Most folks say the brother was killed by savages years ago, but Frederic wouldn't believe them."

Dutch reached for his sea knife and showed it to the smithy. "Samuel made this blade for his son, over twenty years ago. That son, Joseph, was my father, and he was killed by renegade Indians less than a year ago, on the Pacific Coast."

Stunned by the story, the blacksmith took the blade in his hand and examined it. "Samuel did fine work when he was sober. This be some of the best I've seen. But the handle is loose. Let me fix it, lad."

Dutch's thoughts sank into a gloom of uncertainty as he watched the smith work on his sea knife. With his only living relative gone, and no family Boston, why was he here?

Once the repair was complete, Dutch wandered aimlessly back up Fulton Street in the hot afternoon sun. His mind was still reeling from the disappointing news of his family. This adventure to his father's land had proven to be a bad notion. Stopping in the shade of a building close to the wharf, he gazed upon the people in the street. They all looked painfully unfamiliar, as did the city itself. Why was he here…and where was he going?

Slowly, his gaze came to rest on a public house across the road. The sign above the door proclaimed the tavern to be the *Sea Witch*. At least the name was something familiar. And so it was, with his mouth parched and his mind still racing, that he crossed the way and stepped inside the open doorway.

The pub was large and narrow, with round tables and chairs on one side, and a long wooden counter with stools on the other. Behind the counter was a side bar, with open windows that faced a brick alley. The only light inside the room came from the open doorway and the dirty glass of those windows. The saloon held a few patrons, and Dutch took a stool at the bar, close to the open door.

The place smelled much like Captain Harrison's stateroom, stale from tobacco and spirits. When he was seated, Dutch was approached by a rawboned bartender wearing a black vest and a clean white apron. The older barkeep was hunched over and shuffled his walk. "Would ye be of majority, lad?" he asked in a shrill voice.

"Aye," Dutch answered firmly.

"Very well. What be your pleasure?"

"A tankard of ale, as cool as you have it."

The barkeep nodded his bald head and stumbled to the opposite end of the bar to pour the drink. As Dutch waited, he removed his knife from its sheath and inspected the blacksmith's work. The man had fixed the rivets that held the handle together, and had polished and sharpened the blade. The smithy had even wrapped the grip with a new length of rawhide twine. All in all, he had done a fine job, and he had refused any payment for his labors. Dutch guessed that his sad story of loss and disappointment had gotten the best of the blacksmith.

When the barkeep returned with the ale, the old man commented on the sea knife that Dutch held. "Are ye some kind of Indian fighter, lad?" he asked in his high-pitched voice.

"Nay, just a traveler from a far land," Dutch answered.

"Can I see your blade?"

Dutch looked up at the barkeep and hesitated. Then he flipped the handle toward the bartender so he could grasp it.

The old man carefully checked the shank's balance and craftsmanship. Then, with an odd expression, he stared at the boy. "Strange to say, I've held this knife before. How did you come by it, lad?"

Dutch took a swig from his tankard and wiped his mouth. "That cannot be, sir. While it's true that the blade was made here in Boston, for over twenty years it has been carried on my father's hip."

"And who might your father be?" the barkeep asked in a keen voice.

"A sailor and trader named Joseph Blackwell."

The old man's mouth fell open, and he dropped the blade to the bar. Then the elderly fellow stumbled backwards a few steps, until he bumped against the back bar. His face was pale and his eyes wide with the look of an awful surprise. He mumbled to himself for a moment, then regained his voice. "Tis my turn to say that cannot be. Joseph Blackwell died at Murderous Harbor in '88. I know this because I was there."

Dutch returned his look, bewildered. His mind was reeling as he searched for the right words. "I know nothing of a Murderous Harbor. What I do know is that Joseph Blackwell was my father, and that he died less than a year ago, at the hands of some Chinook renegades on the Columbia River."

The barkeep stepped forward, looking more troubled than before. Reaching into his pocket, he drew out some spectacles and fixed them on his bony nose, then peered more closely at Dutch. "Murderous Harbor is on the Northwest Coast… but then, so is the Columbia River. But ye don't look much like the Joseph Blackwell I knew. He and I sailed there with Captain Gray."

Like a lighting bolt, a flash came to Dutch's quick mind. "Then you would be Sandy, from the *Lady Washington*! Father spoke of you often. Indeed, he said you were a bald, slight fellow with a pitchy voice…and a heart of gold."

Sandy's eyes welled up with tears, and his hands began to tremble. Another customer called out for more spirits, but the bartender only stared squarely at Dutch. "One of the crew swore to us that he saw Joseph and the boy Marcus murdered by the Indians. The Captain and I believed him, and so we sailed away. My God, what have we done?"

"The man was wrong. Both Marcus and my father thrived for many years among the Tillamooks. They were my tribe."

As fate would have it, Sandy owned the public house. He had purchased it with the profits from a second trip to the Northwest Coast. Captain Gray had not been so fortunate, dying in 1806 from yellow fever.

Soon, help arrived at the saloon, and Sandy stepped out from behind the bar and ushered Dutch upstairs to his living quarters. There the two men talked for hours. Sandy wanted to know all the details of Joseph's life with the Indians, so Dutch showed him the story he had written while sailing to America. When Sandy shyly told his new friend that he could not read, Dutch read the account aloud. By the time he finished the tale, Sandy was slumped in a chair, with tears rolling down his cheeks.

"That is truly an amazing story," he said in a choked voice. "One of my patrons is a printer. If you will give me leave, I will see to it that your father's story is told to all of Boston."

"That would be splendid," Dutch replied, warm with pleasure and pride. "With that done, I will be able to return to my mother's land."

Sandy's sad face lit up indignantly. "Don't be foolish, lad. I owe you much. Stay here with me. I have a bar full of spirits and a pantry full of food, so we will have a grand time. And this city has much to offer a young lad like yourself."

Dutch thought a moment and then answered, "Father was right. You do have a heart of gold. I will stay for awhile, since you ask so kindly. But then I will return to the Indians, as it is their ways that I know best."

A few days later, Joe Blackwell's story became front-page news, and the tavern filled with people wanting to meet the now-famous mariner's son and hear more of life on the Northwest Coast. Sandy loved the crowds, as they were good for business, but Dutch hated the notoriety.

To his surprise, written offers of prospects also came. One invited him to write a book about his father's life, while another proposed that he undertake a speaking tour about the coastal Indians. But the most intriguing suggestion came from a New York man named John Jacob Astor. He wanted Dutch to open trading posts on the Columbia River. To Dutch's young mind, this sounded like the most reasonable enterprise.

A few days after these written offers, Dutch sat quietly in a dark corner of the tavern, eating his morning meal. Just as he finished with his last cup of coffee, Sandy approached and handed him an envelope with his name written across it in a delicate hand.

Opening the envelope, he found a short note inside.

Dutch Blackwell,

I am an old friend of your father's. My maiden name was Becky Barrel. I have something of Joseph's that I would like to return. Can we please meet at two o'clock today on the stone wharf from which the Lady Washington sailed? (Sandy knows the place.) I will be wearing a yellow dress, with a red rose in my bonnet.

Faithfully Yours,

Becky

He read the note aloud to Sandy, who told Dutch more of Becky and how she had been his father's first love. This was surprising news to learn about one's own father but, brimming with curiosity, Dutch decided to meet her.

That afternoon, he walked up Fulton Street towards the harbor. The summer sun glared, and beads of sweat drenched his body beneath the waistcoat. He cursed his English togs, but wanted to look like a gentleman when he met his father's friend.

Reaching the stone wharf, he slowly walked the vacant dock, looking about for the lady. Soon, across the way, a woman appeared; as promised, she wore a bright yellow dress and carried a white parasol. Under the umbrella, she sported a bonnet that was adorned with a red flower.

Dutch walked in her direction, and they soon came face to face in the blazing sun.

"Would you be Miss Becky?"

"Aye, and you would be Dutch," she replied in a soft, sweet voice.

"Let's move to the shade," Dutch suggested. "Your Boston heat is stifling."

She smiled at his request and nodded. As they moved next to a nearby building, Dutch noticed the beauty of this woman. She had creamy skin, and her delicate face showed little age. The slender shape of her body was as graceful as an Indian canoe.

As they stopped in the cooling shade, Becky's gentle green eyes looked Dutch over carefully.

"Thank you for meeting me," she said with a friendly smile. "You look much like your father. You have his eyes and color, although not his red hair."

"Aye, my mother had shiny black hair, so I have reddish-brown. She was a Tolowa Indian and half Spanish. I miss both of my parents very much."

Becky looked surprised at Dutch's honesty about his lineage. "Your father was about your age when he shipped out on that faithful voyage."

"He was nineteen, while I'll turn eighteen next month. He took me fishing for my birthday, last year. It was a day I will never forget."

"I read your account of his story in the newspaper," she confided, "and it troubled me greatly." She reached into her small handbag and pulled out a gold chain and cross. "Joseph gave this to me before he departed. I want you to have it back. It belongs in your family."

"Thank you, ma'am." Dutch took the chain and held it in his hand. "I will cherish this always."

"So then, young Dutch, what is in your future?" Becky asked with an air of friendly curiosity.

"I'm not entirely sure…but a man named Astor has contacted me. He wants to open trading posts on the Columbia River, and he has asked for my help. There is something about that mighty river that draws me back, like a bee to a flower – to be among my mother's people again, to see the vast beauty of the land and smell its clean air. It is there that I hope to find my way."

"So you won't consider staying in Boston?"

"No offense, ma'am, but no. The people here mill around like a herd of elk without a bull."

Becky's rosy lips parted in a slim grin. "In that case, I hope you will make that journey. I have a notion that it's something your father would have done. He always did love a great enterprise."

Opening the pouch that hung from his shoulder, Dutch reached into it and carefully removed the golden locket. "Ma'am, I found this among my father's things. But the likeness inside doesn't do you justice," he said shyly, and held out the brooch. "This be rightfully yours."

When he handed the pendant to Becky, she grasped it tightly, with tears shining in her eyes. There was a long, silent moment, as if time were standing still.

"It seems like only yesterday that he sailed away. We were so full of hope… and love. I waited, but then, years later, we heard the news of his death. It about broke my heart."

Becky ran her fingertips across the surface of the brooch with a wistful look of days gone by. Then she turned the pendant over and once again, after so many years, read the engraving: *Why Is The Eagle Feared?*

"I wonder if Joseph ever learned the answer to the riddle," she mused, rubbing a fingertip gently over the etched letters.

"Aye, he told it to me many a time," Dutch humbly replied. "The eagle is feared because he is fearless."

End

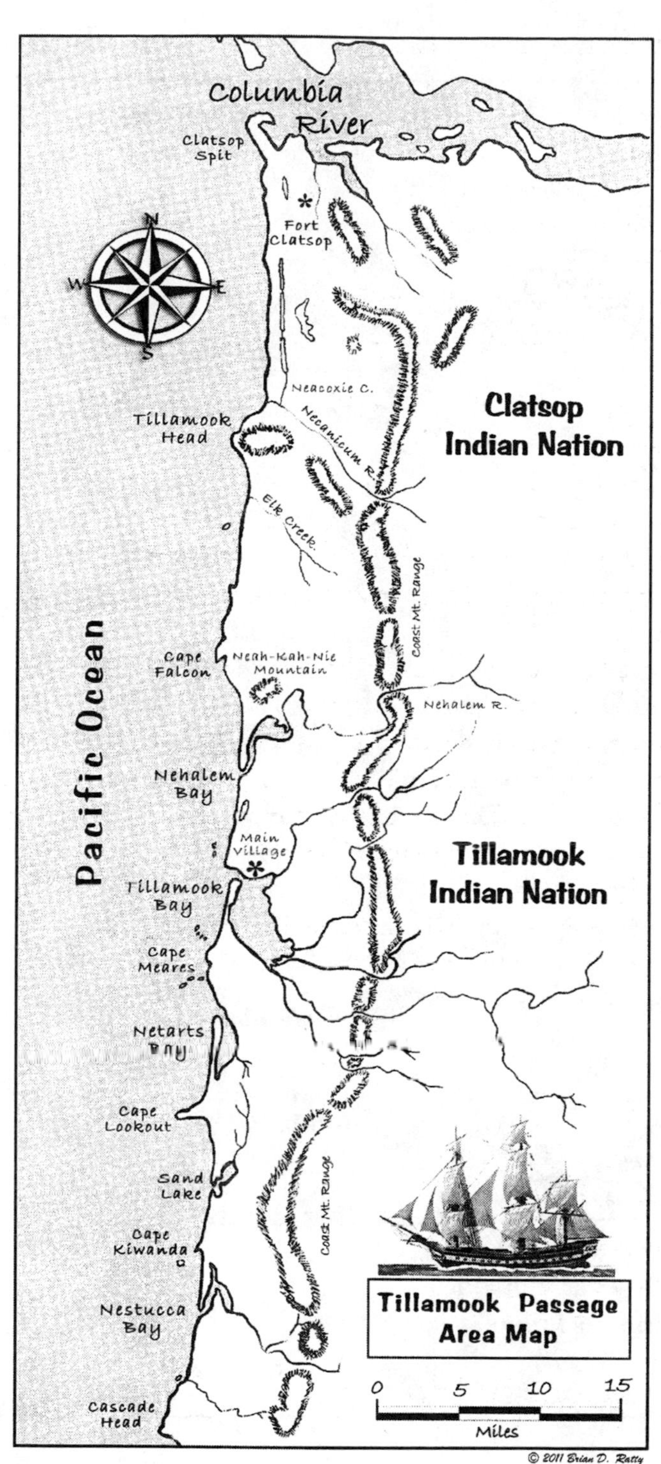
Columbia
River
Clatsop
Spit
Fort
Clatsop
N
W
E
S
Neacoxie C.
Necanicum R.
Clatsop
Indian Nation
Tillamook
Head
Elk Creek
Coast Mt. Range
Cape
Falcon
Neah-Kah-Nie
Mountain
Nehalem R.
Pacific Ocean
Nehalem
Bay
Main
Village
Tillamook
Indian Nation
Tillamook
Bay
Cape
Meares
Netarts
Bay
Cape
Lookout
Sand
Lake
Coast Mt. Range
Cape
Kiwanda
Nestucca
Bay
Tillamook Passage
Area Map
0
5
10
15
Miles
Cascade
Head
© 2011 Brian D. Ratty

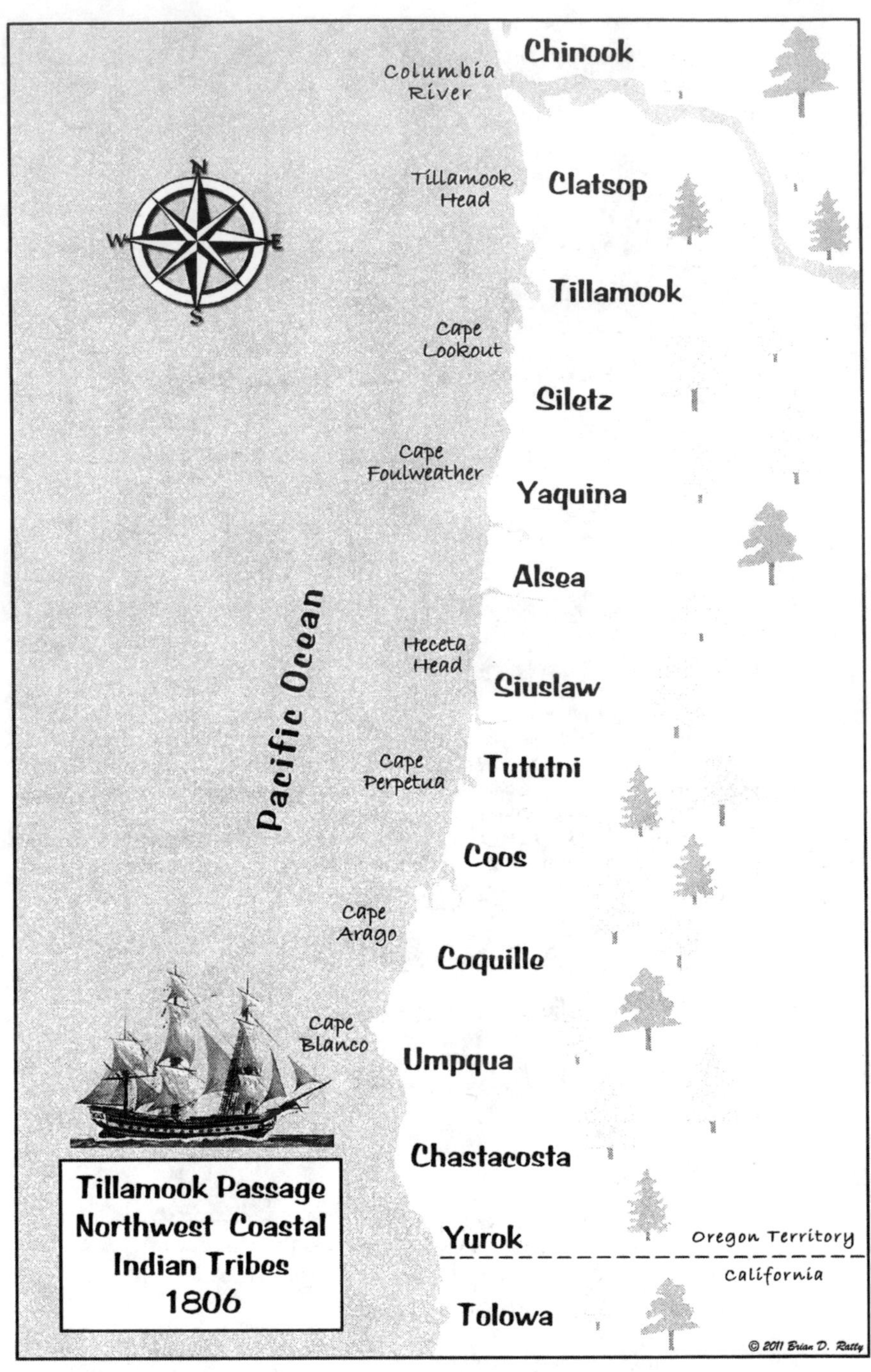
Chinook
Columbia River
Tillamook Head
Clatsop
Tillamook
Cape Lookout
Siletz
Cape Foulweather
Yaquina
Alsea
Pacific Ocean
Heceta Head
Siuslaw
Cape Perpetua
Tututni
Coos
Cape Arago
Coquille
Cape Blanco
Umpqua
Chastacosta
Yurok
Oregon Territory
California
Tolowa
N
S
E
W
Tillamook Passage
Northwest Coastal
Indian Tribes
1806
© 2011 Brian D. Ratty

Books by Brian Ratty

Dutch Clarke—The Early Years

We all come into this world alone and go out the same. Between coming and going is life. This is a story about life and how a year long adventure defines the future for a young man named Dutch Clarke.

Manipulated by his Grandfather, Dutch undertakes a one year ordeal in the wilderness of British Columbia in 1941. Set against the backdrop of the opening days of World War II, this is a classic story of a personal struggle and coming of age against all odds.

Book Length: 376 Pages
Action - Adventure
Audience: Young Adults 12 and up

Quarter Finalist
Amazon Breakthrough
Novel Award
Forward Mg. Book of the Year

Dutch Clarke—The War Years

In 1942, as American blood is about to be spilled in far off Guadalcanal, a young man boards a train and blindly heads towards his destiny: boot camp with the United States Marine Corps. The tragic times of World War II were the defining years for millions of cowboys and plowboys, and 'Dutch Clarke - The War Years' is a compelling chronicle about these years and one not so ordinary, young man.

This is a uniquely different war story about men who fought their way across the Pacific, not with guns but with cameras. Dutch's story is as fresh as today's headlines and as true as yesterday's sins.

Book Length: 512 Pages
World War II Historical Fiction
Audience: Adults 18 and up

Winner: 2009 Eric Hoffer Award
Finalist: Forward Magazine Book of the Year

Available From:
AuthorHouse.com
Amazon.com
DutchClarke.com

CPSIA information can be obtained at www.ICGtesting.com
Printed in the USA
239719LV00002B/9/P

9 781463 406158